DESTINED RADIANCE

NEPHILIM'S DESTINY: BOOK 5

TESSA COLE

Gryphon's Gate Publishing

Destined Radiance

Gryphon's Gate Publishing

550 King St. N.

PO Box 42088 Conestoga

Waterloo, ON

N2L 6K5

ISBN 978-1-988115-74-0

Print ISBN 978-1-988115-73-3

CHAPTER 1

THE WORRY IN MY HOSPITAL ROOM AT OPERATIONS DROPPED the temperature. All my guys stared at Sebastian standing in the doorway, his posture casual, his hands in the pockets of his slacks, as if he hadn't just reminded us that there could be a powerful goddess out there determined to finish Michael's war and kill all humans and supers.

"You've already lost a day," he said, leveling his pale, exhausted gaze on me. Even the soft blue-white glow that usually emanated from his translucent skin was dimmed. He didn't look like he was made from tissue paper any more, not like he had after pouring all his magic into the glyph witch's power-leaching spell to save us, but he didn't look close to being recovered, either.

Marcus, who lay behind me in the bed—my back against his bare chest—tightened his grip around my waist, shifting my hospital gown under the blankets a little higher up my thighs, and growled low in his throat. "Not Essie's fault."

"Hey." Sebastian raised his hands in defense. "Not saying everyone didn't need a day, but you don't even know the true extent of the source of the glyph witches' worship magic. How many followers are there? How many witches have access to the source?"

"Not to mention whether their goddess is awake or merely a catatonic vessel for the worship magic spell," I said, fighting a shudder.

I didn't want to think about the source of the glyph witches' power. We'd barely managed to survive stopping them from assassinating Ambassador Hollaway, and God, couldn't I just get a day with my guys when nothing happened?

But that wasn't how the team worked and the angel half—or rather, my angel entirety—couldn't ignore the danger.

And yeah, I still wasn't sure what I thought about being a full angel. Learning the truth had happened so fast and during so much chaos that I hadn't had time to let that really sink in. And it seemed I still wasn't going to have the time.

Jeez, I didn't even have time to give in to the need thrumming through all my soul bonds. A need that was still so strong, I ached for them. Especially Gideon. Yes, we'd solidified our bond yesterday, and the pieces of my soul bound to his were no longer fractured, but I needed more, needed to give myself over to the magic binding us together. I needed to give myself over to the magic binding me to *all* my guys. The urge was overwhelming, and it took everything I had not to turn in the bed and start making out with Marcus. Especially since I could tell I was in a hospital gown and nothing else.

Angels said the mating brand was beautiful and sacred, and while I had to agree—I was still in awe at how amazing having my guys felt—it was also a pain in the ass right now.

How was I supposed to do my job when all I wanted was to take my guys to bed and stay there?

My job.

As a JP agent.

Which was another thing that shocked me... and was possibly uncertain... since I'd been assigned to the team as their required human agent.

I pulled my gaze from Sebastian and slid it over to Kol. Much to my surprise, he was actually making eye contact with me.

The hellfire in his eyes flared for a second, sending a thrill of desire mixed with hope through me. Maybe we could work things out, get our friendship back... get more. But realization slid over his breathtaking features and his hellfire snapped to barely-there pinpricks, his magic and emotions grasped tight as he pulled his attention back to Sebastian.

My hope wavered. Yesterday's issues hadn't been forgotten. Thinking I was a nephilim had still triggered horrible memories, and I'd still lied to him. And really, it was too soon. Shock and betrayal, especially around what had to be PTSD, wasn't something that someone just got over.

But God damn it, I just wanted to grab him and scream at him. Sure, we didn't have a soul bond, but I couldn't help feeling like we were supposed to have something more, like he was as much mine as Marcus and Jacob and Gideon.

And that wasn't just a human— er, woman craving an incubus.

But screaming at him wouldn't help. As much as I wanted everything to go back to the way it had been, that wasn't going to happen right away... if ever.

Jacob shifted from his position sitting at my feet, sliding his hand on top of the blanket higher up my calf and drawing my attention. His vampiric intensity sent a shiver of desire racing over me and made my pulse pick up, which made Marcus release a soft, sensual growl that vibrated through my back and shot heat to my core. Gideon, who sat in the chair beside the bed, squeezed my fingers, a mix of yearning and worry in his summer-sky eyes, clearly torn between protecting innocents and giving in to the urge of our bond.

I was just as torn. My guys weren't seriously injured, we weren't fighting for our lives, and I finally felt good. Yeah, my inner magical channels were still a little raw, but I didn't feel like my magic was going to explode and take out the building, and my buzz was gone. Gone! It had been years since I hadn't felt like I was holding a low voltage electric fence. In fact, I felt powerful, like a light had been turned on inside me and it radiated heat and strength and magic through every cell in my being.

And those cells wanted my guys. Now.

"So," I forced out, my voice embarrassingly breathy, "what's the plan?"

"You're going to take care of that." Kol gestured at the three of us, his whole body tense. "And I'm going to take a walk on the other side of the Quarter."

Gideon's gaze captured mine, and my pulse stuttered at his heated desire, then the muscles in his jaw flexed and he yanked his gaze away. "What we *need* is to figure out how to find the source of the witches' power."

Sebastian sighed. "I can help with that."

"And how much is that going to cost us?" Marcus asked.

"*You're* not helping with anything," Amiah said as she stormed into the doorway, her voice sharp. "You're going back to bed."

"I'm fine," Sebastian said.

"Oh, don't tell her you're fire," Kol warned. He'd told Sebastian that Amiah would be upset seeing him walking around, and... well... as predicted—

She grabbed Sebastian's elbow. "You're not fine, and I don't even need my magic to see that. Your essence is still low and your magical channels are raw. Do I need to sedate you?"

Sebastian glared at her. "I'm not an agent, so I'm not a patient."

"You're in my hospital."

"I'm visiting a friend." He jerked his chin at me.

Amiah followed his motion and glared at me, probably because I was in Marcus's embrace. A strange, honest-to-goodness emotion, not a temperature change, whispered through me, but it came and went so fast I had no idea what it meant, even if I could clearly tell—how, I didn't know—that it was Amiah's emotion.

She yanked on Sebastian's arm with enough force to make him stumble a step into the hall. "You came in on a gurney. That makes you a patient."

He jerked his elbow free. "I'm fine enough to do this."

"No, you're not."

"I am. Especially if Esther is going to supply the juice." He flashed his wicked smile, the sexual invitation clear. All of my guys—including Kol—shifted and the temperature rose to ever-so-slightly too warm.

"What are you proposing?" Gideon asked, his tone edged with ice.

Sebastian's smile deepened—as if his invitation hadn't been clear before—and his eyes filled with mischief. "Well..."

"Bane," Marcus snarled.

Sebastian laughed and Amiah huffed.

He rolled his eyes at her. "I propose casting a spell to locate the source of the witches' magic."

"No doubt the source is hidden. You're going to need to channel too much magic." Amiah grabbed his elbow again. "No one is burning up in Operations on my watch."

"That's why Esther is going to do most of the hard work," he said.

Marcus's snarl turned into an outright growl and a whisper of his cold fear swept over me. "I don't think so."

"She's not a spellcaster," Jacob added.

"But she's got power and she's magically sensitive," Sebastian said.

"Her sensitivity hasn't been trained." Gideon frowned. It was clear he was weighing the pros and cons of going ahead with the plan.

And I couldn't blame him. If it was the fastest way to find the source of the witches' power and it stopped them from killing any more people, the angel in me was going to agree to it no matter how dangerous. Of course, it was also better to know exactly what I was getting into. Jacob's vampiric claim on me being a perfect case in point. I hadn't known exactly what being claimed by a vampire meant, and now Jacob's hunger was focused entirely on me and I was bite-locked.

"How dangerous is it?" I asked.

"Very," Jacob said as he turned his attention to Kol. "Unless you have help."

"But I've never assisted with a tracking spell before," he said.

"You know how to hone in on a magic source?" Sebastian pursed his lips, his gaze going unfocused. "I can make that work. I'll link the three of us and—"

"That's a terrible idea." The muscles in Kol's jaw flexed and the air around me chilled.

"No, it's perfect," Sebastian said. "I cast the spell and you guide her. The danger will be minimal."

"To her," Amiah said. She leveled a hard glare on Sebastian. "You're still going to need to manipulate raw energy and risk burning up or draining your essence to unconsciousness. Neither is acceptable in your condition."

"You saw what three of those witches could do," Gideon said. "We need to move on this." He stood, the yearning in his gaze deepening, making my pulse stutter, and glanced at his phone. "The team from head office is just about to leave. I'll tell them to stick around."

"Just great," Marcus said. "We're never going to hear the end of it from them."

"Put your pride and ego aside. We need all the help we can get." Gideon shoved his phone back into his pocket. "Essie? Kol? You up for this?"

"Yes," I said. We had to know if there were more of those glyph witches out there.

But resignation tightened in my chest.

What the hell was I resigned about?

Then Kol shifted and I realized the emotion wasn't mine.

"Fine." His gaze started to slide back to mine, but he jerked it to Gideon instead, his body so tense it hurt to look at him. "But I can't do it until the four of you release some energy."

"We don't have the time for that," Gideon said.

A whisper of Kol's seductive magic slipped over my skin. He shuddered, which made me shudder, which make Marcus's breath pick up and his hands slide down to my hips.

"If you want me to be able to concentrate enough to

guide Essie during the spell, make time. I'll be back in an hour." Kol rushed out of the room and down the hall.

"I need to pick up a few things from my apartment," Sebastian said, shooting Amiah a just-try-and-stop-me look, and followed Kol out the door.

"Idiot," Amiah huffed, and she headed down the hall in the opposite direction, leaving me with Marcus, Jacob, and Gideon.

The temperature rose and Marcus's breath didn't relax. Gideon and Jacob turned their attention to me, one bright and filled with light, the other dark and filled with intensity. Both blazing with need.

My pulse stalled and heat pooled low within me. These were my guys and they wanted me as much as I wanted them.

"We shouldn't do this here," Marcus said, his voice husky.

His hot breath feathered across the back of my neck, sending a tremor of desire racing down my back, and I bit back a moan.

"We have an hour. How do we want to work this out?" We hadn't had a chance to talk about our situation, or how sex with the four of us was going to work. What were everyone's boundaries? Had the moment yesterday with Marcus and Jacob been a one-time thing?

If I was being honest with myself, I hoped it wasn't. I didn't want to have to pick, or keep a schedule. I wanted my guys, now, all of them. And I *really* wanted more than just an hour.

The guys glanced at each other, and a flicker of uncertainty cut through my desire. They'd had a conversation without me. But what had they decided on?

"Was the threesome yesterday because of extenuating circumstances?" Gideon asked me.

Jacob's intense stillness billowed, radiating through his brand, and Marcus stiffened behind me. The temperature in the room rose a few more degrees with their desire, but their uncertainty grew stronger.

"I won't ask any of you to do something you're not comfortable with," I said.

"For fuck's sake. Be more direct, Gideon. We're wasting time," Marcus growled. "Essie, I'm taking you up to have a shower. I'm sure Gideon and Jacob would like to join us. Are *you* comfortable with that?"

The temperature jumped to sweltering and a need as strong as mine, a mix from all my guys, rushed into me. I gasped and bit back a groan. "What are we waiting for?"

"Finally." Marcus climbed out of bed, dressed only in his jeans—since he'd just come back from a run in his wolf form—looking sexy as hell, and picked me up, cradling me against his firm muscular chest.

"I'll go tell the head office team to meet us in the cafeteria in an hour," Gideon said.

"Meet us in my room," Jacob said. "My shower is bigger."

"And your bed," I added.

Marcus's piercing green eyes darkened, his wolf rising to the surface, and he released a low, sensual growl. God, I loved that sound, loved his ferocity. I slid my hand along his jaw, savoring the rasp of his sexy scruff on my skin, and captured his lips with mine. His grip on me tightened and he raked his tongue into my mouth, fueling my desire, kissing me with a breathtaking kiss that left me panting.

"Jesus, Essie," he gasped. "If you keep that up, we're not going to leave the room."

"The bed isn't big enough for the four of us." I sucked on his lower lip, drawing a throaty moan from him.

"And it doesn't have a shower." Jacob pulled me out of Marcus's arms and strode out of the room.

With a groan, Gideon ran a hand over his buzzed blond hair and marched in the opposite direction. Marcus, his T-shirt clutched in his hand, hurried after us as we took the smaller halls to the elevator and hit the call button. Thankfully the halls were empty. Gideon had said I'd been unconscious for a full day. That meant it had to be after nine at night.

Jacob's grip on me tightened as we waited, his breath coming a little too fast. If he'd had a pulse, it would have been racing. The air around me simmered, hot and muggy, slicking my skin with sweat, and flickers of electricity from Gideon's brand nipped up my right arm into Jacob's brand and swirled with his powerful stillness.

"I can walk, you know." I pressed a hand against his chest and his gaze, his eyes intense black pools, captured mine.

"I need to do more than just hold your hand," he said, his voice a low rumble that sent my essence into glorious resonance with his.

The door opened and he carried me into the elevator, his attention still locked on me. My pulse picked up, pounding in a chest overflowing with desire, mine and theirs.

"I need more, too," I said, and he dipped in and kissed me, the kiss slow, sensual, lingering. It flooded heat through my body, ratcheting up the temperature even more, and left me just as breathless as one of Marcus's ferocious kisses.

The elevator door slid open and we hurried past my assigned room to Jacob's suite. He unlocked his door with his thumbprint and opened it without barely shifting my weight, and carried me straight to his cream-and-gray bathroom with his large standup shower.

Something flashed at the corner of my eye and I jerked my attention to my reflection in the mirror. My thoughts stalled. Brilliant white light with gold flecks radiated from my eyes, and I had no idea if the glow was at its usual bright state or brighter because of my heightened emotions.

The stunned, scared nephilim I'd seen in the mirror the last few weeks no longer looked back at me. In her place was an angel radiating tremendous power. I brushed a finger over the scar along my cheek where I'd almost been shot, then slid it over the ugly ragged scar on my neck where I'd been bitten.

A lot had happened in a little while and so much had changed.

"Amiah might be able to remove those," Jacob said, sitting me on the counter. He cupped his massive hand over my neck, capturing my hand and covering the feral vampire bite. A whisper of regret and worry slid through me. He thought my scars upset me, made me think I was less attractive. But it wasn't the scars bothering me. My whole life had been turned upside down, ripped to shreds, and set on fire.

And I had the scars to prove it.

I also had the soul bonds.

I tangled my free hand into Jacob's shoulder-length hair, pulling it free from the elastic holding it back, and leaned forward.

He captured my lips with another slow, breathtaking kiss. His hand slipped under my hospital gown and skimmed a teasing trail along the top of my thigh. I shifted forward, spread my legs apart, and tugged him close, pressing myself against the bulge in the front of his pants.

With a groan, he deepened the kiss, his tongue raking against mine, his desire weakening his control. I pushed my hands under his shirt and ran my nails over his bulky chest. God, I loved the feel of all that powerful muscle. I didn't think I'd ever get enough of it. Behind him, Marcus had taken off his clothes and started the shower. His wolf's ferocity filled his eyes, capturing my soul, as he stepped into the spray and pumped a hand down his full erection.

A shudder swept through me at the thought of all that ferocious power focused on me. Jacob's hand on my thigh shifted inward, teasing oh so close to my core, and my breath hitched.

Marcus growled and slid his hand back to his tip and pumped again, and I imagined it wasn't his hand he was thrusting into. I squirmed against Jacob, brushing myself against his fingers, sending a shiver of need racing through me. Now all I could think about was getting him out of his clothes and dragging him into the shower with Marcus.

I grabbed his T-shirt. "You should take this off," I said, my voice husky.

"You should take that off," he replied, his gaze raking over my body.

"You should both get in the fucking shower," Marcus snarled, his heated desire mixing with the steam from the shower.

A wicked smile, almost as wicked as Kol's, tugged at Jacob's lips. He slowly dragged off his T-shirt, his body still tucked tight against mine, making it impossible for me to get out of the three-sleeved hospital gown.

"Essie—" Marcus said, his voice low.

Jacob slid both of his hands under the gown, teasing close to my core again, but not making contact.

God, just touch me already.

"Possessive shifter sex," he rumbled in my ear. "How wild do you want him?"

Holy fuck. "You sure you're not Kol?" Getting Marcus riled up was definitely something Kol would do.

The memory of my dream of Kol and his magic sliding into me sent another shiver racing through me.

"I may have asked for a few pointers when our brand first appeared." His thumb whispered against my clit and I gasped in surprise.

"You asked Kol for pointers?" And he gave suggestions? I didn't know if that made our sooner-rather-than-later necessary conversation more awkward or not.

"I like to learn new things." He bit my neck hard and plunged a finger inside me.

CHAPTER 2

Sensation shot through me, pain and pleasure. A rush of aching hot need on a giant wave of Jacob's magic. I tipped my head back, my eyelids fluttering shut, and Jacob took a long pull on my vein, tugging all the way to my core. He slid a second finger into me, drew them out, and slid them back in, slowly. My breath picked up and his magic spiraled tighter within me.

God, this was what I needed. Sure, we only had an hour, but the world wasn't going to end and I wasn't going to explode and take out a building. I could give in to the pull of our soul bonds.

Another thrust of his fingers, matched with another pull on my neck. My essence throbbed, a breathtaking mix of my desire, Jacob's magic, and surging need from Marcus. I felt all of it with my empathy, a mix of heat and steam and honest-to-goodness emotions.

I shoved my hands down the front of Jacob's pants and grasped his erection, drawing a moan from him and a growl from Marcus.

Jacob ground his thumb over my clit and his fingers

worked faster, spiraling his magic tighter within me. My breath picked up. I was flying on blazing need, spiraling higher and higher.

A whisper of a climax shuddered through me, not enough to release his magic, and he tugged me off the counter. His healing magic sealed the bite on my neck shut, and with my head still spinning with desire, he backed me into the shower, the hot spray soaking the hospital gown and pasting it to my body.

My back hit hard muscle, and another whisper of climax made my muscles clench in anticipation. Marcus grabbed my shoulders and wrenched me around. He seized a fistful of my hair and slammed his mouth against mine with a possessive, demanding kiss. The ferocity of his passion stole my breath, blazed across my skin, and flooded me with emotion.

He shoved me against the tiled wall, his free hand raking up under the gown. I hooked my leg around his waist and ground against his erection, showing him how much I needed him inside me.

"Mine," he snarled, and for a second, all I could see in his eyes was his wolf. His pupils had slitted and his canines had started to extend. He was incredible. The attraction that had been sizzling between us from the moment we'd first met had nothing on this. I was burning up with his need and I couldn't get enough.

I dug my fingers into his scalp and snarled back. "Mine."

"Fuck, Essie, you're incredible." He crushed his mouth back against mine and thrust into me, burying to the hilt in one powerful, glorious stroke. With a growl, he grabbed my hips, forcing me to wrap both legs around him and driving him deeper inside me.

Jacob's magic swelled, stealing all breath and thought.

There was only sensation. The soaked gown clinging to my skin, the tile at my back, Marcus's fingers digging into my butt, the feel of him filling me, and his passion blazing around my heart.

He pounded into me with forceful, wild thrusts, making Jacob's magic twist tighter and tighter. Every cell sang with it, spinning into a supernova until it ripped my orgasm free. Every muscle in my body contracted. I cried Marcus's name as he tensed within me, his own climax seizing him. Stars danced behind my eyes, I couldn't catch my breath, and magic swelled around my heart, strengthening our soul bond.

Marcus gasped and his body trembled, but Jacob, now fully naked, drew up tight behind him and steadied us against the wall. The intensity in Jacob's eyes sent another shuddering climax through me, making Marcus groan.

I slid my legs from Marcus's waist, and he wrapped his arms around my back and turned us, capturing me between him and Jacob. One lithe muscular body thrumming with passion even after he'd just come, and the other bulky, powerful, encompassing, radiating an intensity focused entirely on me.

"You're still wearing too much clothing," Jacob said, his voice rumbling through me, reigniting my aching need.

"I can help with that." Marcus yanked a claw through the thin fabric, ripping it open.

My pulse tripped, and Jacob tugged the gown off. A low, sensual growl rumbled in Marcus's throat and his pupils dilated. He slid his hands up my belly and cupped my breasts. I leaned into him. God, I'd just had a mind-blowing orgasm and I wanted more with him, with Jacob... with all of them.

Jacob pressed tight behind me and I ground my butt

against his huge erection. He reached around and found my clit as Marcus rolled my nipples, pinching them into tight, aching buds.

I moaned into Marcus's mouth, and Jacob's tip brushed my folds, teasing me.

Oh, fuck, yes.

I arched my back, giving Jacob a better angle. He slid inside me, slowly, stretching me with his girth, his thumb rubbing my clit while Marcus pinched my nipples and plunged his tongue into my mouth. It was sensation overload. I'd never experienced anything like it before.

Jacob drew out and agonizingly slowly pushed back inside. My breath picked up and my body trembled. I didn't even have his magic inside me, and I throbbed with a burning, consuming need.

"Jacob, please," I begged, grinding against him and pressing my hands against the wall on either side of Marcus's head to keep my balance.

He drew out again, and Marcus slid lower down the wall and sucked hard on my nipple. I gasped and Jacob pushed back in. He built up his pace, growing my desire until I was trembling on the edge again. Then he drew me back and sank his teeth into my neck.

His power exploded through me and another glorious climax crashed over me, stealing my breath and sending stars snapping across my vision.

More heat seared around my heart and strengthened my bond with him, and his intense stillness surged from his brand, rushing up my arm, his magic manifested in my body.

He tensed with his own climax, sending glorious aftershocks rippling through me, and we breathlessly sagged to the shower floor with Marcus.

"Wow—" It was all I could think of to say. "Oh, wow."

The bathroom door opened with a whirl of mist, and Gideon stepped in. His angel glow blazed from his stunning blue eyes, and a flicker of electric magic crackled through our brand.

"You're just in time," Jacob said.

Marcus rumbled a satisfied agreement. "But you're wearing too much clothing."

Gideon's gaze locked with mine and I could sense uncertainty and need. A need that made my pulse trip as if I hadn't just had another amazing orgasm.

"Essie?" he asked, his uncertainty breaking my heart, sending miniature fractures through my bliss.

"I agree. You're wearing too much clothing." I reached out a hand to him. "Help me to bed, Gideon. I'm not sure I can actually stand any more."

Marcus captured my lips in a quick, fierce kiss. "You're welcome."

"You can't stand either, buddy," I said back.

"Oh, I'll be able to stand again soon enough." He shifted, drawing my attention to his already growing erection.

Oh, my!

Gideon's uncertainty flared stronger. In a way, he was the newest to the relationship, even though we'd shared a brand first. And just like I'd needed to reassure Marcus's wolf that he was mine, it looked like I needed to reassure Gideon that he was mine, too.

I turned my attention back to my angel and started to stand. My legs trembled and—as I'd hoped—Gideon rushed forward to steady me. For a second, I was soaring in a blazing summer sky, my soul captured by Gideon's gaze. And now I really did have wings. Flying with him was no longer just a dream.

"Mate," I breathed, and pressed my lips to his.

He groaned, swept me still dripping wet into his arms, and carried me to Jacob's bed. More electricity nipped through our brand as Gideon stared down at me, laid out on Jacob's comforter, waiting for him to join me.

"You're so beautiful." He flicked open the top button of his shirt. The front was wet from carrying me out of the shower and clung to the perfect contours of his chest. "And generous." Two more buttons. My breath hitched. "And brave." Another button. "And strong."

I squirmed. Good lord, he was just unbuttoning his shirt, but with the searing desire in his eyes focused entirely on me, he was lighting me up and making me ache.

I sat up and slid my hands inside his shirt and across his sculpted pecs, making him draw in a sharp breath, and pushed his shirt off his shoulders.

He ripped open the last button and shrugged out of the shirt, his gaze never leaving mine. "Even if fate hadn't bound us together, I still would have fallen in love with you."

He cupped my cheek and brushed his lips against mine. Desire shivered through me at that whisper of a kiss, and our bond throbbed inside me. I could feel how much he wanted me. The room was practically a sauna, and his emotions flooded my chest.

"But fate *did* bind us together," I said.

His uncertainty flickered through his desire.

"Because we were destined for each other all along." I pressed my hand over his heart, willing him to feel how much I wanted him, how much I cared for him.

Heat swept down my arm, picking up some of Jacob's stillness and Gideon's electricity, and swelled around my palm. For a second I feared I was going to blast him with divine light, but the power felt different, not the blazing, roaring magic I always felt when I shot a light strike. Yes, it was still warm, but not burning. Still strong, but not destructive.

It sank into Gideon's chest and his eyes widened with surprise. "You feel that for all of us," he gasped. "For me?"

"Yes." I returned his kiss and he took the invitation, leaning forward and kissing me in full.

I let him nudge me back to the bed and plunge his tongue into my mouth. His passion wasn't as ferocious as Marcus's nor intense as Jacob's, but there was a certainty in it that made the divine light in the core of my being light up. And his control was insane. I knew how much he ached for me. It made my desire burn hotter, and yet he kissed me as if we didn't have less than an hour left. He kissed down my neck to my breasts, sucking on one nipple and teasing it into a tight bud before turning to the other one in a slow, sensual way that had me squirming and panting beneath him.

Then he sat back and undid his pants. Marcus climbed onto the bed beside us and stole a kiss as Gideon undressed. Jacob knelt on my other side. I turned my head to kiss him, and Marcus switched his mouth to my nipple.

The weight on the bed behind my legs shifted and I returned my attention to Gideon, gloriously naked and ready for me. He grabbed my hips and slid into me with a slow powerful stroke, his gaze never leaving mine. We were connected, body, magic, and soul, and our power crackled over our brands, divine light dancing over our forearms.

He pumped into me as Jacob made love to my mouth and Marcus sucked on my nipples. My desire ratcheted higher, my breath so fast I was dizzy, and I rocked my hips, meeting Gideon, driving him as deep as he could go.

My climax built fast in part because I was already aching

for Gideon and his desire flooded me, and because of Marcus and Jacob caressing and kissing me.

Gideon's pace picked up and grew frantic, then Jacob rubbed his thumb over my clit and I shattered. Light blazed from my brands and eyes, hell, my whole body. My bond with Gideon surged strong and sure. He came, his body tense, his wings exploding from his back, at the same time the full force of my climax made every muscle clench.

With a shuddered groan of satisfaction, Gideon pulled his wings back in and Marcus shifted so he could collapse beside me.

"That was—" Gideon gasped.

"Amazing," Marcus finished.

"Yeah," Jacob said.

That was one way to put it. It'd also been incredible, sexy as hell, and utterly satisfying. This was the way it was supposed to be. I could feel my guys, their bonds pulsing around my heart and their emotions filling me.

Jacob nudged me—then I nudged Gideon who nudged Marcus—and we all shifted over to make room for Jacob on his bed.

I could lie with the guys like this, naked and boneless, forever. Add Kol and it would be perfect—

Jeez.

I fought to shove that thought aside.

Kol wasn't mine.

I had to remember he wasn't mine.

Except a small voice kept whispering, *he should be.*

Gideon ran his hand over my belly, drawing a shiver of renewed desire—which surprised me since I'd just had three amazing orgasms—and pulled me close. He planted a soft, lingering kiss on my lips that made my breath pick up again, then, with a sigh edged with regret, he sat up.

"We have to get back to work," he said.

Marcus groaned. "I hate those glyph witches more than I did before." But he too sat up and headed into the bathroom.

Gideon grabbed his pants off the floor and stepped into them. "I brought you a change of clothes." He set my duffle bag on the bed.

I sat up and reached for the bag. "Are there actually clean clothes in there?" I couldn't remember if I had any remaining changes that I'd originally brought from my apartment yesterday...? The day before...?

Jeez. I had no idea when I'd last been home.

"I ran over to your place and grabbed a few things earlier today," Jacob said. He hooked a finger under my chin, raised my head, and kissed me before getting off the bed and heading to his closet.

"Thanks." I returned to the bathroom, was kissed sense-less again by Marcus, and had a quick proper shower, since a lot had happened between now and my last shower at Sebastian's.

With my wet hair pulled back in a ponytail, and dressed in a clean pair of jeans and a T-shirt that revealed all of Gideon's brand and most of Jacob's, I joined my guys striding down the hall to the elevators. I'd never felt more sure about my place. It was here with my guys, helping people as a JP agent. And yet I had no clue if I was still an agent.

The elevator door slid open and we stepped in. Marcus snaked an arm around my waist and drew me tight against his body, while Gideon and Jacob pressed close on either side.

"So am I just helping out with this spell or am I still an agent on the team?" I asked.

Marcus huffed. "Of course you are. Why would you ask something like that?"

"Because I was assigned as the *human* member of the team and I'm no longer human. I really want to know where I stand."

"Beside us," Gideon said. "Your paperwork went through this afternoon while Amiah had you sedated. You're officially a JP agent assigned to our team."

"Even though I'm your mate?" That was the other issue. Although I wondered how Cassius felt about that now that I was actually a full angel.

"Head office knows everything," Jacob said. "And the mayor has rescinded his demand that a human be assigned to our JP team."

Thank God. Because I didn't know how any human would survive chasing the city's most dangerous supers. I had some power and I'd barely managed to survive the last few weeks.

Gideon gave me a warm smile that made my soul sing. "Once we've found the source of the glyph witches' power, we'll get you proper training."

Once we'd found the source. That sounded suspiciously like I was going to help with the spell and nothing more. I resisted the urge to fight him on that. I might now be a powerful super, but I still had no idea how to control that power, or the best way to apprehend supers. There was a lot I needed to learn before I could be a good agent.

"Hopefully now that the spell blocking your magic and true essence is gone, you'll have more control over your light strike," Jacob said.

"So my essence now says I'm an angel?" It was going to be even more challenging to be an agent if my essence still said I was a human and my eyes glowed. Everyone would mistake me for a nephilim. And while I knew my guys had my back, the average-Joe-super wouldn't.

"More or less," Marcus said.

"What does that mean?"

"If you look closely, there's still something a little wonky with it, but it does say you're an angel," Jacob said.

"Bane says it's just the remnants of the spell," Gideon added. "It'll eventually pass."

Well, that was a relief. Finally something was going right. There was just one more thing—

"What about Cassius? Is the team still under review?" He'd been against me since the beginning... then he'd arrested me and been poisoned and nothing with him had been cleared up.

Jacob shot Gideon a worried look.

Oh, that wasn't good. Maybe nothing *would* be cleared up and he'd always hate me.

"Cassius is still unconscious," Gideon said, his angel glow dimming with worry.

"But we removed the magical poison," I said. "And the glyph witch who cast the spell died." Surely that had been enough to destroy the spell poisoning him, and, although things were a bit of a blur, I thought I recalled Amiah saying the poison was gone. As much as I didn't like Cassius and he'd been a real asshole to me, he was still Gideon's brother —and all that assholeishness had been a misguided attempt to protect Gideon, something I could fully understand.

"And Willow worked through me to pull it all out." The muscles in Jacob's jaw flexed, but I wasn't sure if it was because Cassius hadn't woken or because he'd let Willow use him to save Cassius.

Gideon squared his shoulders. "He'll wake eventually." But I could feel his worry.

The door slid open and we headed the short distance down the wide hall to the shallow steps leading down to the cafeteria.

It was empty. Thank God.

I wasn't ready to face all of the angels in Union City, as well as my non-angelic co-workers, as a full angel. Especially since everyone had believed I was a human. Just the thought of how much attention that was going to get made me shudder. I'd spent my life hiding, striving to not be noticed, and now I was sure everyone was talking about me.

The rock wall feature was still under construction, surrounded by scaffolding, the water still off, and only half of the decorative plants were in their crannies. But the bank of windows at the back and the door leading to a patio had been replaced. If I ignored the rock wall, I could pretend the archnephilim hadn't destroyed the room and murdered Zella.

I slid a glance at Gideon, threaded my fingers between his, and gave his hand a squeeze. I knew he was in love with me. I could feel it in our bond. But that didn't mean he hadn't been in love with Zella. Love was complicated. There wasn't just one person—my bonds were proof of that—nor was there one way to love someone.

Jacob headed to our usual six-seater table while Marcus, Gideon, and I went to the fridge containing the wrapped sandwiches and salads. I picked a turkey club sandwich and a bottle of water, and took the chair beside Jacob as he slid his phone back into his pocket.

"Just letting Kol and Bane know where we are," he said as Gideon sat at the head of the table and Marcus sat across from me.

"Good." Gideon cracked open his water bottle. "We need

to figure out what we're going to do once we locate the source of the witches' magic."

"Let the professionals handle it," a raspy alto said, as a tall woman strode down the steps toward us. She was strikingly beautiful, even with the sneer curling her lips. Not quite succubus beautiful, but close, with black hair pulled back into a long braid, sculpted cheekbones, and large black eyes that glowed with a prick of hellfire. She wore a tight tank top that showed off her muscular arms and gave a hint of what had to be a perfect six-pack. But what shocked me was her power. It filled the room, pushing out the air and crushing inside me. Whoever she was, whatever kind of demon she was, she was powerful.

CHAPTER 3

THE FORCE OF THE WOMAN'S POWER STRENGTHENED AS SHE drew closer, and I could barely breathe by the time she stood beside Gideon and stared down at him.

"Would you mind pulling it back?" Marcus growled, his anger curling tight in my chest. "Our mate can't breathe."

The woman cocked a black eyebrow. "I didn't think you were sensitive, agent."

"You *know* I'm not." He and the others looked fine. But then they weren't magically sensitive and couldn't feel the woman's power like I could. "But that doesn't mean you can just let it all hang out."

Wisps of red demonic magic curled around her forearms and sank back under her skin, and the force of her power billowed. It stole what little breath I had left, and I clutched the edge of the table to keep from collapsing.

"Zuri." Gideon shoved out of his chair, the light in his eyes blazing, his emotions turning the air hot.

"I outrank you," she hissed. "Sit back down."

Black specks crept around the edge of my vision. She was doing it on purpose. I had no idea why, but it pissed me off. I was sick and tired of being in pain and out of breath and the weak link.

Well, no more.

My magic roared inside me, ignited by my determination. It seared in my chest, shoving the woman's power out of my body, and blazed from my palms. I drew in a deep, ragged breath and stood, my chair's leg screeching on the floor.

The woman's eyes widened, her hellfire flared, and her power pounded with enormous force, but couldn't get back inside me.

"I'll give you a pissing contest if you want one." I met her raised eyebrow with my own. I had no idea if I could win a fight against this woman, but all the frustration and fear from the last few weeks now burned in a powerful rage inside me. I was done running and hiding. My guys had stood by me even when they thought I was a nephilim, and now it was time for me to stand my ground.

The woman's sneer deepened and with a flash her crushing power vanished. "Strong enough to withstand a greater demon. She *is* an archangel. I'd say a full one, too." She grabbed a chair from the table behind her, pulled it beside Gideon's, and sat in it backwards.

Gideon glared at her and the temperature stayed hot. "Was that really necessary?"

"Head office requested it," a broad-shouldered guy with angelic glowing eyes said from the top of the cafeteria stairs. Beside him stood a rake-thin woman radiating the feral intensity of a shifter, and another guy, who looked to be in his mid-twenties and was built like Marcus with a lean-muscled body. I couldn't sense any power radiating from him, and he didn't give off vampiric intensity or shifter feral-ness, so I had no idea what kind of super he was.

"I really want to tell head office to fuck off," Marcus said under his breath.

"It's not that they don't believe your reports..." the angel said as he headed down the stairs toward us.

"But there hasn't been a new archangel in generations." Gideon sat back down. The temperature eased a bit, but didn't fully return to normal. In fact, if I looked closely—because I could also *feel* it with my magic—all of my guys were tense with anger and worry.

"Just like there's only been one other mated pair in over a hundred years," the demon-woman said. Her gaze slid to Jacob's arm and his brand. "Mated trio?"

"Plus an extra," the female shifter said with a sniff. "Your incubus must be in heaven."

"Or he's stoned out of his mind," the demon-woman said. "You said he'd be back in an hour."

"There are still a few minutes left," the angel said, taking the empty chair beside Marcus.

The demon-woman rolled her eyes at him.

"I'm sorry about your welcome to the JP," the angel said, holding out his hand to me. "I'm Ephraim, Zuri's second in command, that's Regan—" He jerked his thumb at the shifter, who took the other empty chair, leaving the human-looking guy to grab one from another table. "And that's Xavier."

"Who can just as easily cast this location spell as your guy," the demon-woman, Zuri, said.

"I don't know about that." Xavier rubbed the back of his neck, looking embarrassed.

"You're powerful enough to be on an elite team, kid. Start acting like it," Regan growled at him.

"I just mean Sebastian Bane is known in witching circles to be powerful and he's already felt the magic we're looking for. I'd need even more power just to figure out where to start looking."

"He's also rumored to sell illegal goods to known criminals," Ephraim said. "We can't look the other way because he's helpful."

"Rumored," Sebastian said as he entered the cafeteria with Kol at his side. They were both breathtakingly sexy, Sebastian the ice to Kol's fire, but I couldn't keep my eyes off of Kol.

"Are we finding the source of the worship magic or not?" Sebastian asked.

"We're waiting on you." Zuri shoved out of her chair and marched right past Sebastian to the stairs, as if she knew exactly where she was supposed to be headed.

Her team fell in line behind her, and Gideon rose and glanced at me. Love and desire swept across his expression before he gave me a nod of encouragement and squared his shoulders.

"Always great to have an elite team visit," Marcus growled, his voice low.

"We need them," Gideon said. "Especially if those weren't the only witches able to access that worship magic. Those glyph witches nearly killed us twice."

I shuddered at the memory of my guys bleeding and gasping, my soul screaming that they were dying, while I'd been unable to help them. I was never going through that again.

"Three times," Jacob said. "We didn't fare too well at the airport."

Marcus shot him a dark look. "Don't remind me."

"Come on." Gideon jerked his chin to the cafeteria stairs. "Let's not keep the *elite* team waiting."

"Just give me a minute with Esther and Kol," Sebastian

said, his gaze leaping past Gideon to the hall where Zuri and her team had gone. "I want to set up the necessary links without the audience."

"I'll go keep them distracted." Jacob headed out of the cafeteria.

"Marcus, go with him," Gideon said.

"Really?" Marcus asked. "They're not a threat."

"Yet," Sebastian said.

Marcus glared at him. "They're assholes, but we're all on the same side."

"Come on, Marcus." Gideon's angel glow flared. "Given how we were greeted, I don't want any of us alone with them."

"You think we're still under review?" Kol asked.

"Cassius—" Gideon said, and a swell of grief misted the air around me. "Cassius is still unconscious and we called for help. It's not a question of whether we're under review or not. It's for how long. And we can't risk being reassigned to different teams. I don't want any of us to have to choose between Essie or our jobs."

"Then why the hell did you ask them to stay?" Marcus asked. "They were supposed to be on a plane by now."

"Someone else would have shown up in a day, probably less, and I'm not going after the source of the glyph witches' power with just one senior agent. I want that team." Gideon ran his hands over his buzz cut. It was a little longer now, but not anywhere close to what it was before I'd burned him to a crisp during a drug-induced suicide attempt.

"Are you coming?" Jacob asked from down the hall. I could still see his legs, so he hadn't gotten far. He'd probably heard the debate and waited for Marcus.

"Yeah." Marcus shot me a heated look that sent a shiver

of desire down my spine, and hurried to catch up with Jacob.

Kol dropped his gaze to the floor for a second, his body tense, then raised it, his expression tight, his hellfire still small, barely there, pinpricks. "So how does this tracking spell work?"

"First," Sebastian said, sitting in the closest chair and placing a large coin with a complicated glyph on it on the table, "Essie needs to connect to the link charm."

"Kol?" Gideon asked, and Kol picked up the coin and shut his eyes.

"Feels like a temporary link with nothing else attached," Kol said, opening his eyes.

"You still don't trust me." Sebastian gave an exaggerated sigh. "I've already had access to her essence. If I wanted to control her, I would."

Gideon's eyes narrowed. "That doesn't make me feel better."

"And it doesn't mean we shouldn't be careful," Kol added.

"They don't trust me." Sebastian flashed me a wicked smile filled with heat and mischief. He took the charm from Kol and held it, resting it in his palm.

"Probably because you keep messing with them," I said.

"Everyone has to have a hobby." He cocked a white eyebrow, drawing my attention to a gaze so pale blue it was almost colorless. A flicker of his power danced across his eyes. Even with his essence low, I could glimpse the vast, icy universe of magic in his pupils. "Place your palm on top of mine and we'll get this link set."

"So I'm *not* giving you magic?" I asked. I'd thought I was going to transfer power into him like I had yesterday, when my guys were dying and he needed to teleport them to safety.

"You're not," he said. "I'm not dumb enough to try a transfer with an untrained archangel who's used to using extra force to get her power out. I'd be fried before I could blink."

"Which means I'm still a bomb waiting to explode." Just great. I thought I was past that. My buzz was gone and I couldn't feel my power threatening to erupt, and while my head was still sore from channeling too much magic, I'd thought I was finally fine.

"You're not going to explode," he said. "The pressure building within you as your magic was trying to break the spell on you is gone."

"But an energy transfer to a person is a delicate thing, and you don't have that kind of control yet," Gideon said.

"If you weren't as powerful as you are, it wouldn't be a problem." Sebastian shifted his hand closer to me, reminding me I was supposed to place my hand on his. "If I wasn't in my... *current* condition, your lack of control wouldn't be a problem, either."

Great. So I wasn't a ticking bomb, but that still didn't mean my light strike wasn't going to accidentally hurt someone.

"We should get on with this," Kol said, shoving his hands in his pockets. "Zuri isn't going to wait forever."

Right. We were supposed to be playing nice with her so she wouldn't break up the team.

I placed my hand over Sebastian's. He captured it, setting his other hand on top, and murmured something, his voice so low I couldn't make out the words even with my vampire-enhanced hearing.

A shiver of ice, somehow soft and sensual, crawled over

my hands and snaked up my arm. Miniature magical ruptures sparked under my skin, frozen and powerful. This was what Sebastian's power felt like. Or at least this was a glimpse. I got the feeling this was merely a fraction of the whirling power that lay inside him.

He turned my hand so the charm lay in my palm and looked at Kol. "Your turn."

"Yeah," Kol said, his tone sharp.

He pressed his warm palm to mine, the heat from his demonic body temperature sinking into my skin and swirling with Sebastian's ice. My gaze lifted to his of its own volition. The hellfire in his eyes grew, simmering and stealing my breath like it always did, and for a second, the connection between us felt like it had before my wings had appeared. Warm. Sensual. Right.

Then frustration cut into the feeling. The muscles in Kol's shoulders stiffened, his hellfire tightened, and he shifted his gaze to Sebastian, who captured our hands between his and murmured the spell again.

A caress of heated desire entwined with Sebastian's ice, and need swelled in my chest and lower. I bit back a moan. I was pretty sure this wasn't supposed to turn me on. There wasn't even close to enough of Kol's magic to fill me with yearning, but I remembered what the full force of his power felt like, hell, what even half of his power had felt like when he'd poured it into me to save my life, and my body craved him.

Maybe Kol wasn't really mine. Maybe my reaction to him *was* just a woman, reacting to an incubus.

The heat swelled and another slice of frustration cut through it.

Kol pulled his hand back and my yearning billowed, aching with the loss of his skin against mine. The curls of his magic and Sebastian's were still there, but it felt as banked as the hellfire in his eyes.

Sebastian sat back and ran a hand over his face, looking exhausted. "Okay. When we get to—" He turned a questioning look at Gideon.

"The clean room," Gideon said.

"Good call. Lots of wards and no magical residue. We might need those." Sebastian drew in a sharp breath and squared his shoulders. "When we get to the clean room, I'll initiate the spell and link you to it. Essie, just relax into it and let Kol guide you." He stood and shoved the charm into his pants pocket.

I stood and Gideon threaded his fingers between mine. I hadn't thought he'd be a handholding kind of guy, but perhaps he was trying to make up for the weeks he'd tried to stay away from me.

We headed out of the cafeteria and down the hall, going past the elevator and deeper into the 19th century warehouse half of Operations. The first time I'd been there, I'd been in pain and afraid my secret would be discovered. I'd just had the crap beaten out of me by the archnephilim and Gideon had all but gotten a court order to have my memories read. I hadn't wanted to go to the place where every angel in Union City lived and I certainly hadn't wanted to get close to Marcus again, not with the attraction still sizzling between us.

Just a few weeks later and everything had changed. Now I walked hand-in-hand with Gideon, craved all of Marcus's ferocious passion, yearned for Jacob's intense stillness, and ached for Kol.

I'd dreamt again of Kol while doped up on Amiah's sedatives, of his embrace, his kiss, his caress. Dream Kol had told me that he craved me as much as I craved him, that I should talk to him and shouldn't assume it was all in my head.

Which, ironically, had *been* all in my head.

But every interaction I'd had with him so far indicated he wasn't ready to talk. Even if it was to just tell him I understood his reaction when I'd triggered his PTSD and was there for him when he was ready.

We reached a nondescript door in a hall of nondescript doors and entered the all-black windowless room where I'd first had my memories read. The light was still low, the room illuminated by a single-bulb fixture in the center of the ceiling, and the four benches, one along each wall, still the only pieces of furniture.

Jacob and Zuri stood by the door. It looked like they'd been talking but their conversation had stopped the moment we'd entered, and I felt Jacob's essence focus on me. It was subtle—I was pretty sure no one else noticed—and it settled nerves I hadn't realized were thrumming.

The rest of the elite team sat on the bench on the right-hand wall, Ephraim posture-perfect, Regan managing the lotus position on the narrow bench, and Xavier leaning against the wall. He sat up when Sebastian—who'd been behind me—entered.

Marcus, sitting on the bench on the other side of the room from the elite team, sat forward as well, his gaze locking with mine for a second, his wolf slitting his pupils. A wave of fierce protectiveness flooded my chest and the temperature rose a few degrees.

Sebastian went straight to the middle of the room, sat cross-legged, and motioned for me and Kol to join him. We sat, and Xavier leaned forward, his elbows on his thighs, as if he wanted to get closer but had been told to stay where he was.

"Just let the spell work through you," Sebastian said, leveling his icy gaze on me. "Don't fight it."

I didn't like the sound of that. "Will I want to fight it?"

I'd had the archnephilim, a hellfire prince, and Victoria try to control me, and I'd hated that feeling. I never wanted to go through that again, the helplessness, the terror. Thinking about it still made my stomach churn and my pulse race. I really hoped this spell wasn't anything like that.

Sebastian pressed two fingers to his neck, activating one of the glyphs tattooed on his body. Light burst from it, turning his white button-down see-through and revealing that the glyph snaked down his chest, between thicker glyphs, in a thin, complicated design. More glyphs covered his torso, a mix of thick and thin mesmerizing black swirls. "Just concentrate on relaxing."

"Sure," I said. No problem. Even if concentrating seemed the opposite of relaxing.

He activated another glyph that curled over his right biceps, and a third at his hip, at the waist of his slacks.

"He's combining spells," Xavier said, his voice breathy with awe.

"Take a breath and release it, Esther." Sebastian held out his hands, one to Kol, the other to me.

I drew in a slow breath and took his hand as Kol took Sebastian's other hand.

Just relax and let the spell flow. That was all I had to do.

Sebastian jerked his chin at the space between me and Kol. "Now complete the circle."

Kol grabbed my hand before I could reach for him and a blast of ice, Sebastian's frozen magic, sliced into my chest. My power erupted in response, exploding into a consuming inferno that threatened to burn Sebastian and his magic into ash.

CHAPTER 4

My pulse raced and the twin fears that I was going to hurt someone and I was being controlled by someone seized me. My power roared stronger, blazing through magical channels still raw from the last couple of days, fighting the thread of ice determined to wrap around it and control it. I couldn't let it. Never again. The ice had to get out.

Get out. Get out get out.

My heart slammed in my chest and I couldn't catch my breath.

Get out. Please, get out.

Except this was what was supposed to happen. Sebastian had told me not to fight it.

I gritted my teeth and struggled to give in to his magic. We needed to find the source of the glyph witches' power and this was the only way to do it.

But God, everything within me howled against the feeling of being possessed, of letting someone take over.

"Just take a breath." Sebastian's grip on my hand tightened. The glow from his glyphs now radiated so brightly he was engulphed in their light and looked like a being of pure illumination.

On my other side, Kol had bent forward, his forehead pressed to the floor, his face scrunched with pain.

"Take. A. Breath," Sebastian gasped.

I forced myself to take a slower breath. It wasn't as long and calming as it could have been, but it was the best I could do.

Sebastian's ice twisted, sliding against my blaze, trying to gain purchase inside me. He rolled his shoulders as if he, too, was trying to relax, and his icy blue-white glow rippled down his body. "Another."

I drew in another breath, slower than before, willing my power to calm. It didn't have to be an inferno. It could be a banked fire, or an electric blanket, or something God damn calm and controllable.

Just let him in. That was all I had to do. My power heaved, and I imagined the swell as a great wave sweeping over me, followed by a smaller wave, and then an even smaller one. There were still swells, I didn't think the magical burning ocean within me was ever going to be a perfectly still lake, but I managed to wrench it back so it was now no longer a ferocious storm.

Sebastian's ice curled into my ocean, twisting my power into his spell. The sensation grated on my nerves and made my soul scream to push him out, keep control. He didn't belong. He wasn't supposed to be inside me.

Then a whisper of sensual heat blended with the ice and my essence instantly focused on it. The ice, the fear, the inferno, were gone. There was only Kol's magic, warm and aching and right. I didn't want to kick him out, felt no need to fight him... because he wasn't trying to control me, not like Sebastian. But I couldn't help wondering if it was because I wanted Kol as much as I wanted Marcus and Jacob and Gideon.

The ice and heat wove deeper inside me, bringing with it a flood of emotions from them. Sebastian was exhausted and worried. Kol was afraid and hurting, a pain that reached soul deep. I gasped, drowning in feelings that weren't mine, fighting to breathe, to think, to do anything beyond *feel*.

My power surged again, instinctually defending me from the *emotional* attack. I scrambled to control it and managed to refocus the blast into a rope and twist it deeper into Sebastian's spell. The sudden burst of power shot my consciousness out of my body and into the sky floating above Operations.

Below lay the helicopter pad and the rooftop patio where Gideon had first agreed to let me be on the team. Ahead stretched the park ringing the Supers' Quarter and beyond that lay the rest of Union City. Fifteen minutes to the north was my apartment in its four-story walkup in its neighborhood of four-story walkups.

This is what the glyph witches' source feels like, Sebastian said in my head, his voice strained as he struggled to keep the spell together. *Kol, guide her.*

Kol's heat sank deeper into me, his essence entwining with mine like how Jacob had entwined our essences when he claimed me. My soul sang with joy and grief and a churning mix of emotions that I wasn't sure were mine, until his sensual magic overwhelmed it all with bone-melting desire. I swallowed a moan, my pulse picking up again, and strained to concentrate.

We were supposed to be doing a spell. Weren't we?

Can you feel the witches' magic? Kol asked.

God, I couldn't feel anything but Kol's strong, aching, liquid desire flooding my every cell.

Esther, Sebastian gasped. *Concentrate. You might be powering this, but I'm still holding the spell together.*

Which meant I needed to hurry up. He was still weak, and out of all of us in this spell, he was the one risking burning up by channeling too much magic.

I fought to mentally push past Kol's magic but couldn't make myself leave him. I wanted to stay embraced in his heat forever.

An aching slice of frustration cut through my desire and Kol's heat turned brittle, losing its sensual slide through my essence.

Reach out with your senses, he said, his voice tight as he gave me a mental shove.

My senses spiraled out. For a second, all the magic in the city flooded me, bright, dark, cold, burning. There was so much. The Quarter was one big churning ocean threatening to drown me, but there was also magic in the human part of the city. Protective wards and charms and a few supers who'd chosen to live outside of the Quarter. So much magic, all if it calling to me.

And then I plunged into a sticky black crushing smoke. It clung to me, threatening to ooze into my magical pores and foul the brilliant light at the core of my being. It was more powerful than anything I'd encountered before, even when sensing the glyph witches' magic. It was as vast as the universe in Sebastian's eyes and more, a swirling, writhing force that could devour me and everyone in the room in an instant, which awed and terrified me, since I hadn't thought I'd ever encounter anything more powerful than Sebastian.

That's it, Kol said. *Hard as a rock and impossible to access.*

Rock hard? It didn't feel hard or inaccessible at all. It curled in and around me, cajoling and begging me to embrace it, draw it in. I'd be more powerful than anyone alive. I could right all the wrongs in the world. I'd be worshiped, adored, feared.

Except I didn't want to be worshiped and I certainly didn't want to be feared. And how had I so easily forgotten the threat of being consumed by it? It mesmerized and terrified and spun my thoughts until I wasn't sure what to think.

Esther, please, Sebastian groaned. *Find its source so I can end the spell.*

I struggled to push out of the smoke, but it wouldn't let me go.

Esther.

I'm stuck. I mentally wrenched harder, and the smoke thickened, grating against my magic with a shifting buzz, faster one moment, slower the next, as if trying to find my core resonance. My internal light dimmed and my pulse stalled. It was trying to gain a hold within my soul, trying to take over.

How can you be stu— Kol's heat swelled, but the smoke hit the grating burn of what my buzz used to be and a wave of darkness crashed inside me.

Shit. Bane. What the hell is happening? Kol asked, his voice small and far away.

Esther, fight it, Sebastian yelled, sounding as if he were standing on the opposite side of a great chasm. And that chasm was getting bigger by the second.

His and Kol's fear sliced frozen inside my chest. So, too, did Gideon's, Marcus's, and Jacob's.

The smoke flooded my essence, pounding into me and drowning me in darkness. It tossed me, a soul adrift in a sticky miasma, each second staining my cells darker and darker.

I heaved and yanked and clawed, but couldn't find my way out. There was no up or down, and no light. Only a clinging, exhausting darkness.

My thoughts stalled. For a second I was in the water-that-wasn't-water of my dreams. Asleep but not asleep. Then I was back to drowning in a black void, my soul screaming, my power stuttering.

Blazing white.

Darkness.

Blazing white. Dark—

Blazing fucking white.

I grasped at my light and pumped every bit of my willpower into it. I pulled strength from Gideon and Jacob and even Kol. I could sense extra power from Sebastian but I could also feel the fiery agony inside his head and the strain on his body to keep the tracking spell active so I left him alone.

I spun all that power into a supernova, twisting it tight, and released it in a massive blast inside my body. Sebastian screamed and his magic clenched around mine. Kol's magic faltered and started to fade away. I mentally seized it and it shot me out of the smoke, racing through floor after floor of some kind of building and rushing out the top of a shiny copper peak.

Got it, Sebastian gasped, and his spell burst apart.

I slammed back into my body, staring up at three—? one —? four—? light fixtures, with the room spinning around and around and around.

Out of the corner of my eye, I saw Kol bent forward with his forehead on the floor. With a groan, he sagged to his side and rolled, spread eagle, onto his back.

"What the hell?" Marcus said as he appeared above me, blocking out the too-many light fixtures. He cupped my cheeks with his strong hands, his eyes filled with worry. "Are you all right?"

"Bane?" Gideon asked, and I caught a glimpse of my angel past Marcus's shoulder as he drew close. "How come Essie and Kol are down, but you're not?"

Marcus raised his gaze—presumably glaring at Sebastian—and I managed to turn my head enough to look at the fae sorcerer. He held his head in his hands as if it hurt, his glow dimmer than before, but he didn't look as if the room was spinning and he hadn't collapsed.

"I'm not sure. Something happened and for a bit they were caught up in the worship magic spell, not just the power it's collecting," he said.

"Which is where?" Zuri asked.

"The Cromer Building," Kol gasped.

"Shit." Marcus's wolf rose under his skin, threatening to break free. "We have to assault the mayor's pride and joy, the jewel of Union's newly built downtown?"

"We're not assaulting anything until we have more information," Gideon said.

"That's not your decision, agent." Zuri stepped into sight and glared at Gideon.

The light in Gideon's eyes flared. "You're here on my request. Pretty sure it is."

"I outrank you."

"Not in this situation," Jacob said as he knelt beside me and brushed a strand of hair that had slipped out of my ponytail off my forehead. His dark eyes were filled with concern, and his worry wormed chilly around my heart. "Are you okay?"

"I've been worse."

"Not helpful," Marcus growled.

"Bane, how long will Essie and Kol be down?" Gideon asked. I could feel his need to touch me, reassure himself that I was okay, conflicting with his certainty that he had to stay in control of this situation, not look weak or distracted, and make sure Zuri didn't think she could take over.

"The effects of the worship magic spell will leave their system in about twenty minutes since the spell isn't focused on them." Sebastian rubbed his face. "Given that they're close to passing out, I'd say the spell has also knocked out the super it's focused on, which means we're just dealing with juiced-up witches and not also a goddess."

Which was good. We'd been looking at two outcomes with the source of the witches' power, a comatose super used as a vessel to store the worship magic or a super strong enough to stay conscious while maintaining the spell, along with having access to all that extra power.

Marcus looked up at Gideon. "We should call Amiah."

"No." I grabbed Marcus's wrist, drawing his attention back to me. "We need her at full." Especially if the team was going up against any more witches powered up like yesterday's witches.

"She can spare a little right now. We're just going to start with surveillance," Marcus said.

I gave him the driest look I could muster, which probably just came out as exhausted. "And what happened the last time we just did surveillance?"

Marcus's pupils slitted. "Right." The last time we'd done surveillance, we'd gotten into a fight and a building had been dropped on me and Gideon. "Let's just wait twenty."

"Okay." Gideon nudged Marcus aside, knelt, and offered

me a gentle smile. "Are you good to stay here while we go to Summer's lab and figure out the op?"

"As long as I'm not required to stand." The room had stopped spinning and my vision was no longer double, but I was so exhausted I didn't know if I could raise my head.

Gideon's gaze lifted. "Kol?"

"Sure thing." He raised his hand, thumb up, then dropped it back to his side, as if it were too heavy to hold up.

"Meet us in the lab." Gideon brushed his thumb along my jaw, his gaze wistful. "If we're done before you're up, we'll come get you."

"You're not taking those two anywhere," Zuri said.

"We'll discuss this in Summer's lab." Gideon straightened and marched out the door.

My guys, Sebastian, and the elite team followed, leaving me alone with Kol.

Stillness filled the room, the only sound the soft buzz of the overhead light and Kol's slow, ragged breathing, both dragging me closer to sleep. I couldn't feel anything from Kol, not inside me or as a temperature change, and I didn't know if that was because he'd locked down his emotions or if I was just that tired.

This was the first time we'd been alone together since my wings had appeared, and I knew I needed to talk to him, but I didn't know what to say. I couldn't just say I was sorry I reminded him of the monsters who'd tortured him during the war, but I was madly attracted to him.

And even if he was attracted back, how would that work? He'd said incubi didn't have romantic relationships like humans or other supers, and I got the impression what he'd really meant was that they didn't have romantic relationships at all. I suppose you couldn't really have one if you didn't know if your partner was actually in love with you or if her feelings were just your magic influencing her.

He also still acted like he didn't want to talk to me, hell, he'd barely looked at me since I'd woken in my hospital room, and I was torn between broaching the subject to get it out of the way and giving him more time to sort out his emotions.

"Kol?"

A whisper of hurt and longing and frustration slid across my senses. I rolled my head, almost too heavy with exhaustion to move, to look at him, but his face was turned away from me so I couldn't read his expression.

"I'm sorry I lied to you."

His breath shuddered.

The bulb in the fixture continued to buzz and my thoughts grew fuzzy, except I didn't know when we'd have another moment alone to talk. I had to say something. Now.

"I thought— I wanted—" Him. I wanted him. Marcus, Jacob, Gideon, *and* Kol. That was the way it was supposed to be. But I didn't know how to fix what I'd broken between us.

My enhanced hearing picked up the mumble of voices in the hall, a conversation between at least two people. But they weren't close enough for me to make out who they were or what they were saying.

"Kol, please." I fought to keep my eyes open.

He released another couple of shuddering breaths, each one coming farther apart, slowing with the same exhaustion that pulled at me. I wanted to think that was why he wasn't answering me, but I feared it was because he didn't want to talk with me.

Now just isn't the time. And really, it was selfish of me to try to force this on him. He was the one with the PTSD. He was the one who'd been triggered. Just like facing Marcus's rage over turning him into a werewolf, my conversation with Kol had to be on his terms. Which was going to drive me crazy.

I dragged my eyes open, not realizing I'd closed them. They slid shut again and with a heavy sigh I gave up trying to stay awake.

I drifted into a warm darkness, bobbing up and down... up and down... in the thick water that wasn't water. I was safe, secure, and alone. For the second time in as many days I felt empty in my not-water dream. I was missing something.... or someone. I didn't know which, and my mind just kept bobbing with my body, soft and out of focus, unable to figure it out.

The handsome angel with the light brown hair and the gold flecks in his angel glow appeared before me. My father. He *had* to be my father. We had the same hair, the same gold flecks. Everything within me *said* he was my father.

He pressed his hand on something between us, and said something, but I couldn't make out his words.

A boom sounded far off in the distance. My father glanced over his shoulder, but I could only see darkness behind him and I had no idea what he was looking at.

Another boom and a flurry of sharp cracks.

A sob quickly followed, coming from the darkness.

The sharp cracks drew closer and my thoughts clicked. Gunfire. I was hearing gunfire.

More cracks. Another boom.

The sobbing grew louder, heartrending, and I strained to see in the gloom, find whoever was crying, help them.

Please, he sobbed.

My father vanished. So too did the not-water, and the sobs turned into ragged pleas.

Stop, please. Please. No.

My pulse picked up. I needed to help him. I couldn't just lie there and listen. But I couldn't see him. I couldn't see anything.

No! The sobber begged and released a raw, desperate scream. It tore into my soul and wrenched me out of the darkness as Kol screamed again.

CHAPTER 5

I YANKED MY GAZE TOWARD KOL, WHO WAS STILL ASLEEP, AS another sharp, panicked scream tore from him. Curled in the fetal position, he whimpered and pleaded with his nightmare, his breath desperate gasps, tears leaking from his eyes.

Real fear and agony poured into me, while also frosting my hands and arms and making my breath mist. So much pain and terror. I could barely breathe against its crushing weight. God, how could he even live with it?

"Please. I promise I'll be good," he begged, his voice raw and cracking, sounding shockingly young.

I had guessed he'd been young when Michael had manifested him in this realm to control the women used to create the nephilim army. Kol could have been as young as thirteen or fourteen, fresh into his power to enthrall multiple people at the same time. And now I had proof.

"Please. I promise. I promise."

Bile burned the back of my throat. To do that to a kid. To—

"I promise," Kol sobbed.

"Kol, wake up." I pressed my hand to his warm back, not wanting to startle him but needing to wake him and unable to resist the desire to comfort him.

He stiffened, still asleep, his breath catching, his fear turning the frost on my hands and arms into a thick ice despite the warmth radiating from his body. His pain slammed into me, and my power flared with the strange heat that wasn't my destructive light strike but that something else I'd used when I'd shown Gideon how I really felt about him. It flowed out of my hand into Kol and spun a gauzy golden net around his terror.

He drew in a ragged breath but didn't wake and didn't stop sobbing. The ice on my arms cracked and fell off, and the net thickened, ever so slightly softening the edges of his fear.

A shuddering sigh escaped his lips, and the ice on my hands crumbled.

My pulse skipped a beat. My magic wasn't just a strange energy. This was my empathy easing his emotional agony. I could make his memories of the war seem like a dream, take away all of his fear. I could make him feel relaxed and joyful—

I could make him fall in love with me.

But I didn't want to *make* him love me. I wanted him to love me because *he* loved me.

"Kol, wake up."

My magic seeped deeper into his essence and soul, drawn to a horrible, infected darkness. A ragged tear that had never healed, and made me want to scream at the injustice.

Beautiful, mischievous, amazing Kol carried such pain, every day, and no one knew. I wondered if he even knew. The tear was buried deep, hiding among emotional and psychological scar tissue. He probably knew there was something wrong, but not what, and thought it was something he just had to live with.

Heat fluttered around me, Kol's magic caressing mine, and aching desire sank into my core. He groaned, the sound low and sensual, making my nerves thrum in anticipation, and his eyes cracked open. His hellfire blazed in full, dancing along his cheekbones, and accentuated an expression that was filled with an aching yearning. A yearning that stole all breath and thought. There was only him, his passion, his need, and that tear in his soul that I wanted—no, *needed* to mend.

My magic swelled, curling around the tear's edges, and his heat flared in response. His breath picked up, his desire fueling mine for a breathtaking second.

Then he wrenched his gaze away from me and squeezed his eyes shut. "Essie, stop."

But I hadn't even begun to mend the tear, hadn't even managed to soften the painful ragged edges. "Kol—"

"Please," he begged, his voice heartbreakingly similar to when he'd been begging in his nightmare, his emotional pain overwhelming.

I pulled my hand away and released my magic. I didn't know how I was causing him harm, but it was clear I was. "You were screaming in your sleep."

"Sometimes I scream," he said, panting, his pain still raging through me. "Don't do that again."

"But I can help you." My empathy was finally good for something. He'd helped me so much, dealing with Marcus and Gideon, and had welcomed me with open arms to the team. Now I could help him in return.

"Let it be."

"Kol—"

"I've worked with empaths to ease the emotions and lethe demons to dampen the memories," he said, his voice tight, his whole body tight. "It's fine."

"It's not fine."

"The nightmares will pass in a week or so. You're not the first to trigger me and you won't be the last." He sat up, drawing farther away, the hellfire in his eyes back to barely-there pinpricks. "It is what it is. The sooner I move on, the better."

"Pretty sure that's not how it works."

"Just let it be." He stood and headed to the door, taking a page out of Gideon's book and walking away to end the conversation.

I scrambled to my feet, surprised that I still wasn't completely exhausted, and hurried to catch up with him. I could help him. I knew I could. He didn't have to suffer. "Kol—"

His back stiffened and a mix of yearning and horror swept through me, confusing me even more.

"Leave it," he snapped.

"Wasn't what I was going to talk about," I snapped back, even if it was. A part of me was frustrated that he didn't want help, but another part, a part that had lived through a few horrible events—although not nearly as horrible as Kol's—understood the desire to just shove everything down deep and carry on. Not to mention right now he was probably still reeling from that nightmare. Better to bring the conversation up when he wasn't feeling on edge.

"How much do you know about Zuri and her team?" I asked, jumping on the first topic change I could think of.

The tension didn't leave his body and he kept walking down the hall toward the elevator. "I've met them a couple of times before but never worked with them. They think they're the best, probably because they are."

"So they can back up the attitude?"

"Oh, yeah." Kol hit the call button and we waited for the elevator door to open.

My whole essence yearned to step closer to him, not just to let my empathy heal the wound in his soul but to be close to him, while his stiff posture and averted gaze said in no uncertain terms *keep back*.

"They're the best of the best," he said, his gaze locked on the closed elevator door. "Zuri's elite team is the best of the elites. I'm surprised they have that new guy, the human witch. He's awfully young to be an elite."

"And he didn't strike me as powerful."

"I think he is. I just think he's really good at hiding it." Kol gave a sensual shrug and a bit of tension eased from his posture for a second. "Of course, after seeing past Sebastian's concealments to his true essence, every witch you come across is going to seem weak in comparison."

The door slid open, revealing Jacob inside. His dark gaze leaped to mine and quiet certainty flooded me through our brand.

"You're up," he said with his soft low rumble that always made my essence thrum with desire.

"They send you down to get us?" Kol stepped into the elevator and I followed.

Jacob wrapped an arm around my waist and drew me tight against him. He didn't scold me like Marcus would have, but I could feel his worry for me. "It's been half an hour. Gideon and Zuri have agreed on the op and we're getting ready."

Kol shoved his hands into his pockets.

"What's the plan?" And was I going to have to fight to be

a part of it... and did I want to? Even if I now had incredible power, I was still untrained.

Except no way in hell was I letting my guys face anyone as powerful as those witches again without me.

Guess I'd made my decision. I was fighting for my place on the op.

"Xavier is setting us up with short-term concealment spells, then we're gearing up and going in through the Underground."

"I didn't think the Underground had been restored all the way to the Cromer Building." The Underground had been a series of underground halls between some of the bigger buildings in the downtown core and a couple of the downtown subway stops. It used to be just as busy as above ground, with shops and restaurants, but only a fraction of it had been restored when the downtown had been rebuilt. And while the original building in the Cromer Building's location had access to the Underground, it sat on the very edge of the core. Access had been cut off halfway between it and the next high rise and had yet to be restored. Or at least I thought it hadn't been restored.

"Construction started middle of last week," Jacob said.

So just about the time when things had really gone to hell for me. No wonder I didn't know about it—because I was sure the mayor would have been all over the local news the moment anything with the Cromer Building had come up.

Although I suppose I couldn't say any more that things had gone to hell. Sure, I'd been attacked by a feral vampire and that had just been the beginning, but I had my guys, I wasn't alone any more, and I'd found where I belonged.

I leaned into Jacob, savoring the feel of his massive body against mine. I always felt so safe when I was in his arms.

Even before our mating brand had formed, he'd made me feel that way.

"An access tunnel was established for the construction workers," Jacob said. "We'll go in through there."

The doors slid open and Kol hurried out. "How many are going in?"

"All of us," Jacob said as we followed Kol down the hall to Summer's lab. "Those were Gideon's conditions. You, Essie, even Bane. It's a ten-man team."

"If I didn't know what we were up against, I'd say it was overkill for just surveillance," Kol said. "How did Gideon convince Zuri?"

Jacob's expression darkened. "He reminded her that Cassius is still unconscious and showed her the surveillance footage of our arrival at Operations last night after the fight at the airport."

"That would do it," Kol said.

We reached Summer's lab, a large room with stainless steel tables and shelves, and humming machinery. The petite angel stood at a computer, her fingers flying across the keyboard, her expression tight with concentration. Beside her, the large screen hanging on the wall had its image split between a satellite picture of downtown with the Cromer Building dead center, a map of the Underground, the halls colored red, yellow, or green—no access, partial access, full access—and a muted news report about the preparations for this year's unification ceremony.

Jeez, the last time I'd looked, the ceremony marking the day the treaty between supers, humans, and the Angelic Defense had been signed and turned the tide of the war against Michael had been over a week away. That had been before I'd been thrown back into the supernatural world by running across that feral vampire's nest. God, it had only been a week and yet it felt like a lifetime ago.

Gideon, Zuri, and Ephraim stood staring at the screen, discussing the advantages and disadvantages of different search options and splitting the teams into groups. Regan sat on an empty table beside them, and Sebastian leaned against it, his weak glow belying his relaxed I-don't-give-a-shit posture. Behind them, Marcus sat on a foldout metal chair at another table across from Xavier. He turned to me the moment I entered, even though his back was to the door, and his wolf gave a soft huff of contentment.

Xavier raised his gaze to me and Kol and tapped the butt of a permanent marker on the table. "Next."

"I'll go." I headed to the table and Marcus gave up his seat, sliding his palm across the small of my back as we traded places and sending a shiver of attraction racing over me.

"Hold out your wrist," Xavier said.

I set my arm on the table wrist up, my stomach churning. Mavis's spell yesterday, where my power had roared out of control and started devouring her magic, had scared me, and I didn't want a repeat of that, especially not with Zuri's team watching. I needed to prove I could control my power, at least well enough not to hurt an ally.

Xavier quirked an eyebrow, making him look even younger than the mid-twenties I'd originally assumed. "You don't have to hold your breath. It's not going to hurt."

"You sure?" While I didn't see a knife or a box of coins, I wasn't going to assume it wouldn't hurt. So far almost everything in the supernatural world had hurt.

He held up the marker. "It's just a temporary glyph. I draw it on and the spell will last about six hours."

"What about topping up the concealment charm we got yesterday?"

Xavier's other eyebrow joined his first. "You got charms yesterday? Who set them?"

"It was kind of an emergency." Marcus placed a hand on my shoulder and gave it a reassuring squeeze. "The glyph witches had a tracking spell on us, and he can't top up the charms because once the spell ended, the coins disintegrated. Besides, he's casting a concealment against magic *and* video surveillance, which the charm didn't have."

"But if you got them yesterday..." Xavier said.

"Trust me," Kol said, "they're dead."

"Pretty sure you would have sensed them," Sebastian added over his shoulder.

Xavier's gaze dipped to the table. "Not if a more powerful witch cast them."

"Jeez, man," Regan growled. "Grow a pair."

"And no," Sebastian added. "I can't set charms. So you've got one up on me, kid."

"Not even close," Xavier said under his breath, only audible because Jacob's claim enhanced my hearing... or was that because I was part archangel? I wasn't quite sure which.

"You're obviously powerful enough to be on an elite team." I nudged my hand closer to him, reminding him he was supposed to be casting a spell on me—as much as I was afraid I'd react badly to his magic.

"I specialize in support magic." He took my hand and drew a complicated glyph on my wrist with his extra-fine tip black marker. "Concealment charms, wards, extra power, that kind of thing. Trust me, you don't want me beside you in a fight. You want me about six feet back. But Sebastian Bane is—" His voice dropped low but I was pretty sure everyone in the room could still hear him. "Sebastian Bane is a legend. A faekin with more glyphs than any known glyph witch."

I bit my tongue against telling him that was because Sebastian wasn't a faekin but a full fae and a sorcerer able to channel raw magic power, something most witches and supers couldn't do.

"He just combined glyphs to cast the tracking spell. I've never seen a witch do that before." Xavier set the marker aside and grasped my hand with both of his.

I instinctually tensed.

"Just take a breath," Marcus said, releasing my shoulder and stepping back. Guess he couldn't be touching me while Xavier cast the spell.

I drew in a slow breath, willing my power to remain calm. I wanted this spell. I needed the spell.

Jeez, maybe if I thought about it hard enough, I wouldn't lose control.

Xavier said two soft sibilant words I didn't recognize, and a gentle heat swelled over my wrist.

My power didn't blaze out of control.

In fact, it didn't react.

Finally!

Xavier said another soft word. The heat grew a little and a wisp of white smoke, just a breath of magic, curled from the glyph's lines and wrapped around my forearm in a gentle gauzy net.

Another word and the net swelled, brushing the bottom of Gideon's brand. The brand lit up with brilliant golden light that surged past my elbow into Jacob's, making it glow as well and filling me with glorious, brilliant power. I was alight with it, filled with the promise of being a super of pure light, like when Sebastian had first discovered I was a full angel. Both of my guys gasped as the brands on their arms lit up, and Xavier's eyes widened with awe.

"Amazing," Ephraim said, his voice breathy.

Zuri huffed. "Yeah, yeah. Beautiful and sacred. Finish the glyph. We need to get a move on."

Xavier rushed through three more words. The power in my brands grew stronger, filling me with Gideon's certainty and Jacob's calm, and the smoke of the concealment spell sank into my skin, taking the marker's ink with it.

I pushed out of the chair, a little stunned, my inner light blazing. I hadn't felt that good in a long time, years, and I could feel the strength of my bonds with not just Gideon and Jacob, but Marcus as well, powerful and sure and right.

Marcus pulled me into his arms and Kol took my place, sliding into the chair without his usual sensual grace. His body remained tense for the whole time Xavier was casting the concealment spell, and then he shoved out of the chair and headed toward Gideon.

"Gideon, a word," Kol said, his voice low.

"All right." Zuri squared her shoulders, distracting me from Kol and Gideon's quiet conversation, and swept her gaze over everyone in the room. "Get your gear and meet in the garage."

Gideon glanced past Kol, met my gaze, and jerked his chin toward the door. "I'll take you to the armory."

"Grab the faekin a vest while you're down there," Zuri said as she strode from the room.

I turned to Sebastian. "Are you sure that's a good idea?" The light that usually radiated from his skin was still dim—I barely caught a glimpse of it from the corner of my eye— and exhaustion still pinched his expression. "You're running on fumes."

"Oh, I've got more than fumes." He flashed his wicked

smile, making Regan snort as she, Ephraim, and Xavier followed Zuri out of the lab. "There's still magic stored in some of my glyphs and if things go south, I can use Xavier's magic to power my bigger glyphs." His expression snapped to serious. "We know what we're up against. The elite team doesn't. This dangerous source of magic needs to be eliminated and I'm not going to sit by and let their ego fuck this up."

"Hunh," Marcus said. "Didn't know you cared."

"These witches are still fighting Michael's war and if his side wins, I'm going to have to go home—" His expression darkened and he shoved past us. "I've a lot invested in this realm. I'd hate to lose my money," he said, his tone flippant. But I got the impression his grim look hadn't been because of the money.

"Well, Agent Shaw," Marcus said, kissing the back of my head and releasing me from his embrace. "Let's do this."

"Meet you in the garage." Jacob gave me a warm smile that heated from his brand to my heart and lower, and he and Marcus left.

Kol hurried after them and I joined Gideon, taking the stairs two floors down into the basement so the guys could take the elevator up to the top floor to get their gear from their rooms.

We emerged from the plain concrete stairwell, rounded the corner, and stepped into the study area just outside the elevator doors. With a soft *click*, the overhead fluorescents flickered on, the sensor registering our movement and illuminating the wide wooden table, old couch, and shelves upon shelves of books in the Operations' library. Directly across from us sat the armory's metal door, with its thick security glass and fingerprint reader.

Gideon pressed his thumb to the reader and unlocked the door.

I hurried inside and headed to the locker with the sidearms, but he grabbed my wrist as I passed him and tugged me around to face him. "Are you up for this?"

Really? I rolled my eyes at him—as much as a part of me did wonder if I was up for this. "You didn't just ask me that."

The muscles in his jaw flexed. "I'm team leader and it's my job to ask." His expression softened and a hint of worry dimmed his angel glow. "I'm also your mate and you've had a tough few days."

"And so has the whole team." I thought he knew me, knew I couldn't sit this out. "Are we going to have the you-can't-be-on-the-team argument again?"

"No. I'm just checking in. I can feel through the brand that you're worried, but I don't know why or over what."

"Gideon, three witches kicked our asses and we don't know what we're walking into in the Cromer Building. Of course I'm worried."

"Well, yes." He frowned. "But it feels deeper than just that."

"Deeper than maybe losing one of you?"

The concern in his expression grew and he pulled me into a firm embrace. "We've just found each other. No one is dying." He said it with such conviction that I desperately wanted to believe him. Except this wasn't a situation he could control.

I leaned into him. Just thinking about losing any of them made my heart pound. But our job was dangerous, and if I couldn't even consider giving it up, I couldn't ask them to give it up, either.

And while that was a huge concern, if I was being honest with myself, my most immediate one was Kol. He wasn't acting like himself and I feared being off his game would endanger him.

"What do you think about Kol?" I raised my gaze to Gideon's. "You know him better than I do."

Gideon's angel glow dimmed even more and the air around me misted.

Damn. My heart sank. "What?"

"He just asked for a transfer," Gideon said.

My essence stalled, my mind unable to fully register what he was saying.

"He'll help us deal with the source of the witches' power," Gideon continued, "and then he wants to be reassigned. Out of town."

CHAPTER 6

"REASSIGNED? OUT OF TOWN?" MY THROAT TIGHTENED. HE couldn't leave. Not now. Not when things were working out. He belonged on the team. I knew that meant everything to him. He belonged with my guys. With me.

I also knew I was the reason he was leaving.

That, and the horrible scar Michael and his nephilim had left on his soul.

The urge to find him, convince him to stay, God, just fix that tear in the core of his being before he left for good, made me push out of Gideon's grasp before I could stop myself. "It's because of me, isn't it?"

"He didn't give a reason and I didn't press."

"Does the rest of the team know?" I asked, forcing myself not to rush out of the armory. Kol had already refused my help. I had to respect that. Just as I had to respect his desire to leave. But I'd thought I'd have more, that I'd just have to wait it out and things could go back to the way they were. The way they were supposed to be. Not him leaving.

"I haven't told them. I'm hoping he'll sort himself out by the time this op is done." Gideon released me and opened the locker with the bulletproof vests, pulled out three vests, and set them on the long, narrow standup table in the center of the room. "I haven't seen him this shut off since Jacob and I pulled him out of that hellhole. It took over two years before an angel could get into the same room with him without him completely shutting down."

"That's horrible." I stared at him, stunned. I didn't know why. I already knew whatever Michael and his nephilim had done had left a festering hole in Kol's soul. And then I'd brought up all those memories again.

Gideon must have seen something in my expression because he wrapped his arms around me again. "It's not your fault. It's Michael's." A whisper of his anger slid through me. "And mine. I didn't realize how bad Kol was. I thought with how well he'd handled the other day with the witches that the trigger had been manageable and he was pulling himself together. I wouldn't have asked him to help with the tracking spell if I'd known."

I wanted to scream with frustration, at the injustice of what he'd suffered, and, selfishly, at how much it hurt me. I didn't want him to leave, and I didn't want him afraid or hurting. I wanted my Kol back. And there wasn't a damned thing I or Gideon, or anyone, could do about it right now. He needed time and therapy and—

God, I didn't know what else. He needed everything I could give him and more to take away this hurt. And even then, none of it would matter if he didn't want my help.

The thought stung, but it was the truth. I couldn't force help on him and he'd decided getting away from the situation was best for him. And if I wanted my guys to get through dealing with any more witches alive, I couldn't be distracted by that. Focusing on Kol's PTSD right now would only get someone hurt.

I eased out of Gideon's embrace and squared my shoulders. "Do you think he'll be able to hold it together during the op?"

"He's assured me he can and he handled the other day fine." The temperature dipped and worry slid through me. "If push comes to shove, I know he'll have our backs."

"And if push comes to shove, we might need everyone." A shudder of fear swept through me.

"Exactly," he said. "Which is why I've reluctantly agreed to keep him on. Now, before we head up to the garage, prove to me you can make a blade of divine light. It's not as powerful as a light strike, but it's safer for the rest of us and I'll feel better knowing you've had a little practice forming one."

I doubted it was a good idea to keep Zuri waiting, but I could sense that confirming the divine light blade that I'd only summoned twice before was important to Gideon. Both of the times I'd formed the blade, I'd been desperate, with my adrenaline pumping, and had been working purely on instinct. But that didn't mean I'd be able to summon one next time I was desperate.

"Hold your hand as if you're holding a knife," Gideon said.

I fisted my hand and held it out. Gideon clasped his hands over mine and I met his warm gaze. A shiver of desire swept over me along with the memory of how he'd kissed, caressed, and filled me only a few hours ago.

"Aren't you supposed to be behind me?" I asked, my voice suddenly breathy as I imagined him tucking up close, his body hard against mine.

The warmth in his eyes turned sizzling. "We'd never make it out of the armory and I really don't want Zuri walking in on us."

He had a point. If he got any closer, I'd give in to the yearning of our bond and rip his clothes off. Hell, he didn't have to get closer. My pulse had already picked up and the rising temperature was revealing his.

"Just like when you pulled in your wings, flood your hand with power," he said, his voice husky. "Imagine it turning into a blade."

"A blade." I could do this. I'd done it before. I imagined my magic rushing to my hands and raised my gaze from our joined hands to his eyes. For a second I was drowning in his perfect summer-sky, captured body and soul. It stole all breath and thought and filled me with warmth and certainty and need. This was where I belonged and who I belonged with. I could do anything with him and Marcus and Jacob and Kol—

My thoughts tripped, stuttering over that, and my power exploded in a blazing inferno in my palm, and Gideon released a strangled cry.

Shit.

Shit shit shit.

I slammed my power back into the core of my being, fear making my pulse pound. "Did I burn you?" *Please say I didn't hurt you.*

"I'm fine," he said, but didn't release his hands so I couldn't tell if I'd burned him or not. "Flood might not have been the best word. Try imagining your power as a marble in the palm of your hand."

"Not until you show me your hands." I'd hurt him. The sultry heat that had been warming the air around me was gone, replaced with an ever-so-slight unnatural chill and a whisper of real-emotional worry.

"You didn't burn me."

"Gideon."

"I'm fine." He peeled back an unblemished palm, letting me see, then retightened his grip. "Just should have been thinking about what we were doing and not—" He cleared his throat. "Marble. Blade. We don't have a lot of time and I know you can do this."

Right. Zuri was waiting.

I drew in a breath and imagined a pinprick of power, not even a marble. Just a spark. If it wasn't big enough, I'd add another spark and another until it was, but I wasn't going to risk a blaze again.

The spark formed, bigger than I expected, and Gideon's face lit up with a stunning smile.

"Good." His electric magic swelled in my brand and slid into my hands, making my skin tingle. "Imagine that marble forming into a knife. Just something small to start."

I closed my eyes and concentrated on stretching my spark into a blade.

"Yes," Gideon breathed.

My concentration slipped, the spark flickered, and my eyes flew open. Gideon's lips quirked in a smile and he sent a pulse of magic into my hands. I regained control on the spark and it lengthened into a three-inch blade.

"Good." He released my hands and stepped back. "Now do it again without me."

I fought to ignore my disappointment at the distance he put between us—now wasn't the time to give in to the brand —released my hold on the blade, letting it disappear, and reformed it.

Gideon made me form it four more times as he grabbed a Glock from the locker securing the sidearms and an M4 carbine from the rack. If I hadn't already known how dangerous anyone we might meet in the Cromer Building could be, I'd have said all the weapons were overkill, just like the ten-man team.

But just like making sure I could form a light blade when I needed to, I also knew Gideon wasn't taking any chances with our weapons. And since I'd yet to be fully trained in my powers—hell, we might not even know all the powers I possessed—I was going to be armed as before, which was just fine with me. Even if it meant causing another incident with the mayor if I was spotted, armed to the teeth, in his pride and joy.

With my Glock holstered, the M4 on a sling across my chest protected with a bulletproof vest, and two extra magazines with ammunition enspelled to stun for each weapon, I left the armory with Gideon. We took the elevator up to the first floor and headed down the long hall to the garage where everyone waited for us.

Everyone, even Zuri's team, wore vests. Of my guys, Jacob was the only one with visible weapons, with his paired Berettas at his hips, but I knew Marcus wasn't unarmed because of his wolf's claws, and Kol, without a doubt, had at least half a dozen blades—probably more—hidden on his body.

Marcus took a step forward as Gideon and I entered the garage, his wolf slitting his pupils, and Jacob's hold on his vampiric intensity slipped a little. My soul sang, my bonds making me ache for them. Kol, leaning against the side of an SUV, crossed his arms and kept his attention on Zuri, with not even a glance in my direction.

"Let's go," Zuri said with a jerk of her chin to the medium gray JP SUV behind her. Her team piled in and we, plus Sebastian, got into the SUV parked beside it.

"Did you figure out your blade?" Jacob asked as he got into the back.

Gideon reached between the front seats and handed Sebastian his vest. "Yes."

Kol got into the back with Jacob, and I slid onto the seat beside Sebastian, keeping close to my door to avoid getting an elbow in the face as he put on the vest.

"You should have taught her how to fly." Marcus, in his usual spot in the driver's seat, shot me a dark look in the rear view mirror and pulled out of Operations' secure garage. "I'd rather know you can get the hell out of there."

"We already know I'm terrible at running if it means I'm leaving someone behind," I said. "Learning to make a blade was a better choice." Even if I really did want to learn to fly.

"And we're going into underground hallways," Sebastian said. "Flying wouldn't be very useful."

"I *know* that," Marcus growled, driving through the Quarter toward the human part of Union City with the other SUV following. "But my wolf really disagrees."

Kol shifted, the tension radiating off him making my stomach churn.

"You're going to need to learn to get it under control." Jacob opened a small black plastic case with the team's coms, pulled one out, and handed it to Kol.

Kol took a com and handed the case to Sebastian.

"This is why soul bonds are a bad idea." Sebastian took a com and passed the case to me. "No one can think straight. You guys need a month to fuck and get the crazy out of your system."

Kol stiffened.

"Gee, what a beautiful way to put it," Marcus said.

Sebastian raised a sculpted white eyebrow. "Don't tell me your wolf doesn't like that idea."

Marcus growled.

"So the source of the witches' magic." I took a com and

passed the case to Gideon. "Did you get a better idea of where it might be instead of just in the Cromer Building?"

Sebastian rolled his eyes at my not-so-subtle change in topic. "Underground."

"Like a basement office?" Marcus asked.

"Deeper." Sebastian frowned. "I think. I'm hoping because I've cast the spell that once we get close, I'll be able to sense the magic even if it's concealed."

"Below the expected basement means less chance of accidentally being seen by civilians," Jacob said.

"But that means if we run into someone," Gideon said, "they're most likely involved with the worship magic. That might make it harder to get in, get the lay of the land, and get out."

Jacob's hold on his vampiric intensity slipped a little more, building a pressure inside my chest. It wasn't crushing, not yet, but if I didn't get out or he didn't pull it back soon, it would be. "Zuri will want to split us up to cover more ground."

"I've already told her that isn't a good idea," Gideon said.

"Yeah, well, let's just hope she believes you," Marcus growled.

Twenty minutes later, we drove into the downtown core and reached the most discreet and easiest access point into the Underground: the entrance to the subway four blocks from the Cromer Building.

I didn't like that we were so far away. If things went south and someone got hurt, we were going to have to drag them four blocks to get them to a vehicle. But if there were a lot more witches connected to the glyph witches' cause to restart Michael's war, we couldn't risk them seeing us enter the Cromer Building. Just because we couldn't be seen by magic or security cameras didn't mean we were invisible.

Marcus parked on a shadowy side street around the corner from the busier street where the subway's entrance lay, and we gathered in the shadows as Ephraim pulled up behind our SUV. Tension from my guys crackled against my senses and the summer night was cooler than I'd expected, given how hot the last couple of days had been—and I couldn't tell if that was because of my empathy or not.

Zuri's team, however, was more relaxed. In fact, Zuri and Regan looked more than ready for a fight. Even Xavier, with his Glock drawn—the only one of Zuri's team who had a weapon—looked more 'ready to do business' than worried.

They had no clue what we were up against.

And I prayed they wouldn't find out.

Not until we had more information, like how many witches remained, and how many worshipers were sacrificing their essence into the pool of magic controlled by those witches.

CHAPTER 7

"COM CHECK," ZURI SAID AS SHE SWEPT HER GAZE OVER THE area, and we all sounded off. "Form up as planned."

She gave Jacob a tight nod, and together they headed around the corner to the stairs leading down into the subway.

Kol and Regan were next, followed by Xavier and Sebastian. Marcus jerked his chin at me and we fell into line, leaving Gideon and Ephraim to take the rear.

As I hurried onto the brighter main street, I glanced up and down the road looking for possible danger as well as bystanders. Thankfully the street was empty. Most of the downtown clubs were on the other side of the core and at this hour there was little traffic, which was one of the reasons Gideon had picked this subway stop.

So far, so good.

I wondered if Gideon had followed protocol and alerted the UCPD of our operation or if, like at the airport, he'd decided breaking protocol was better than endangering human cops—which a few weeks ago would have shocked the hell out of me. Angels didn't lie. They followed the rules. But Gideon, at least, understood that sometimes a rule had to be ignored to save lives.

Zuri and Jacob hustled down the stairs. I took another glance up the street, then followed. This subway stop had miraculously managed to avoid destruction, even though most of the buildings around it had been damaged beyond salvation or outright leveled during the war.

But that meant the stop hadn't received revitalization money, and while it wasn't in rough shape, it still looked old and tired. Grime had built up on the corners of the stairs and the tiled floor at the bottom was chipped in a few places and scuffed all over. A ghost of black graffiti stained the wall, either bleeding through a too-thin layer of paint or not completely scrubbed away, a strange contrast to the large, bright poster beside it touting tomorrow's unification ceremony in Unity Park.

There wasn't a soul in sight, but a rumble far off down the tracks told me a train was on its way and we might not be alone in the station for long.

To my right stood the turnstiles and self-serve ticket station separating the Underground from the platform, and ahead lay a wide, dim hall, most of the lights off, blocked off by a floor-to-ceiling metal security gate.

"Xavier," Zuri said as she swept her gaze past the turnstiles to the platform.

Xavier holstered his sidearm and hurried to the lock on the far side of the gate. With a few hissed words and a pulse of power that rippled through my chest, he unlocked the gate and stepped back.

Jacob pushed it open just wide enough for him to slip through—which was more than wide enough for everyone else since he was the biggest member of the group—and hurried inside.

The rest of us followed in order, reformed our formation on the other side, and Gideon pulled the gate closed, covering our tracks. The only way someone would know something was different was if they tried to open the gate and discovered it was no longer locked.

Half a dozen small stores, also locked behind security gates with only a light or two on inside, lined the hall on either side. Beyond stretched a long expanse of plain hall leading to the next section of the Underground, half a block over in the basements of a pair of twin office towers.

I peered into the darkness ahead of us, seeing farther than I would have if I was a normal human. Thanks to Jacob's claim—or my angelic nature, I wasn't sure which—I didn't need help seeing in the dark.

There wasn't a soul around. Which was expected, since we were in an area closed down for the night.

Except I couldn't shake the feeling that something wasn't right.

I brought the scope on the M4 to my eye and searched the hall for heat signatures.

No one.

We reached the next building over, crossed an area with a food court, and headed into a narrow, concrete service hall. Zuri must have memorized the route because she took us without hesitation down four more narrow halls to one blocked off by a temporary security gate.

A large plastic sheet, with multiple slits in it to allow access but keep dust in, hung just past the gate, and a mess of dirty footprints led to and from the entrance.

I continued to scan everything with my scope, confirming we were alone.

But I just couldn't shake the sense that something was wrong.

Except I didn't know what, and just saying something was wrong without giving actionable intel was useless. Everyone was on guard. Even if Zuri and her team didn't fully understand the danger we were in, my guys and Sebastian did. No one needed to be warned to watch for danger. They already were.

Xavier unlocked this gate and we pushed past the plastic, hustling down a dark hall with construction equipment and crates and rubble.

The worry in my chest grew the closer we got to the end, and I still couldn't see any heat signatures with my scope or explain what was off.

We reached another locked security gate and stepped into a wider, cleaner hall. A few feet down stood a solid metal security door with a glimmer of light seeping under the crack at the bottom.

"Eyes open, everyone," Gideon said. "This is the Cromer Building."

Jacob opened the security door a crack and Zuri peeked out.

"Clear," she said, and without making a sound, she hurried into the main basement of the Cromer Building.

The guys ahead of me followed her and fanned out into an area that was still dim, but brighter than the maintenance halls. It was a big space, with a large food court with five wide halls branching away, a restaurant—still under construction—and a dozen shops. A large set of metal and glass stairs trailed up the far side to a glassed-in second-story—or rather main floor—promenade that ringed the area, and the ceiling rose at least two stories above that.

Pale moonlight shone into the area through the many large windows above on the first-floor lobby. Most of the food court kiosks were covered with plastic tarps, empty spaces waiting to be finished, and only two stores looked like they had businesses in them. The floor was plain concrete not yet tiled, and half of the drywall had yet to be painted.

I hustled out of the hall with Gideon and Ephraim close behind, and the massive weight of the witches' power slammed inside my chest, stealing my breath.

My knees buckled and I fought to keep standing. Kol gasped, Sebastian groaned and sagged to one knee, while Xavier screamed, clutched his head, and dropped to both of his knees.

Zuri jerked around to look at us. "What the hell?"

"Ambush." Gideon grabbed the back of my vest and hauled me back as a massive ball of fire exploded in our midst.

Sebastian slapped his chest, activating a glyph, and a shimmering magical shield swept around him and Xavier. Kol leaped back, and the rest of the group scrambled to get out of the way. The fire seared the air then vanished in a flash. Regan's pants caught on fire and she dropped and rolled as Marcus slapped at the flames, putting them out.

Gasping for breath, Sebastian sagged forward, down to both knees, his hands pressed against the floor. "Fucking hell."

"Here." Xavier grabbed Sebastian's arm and hissed a quick word. Sebastian's head jerked back and light blazed from his skin for a second, turning his button-down see-through, revealing all the black tattoos covering his arms and torso.

Another *thu-thud* of power crashed into me, and six people—four men and two women—with bat wings flew down at us, shadowy swords of darkness in their hands. Their wings vanished with a puff of black smoke and they attacked Zuri and Jacob, two on each, while the remaining two went after Kol.

Regan and Marcus lunged into the fight with Zuri and Jacob, and Ephraim shot a whip of water at one of the bat-witches on Kol.

More witches, a mix of men and women, barreled out of the shadows from down the halls and out from behind the counters of the unfinished food court kiosks. They all had tattoos on their right arms, indicating they were glyph witches. Some had more complicated tattoos than others, but while those with less ink likely had fewer spells at their disposal, that didn't mean they were any less dangerous.

I turned to the group coming from my left, while Gideon shifted to cover my back and take the other side.

A witch with an all-red tattoo curling up her arm screamed and raced toward me. I fired my M4, set to a single shot, and hit her in the chest, the stun spell activating and dissolving the round before it punctured flesh. Red lightning crackled around her, but she didn't drop.

Crap.

They were like the other supers I'd come across. One shot didn't take them out.

I flicked the switch on the M4 to a three-round burst.

The red-tattooed witch was almost on me, and another big guy was close behind. I fired again, dropped the woman with a larger blast of red lightning, and aimed at the big guy. But another *thu-thud* of magic slammed into me.

The world shuddered. A wisp of sticky, smoky darkness

crawled against my soul and my magic flared in response, blazing through the miasma and pressure.

Out of the corner of my eye, I saw Kol stumble and barely get out of the way of a shadow blade, and Xavier bit back a strangled scream, his body trembling.

Gideon shot a blast of divine light at the big guy barreling toward me, knocking him back.

Two of the witches who'd rushed out of the shadows grasped hands and in unison yelled a harsh word. A writhing mass of smoky tentacles erupted from the concrete, very much like the vines the glyph witch had summoned at the airport but without all the damage to the floor, and shot toward us.

My pulse stalled for a second at the memory of the arch-nephilim and all his writhing smoke, but I shoved that thought aside. I'd handled him. I could handle this.

Sebastian dragged Xavier back to me and Gideon, and activated a tattoo on his neck. Marcus snarled and tossed the witch he was fighting into one of the witches on Jacob, who swiped his short vampire claws at another witch. But a tendril of smoke seized Jacob's wrist and yanked him off balance before he could strike.

The witch, a bulky guy not quite as broad or tall as Jacob but close, jabbed his shadow blade at Jacob's heart.

Jacob jerked away with his enhanced speed and wrenched free of the smoke tendril.

I shot a three-round burst at one of the hand-holding witches, a squat woman with a thick colorful tattoo. Red lightning burst around her. She sagged to her knees and her partner, an average looking guy in every way, screamed. But she didn't go down, and the smoke tendrils whipped toward me.

"Really? More than three?" Shit.

I fired another burst, but the smoke devoured the rounds and the tentacles didn't vanish.

I hadn't hit my mark.

A tendril seized my leg and the sticky smoke, the source of the witches' power, oozed around my cells, trying to gain purchase inside me like it had during the tracking spell.

Gideon swept his divine light sword through the tendril around my calf then severed another one going after Sebastian.

"Call your blade," he said to me, slicing through a third tendril reaching for Xavier. "Anyone got eyes on the smoke pair?"

"Little busy," Kol gasped.

Someone else grunted, but I couldn't tell if that was an affirmative or a negative.

The witches' power thudded again, and my knees buckled.

"Xavier, pull up your extra internal shields and give Esther one," Sebastian said, and a pulse of his power, wild and icy, crashed through my back and out my chest.

I dropped to both knees, my legs too weak to hold me.

Sebastian's magic whirled into a raging vortex and swept into the smoky tendrils. It wrenched the smoke to the ceiling high above and ripped it apart.

Xavier scrambled to my side and grabbed my arm, but his eyes widened with surprise. "You don't have any shields?"

"That's why I asked for one," Sebastian said, and another pulse of icy power shuddered through me, making the world darken and my power roar in response. It swelled in my palms, blazing divine light, and I shot the blast at a wiry man with a thin tattoo on his arm before it could build up.

The blast hit him in the chest and slammed him back into an empty store's security gate fifty feet away. The gate ripped free, buckling around him, and he skidded deeper into the store's shadows.

"Oh, my God!" Xavier gasped.

"Shield," Gideon snapped at him, and Xavier mumbled a longer sentence than he'd used before in a language I didn't understand.

Heat wrapped around me as another *thu-thud* of power pulsed into me, but this time the thud felt far away, like it had when the witches had been within the area containment master ward at the airport. The force didn't steal my breath and I had no trouble standing. Thank God.

"Thanks," I said to Xavier as I stood.

But the sense of inky dark magic oozing against my soul and searching for a way in grew. I could put an end to all of this if I just let the power in. I'd be powerful, feared, adored if I just embraced it.

I'd be consumed and there'd be nothing left.

I gritted my teeth against its begging and fired my M4 at a witch barreling toward Regan.

Lightning exploded around him and he dropped. Regan raised her gaze to me, gave me a tight nod, and lunged at a woman with a long black ponytail.

Beside him, Kol sliced the hamstring of a bulky man, while Ephraim seized another man with his water whip and slammed him into a third man.

Above, witches lined the promenade, shooting blasts of shadow at Zuri, Jacob, and Marcus. Their magic thudded softly, like an explosion far off in the distance.

With a burst of misty red demonic magic, Zuri released her massive leathery wings—not the magical constructs like the glyph witches. Twisted horns extended from her forehead, and red wisps of magic whipped around her. Snarling, she flew up to the promenade, and grabbed the closest witch, and threw her over the railing.

The witch screamed and landed with a sickening crunch on the concrete floor. Blood pooled around her body and her half-open eyes were vacant.

The other witches on the promenade turned the force of their shadow blasts on Zuri, but she buffeted them away with a ferocious flap of her wings and wild gust of demonic smoke. And while she knocked the four witches in front of her to the floor, the three farther back merely stumbled.

More witches rushed out of the darkness, and with a strangely distant thump, and seductive swell of inky magic inside me, another fireball exploded around Marcus and Regan, encompassing them and the witches they were fighting.

Xavier yelled something. His power rippled through me, and Marcus and Regan screamed.

My pulse stalled. *No, please.* I couldn't lose him. *Please be alive.*

I ran toward them before the fire had fully dissipated, the heat threatening to burn my skin.

Both of them were on the ground, their clothes burning, along with the five witches they'd been fighting. Everyone was screaming, their gut-wrenching cries filled with agony.

Ephraim doused Marcus and Regan with his water magic, putting out the fire on their clothes. Somehow—it had to have been what Xavier had cast—they weren't completely burned. A nasty burn scorched up Marcus's ribs on his left side, his shirt nothing but blackened tatters. The burn ran along his left biceps, with a small trail up the side of his face, but other than that he was unharmed. Regan was in similar shape, with her hands and most of her back burned.

"We need to take cover," Gideon said. "Regroup."

"No, we stay," Zuri snarled, leaping into the air and jerking out of the way of a blast of lightning.

A swell of Sebastian's icy magic pulsed, and the witch with the lightning collapsed. I didn't know what he'd done, but that was at least one more witch down.

"Clear this coven out for good," Zuri said.

"Are you crazy?" Marcus gasped. "Didn't you listen to anything we said?" His ferocious gaze met mine before he wrenched a still-stunned Regan out of the way of a witch's shadow sword.

She staggered, and I scrambled to her side, catching her as she crumpled to the floor.

"Regan is down," I said.

"Xavier, to Regan," Zuri snapped. "Ephraim, to me."

Light exploded from Ephraim's back as he released his brilliant white wings and swept up to the first floor balcony.

Xavier scrambled to my side, and I pulled my attention from Regan and searched for a witch to shoot that was far enough away from my teammates that I wouldn't accidentally hit them.

"There are too many," Gideon said. "We need to pull back."

"There are only thirty." Zuri dove for a witch and tossed her over the railing to join the others. "And most can only summon shadow swords, so they're not that powerful. Take out your share and we'll be done with them."

The witches' power thudded again, the sign of a more powerful spell, and I wrenched my attention over the chaos, searching for the spellcaster.

There. Half in the shadows down one of the halls. A

man, close to my age, with stylishly mussed blond hair, wearing a black robe, holding his hands above his head.

The inky magic in my soul swelled as his mouth moved, saying the quick words of his spell, and something inside me sparked. My pulse lurched and a massive ball of fire exploded around me, Marcus, Xavier, and Regan.

Fiery agony seared my skin for a blazing second, then my magic roared through me. It exploded from my body with a massive wave of power and light that consumed the inky magic inside and the fire searing my skin, and slammed into anyone not standing close to me.

Everyone, including Gideon, Jacob, Kol, and Sebastian, was tossed to the ground, stunned. Zuri and Ephraim hovered at the top of the ceiling two stories up, while Xavier and Marcus—who hadn't been hit with my wave of power while propping up an unconscious Regan—stared at me, wide-eyed.

Ice, not just frost, swept over me, snapping my inflamed, thankfully not-scorched skin, from burning with heat to burning with cold, and overwhelming fear squeezed tight in my chest.

Shit.

Gideon, who I'd slammed against the wall beside the security door and who'd sagged down the wall onto his butt, blinked, his angel glow flickering for a second and making my pulse stall. "Pull back. We're getting out of here."

"Copy that," Jacob said, crawling to his hands and knees, his breath ragged.

All around us the witches I'd knocked to the ground moaned. But the inky power thudded again, still a far-off feeling, and they all drew in a quick, reviving breath and stood.

Shit shit shit.

I pumped strength into Gideon and Jacob through our brands to get them standing. There wasn't anything I could do for Kol, who was climbing to his feet, using a pillar to keep his balance, so I shot the witch closest to him.

Behind him, still partially in the shadows, the fire witch sneered.

"Stand your ground," Zuri yelled. "They're down, cuff or kill them. I don't care which."

Gideon jerked to his feet, his gaze leaping to me, and the strength pouring through our brand hit a mental wall. "Don't."

He'd blocked me off.

I mentally pushed, but he held firm.

"You need it," he said.

"I wasn't just slammed onto my ass." I shot at a witch lunging for him, missed the woman's torso, but nicked her shoulder with one of the rounds. The strike and small flicker of red lightning was enough to make her stumble, giving Gideon time to ram his light blade through her chest.

"Thanks for that," Sebastian groaned, lying face first on the floor, his tone thick with sarcasm.

"No one got burned to a crisp. Deal with it," Marcus snarled, lunging at a witch and ramming his claws into the man's gut. "Xavier, get Regan to Gideon."

Xavier slung Regan over his shoulder and staggered under her weight. Jacob ripped out the throat of another witch and grabbed the arm of a woman, stopping her from running Kol through the back with her shadow blade.

Three witches on the promenade above shot a barrage of shadows at me, and I jerked out of the way. A blast slammed into my shoulder. Screaming agony ripped through me and my whole arm went numb. I fought to keep hold of my M4, but my hand slipped away and my arm hung limp at my side.

The inky magic seeped deeper into me.

Embrace me. Use me. Be powerful.

I could end it with a thought, flatten everyone. My magical blast against the ball of fire had been powerful, but the inky magic was stronger.

The witches fired another barrage and I dove out of the way. A shot hit my thigh. More agony. Darkness teased my vision for a second. My leg went numb, and I sprawled, face first, across the concrete. Another blast skimmed Kol's back. He stumbled and the witch fighting him rammed his shadow blade into Kol's chest as if he weren't wearing a Kevlar vest.

He screamed and dropped to his knees, blood gushing from his chest and splattering on the floor. The witch swept his sword up to decapitate Kol, and instinct wrenched my good hand up. Divine light shot from my palm and tossed the witch across the courtyard.

Kol clutched his chest, but blood still rushed through his fingers. He staggered to his feet, lost his balance, and I hurried to help him, but Marcus pushed me aside, catching him before he fell.

"You've got the range weapon," he said, wrapping one of Kol's arms across his neck and taking the incubus's weight.

I reached to draw my Glock. It was easier to shoot one-handed than the M4... but still, not as accurate as a one-handed divine light strike. I left my Glock holstered and raised my palm.

Zuri and Ephraim dove into the witches on the promenade and Gideon shot a light blast at a witch running toward me. The blast hit the woman in the center of her chest. She screamed and dropped to her knees, bent forward in agony.

"I said stand your ground," Zuri yelled.

Jacob bolted up beside me, helping me cover Marcus's and Kol's retreat. He gave me a grim glance, his worry flooding me and stealing my breath for a second.

Sebastian was back on his feet, a long tattoo curling over his left arm blazing under his shirt. He raised his hands and his icy magic swept over me, but a blast of searing magic engulphed it, killing whatever spell he was going to cast.

I wrenched my attention to the fire witch and shot a bolt of divine light at him, but the witch's magic thudded stronger, almost as strong as it had been before Xavier had given me a shield, and wrenched me to my knees.

The inky magic, desperate to get inside me, howled. *Use me and end it. Let me in. Let. Me. In.*

Kol screamed and Marcus dropped to his hands and knees beside me. Jacob went down on one knee, while Zuri and Ephraim dropped from the air and crashed onto the concrete.

Xavier went down face first with Regan and all the witches went down as well.

Gideon and Sebastian staggered forward a step, but the weight of the fire witch's spell pulsed again, pounded them to their knees, drawing screams from everyone already down.

The power crushed me to the floor. I couldn't move, couldn't think, and couldn't draw breath. Something in my chest snapped and agony sliced through me.

My power erupted and blazed against the spell, but the fire witch's power just kept growing, squeezing me tighter and tighter, and I couldn't push past it like I had with the ball of fire.

If I just let the inky magic in, I'd be able to stop him.

But if I let the inky magic in, it'd take over.

I couldn't forget that. No matter how much it cajoled and begged and promised me unimaginable power, my essence and soul would be devoured.

The fire witch strode out of the shadows, his dark eyes filled with malice, and he wove his way between his fellow dead and unconscious witches, and crouched in front of me.

"That's it, fight it," he said, his voice a raspy hiss.

His magic swelled and mine surged in response, raging through every cell, burning at the inky magic, pressing against the fire witch's crushing spell. But I couldn't blast free. He was stronger than me—

No, the external source he was drawing from was stronger. I could feel the same sticky magic desperate to possess me also inside him, pouring into him without end. And while I still had power and could draw from Gideon and Jacob if I needed to, it wasn't going to be enough.

Except it had to be enough. If we didn't break free, the witches would kill us.

Behind him, a stunningly beautiful woman, with skin so pale it was pure white and long black hair, dressed in a black body-hugging gown, stepped out of the shadows.

Red demonic mist curled from her skin, caressing her, and hellfire consumed her eyes. Heat filled the room as if a massive furnace had been turned on, and the witches' crushing power swelled.

Whoever this woman was, she was the most powerful super I'd ever come across, and that said a lot, given the supers I'd encountered in the last couple of days.

The ice on my arms evaporated in her heat, and the heart-stopping fear from my guys and the rest of the team squeezed tighter.

I fought to breathe against the power and fear as darkness danced at the edge of my vision.

The woman knelt before me, her radiating heat making the air ripple around her, and grabbed my chin with a searing hot hand. Agony screamed through my face and neck and the acrid sent of burning flesh filled my nose.

"I bring you sacrifices," the fire witch said, "my goddess."

CHAPTER 8

OH, FUCK.

My whole essence stalled, pulse, breath, and thought, and that one word raced over and over again in my mind. Goddess. We were up against a real goddess. The super— or rather demon powering the worship magic spell was strong enough to contain it *and* remain conscious. How the hell were we supposed to stop a goddess? We couldn't even stop her witches.

The goddess's power surged, slamming into me, and the darkness at the edge of my vision engulfed me.

The fire witch hissed something else and the woman murmured a reply, but crushing pressure muddled my thoughts and I teetered on the edge of unconsciousness. If I'd heard what they'd said, I didn't remember a second later.

People moved around me, groaning and shuffling. The crushing magic continued to squeeze my chest and I struggled to breathe.

For a second I was in the not-water, but the bobbing wasn't soothing. It was jerky and shot through with slicing agony.

My eyes fluttered open. Pain screamed through my chest and along my jaw and pounded in my skull. I stared down at someone's butt, legs, and bootheels as they walked across granite flagstones, and with sluggish thoughts, I realized I'd been slung over someone's shoulder.

He shifted my weight, digging his shoulder into my ribs, slicing more pain through me. I had no idea if the crush in my lungs was from my position or the witches' magic, and I was in too much pain to care.

Out of the corner of my eye, I caught a glimpse of two bulky men, each holding one of Jacob's arms, dragging his unconscious body across the floor. I couldn't feel past the pressure and dizziness to tell if he was pulling strength from me or not, or if Gideon was, and I couldn't get an empathic sense of emotions from anyone.

Please let him be okay. Let them all be okay.

I strained to raise my head and look for the others, but a wave of dizziness swept me back into the darkness and I was bobbing again in the painful no-longer-comforting not-water. I couldn't breathe, when, like with the strangeness of dreams, I'd been able to breathe in the water before. A vise squeezed my chest and the inky magic, the clinging miasma of the witches' power, taunted me.

If I'd just let it in, my guys would be safe.

If I'd just let it in, I wouldn't be in pain.

If I'd just—

Someone called my name, but I couldn't tell which of my guys it was, only that it was one of my guys.

I shoved at the inky, sticky magic, but couldn't get it out of my head and could feel my resistance to it weakening. It was going to take over and I was going to lose myself.

Embrace me. Let me in.

No.

My guy called me again, and a whisper of warmth from my brands strengthened my soul for a moment.

Let me in.

I whipped my power around the inky magic, but couldn't force it out and could feel myself slipping away.

I strained to focus on my connection with my guys, and my sense of self returned.

Let me in.

Except I didn't have enough power to force it out right now.

Fine.

I'll wrap you up so tight I won't be able to hear you.

With a mental scream, I spun my power, tighter and tighter, squeezing the voice of the inky magic until I could barely hear it.

"Essie."

I jerked awake, shooting agony through my head, chest, and neck. The pain stole my breath and made my vision waver.

Holy hell. I knew that feeling all too well. Broken rib. At least one. Probably more. The fiery agony in my head felt like my magical channels had been scorched raw, and the pain in my neck felt like...

I wasn't sure.

My memory lurched to the demon-goddess grabbing my chin with her too-hot hand.

She'd burned me. Her internal demonic power was so strong, her touch had burned my skin.

This was bad.

"Essie," Jacob said from behind me, but not in my ear through the coms. "Wake up."

"I'm awake," I gasped, knowing the longer I stayed silent, the more my guys would worry.

I dragged my gaze around me, my thoughts still whirling and my vision clouded with darkness.

I sat, propped up against a metal wall in a plain, all-metal, ten-by-ten box with a stainless steel single-unit toilet and sink, very much like the cell in Operations. Harsh fluorescent light, from an exposed fixture in the ceiling on the other side of narrow metal bars and a solid metal door, glared off the metal floor and walls. My weapons, extra magazines, cell phone, and vest were gone. So too was the com that had been in my ear.

Across the hall, Regan and Ephraim lay on the floor of their ten-by-ten cell, but I sat too far back in my cell to see into the other cells or down the hall.

"Thank God," Jacob said from the other side of my cell wall, his relief creeping into my chest.

But my chest didn't feel right. The agony of broken ribs aside, there was something wrong. I was cold and hollow and—

My stomach bottomed out. A hollowness in my chest meant I was either out of power or cut off from it. And that hint of emotion had to have come from the soul bond I shared with Jacob, not my empathy.

"How badly are you hurt?" Gideon asked, his voice tight, also coming from somewhere to my right. Except he sounded farther away than Jacob so most likely in the next cell over.

"How badly are *you* hurt?"

He snorted, which turned into a ragged wet cough, and then gasping shallow, rattling breaths.

That didn't sound good. I closed my eyes and fought to concentrate past the pain on my brands. Neither Jacob nor Gideon were pulling strength, and I wasn't pulling from them, but that didn't mean we weren't seriously injured. The brand wouldn't pull strength if it jeopardized a mate's life, even if the other mate was in critical condition.

"I asked you first," Gideon gasped.

"At least one broken rib, my head throbs from all the magic I used, and—" A shudder swept through me at the memory of the power and heat radiating from the demon-goddess. "My neck is burned."

"I think we all have broken ribs," Jacob said. "That spell that took us out literally crushed us."

"Yeah." Another shudder shook me. With all that power, the goddess could have smashed every bone in our bodies and killed us. Which scared me even more. She wanted us alive.

You can be stronger than her.

But that was a lie. I couldn't be stronger than her by tapping into her worship magic like her witches did... could I? No, it was still her magic. She controlled it.

"How long was I out?" I asked, struggling to ignore the inky magic's lure. "And who's in which cell?"

"You weren't out much longer than us," Jacob said.

"But we have no idea how long we were out," Gideon gasped. "As for who's where... Zuri is with me. She's still out and in rough shape. I haven't been able to stop her bleeding. She might have only taken a one-and-a-half-story fall, but with that spell and from the look of how many bones she's broken, I'd say the impact was more like a five- or six-story fall."

"Greater demons heal quickly," Jacob said.

"Not *that* quickly," Gideon shot back. "Anyone in the cell with you, Essie?"

"No."

"I don't have anyone, either." Worry darkened Jacob's

tone. "Bane and Marcus are across the hall, and I can see Regan and Ephraim across from you."

"They're both unconscious," I said.

"We figured, since they weren't answering us." Sebastian groaned. "Your wolf is also still out of it and is pretty beaten up. His burns are serious and he was stabbed a few times during that fight. I've managed to stop most of the bleeding for now, but..."

My pulse lurched and I fought to slow it down.

Come on. Control your fear and think straight. Fear wouldn't help us out of this mess and we needed to get out of there. Everyone needed medical attention and—

Oh, God.

"Where are Kol and Xavier?" No one had said they were in a cell.

If they weren't in a cell, where were they? Were they dead?

I lost what little control I had on my emotions and my breath turned to desperate pants that sliced agony through me.

Please don't be dead. Please. Kol couldn't be dead. I needed him. Just like I needed Marcus and Jacob and Gideon. *He had to be alive. He had to.*

I didn't know what I do if he wasn't.

My throat tightened, and a whisper of inky magic broke free from my mental hold and crept along my senses.

He could be alive if I just let it in.

Which was a lie. It was all lies. Only a master vampire could bring someone back from the dead and only if they performed the ritual to turn him into a vampire.

"Where is he?" We had to get out of there. Find him. Now.

Now now now.

And the only way to do that was to fucking focus!

I gritted my teeth and tried to draw in a slower breath, but that only shot more agony through my chest. The only way out, the only way to find him, was to get more information. Hell, even just answers to basic questions like where we were would be useful.

"What do we know?" I forced out.

"We're all injured," Jacob said.

Sebastian huffed. "And our magic is contained with one hell of a powerful containment spell."

Which was why I felt so hollow. But I knew that already. "Will it affect personal magics? Like Kol's healing or Marcus's shifting?"

"No, but that's about it," Sebastian said.

"We also don't know where we are or why they've kept us alive, how many of them are left, or even how powerful they are," Gideon added, his voice grim.

Jeez, this was bad. Beyond bad. Even if we could figure out how to get out of those cells, we were running on no information. We could just as easily be captured again. "And that doesn't even take into account their goddess."

"Oh, fuck," Sebastian hissed, reminding me that they'd all been knocked out before she'd stepped into sight. "Let me guess. She isn't asleep."

"She isn't."

Someone groaned, the sound a low, throaty growl. Marcus. A glimmer of relief rushed through me, but it was squashed by the fear that Kol was missing, possibly dead.

"Don't move," Sebastian said. "You'll start bleeding again."

"Essie? Where's Essie?" Marcus gasped.

"I'm right here." I shifted closer to the bars at the front of the cell to try to look at him. He lay with his head close to his bars and I could see the oozing burn trailing up the side of his face, mixed in with red, swelling bruises. "I'm in better shape than you."

"Thank God." He rolled his head to look at the ceiling. "Where the fuck are we?"

"Better question," Gideon corrected. "Why aren't we dead?"

Sebastian shifted into sight, his glow barely there, his skin like tissue paper. "I'd rather know how to get out of here. Anyone know how to pick a lock?"

"Sure," Jacob said, his voice a dark rumble. "If I had something to pick it with."

"We have to wait for someone to show up and unlock our doors," Gideon said, breaking into a fit of wet coughs that made my heart stutter again with worry.

I concentrated on our brand and imagined strength seeping into him, but there wasn't even a flicker of electric magic or heat or anything to indicate it was working.

"I hate waiting," Marcus groaned. "Come up with a better plan."

Footsteps sounded down the hall, at least two people, men from the weight of their tread, but possibly more, and with them was a strange *shushing* sound that I couldn't identify.

"Someone's coming," Jacob said.

Marcus started to sit up and Sebastian pressed a hand to his chest. "I said don't move."

"You going to jump whoever opens our door?" Marcus growled.

"I've got more than magic up my sleeve, wolf," Sebastian shot back as he stood and grabbed the bars.

"Get ready," Gideon said.

I clutched the bars in front of me and staggered to my

feet, the pain in my chest overwhelming. Darkness flickered at the edge of my vision, but I was God damn not going to pass out.

Someone moaned, and I strained to see farther down the hall.

The first of the glyph witches stepped into sight, a thin woman, her right arm covered with a thick tattoo, her expression hard, unreadable. Behind her, two burly guys gripped a barely conscious, moaning Xavier under the armpits, his feet dragging on the floor.

The woman slid a key into the lock on Jacob's cell door and opened it.

Jacob wrenched toward her but she grabbed her forearm and her power thudded in me. My knees buckled and I slid down the bars as Jacob gasped and did the same.

"Fuck," Sebastian snarled, and he too sagged down.

"Jacob, get up," Gideon said.

"Can't," Jacob gasped.

The woman sneered at him and the men holding Xavier tossed him into Jacob's cell. Her sneer deepened, and she closed that door and opened mine. I clutched the bars, fighting to stand, but another thump of magic swept through me and a massive weight pressed me to the floor.

Another pair of guys dragged Kol into sight, and my heart stopped. His head lolled forward and blood oozed from the gash in his chest—clearly visible because he too had lost his vest—leaving a trail on the metal floor. He wasn't even moaning like Xavier was, and I couldn't see his chest moving. I couldn't tell if he was alive.

Oh, please.

The men tossed Kol face first onto the floor beside me and the woman slammed my cell door shut.

I grabbed Kol's shoulder and rolled him over as our

captors left. His complexion was gray and blood dampened the entire front of his T-shirt, pasting it to his body. I pressed my hand over the wound, trying to stop the bleeding, and everything lurched inside me. He was cold.

"Oh, God. His heat is gone." I didn't think demons could ever have a cold body temperature. I thought the coldest they got was close to human normal.

I strained to feel his pulse beat or his chest rise under my palms, anything to tell me he was alive.

"Essie, is he alive?" Gideon asked.

"I don't know." I pressed two fingers to his neck.

Gideon coughed, the sound ragged and gasping, and his fear joined mine and tightened inside me. "If he's alive, cold means his essence has been drained."

"Which would be why they took him," Sebastian said, as if he'd just realized the obvious. "It's worship magic. And their goddess is awake. She can probably drain someone even if they're unwilling, and he's got the strongest essence out of all of us."

"He won't be able to heal," Jacob said. "Not with his essence drained to the point that he's cold."

Which meant he needed sexual energy to regain some essence.

I pressed my lips against his, praying my desire for him would be enough for me to feel a pulse, a breath, anything. But my heart pounded and not with desire.

Please, take a breath.

I tried to imagine the feel of his sensual magic sliding into me, or Jacob's bite twisting in my core, and push that sensation into my kiss.

But his lips didn't move, just squished against mine, and my throat tightened, taking me farther from any sensual thought that might help him.

I still couldn't feel a pulse or breath. His chill seeped into my hands. Even his blood was cold. How the hell could his blood be cold?

"Essie?" Gideon gasped. "Is he dead?"

Tears burned my eyes.

"Is he dead?"

He couldn't be dead. I wouldn't allow him to be dead. *Please, God. Don't let him be dead.*

CHAPTER 9

I PANTED, UNABLE TO SLOW MY BREATHING AND STOP THE shooting agony in my chest. My hands trembled, the cold radiating from Kol's too-still body deepening my fear. It was impossible to focus and tell if he had a pulse.

Jeez. I had to calm down. Concentrate. But I couldn't. I just couldn't accept that he was dead and it didn't matter if I couldn't feel a pulse. He was alive and I could save him. I just needed to get turned on.

Except my fear was so strong my teeth chattered.

A tear leaked down my cheek. I couldn't lose him like this. Not before he knew how much he meant to me. It was like Jacob all over again. Except Jacob had been alive. I'd been able to do something.

"Essie?" Gideon pressed. "Is he dead?"

"I don't know!"

God, do something. Anything.

Sebastian had said the containment spell didn't affect personal magics. That meant Jacob's bite could still turn me on. I wouldn't be able to release the bite-lock myself, but Kol could do it with his magic when he revived. Because he was God damned going to revive.

Gritting my teeth against the pain in my chest, I crawled to the bars, pressed my face against the metal wall between my cell and Jacob's, and reached around. "Bite me."

"No," Jacob said.

"Jacob, bite me. It's the only way."

"If he's dead, the bite-lock will keep building within you," he said.

"Jacob, please," I begged. "He's not dead. He can't be dead." He was family. He belonged.

He was mine.

"I'm too scared," I gasped. "I can't draw enough desire to help him. Jacob, ple—"

Marcus jerked forward and seized the bars as Jacob grabbed my hand. "Don't—"

Pain sliced into my wrist, and more tears rolled down my cheeks with a mix of fear and hope. His teeth sank into my flesh and with a gentle pull, bone-melting desire shot up my arm and straight to my core.

I gasped at the sudden surge, my body instantly throbbing with need.

Marcus snarled and his wolf turned his expression fierce. "God damn it, Jacob. She's not just *your* mate. If he's dead, we all get to listen to her lose her mind."

Jacob took a longer pull, sinking his magic deeper into me. It twisted around my heart, burning away all fear and thought, leaving only aching, desperate need. Then as fast as he bit me and flooded my essence with his magic, he withdrew his fangs, sent a whisper of healing magic into his bite, and released my wrist.

I sagged against the metal wall, my breath too fast, each inhalation slicing sharp agony through me. But the pain didn't diminish Jacob's magic. It kept growing, twisting until I could barely feel the pain

With a shuddering groan, I crawled back to Kol, pressed my hands against his wound—not that it'd help slow the bleeding, I just couldn't stop myself—and kissed his too-cold lips again. The memory of his magic pouring down my throat when he'd saved me, and again when he'd helped me save Jacob the other day, made me shudder and twisted Jacob's magic tighter.

Come on. Work. Please work. Please don't be dead.

Kol's blood continued to ooze through my fingers.

"Please," I begged against his lips. "Come back to me." *Don't leave me.*

But he *was* leaving. He'd asked for a transfer because I'd reminded him of all the horrible things he'd gone through during the war. And because of that terrible tear in his soul that I had to heal before he left. That I'd never be able to heal if he was dead.

"You can't be dead."

A tear fell from my lashes and plopped onto his face. It rolled over his breathtakingly beautiful cheek and trailed a line along his jaw. I'd been attracted to him the moment I'd seen him, but that wasn't why I desired him, why he belonged. It was everything else after the moment I'd woken in the hospital. All his wicked smiles, his playful teasing, his unwavering support and kindness.

Something fluttered under my hands. Was that a breath? His pulse? He was still so cold.

I sat back on my heels. Jacob's magic billowed and sank low, teasing me on the edge of a climax I knew wouldn't come. I fought to concentrate on Kol's chest, desperate to feel another flutter, terrified it had all been my imagination.

The ragged, shallow flutter under my hands came again.

It was a breath. He'd taken a breath.

"Oh, thank God."

I yearned to embrace him, kiss him, rub my aching body against his, but I forced myself to take his hand in mine and lean against the wall. I didn't have his consent to keep kissing him, and holding his hand and letting him feed off my desire from Jacob's bite would be just as effective as anything else.

"Is he alive?" Gideon asked.

"Yes," I said, my voice breathy. "He's going to be all right." I just needed to wait until he'd gotten enough sexual energy to warm up and seal the gash in his chest shut.

"Will you be?" Marcus asked.

"I'll be fine." A shudder swept through me, surging Jacob's magic and making my breath hitch. "I just need to wait."

I tipped my head back, but that made me think of Jacob sinking his fangs into my throat and the glorious rush of his magic. A magic that twisted tighter and tighter.

Seconds... minutes... an eternity dragged by, trapping me on a razor's edge of pain and pleasure, and not the good kind. I just needed to wait it out. I could wait it out.

Please, God, let me be able to sit here long enough for Kol to wake up.

Then Kol groaned and my pulse leaped, the urge to throw myself on him and beg him to take me overwhelming. I fought to stay put and another shudder taunted me with a climax that wouldn't come. I ached with need, every nerve hypersensitive, every breath and twitch and thought ratcheting up my desire. My breath kept speeding up and was now short, sharp gasps, and the small cell spun around me.

"Essie," Jacob said, his voice rumbling through me,

twisting his magic tighter. "Slow your breathing. You're going to pass out."

But I couldn't slow anything. The only control I had of my body was to stay where I was. *Just God damn stay put and hold Kol's hand.*

I tightened my grip on his hand and added my other hand, clinging to him as if that would somehow ease my pain.

"Focus on my voice, Essie,' Jacob said, his voice that sexy, deep rumble I loved so much, sending another shudder of need through me.

"I can't. Stop talking. Please.'

Marcus pressed his face to the bars, his eyes wild. "Gideon, use your brand. Do something. Kol isn't waking up fast enough."

A hint of Gideon's electric magic whispered over my right forearm, adding to my agonizing desire. "Oh, fuck, Gideon," I whimpered.

Kol groaned again and his hand twitched, shooting another taunting tremor through me.

I squeezed my eyes shut. I couldn't fight or ignore the feeling of Jacob's magic, because that was what was saving Kol, but God, I was going to shatter into a million pieces and there wasn't going to be anything blissful about it.

"Kol," Marcus said, "wake the fuck up."

Kol groaned again.

"Wake up!" Marcus barked. "Please, God, wake up."

Kol gasped and his hand on mine tightened. My eyelids flew open and I was drowning in hellfire. It blazed in his eyes and licked across his cheeks. Cheeks I wanted to lick. *Needed* to lick. *Oh, God.*

"What did you do?" he gasped, his eyes filled with horror.

A whisper of his sultry magic slid up my arm, drawing another whimper.

"You have to release the bite-lock," Marcus said.

"I what?" Wild emotions—fear, anger, pain—flashed across his face and he jerked away from me. Just the idea of releasing Jacob's magic hurt him.

"Kol, please," Marcus begged.

The anger deepened, and Kol squeezed his eyes shut and dragged in a deep breath that didn't seem to calm him. He dragged in another breath and the muscles in his jaw flexed. The frustration and anger deepened and he glared at me.

"Fine."

But it wasn't fine. I didn't know what Michael and his nephilim had done to him, but they'd forced him to do things he hadn't wanted to do. And now so was I, and he hated me for it.

"Just use your magic and release it," I gasped. Then he wouldn't have to come any closer. Hell, he wouldn't even have to look at me.

"It doesn't work that way," he snapped, shifting farther away from me. "The bite-lock will absorb my magic before your body can use it to set you free."

"You mean you have to—?" My breath hitched with a mix of yearning and dread at the thought of Kol doing more than just using his magic and releasing Jacob's power.

"It's fine. I'll deal with it." He dragged his gaze up his body, over his bloody T-shirt and arms, then jerked it around the cell, stopping at the toilet-sink unit. "I'll fucking deal with it," he said again, his tone hard, breaking my heart, as he crawled to the sink.

But it wasn't fine and there wasn't anything I could do

about it. My throat tightened and even that made me gasp with another torturous tremble of climax.

God damn it. All of me, body and soul, burned with a desire soured by heartache at what needed to happen. He didn't want to touch me. Just being near me hurt him deeply. And still I yearned for his touch, his kiss, his body filling me.

He scrubbed the blood off his hands and arms. The water ran over his skin, making me think of sex with my guys, all of my guys, in the shower.

I squeezed my eyes shut, but that only deepened the fantasy. Water running over their sculpted muscles, slicking their erect—

Fuck.

I forced my eyes open to find Kol glaring at me, his body tense. "Let's get this over with." He stood and, using the wall to keep his balance, shuffled the few steps to my side and glared down at me. "Just— look away or close your eyes or something. I can't— not with that look on your face."

"What look?" But I knew what look. I ached for him and I ached for more than just releasing Jacob's bite-lock. He belonged with me and the guys. He needed the team and quite frankly the team needed him. I needed him.

"The look you give *them*," he snarled, his voice low and dark. "It's not real. It's Jacob's bite and my magic and you don't mean it."

"What are you talking about?" The magic in my chest billowed, the sensation fierce and painful. *Oh, fuck.*

Please, yes.

He sagged to his knees beside me. I wanted to scream at the anger and pain in his eyes, at being just as bad as Michael and making him do something against his will.

And yet my body didn't care. It screamed for his touch, for his kiss. For God damned anything. *Just please touch me.*

"You don't actually want me," he said between gritted teeth. "You don't really love me."

My thoughts stalled. Even my desperate need for release caught on that one word.

Love.

He thought I didn't love him?

"You want me to love you? But I triggered you, I reminded you of—" Of all the horrors he survived. "You asked for a transfer."

"And I'm God damned taking it." His expression hardened and filled with frustration. "I have to get away from you. You've fucked everything up. You've fucked me up." He slammed his fist into the wall beside him. "I want to scream every time they touch or kiss you. Every time they make love to you."

The hellfire in his eyes flared, and a shot of searing, sensual magic whipped into Jacob's magic and blazed through my core, making me whimper.

"Incubi don't get jealous. It's not in our nature. You're a free meal. Fuck, with the four of you, I'm going to be riding high for the rest of my life with no risk of draining anyone to death. But I can't do it."

His breath picked up and frustration and need swelled in my chest. His emotions were so strong I could feel them despite the containment spell, and they merged with the agonizing pleasure in my body.

"I can't keep riding your desire for *them*." He raked his hands through his hair. Hands that needed to be on me, caressing me, releasing me. "I want your desire to be for *me*. I want you to love *me*," he yelled, his voice breaking. "Like you love them."

"But I do love you." I was more certain now than I'd ever been before. The thought of him leaving— God, of him dead or dying, filled me with as much panic as it did for the rest of my guys.

"That's just my nature influencing you. You only think you love me. No one loves an incubus. They only think they do." The pain in his eyes turned to full, desperate grief. "And incubi don't fall in love. How can we? It'll never be real. We don't need it to be real. But I want it to be fucking real. I want something I'm not supposed to want or can ever have."

"Kol." I captured his cheeks with my palms, still sticky with his blood, and forced him to meet my gaze. "I do love you. And it is real."

I smashed my lips against his and kissed him, willing him to feel all my love and desire and need for him. A desperate kiss had convinced Jacob how I felt about him. It had to be enough to convince Kol. I had no other way of proving to him that I cared for him as deeply as I cared for Marcus and Jacob and Gideon, that he was just as loved and desired. He was a part of the family I'd ached for, the love I'd been missing since my mom died and more, and no way in hell was I letting him go without a fight.

He stiffened, his body trembling. He was going to reject me. I could feel it in my soul. Fear and hurt and a certainty of what he was supposed to be was going to take over. I'd lose him forever if I didn't do something. But I had nothing else to offer that could convince him of how I felt.

My thoughts leaped to my power, even though I didn't have access to it, and my imagination took over. I envisioned my empathic magic flooding into him, just like it had flooded into Voth the other day when I'd shown the greater demon my love and connection to my guys to get the area containment master ward.

In my mind's eyes, I saw the same gold strands, the primal, brilliant source of the universe that was neither light magic nor dark magic nor essence-based magic and yet all of it. A pure power that recognized true mates and bound souls together.

The power swirled through Kol's soul and essence, then swelled into a ball of dazzling magic around his heart.

He sucked in a startled gasp, his breath stealing mine through our kiss, and my magic surged. I could almost feel it now, a blazing fire in the center of my being, pouring into him.

With a moan, he tangled his hands into my hair and deepened the kiss, sliding his tongue against mine. His hold on his magic slipped and it rushed into me, but my power pulled it in before it could twist into Jacob's magic, adding to the imagined blaze in my body—

No. Not imagined blaze. It was real. Kol's cheeks were cool to the touch but it wasn't because his essence was low. It was because every cell in my body was on fire.

And that fire kept growing, trapped within me, squeezing around my heart. It ignited Gideon's brand, gold light blazing from it, and swept up my arm into Jacob's. The power roared through me, poured over and through my chest, and surged into a supernova about to rip me to pieces.

CHAPTER 10

THE PRESSURE OF MY MAGIC TORE OUT OF ME WITH FIRE AND agony. Every muscle in my body seized, every cell on fire for a torturous eternity, before it vanished with a whoosh.

I collapsed into Kol's arms, the room spinning, my breath fast, painful gasps with my broken ribs. Jacob's bite-lock still held me captive, my body desperate for release, but I was too weak to do anything about it.

The hollowness in my chest returned, along with a bone-deep cold that went beyond just being cut off from my magic. But I knew what that cold meant and my soul sang with joy.

"See. I do love you," I gasped.

"What the hell was that?" Ephraim groaned, his voice weak and filled with pain. Guess he'd finally woken up. My thoughts tripped on that for a second, but with my mind whirling, I couldn't focus on that detail long enough to figure anything out.

"Another one just bit the dust," Sebastian said. "Even with the containment spell on us."

I tried to raise my hand and place it on Kol's heart, but couldn't make my muscles work.

"What did you do?" Kol shifted and looked me in the eyes, his expression stunned. The movement sliced agonizing pleasure through me, drawing a half moan, half whimper from my numb lips.

"Please," I begged. But I couldn't tell if I'd actually spoken, because his expression didn't change.

"Essie?" He moved to hold me with one arm and cupped my cheek with his palm. "Essie, talk to me."

I unclenched my jaw—so I guess I hadn't spoken—and my teeth started chattering. I wanted to tell him it would be okay. That this was what had happened every time I'd claimed one of my guys, but I couldn't pull my focus from my desperate need long enough to form coherent thoughts.

"What's wrong with her?" He clutched me to his warm chest. So warm. Gloriously warm. And yet even the cold flooding me from bonding my soul with Kol's was nothing compared to the agony of Jacob's bite-lock.

"She was stupid enough to bind your souls together within the containment spell," Sebastian said. "She's in shock. Again."

"Pretty sure she didn't have a say in when their bond formed," Gideon said, his voice low.

"Are you saying she just claimed another mate?" Ephraim asked.

"Check her brand." Jacob's voice rumbled through me, and the world spun faster, my not-climax tearing into me.

Tears leaked from my eyes and my twitching made everything worse, an aching, freezing, desperate need.

"No, check if the bite-lock is released," Marcus said.

Kol closed his eyes for a second and sensual heat roared through me. Darkness shuddered across my vision, but

Jacob's magic wouldn't let me pass out. All I could do was pant and twitch, my mind begging, my body numb and weak.

"Shit." Kol shifted, his body sliding against my too-sensitive nerves.

Oh fuck oh fuck oh fuck.

He braced his back against the cell wall and settled me in the V between his legs, my back against his chest. Heat seeped from him into me and a hint of the chill melted from my bones.

"I've got you," he said, just like the times before when he'd held me and I'd been in shock from binding my soul with Gideon's and Jacob's.

He reached down with one hand, undid my jeans, and slid his hand inside. My breath picked up so fast I was certain that this time I would pass out despite Jacob's magic. Just a brush of Kol's fingers into my curls, and I was on fire, the taunting climax trembling within me. Except my body still shivered, and I couldn't get the tears to stop leaking from my eyes.

"We need to do this gently," he said, his breath hot against my neck and cheek. "There's too much magic trapped in the bite-lock."

I weakly squirmed against him, desperate, spinning, freezing and on fire at the same time. Then he brushed his finger over my clit and every muscle in my body clenched in anticipation, but the magic didn't release.

No, please.

"Just let it go, Essie."

He brushed my clit again. My body clenched tighter, every cell screaming in pain, drawing a whimper.

Another gentle brush. The promise of my climax trembled and twisted so tight I couldn't breathe. I jerked in his embrace, unable to draw breath, every muscle seized, and on the edge of a climax that wouldn't come.

"Essie, breathe. Release it." Kol's voice grew sharp and his frozen fear spiraled into my agony.

Tears streamed down my cheeks and I still couldn't draw breath. The darkness creeping at the edge of my vision promised blissful unconsciousness, but it wouldn't come, teasing me like my climax teased me.

"Shit," he hissed. "I'm sorry. Gentle isn't working." He thrust two fingers into me, my body already slick and ready for him, and ground his thumb against my clit.

I shuddered. He withdrew and thrust again and again, the strokes fierce and fast, his thumb hard against my clit until my climax exploded with a blazing agony that threatened to tear me to pieces.

Blinding light burst across my vision, and all breath and thought vanished, consumed by pain. Someone screamed. A great, heartrending wail, and I realized it was me.

Kol stiffened and his magic roared through me. For a second there was only sensual, agonizing pain, then his power rushed out of me into him, taking the destructive release of Jacob's bite-lock with it and leaving me limp in Kol's arms.

Someone gasped. Not me. But with all the whirling darkness, I couldn't figure out who.

Marcus growled, the calm stillness in Jacob's brand shuddered, and a single snap of lightning surged through Gideon's brand.

"What the hell?" Marcus asked with a throaty groan.

Gasping, Kol pulled his hand from my pants and cradled me against his chest. I should have been bothered by the fact he was still covered in blood and getting it on me, but I didn't care. The pain from Jacob's magic was gone, leaving just the agony of broken ribs, and I was right where I needed to be, wrapped in Kol's warmth and love.

"What was that?" Gideon gasped.

"It was too much," Kol said, his voice ragged. "I needed to send it somewhere. Her soul bonds were the easiest way to disperse the bite-lock's release "

"I owe you a serious apology if that's what you feel every time my bite-lock releases," Jacob said, his words slurred.

"That was a lot stronger than usual. There was just too much magic built up this time." Kol pressed his lips to the top of my head. "You okay?"

I opened my numb lips to respond, but footsteps clattered toward us from down the hall and Kol tensed.

"They must have felt Essie form her bond with Kol," Gideon said.

"Gee, you think?" Sebastian huffed. "Anyone sensitive in a ten-mile radius probably felt that."

Kol shifted out from under me and leaned me against the wall.

"Which one of them released the power?" a male voice asked from down the hall.

"Check all of them," a woman replied.

Three men and a woman rushed into the prison. The first man, a bulky guy with a buzz cut, opened my cell door, and Kol dove at him, moving as if he were completely healed.

The woman reached for her arm, but Kol's magic surged, sending a shudder of desire through me, but not enough to reignite my passion. The woman, the real target of Kol's magic, dropped to her hands and knees, panting, as Kol slammed his fist into Buzz Cut's throat and snapped his heel into the next man's temple. Buzz Cut staggered back choking and the other guy dropped to the floor unconscious. With a snarl, Kol seized the front of the third guy's shirt, but the woman reached for her arm again.

Kol tossed the man in his grasp at her, sending both of them crashing to the floor in a heap. But Buzz Cut had recovered and lunged at him. Wrenching around, Kol slammed his palm into Buzz Cut's nose and his eyes rolled back. Kol was turned around and facing the remaining two before Buzz Cut's body hit the floor.

The man Kol had thrown into the woman scrambled back and grabbed one of his tattoos, but Kol whipped a key at him—he had to have gotten it off of one of the witches, although when, I had no clue. The small piece of metal embedded in the man's eye and killed him before he could cast his spell.

The woman screamed and her power thudded into me. Kol lurched forward a step and dropped to one knee.

"They can cast within the containment spell?" Sebastian groaned. "We're fucked."

"No," Kol barked, his determination to save me blazing through my chest. "We're getting out of here."

He fought to rise, his body shaking with the effort. He was almost up. I couldn't believe it. But it wasn't going to be enough to get to the woman. He needed more strength.

And he was God damn going to get it.

I concentrated on my new connection to him and flooded him with what little strength I had left. It rushed out of me with a strange sticky heat, unlike the gentle warmth I usually felt when I gave my guys strength. But the hellfire in Kol's eyes flared, demonic magic misted around him for a second, and he heaved to his feet.

He grabbed the woman's head, breaking her neck, and the pressure crushing me vanished.

"Thank God for too much sex," Sebastian said.

Kol grabbed another key from beside the woman's body and unlocked the rest of the cells.

I crawled to the front of the cell and stood. The world tilted and darkened, and I clung to the bars to keep standing. I might have released the pain of Jacob's bite-lock, but I was still freezing and weak from binding my soul with Kol's and couldn't take a full breath without slicing agony through my chest.

"Who can walk?" Gideon asked, staggering into the hall, his face pale and pinched with pain. "We need to get out of here now."

"We just need to get away from the containment spell," Sebastian said, supporting Marcus.

"Even *you* don't have enough power or strength of will to teleport ten people," Jacob said, heading into Ephraim's and Regan's cell. His complexion was gray, his eyes a little unfocused, but he wasn't bleeding, so the little bit of blood I'd given him must have helped.

"I'm willing to risk Essie frying me to a crisp with a direct power transfer to get the hell out of here," he said. "She's probably still low on juice, so the odds of her burning me up are less than if I channel directly."

"There's not going to be ten of us," Ephraim said. "I can't feel my legs. My back has to be broken. And Regan is still unconscious. Too many of us are down."

"We're not leaving anyone behind." Jacob knelt beside Regan and pressed his fingers to her neck. "She's still alive."

"I can walk on my own," Marcus said, pushing away from Sebastian but clinging to the closest bars to keep standing.

"You can't." The muscles in Gideon's jaw flexed. "And Essie can't give you strength like she can for the rest of us."

And like I could take the strength from them, as well.

Marcus glared at Gideon, his wolf darkening his eyes. "Thanks for reminding me."

If I could pull some strength from Kol, no one would need to carry me.

"If we don't have to go far, I can probably carry one person," Gideon said. "Jacob, can you carry two?"

"Yes, but we're still short one," Ephraim said. "You have to leave. Now."

I concentrated on my brand with Kol. I'd given him strength to defy the witch's spell, but I had no idea how I'd done it. I couldn't seem to push or pull anything through it any more. My trembling increased, and I lost my grip on the bars and slid to the floor.

Kol rushed to me and picked me up.

"Why can't I pull strength from you?"

"Your bond is too new," Gideon said. "It might form quickly, but it's not instant. You can't give or take strength from him right away."

"But I just gave him strength to break through the witches' spell."

Sebastian narrowed his eyes, his look that soul-deep appraising look he'd given me before my angelic nature had been revealed. "Are you sure?"

Well... was I sure? I'd thought I'd given Kol strength... but... it had felt weird. Maybe it had been my imagination.

Jeez, it was so hard to think. All I wanted to do was fall asleep wrapped in Kol's warmth.

"We don't have time to figure this out." Gideon stepped back into his cell and, with a grunt of pain, hefted Zuri over his shoulder. "Jacob, grab Xavier and Regan."

But that left Ephraim. "You can't just leave him," I said. Anyone left behind was dead or kept alive to have their essence drained to the point of death. And I had no doubt the witches would drain Ephraim again and again until he wished he was dead.

"We have to leave someone and he's agreed." Gideon met Ephraim's gaze and a shadow passed through both of their angel glows. "Do you want rescue or death?"

My pulse tripped. Did he just ask—?

"You're going to kill him?"

"If that's what he wants. His back is broken. He can't heal that on his own and we can't get him out. Death is a kindness," Gideon said, but I could feel his horror at what he'd asked through our bond. "The angels Michael captured never got that kindness."

"Rescue," Ephraim gasped. "I might learn something important." But his grim expression said the rest: if the witches kept him alive.

Gideon gave him a tight nod. "We'll come back with a full squad."

"Given what we just faced, bring at least two," Ephraim said.

Gideon coughed, the sound still wet, and grabbed a nearby bar to keep standing and holding Zuri. "Kol, lead the way."

Kol's grip around me tightened, and even with the pain in my chest, I fought to keep my eyes open against the lulling warmth of his body.

We headed out of the small, ten-cell prison into a long hall with the same metal floor and walls. The only lights shone at the entrance of the prison and at the far end at a T intersection, leaving thick shadows in between, and with no other hallways or doors, the only place we could go was the T-intersection.

I strained to listen for anyone nearby, but my teeth kept chattering with the bone-deep cold of magical shock and my thoughts kept drifting back to Kol. My mate. Thank God. Finally. His pulse pounded strong, the release of Jacob's bite-lock having brought him back to full, and his warmth embraced me.

For a second I was drifting in the not-water with my father staring at me, the flecks of gold in his angel glow mesmerizing. He pressed his hand against something between us and glanced over his shoulder.

Far off in the distance, gunfire popped and hurried foot-steps pounded closer.

Shuddering cold sliced through the warm not-water, and I gasped. My eyes flew open, but the footsteps didn't stop.

"They're getting closer," Kol hissed. "Which way?"

We were at the T-intersection and both directions looked identical to where we'd come from: metal floor and walls with low light and a long stretch to the far end. Although this time there were two doors on either side of each hall to break up the cold sleek metal.

"Bane, do you feel anything?" Gideon gasped.

"Until I'm out of the containment spell, I won't be able to tell you its radius," Sebastian said.

"To the right." Jacob jerked his chin toward the right-hand hall. "The witches are coming from the left."

Kol hurried down the hall as the footsteps grew louder. I peered around his shoulder at the others behind us. Jacob's chest heaved with heavy breaths. Even just hurrying down the hall while carrying Regan and Xavier—one on each shoulder—was too much for him in his condition. Marcus didn't look any better, clinging to Sebastian as if that were the only reason he was upright, and the tendons in Gideon's neck were bulging with the strain of carrying Zuri and his face was ashen—and I doubted Zuri would normally be too heavy for him.

The footsteps drew closer. I couldn't see whoever was coming at the far end, but they had to be close and we still had at least fifty feet to the next intersection.

"We're not going to make it," I said. "They're about to round the corner."

Kol raced to the closest door and opened it, taking a huge risk by not stopping to listen for anyone inside. We rushed in and he set me on my feet, just inside the door, clinging to the wall for balance, then stepped back into the hall to cover the rest of the team's retreat.

A cold air swept around me and the only light came from the hall, a weak splash of illumination on a metal floor. The rest of the room lay in complete darkness.

Jacob hurried in through the doorway, and I staggered along the wall to make room for him so he didn't have to move too deeply into the dark.

My hand hit a light switch as Gideon, Sebastian, and Marcus hustled inside. Kol stepped in last, shutting the door behind him, and I turned on the lights.

The fluorescent lights flickered on blindingly bright. I slapped my forearm over my eyes—since my hands were bloody—and squeezed them shut as the guys hissed and groaned.

"A little warning next time," Sebastian said, his voice echoing, indicating we were in a large room. "Better yet, don't."

Marcus huffed. "Or you could go bashing into whatever is in here."

"Or we could just wait for the witches to run by," Sebastian shot back.

I dropped my gaze to the floor and shifted my arm, letting in a little light, trying to get my eyes to adjust as quickly as possible. I could barely stand or breathe or hell, even think. I didn't want to be even more useless by being blind.

Shading my eyes and squinting, I blinked back tears and raised my gaze to check our surroundings. We stood at the edge of a platform with a waist-high metal railing that stretched across the front of a vast room. The unfinished ceiling with exposed metal girders towered above us and the main floor sat one floor down, accessible by stairs on either end of the platform. A massive black circle surrounded by large swirling glyphs had been drawn in the center of the metal floor below, and tables, cabinets, shelves, and tall stacks of crates crowded against the walls on either side. Most of the tables were covered in thick plastic, protecting whatever equipment lay beneath, and with that, along with the lack of electric hum, my best guess was that this was a lab that wasn't yet in use.

It was a lot like the zip lab we'd stumbled across a few days ago that the red-haired glyph witch had brought down on us, except this looked four times bigger and more sophisticated. If this was their new lab, we were in serious trouble. There were already too many deaths from the magically enhanced upper, and an influx of the drug would only make things worse.

"Oh, Jesus," Jacob gasped, his attention on the back of the room.

"No." Kol's back stiffened and frozen fear shot through my still-hollow chest. "We have to destroy them. We can't leave without destroying them."

"Are those—?" Marcus staggered to the railing and pointed to a dozen large glass tanks standing at the back. They were big enough to hold a single person, sealed at the top and bottom with metal caps, and had dozens of pipes and wires trailing out of them.

"Nephilim maturation tanks," Gideon said.

My pulse stalled and more frozen fear from my guys slid through me, defying the containment spell.

A wave of dizziness washed over the fear and I bobbed in the not-water. The inky dark magic that I'd tried to lock away started laughing.

The footsteps in the hall pounded closer, and we froze. Then a soft wet plop filled the silence and everyone's gaze dropped to the floor and the splattered blood on the landing by Jacob, Gideon, and Marcus, then jumped to the trail leading to the door.

Marcus groaned. "Shit."

"There's a door at the back," Jacob said, pointing to a narrow metal door in the corner half hidden by a tank.

"Move." Gideon shifted Zur's weight on his shoulder, groaned, but still hurried to the stairs with Jacob close behind.

"With luck, we won't need the door. The tanks and the circle require a lot of magic." Sebastian slung Marcus's arm across his shoulder and they followed Gideon and Jacob. "They can't be within the containment spell."

Kol flipped the deadbolt on the door—not that the witches wouldn't have a key, but it might slow them down long enough for us to escape—and swept me off my feet into his arms. Agony sliced through my chest, my head spun, and for a second, I was lurching again in the not-water. Then my vision cleared and Kol's gaze locked on mine, his fear twisting in my chest. The edge in his eyes, the one I'd seen when my wings had first appeared, was back.

We rushed down the stairs and reached the magic circle, but the hollowness in my chest didn't ease up.

"Come on," Sebastian said, staggering with Marcus around the outside edge of the circle, careful not to touch the glyphs. "There's got to be a break. There's got to be—" The light under his skin flared then dimmed again, and with a groan, he sagged to his knees, taking Marcus with him.

We were right beside the tanks, with just a narrow strip between the edge of the magic containment spell and the tanks.

Gideon's back straightened as he crossed the invisible threshold of the spell, and the light in his eyes blazed bright and kept glowing. Zuri groaned and he set her on the floor beside Marcus, while Jacob knelt and rolled Regan and Xavier off his shoulders beside Zuri.

Then Kol stepped out of the containment spell and fire rushed through me. I gasped, filled with power, my head throbbing, my body still trembling from magical shock, and freezing with a fear that wasn't mine.

"All right, Esther." Sebastian held out his hand. "Don't burn me up."

Someone said something outside in the hall and Jacob jerked to face the front. "How fast can you do this? They're going to find the blood trail."

Kol set me on the floor beside Sebastian and hurried to the narrow back door. My gaze followed him for a second, but slid back to the tank beside me. It was bigger than I'd first thought, able to easily hold someone Jacob's size. This was how Michael had made so many of his monsters so quickly. It took magic to speed up maturation, and he'd figured out how to do it in the womb in the human women he'd enslaved to create his army, and, once his nephilim had been born, in tanks like these. And he'd had hundreds of women captive and hundreds of tanks.

A shudder swept through me and the inky magic's laughter grew.

Michael had used dark magic to create his monsters. That had to be why they were so monstrous. It hadn't just been demonic magic, but magic warped by pure evil.

Just like the inky magic trying to worm its way into my soul.

You'll be powerful. Worshiped. A goddess.

My thoughts whirled, and I raised a trembling hand and pressed it against the glass of the maturation tank.

"Esther," Sebastian said, grabbing my other hand and jerking my attention away from the tanks. "Think of a stream—" He frowned. "Better yet, think of a very thin thread of magic sliding from you into me."

"The door is locked," Kol said.

"Jacob, can you force it?" Gideon asked.

Sebastian's grip on my hand tightened, dragging my attention back to him. Again. "Esther, focus. We don't have a lot of time."

Right. Escaping.

The voices in the hall rose in volume, and I struggled to block them out. They were at the door, they knew it was locked, and our only means of escape was me giving Sebastian enough power to teleport us.

But there's no escape. You're not powerful enough.

Shut up.

I imagined a thread like Sebastian had said, and connected with my power. The moment I did, my magic erupted into an inferno and roared out of my hand into Sebastian. A scream tore from his throat and his head jerked back. Light blazed from his skin and poured out of his eyes and mouth, and the inky magic howled with pleasure.

I fought to pull my power back, control it, but the guys' fear and the strain to ignore the inky magic, along with the bone-deep exhaustion of binding my soul to Kol's, kept ripping it from my mental grasp. My power was consuming me and I was going to take Sebastian along with me.

My pulse leaped to a rapid tattoo, giving me a blast of mental strength. I wrenched my power out of Sebastian, and it slammed into my chest, stealing all breath and thought. I was a supernova erupting and it took all I had to keep the explosion inside my body and protect those around me.

The inky magic surged, slipping into my cells while I struggled with my power. It consumed my inferno, leaving me trembling and cold and desperate to keep it from sinking into my soul and taking over.

Sebastian sagged forward, his forehead pressed to the metal floor, and I started to fall over and join him when the inky magic seized my body and heaved me to my feet.

My breath caught. *No, please, no.* Not again. I couldn't be possessed again. I mentally clawed at it, desperate to regain control of my body. I had to get it out, had to get free, but I couldn't get rid of it.

My body jerked, slicing agony through me. I clenched my teeth, fighting the movement, but I wasn't strong enough to resist the inky magic's control of my muscles while also keeping it from controlling my soul, and turned to face the front of the room. My guys were a few steps ahead of me on their hands and knees, their heads bowed, their bodies trembling. And on the landing stood ten witches and the demon-goddess.

CHAPTER 11

"That's better," the demon-goddess said, her voice dark, filled with the promise of excruciating pain. Wisps of red mist curled around her and the hellfire in her eyes licked her cheeks, releasing little sparks that snapped around her.

"Ah, fuck," Sebastian gasped, his voice ragged. "That's Lilith."

"What?" Zuri asked.

"The Hellfire Queen herself." Sebastian groaned. "Who the hell let her out of her cage?"

"Now let's have a look at you," Lilith said, raising her hand.

My body stepped forward into the containment spell, and the chill in my soul swelled as the sickening hollow feeling filled my chest again.

"Fight it, Essie," Marcus gasped, and a tear leaked from my eye. He didn't even have to question me, he already knew I was being possessed, knew I wasn't stepping forward of my own free will.

I strode between Marcus and Jacob and stopped in the

center of the magic circle, my body trembling as I fought to regain control. I had to get free—

Or I had to buy Sebastian enough time to recover and get my guys out of there.

"Fight," Gideon said, and I instinctually connected with... I wasn't sure what in his brand. It wasn't like the physical strength we shared when one of us was weak, and it didn't feel as if it flowed from him into me. It was more like a strength of spirit that connected our souls and rooted mine deeper within myself, making the inky magic's hold on me weaken. Just like that same strength had weakened it before I'd regained consciousness in the cell. It lasted a second before the inky magic seized control again, but I'd weakened it. I was sure I had.

"Well," Lilith said, her voice thick with disgust, "you look like *him*."

Look like—? My pulse stuttered. Had she just said—?

"Who?" I asked, even though I had a sinking suspicion I knew who she was talking about.

"Your father." The hellfire in Lilith's eyes flared, showering red sparks around her that hissed when they hit the metal floor. "I should have seen the resemblance the moment you were presented as a sacrifice. Your father's spell hiding you was powerful. I didn't notice the truth until you used your power a moment ago." Her lips curled into a wicked smile. "But even he can't hide all of your magic forever."

"All of my magic?" That didn't make any sense. I'd already broken through the spell hiding my magic.

Oh, you think so? the inky magic inside me asked.

"I know it's in there. Not as locked away as he'd hoped." She flicked a finger and the inky magic inside me jerked me to my knees, jarring my broken ribs and stealing my breath.

Out of the corner of my eye, Jacob tensed, and I concentrated on the spiritual strength in his brand, bolstering my hold on my soul. The inky magic's grip on me faltered again, and I mentally held onto my bond with Jacob, making my body tremble... but because it was partially back in my control. My bonds were the key to pushing the inky magic out.

"He thought he could keep you from me," Lilith said, "thought he could break our bargain."

The image of my father, with his hand pressed on something between us, flashed through my mind's eye. Fear tightened his expression and he glanced over his shoulder.

The red mist curling from Lilith's skin whipped into a vortex around her, and her witches shifted back, their postures tense.

I added concentrating on Gideon's bond along with Jacob's and pushed the inky magic back even further. A little bit more and I'd be free. But when I reached for Marcus, nothing happened.

I tried again.

Nothing.

Crap. Whatever it was that strengthened my soul against the inky magic, it only came from my brands.

"You might be half his," she snarled, "but you're also half mine, *my* weapon, and he'll regret the day he stole you. I'll make him worship at my feet with the rest of them."

She snapped her hand out, and her demonic mist shot across the room and slammed into me. Every muscle in my body seized with fiery pain. My concentration on my soul bonds slipped and her magic, both demonic and worship, ripped through me, tearing into my essence.

Behind me my guys yelled, their fear and anger a churning mix in my stomach.

"All that trouble that he went through, and you still came back to me. And just when things are about to get good."

Specks of shadow and light snapped across my vision. I fought to breathe and stay conscious. I couldn't pass out. If I passed out, Lilith would turn her attention to my guys, and while they might be able to hold off the witches long enough to escape, they wouldn't stand a chance against the demon-goddess.

Please, let Sebastian be okay to cast. Please, they have to get out of here.

"I know it's in there," Lilith said. "I've already felt it."

Her demonic magic reached the core of my essence and my brands lit up. Power from my guys surged into me, and I scrambled to hold onto it, use it to fully force Lilith's magic out of me. But I was too weak from having claimed Kol and her demonic power incinerated it, burning deeper and deeper until all of me was on fire. It scorched my insides and exposed a ball of radiant magic within my heart.

There you are, Lilith hissed in my head. *All that beautiful darkness.*

Her magic contracted around the ball and the pain turned to screaming agony. Tears streamed down my cheeks, my chest heaved, but I couldn't manage to draw a full breath.

Darkness swept over me, stealing all sight and sound, and I bobbed again in the not-water. Gunfire popped off in the distance, and my father glanced over his shoulder. In the shadows behind him stood row upon row of human-sized tanks.

Then the radiant ball of magic hidden in the core of my being exploded and more demonic magic, *my* demonic magic, roared through me.

No. Oh, please, no. It couldn't be true.

I *was* a monster.

I was an impossible creature, born of evil magic. Michael *had* created me, and even if I wanted to deny my memories of being in the maturation tank, I couldn't deny my demonic magic now writhing inside me.

"Now you're a *real* weapon." Lilith flicked a finger and her worship magic, the inky magic howling with laughter inside me, pounded in my chest.

I focused everything I had on my brands, Gideon's crackling magic, Jacob's calm stillness, and even managed to sense sensual heat from Kol. I had to force the inky magic out.

I gritted my teeth. I would God damned force it out.

With a scream, I wrapped the spiritual strength from my guys around my soul and then swept it out from my core in a massive wave and pushed against the inky magic.

The inky magic howled and clawed, but I clenched everything I had, and shoved it out.

I toppled over, too weak to hold myself up, my mind whirling. I'd been made to subjugate and kill. That was my entire reason for existing.

"Get them back in their cells," Lilith said. "I don't care what condition they're in so long as they're alive, since *someone* forced me to change my plans and make my move today."

I hadn't been born to help people or fight for justice. I'd been made to murder and destroy and force people to worship Lilith, the Hellfire Queen and—God!—my mother.

"The ambassador's funeral was going to send the perfect message, and now I have to make do with second best, so I'll take payment for your transgression from your essences."

I dragged my attention back to Lilith. She sneered, her

gaze locked on me. "I'm glad you're finally home, daughter. My war can now begin."

She left with another body crushing thump that made my head spin.

"Surrender," a guy said as he and the other witches stormed down the stairs and raced to the edge of the magic circle to face us.

"Fuck, no," Marcus snarled behind me.

"Zuri," Gideon gasped. "Get Bane steady. We need that spell."

I pushed up to my hands and knees. Demonic mist curled around my forearms, licking around Gideon's brand.

I really was a monster.

Would they still love me?

I shoved that thought aside. It didn't matter. I loved them and they were getting the hell out of there. They had to warn the JP about Lilith, and above all, they had to live.

I jerked my head up and gathered the mist around my hands.

The witches grabbed their tattoos to cast a spell and the *thu-thud* of their magic pounded in my chest. With a yell, I released my power. The force disrupted their spells and crashed them into the tables and crates, drawing screams of pain.

The mist weeping from my skin thinned, and the cold hollowness in my chest where my divine light should have been sank heavier into my soul. My body shook and the unconsciousness I'd been fighting before threatened to overwhelm me. I was running out of strength and magic.

"Sebastian, cast the teleport spell," I yelled without looking behind me. My guys had to go. Now. I couldn't let Lilith drain their essence. "She has to be stopped. You have to get out of here."

A strong arm wrapped around my waist. "Not without you," Kol said, and he hauled me out of the containment spell.

My magic didn't even flare, and the strength of the bone-deep chill of magical shock crashed over me and stole my breath.

Zuri looked at me with horror and shifted away as Kol dragged me closer. Sebastian, his glow so bright it hurt to look at him, had his head down and his burned and bleeding hands pressed against his thighs, so I had no idea what he thought about me. Regan and Xavier were thankfully still unconscious, and Marcus, Jacob, and Gideon stood with their backs to me, facing the witches.

"Bane," Gideon snapped.

"Almost... got it." The muscles in Sebastian's shoulders tightened and his breath grew ragged. A circle of light flickered around him, but had yet to fully form.

One of the witches, still lying on the ground, screamed something and grabbed a tattoo on his arm.

His magic thudded, making the room lurch around me, and I jerked my hand out, praying that I had enough magic left to stop him. Red mist sputtered out of my palm and blew apart in the air. I couldn't get hold of it. I could barely focus.

Just a little more. That was all I needed. I could do this.

The witch's magic thudded again, and a blade of ice shot from his hand straight for my heart. Shit. Without my magic, I had nothing to stop him.

I wrenched my trembling body to the side, but knew as the agony of my broken ribs screamed through my chest that I wasn't going to be fast enough to get out of the way.

With a yell, Marcus dove at me. He tackled me to the

ground. White lightning exploded in my chest and for a second, time froze.

It was just me and Marcus and the ice spear protruding from his back. Then the ice exploded, tearing open the wound and drawing a gut-wrenching scream from both of us.

No no no. Please, no.

Blood rushed over me, instantly soaking my shirt, and he went limp, his weight crushing me, each breath agonizing. But I could barely feel the pain. He couldn't die. None of them could die.

My demonic power burst from my skin and swept into him. It flooded his cells, wove into his essence, and clenched around his soul. I would save him. If Kol could give me his strength through his essence, I could give it to Marcus. Being half whatever-type-of-demon Lilith was had to be good for something.

"Got it." The light around Sebastian flared bright, creating a wide circle on the floor around him. "Everyone get over here."

Gideon and Jacob raced to Sebastian's side, and the teleportation spell tore me to pieces with an agonizing mix of light and darkness and raging red storm.

I was everything and nothing, hurtling through an emptiness as hollow as the feeling in my chest and as searing as my pain. A pain that grew tighter and tighter, until my wings burst free and my back hit something hard.

The air lurched from hot to cold and a wild mix of emotions flooded my chest then vanished as frozen emptiness filled me. The guys hissed and groaned, and Marcus, still on top of me, screamed and convulsed.

Oh, God!

I rolled him off me and pressed my hands over the

wound in his chest. My demonic magic still churned inside him, clinging to his wound and slowing the rush of blood onto the floor, but not stopping it. Mist curled over my forearms and sank into him, burst free from his skin, and sank back in again.

Out of the corner of my eye, I caught a glimpse of my wings, and clenched my jaw in resignation. The tips of my feathers were red. My essence had probably changed, too. I wouldn't be able to hide what I really was.

Beside me, Sebastian, his skin dull with no glow at all, both arms burned past his elbows, threw up blood and collapsed. Gideon tucked his wings back but didn't pull them in, and Jacob's vampiric intensity surged, while Kol's seductive magic caressed my soul, stealing my breath.

Zuri, her horns and fangs revealed because the teleportation spell reformed us in our supernatural states, flapped grit into my face with her leathery wings as she scrambled away from me.

My pulse stalled. We were supposed to be reformed in our supernatural state. Marcus was supposed to be a wolf and he wasn't.

"Oh, my God," a feminine voice gasped. "What is that?"

We weren't alone.

Shivering from adrenaline and shock, I jerked my attention from Marcus to see where we were, and my gaze landed on the shallow cafeteria steps in Operations leading up into the hall. They were only a few feet away, so we had to be at the front of the room. All around us, the tables and chairs had been pushed back and toppled over, the force of Sebastian's spell shoving them aside to make room for us, and half of the scaffolding on the rock wall beside us had collapsed.

There wasn't anyone in front of me, so I turned to the rest of the room. All of the lights were on, but the sky out the back windows was dark, so it was still before dawn. At the far end, a dozen people, along with Cassius, stood around two large tables that had been pushed together, their chairs shoved back, a few toppled over, as if they'd quickly stood up. Half-eaten sandwiches, empty sandwich wrappers, various bottled beverages, folders, phones, and laptops littered the table, indicating we'd interrupted some kind of meeting.

Amiah and Priam, who'd been near a table halfway between us and the others—clearly not a part of whatever late night meeting had been taking place—rushed toward us.

Thank God. Marcus was going to get help.

"Cassius," Gideon gasped. "You're awake."

"That's an archnephilim," a broad-shouldered muscular man said, his eyes bright with an angelic glow. "Amiah, get back. Agents, secure it."

Marcus screamed again, his body jerking under my hands. Something crunched inside him and my demonic magic swelled, surging deeper into his essence.

Amiah stumbled to a halt a few steps from me, her gaze locked on mine. "So you're a—?"

"I am," I said, my teeth chattering and my body shaking so hard it was difficult to keep my hands on Marcus. And my mother was the Hellfire Queen, determined to restart Michael's war, except she didn't want to kill humanity, just subjugate them... and use me to do it.

I dragged my attention to Kol, afraid of what I'd see. He was the closest, still kneeling beside me, and the one most affected by learning that I really was a nephilim. And while his breath was shallow and the edge in his eyes had turned to full terror, he drew closer to me, making my heart swell with love and relief.

"I won't let her take you," he said. "I swear it."

"Who?" Amiah asked as Marcus screamed again and something tore inside him with a sickening wet sound. She dropped to her knees beside him and placed a hand on his leg, her palm glowing with her healing magic.

"Lilith," Jacob said.

Amiah gasped. "Lilith is free?"

My shaking grew stronger, but I didn't know if it was from the cold or fear. "We have to put her back in her cage before she gets stronger." *Before she can use me to kill people.*

"Get that abomination in a cell," the broad-shouldered angel snapped.

Another gut-wrenching scream tore from Marcus's clenched jaw and his body convulsed.

"They need to get to triage," Amiah said, her gaze sweeping over us. "All of them."

"In a cell," the broad-shouldered angel repeated.

"Director, wait," Gideon said, his breath wet and ragged. "Essie isn't a threat."

"But I am if Lilith gets ahold of me—"

"She's not getting ahold of you," Jacob said, taking a step ahead of me and releasing his full vampiric intensity with a breathtaking swell of power. "And neither are they."

Kol gave me a tight nod and stood, taking position beside Jacob.

Marcus gasped, and with another sickening crunch his jaw started to lengthen into his wolf's, then crunched back into a human's, as if his body couldn't figure out how to shift any longer.

"Amiah, please," I begged.

The light from her hand glowed brighter as she pumped more magic into him.

"Agents," the Director said, storming toward us with

Cassius at his side, the others close behind, "secure the creature. It's dangerous."

"Lilith is the real danger," Gideon gasped, staggering to
his feet, his right arm pressed tight against his side. His
complexion was ashen, sweat slicked his forehead, but he
squared his shoulders, ready to fight.

The Director's expression hardened and lightning
crackled around his fists.

"Director, don't," Amiah said. "She's soul bound to half
the team. If Lilith really is free, you'll need them."

"Gideon, listen to reason," Cassius said. "She's clearly an
archnephilim."

"She's my mate."

"She's a war criminal."

"You know that's not true," Gideon said.

"It doesn't matter. The law is the law." Cassius took a few
steps ahead of the Director and squared his shoulders just
like Gideon, emphasizing their family relation. "She's a
monster. An abomination. She only exists because of
Michael's evil magic. I have to arrest her."

"No. You don't." A tremor shook Gideon, and a nause-
ating mix of his rage, fear, and exhaustion churned my
stomach, mixing with the cold. "Even if you didn't know
Essie, you know me. You know my mate would never be a
monster."

"Gideon." The muscles in Cassius's jaw flexed. "Don't
make this harder than it has to be."

"Listen to your brother," the Director said. "You're not
thinking straight, agent. You're compromised."

Gideon's gaze stayed locked on Cassius's, his expression
glacial. "You know I'm not."

"I know your bond is true, but it doesn't matter," Cassius

said, fire curling over his hands and up his forearms. "It's the law."

"Then you're going to have to pick." The light in Gideon's eyes blazed in a brilliant nimbus around his head and his sword of divine light formed in his clenched fist. "The law or me."

CHAPTER 12

CASSIUS STARED AT GIDEON, STUNNED, AS IF HE HADN'T expected Gideon's ultimatum, then anger and horror darkened his expression. In the brief time I'd spent with him, it was clear he needed rules, needed that certainty and structure possibly more than Gideon did. But he'd also shown me that he loved his brother and would twist his precious rules to protect him.

Now he had to choose. He couldn't twist this. The law was clear. Arrest me or don't. Those were his only options.

They glared at each other, Gideon's breath wet and shallow, and Cassius so tense he shook.

The Director shifted a step closer, the eleven others, a mixed party of six men and five woman—four with glowing angel eyes, the rest a mix of vampires, demons, and shifters —only a few steps behind. They stared at us, their expressions ranging from worried, afraid, to angry.

Tension filled the room with a palpable energy that set my nerves on fire and made my pulse race. Everyone waited, the whole room holding its breath to see what Cassius would do.

I didn't want Gideon to fight his brother, but I knew he'd never let Cassius arrest me. Even faced with Voth's enormous power, Gideon hadn't backed down from the greater demon. He'd give his life to protect me. Just like I would for him.

Marcus screamed, breaking the silence, and his shifter magic dissolved his shirt, revealing raw burned skin underneath and the ragged wound in the center of his chest, partially held together by my demonic mist. That was the only reason he was still alive, and I could only hope my power lasted long enough for Amiah to heal him. Patchy fur swept across his chest as his torso expanded, each rib cracking with a resounding snap, then sank back under his blistered skin.

"Gideon, we have to get him to triage," I said. I jerked my gaze over the rest of the group.

Zuri had dragged Regan—who, because of the teleportation spell, was now a sleek panther—and Xavier—still perfectly human—away from us, leaving a wide swath of blood on the cafeteria floor. Priam had rolled Sebastian over and pressed his palms to the unconscious fae's chest, his magic radiating around his hands.

Gideon was in rough shape, and Jacob was too pale with a small pool of blood at his feet. The blood trail we'd left while we were escaping hadn't just been from Regan and Xavier.

Kol was the only one who looked well, but by himself he didn't stand a chance against the Director of the Joined Parliament Bureau of Supernatural Law Enforcement, who was rumored to be one of the strongest angels in the mortal realm, along with eleven other supers, plus Cassius.

Gideon's eyes narrowed, his gaze still locked on Cassius. "Pick."

Cassius glared back.

Marcus screamed, more of his bones shattering.

"Pick!" Gideon yelled, and Cassius roared back at him, the cry desperate and primal.

"God damn you, Gideon." He jerked around, his fire exploding from his hands and sweeping into a massive burning wall that reached from the floor to the ceiling and all the way across.

Sweat instantly covered my body, and the air, blazingly hot, seared down my throat with every shallow breath. Zuri hauled Xavier and Regan farther away, her face a mask of horror, and the supers on the other side of the wall yelled.

"Pick up Marcus and get out of here," Cassius snapped.

Gideon turned to grab Marcus, but gasped in pain.

"I've got him," Jacob said, heaving Marcus, still screaming and writhing, onto his shoulder. My demonic mist surged around him, stretching between us, then split, still billowing and sinking under his skin as well as mine.

Amiah stood as well and placed her hand back on Marcus.

Cassius's eyes widened. "What are you doing?"

"They need medical attention." She turned to Priam. "Stay with the elite team."

"You don't have enough power to heal them all," Priam said.

She squared her shoulders. "I'll have to."

"Kol, get Bane," Gideon said. "He's not an agent. I'm not leaving him here to be interrogated."

I staggered to my feet and the cafeteria lurched, but Gideon grabbed the back of my shirt, catching me before I fell.

"Pull your wings in," he said, pressing his palm against my back.

I squeezed my shoulder blades together and his power exploded into me, forcing my wings back into my chest with an agonizing *thud*. The cafeteria lurched and darkened, and he swept me into his arms. Pain tightened his expression and his body trembled, but he didn't let go.

"Get moving," Gideon barked, waiting for the others to hurry up the stairs first.

"I've got your back." Cassius ran toward us and his fire wall shuddered, his power weakening, taking the searing heat with it.

My bone-deep chill returned and Gideon's body heat taunted me, warm enough for me to feel it but not warm enough to melt the cold inside.

Behind him, lightning shot through Cassius's fire wall and slammed into his back. He staggered, caught his balance, and kept running, but his fire vanished.

Through the smoke, the Director glared at us and barked orders. Half of the other JP agents, or whatever they were, ran after us. The rest summoned magic, their power swelling, crushing inside me and stealing my breath.

There was no way we were going to escape. We didn't have enough of a head start. Cassius needed to put up another fire wall or something to slow them down.

My demonic magic fluttered across my vision, gusting toward the rock wall.

Or *I* had to do something.

God damn it.

I mentally seized my red mist, along with every last flickering ounce of power in my soul.

Gideon and Cassius rushed up the steps, and I whipped my mist around the rock wall and wrenched, the effort burning through my body with glorious heat for a second. The rocks crashed onto the stairs with a boom and a thick cloud of dust, blocking the way behind us, just like they had when the archnephilim who'd started it all had pulled down the wall.

"That won't slow them for long," Cassius said as we barreled past the elevator and around the corner into the long hall leading to the garage.

"We just need a head start," I gasped, leaning into Gideon, desperate for warmth, any warmth.

We ran into the garage and straight onto the street, not taking a vehicle because the Director would be able to use its GPS locator to find us. Thankfully, it was early morning and we weren't near the vampire section of the Quarter, so no one was around.

Gideon's steps jarred my ribs, and the world spun around me with a mix of painful flashes of streetlight, enveloping darkness, freezing cold, and Marcus's gut-wrenching screams. I tried not to think about anything, but my thoughts kept jumping back to the truth.

I wasn't just an angel. I'd been made. My sole purpose was to kill and destroy. I wasn't supposed to exist. And my guys were risking everything, not just their careers, but their lives, to protect me.

We zigzagged from street to alley and street again, until Jacob staggered to a stop near the end of an alley, just deep enough to not be in the band of streetlight shining between the buildings.

"We can't keep running," he gasped. "We need a plan."

"We need to get off the street." Kol ran his hands through his hair. "Some place where they can't hear Marcus."

"Bane's is the closest, but I don't want to go back there," Jacob said, struggling to keep his hand over Marcus's mouth and muffle his screams while keeping him on his shoulder.

"We have to get out of the Quarter," Gideon said as he stumbled. With a groan and hacking cough, he shoved his shoulder against the alley wall and caught his balance.

"I'll take her," Cassius said, his voice gruff.

The light in Gideon's eyes flared and his grip around me tightened, putting pressure on my broken ribs.

I fought to hold back my whimper because he needed to hold me and I needed him to hold me, but it still escaped. He shot me a worried look, eased up his grip, but didn't hand me over.

"Wherever we go, it has to be good," Jacob said. "We're next to helpless in our condition."

And that was the problem. The JP would find us. There was no doubt about that. It was just a matter of time. If we hid well enough, we might have enough time for Amiah to heal all of us, but that was the catch. Where could we go where they wouldn't think to look? And who would help us?

I struggled to focus my whirling thoughts on our options. We could go to Willow, the firebird shaman. No one knew about her, but given how our last encounter with her had gone, the odds of her helping us were slim. I also doubted any of the shifter packs would go against the JP, and I'd destroyed whatever ties we had with Victoria, Union City's master vampire. Which left—

No one. There wasn't anyone else we could go to for help.

Except there was.

Please, God, don't let me be wrong. There was one other person who'd said if I called, he'd help.

The cold surged and my shaking increased, spiking agony through my chest. God, I was never going to get warm. "We have to go to Voth's."

"No." Gideon's angel glow burned brighter. "Absolutely not."

"Even I know that's a terrible idea," Cassius said. "He didn't earn the nickname the Angel of Death for nothing. Voth took great pleasure in killing nephilim during the war. He's going to love killing you."

"He said if I called, he'd come." The conversation flashed through my mind. He'd flattened us with his power, all to figure out why he didn't have a soul bond and we did. "He said they wouldn't understand me, but that he's seen my truth and that I was nothing like them. He already knows what I am."

"Are you sure?" Jacob asked.

Voth had been shocked when I'd shown him my connection to my guys, but then he'd been determined and certain. Not a hint of fear or rage. He had to have known I was one of Michael's creations... and if I really thought about it, Mystic Mavis's reaction to me when I responded to her demonic magic said she'd realized the truth, too. Except she'd been terrified of me and Voth hadn't.

"He knows," I said. He'd searched inside me and seen the truth... and so had Sebastian. Had he known that I was a monster as well?

Gideon's angel glow dimmed with worry and his eyes narrowed. I didn't need my empathy to know he didn't like the idea but knew we didn't have any other choice.

"If you're wrong, he'll kill us," Cassius said.

"I'm not wrong." A wave of darkness stole my vision, and I fought to remain conscious. I couldn't afford to pass out now, and I couldn't be wrong about Voth. *Please, don't let me be wrong.* We didn't have anywhere else we could go.

"He did say he'd help," Jacob said, his voice low.

"He's not an angel. He'll have no problem going back on his word. Especially since she's—" The muscles in Cassius's jaw clenched.

"What?" Kol snapped. "Smart? Determined? Beautiful? Mated to the four of us?"

Amiah gasped.

"He flattened us when he thought she had Gideon, Jacob, and Marcus," Kol said. "I don't want to know what he'll do when he realizes she's branded a demon."

Marcus convulsed and his mouth jerked free from Jacob's grip, his cry loud in the silence.

"We can't keep standing here," Jacob said, the muscles in his arms bulging as he fought to hold Marcus. "Voth said they, whoever they are, wouldn't understand her. He has to know she's an archnephilim. We've got no other place to go."

"Fine." Gideon drew in a ragged breath. "We go to Voth's."

Cassius threw his hands up. "This is insane."

"You can always stay here." Kol adjusted Sebastian's unconscious form on his shoulder, shifted to the mouth of the alley, and glanced out at the street beyond.

"You know I can't," Cassius said.

"Then suck it up, because we're going to Voth's and we're going to break another law to do it." He rushed out of the alley and disappeared from sight.

Jacob and Amiah hurried after him, and the sound of shattering glass followed a few seconds later.

Cassius stiffened and fire licked over his hands. "I'm going to kill your demon."

"Cassius," Gideon said, his voice gruff, jerking his brother's attention back to him. "Thank you."

"You would have died to protect her," he snarled. "I'm not losing another brother."

He stormed out of the alley, and Gideon staggered after him.

"You have— had another brother?"

"We did. Cassius doesn't like to talk about it," Gideon said. "Dominic accepted a mission to infiltrate Michael's army, but he stopped communicating with the Angelic Defense six months in." He pursed his lips. "We haven't heard from him since."

No wonder Cassius had been so determined to protect Gideon from me, and why Gideon had just about had a breakdown when Cassius had been poisoned.

"Cassius blames himself, although I don't know why. It wasn't like he had anything to do with Dominic's mission," Gideon said as he stepped out of the alley.

Kol stood a few feet down the street, reaching in through the now-broken back window of a late model minivan,

"You can't just steal a car," Cassius said.

"You and I might be able to walk to the other side of the Quarter, but no one else can." Kol unlocked the door, set Sebastian on the middle bench—since the back one was down—and climbed into the driver's seat. "Sit your ass down or we're leaving you behind."

Cassius huffed and took the front passenger seat. Gideon set me on the bench beside Sebastian, climbed in as well, and pulled me back into his arms.

Warm, so warm, and yet not warm enough. The world darkened and spun, and when it cleared, Amiah and Marcus were in the back, and Jacob was on the bench with us with Sebastian squeezed between us.

The engine sputtered and caught, and Kol put the

minivan into gear. We sped away as another gut-wrenching scream tore from Marcus's throat, and my pulse lurched. His thrashing increased, and the demonic mist swirling around him grew thicker, more like strands than wisps.

"If it takes everything you have to save him," Gideon said to Amiah, "use it. The rest of us can manage."

"I'm sure you think that," she said, her tone sharp. "But it doesn't matter how much I have, it isn't going to help him. He's in transition, and healing magic can't help with that. I healed the injury in his chest, but now the most I can do is try to make him more comfortable and restart his heart if it stops. It's a matter of waiting and keeping him alive long enough to get through this." Her expression darkened, her worry clear. She didn't know if he would.

My throat tightened and tears burned my eyes. This was a nightmare. I couldn't stop shaking, couldn't do anything, and couldn't lose him. I couldn't lose any of them. "There has to be something we can do."

Marcus screamed and Amiah wrenched her attention back to him. "There isn't."

"How the hell can he be in transition?" Kol asked, speeding around a corner and heading toward Squatters' Row. "He's already a shifter."

Gideon raked his hand over his face. He looked exhausted, and his complexion was too pale and his expression haggard.

Please, God. Help me.

"Something must have gone wrong with the teleportation spell," he said.

Jacob turned in his seat to look at Marcus. "Nine people must have been too much for Sebastian in his weakened condition."

I dragged my gaze to Sebastian, and fought to focus my wavering vision. His breath was so shallow it was hard to tell if he was breathing. Blood crusted around his mouth and the left side of his face—he must have collapsed in a blood pool—and his skin was a flat white, tinged with gray, with no hint of radiance.

"Then why weren't we affected?" Kol asked, taking two more quick turns.

"Because he's a shifter," Jacob said.

Marcus howled and kicked the back of my seat, jarring my broken ribs. A tear broke free. I had to do something, but I couldn't even give him strength, since we didn't share a brand.

Gideon drew in another rattling, wet breath. "Regan shifted with no problem."

"It couldn't be because he was injured," Cassius said. "You're all barely walking." His eyes narrowed. "Except you, incubus. How the hell are you all right?"

"Well," Kol said, his voice too bright, "when a man and a woman, or a woman and a woman, or a man and a man, or, well, a group of naked people love each oth—"

"Kol, please!" Gideon gasped, making Kol flinch.

"Sorry. Trying to hold my shit together. You know, because the Hellfire Queen is free and she has—" His voice broke and a wave of panic crashed through our newly formed bond, as if a wall inside him had just shattered. "She has nephilim tanks and I— The nightmares came back and —" His breath picked up, and his body started shaking almost as badly as mine.

"Just hold it together long enough to get to Voth's," Gideon said. "You can do this."

"I've been holding it together for weeks." Kol jerked the wheel, turning onto a narrow street, squealing the tires, and wrenching us in our seats. "First the archnephilim, then Essie's wings, then— I can't go back to that. I'd kill myself before I go back to that, but then I'd hurt Essie and I— Fuck, I—"

"Take a breath." Jacob reached around the driver's seat and squeezed Kol's shoulder. "You can do this. Think about why... why fate bound you to Essie."

"Because fate is fucked up, that's why. Now she's stuck with me." Kol's breath grew faster, sharp desperate gasps. "God, I love you so much." He released a manic hysterical laugh. "I'm so fucked up. I'm in love. How the hell does an incubus fall in love? And I could still snap again and hurt you. I could—"

"Hey." A tear leaked down my cheek. I couldn't help Marcus and I should have helped Kol. He'd been holding it together since we'd fought the archnephilim and I hadn't noticed. I didn't think anyone had. "You're not going to hurt me."

"You don't know that. I already did and—"

"This isn't working," Cassius growled. "He shouldn't be driving."

Another gut-wrenching scream ripped from Marcus's throat and I gritted my teeth, fighting more tears. Crying wouldn't help anything. But God, I was so tired and cold and my soul hurt for Marcus and Kol.

"Kol, please." Gideon's breath wheezed. "Take a breath and tell me why Sebastian's spell affected Marcus and not us."

"How am I supposed to know?" Kol yelled back.

"Your best guess," Gideon said. "Focus on that and not running off the road."

More of Marcus's bones crunched and the demonic mist sweeping around him billowed to the roof of the minivan.

"Well, I— Okay." Kol slowed to a safer speed, fighting his fear with an effort that made my heart hurt just watching him. He turned onto a side street at the edge of Squatters' Row, avoiding the main strip.

Just a few more minutes and we'd be at Voth's, who —*please, God*—would help us.

Darkness crept across my vision and the cold inside me started numbing everything, the physical and emotional pain, as well as my whirling thoughts.

I needed to hold on just a little longer, just until I knew my guys were safe.

Except if I was wrong about Voth, there wasn't anything I could do to protect my guys.

"We've ruled out being injured and being a shifter." Kol's grip on the steering wheel tightened, making the veins and tendons in his forearms stand out. "Maybe it's because he's not a natural shifter."

The red strands curling up from Marcus twisted and pulled apart, undulating in a breeze I couldn't feel, taunting me. All that power and I was still helpless.

Because that power wasn't in me at the moment. It was in him. Only pale, shuddering wisps drifted from my skin. I was hollow and just wanted to close my eyes. At least I'd put that magic to good use and saved Marcus. Amiah hadn't said he was dying from his injuries. I just had to hope he'd survive this transition. Had his first transition been this painful? This was horrible. I had no idea how anyone got through this kind of pain and came out the other end sane. But he'd survived his first one. He could survive this.

"Okay," Gideon said. "Anyone know if Regan is natural or not?"

"I don't know," Jacob said.

A strand curled over the back of the bench, wrapped

around my arm, and sank under my skin, just like it was sinking into Marcus.

My thoughts tripped on that.

"So that could be it," Cassius said, not sounding certain. "But..."

Oh, no.

Oh, please, no.

But the moment I thought it, I knew it was true. I'd poured my demonic magic into Marcus, desperate to save him when Sebastian had cast the teleportation spell, a spell that ripped us apart and remade us. My magic must have melded inside Marcus during the spell.

I'd done it to him again. I'd made a decision and he was paying for it.

"It's my fault," I forced out between chattering teeth.

"It's not your fault," Gideon said.

"He was bleeding out." I raised my trembling blood-crusted hand and stared at the weak demonic mist swirling around it. There wasn't any other explanation. I'd fucked up. I shouldn't have used magic I didn't under-stand. I should have trusted Sebastian would have gotten us to Operations in time. But I hadn't. I'd just pumped raw magic into Marcus because I hadn't been thinking, I hadn't been able to lose him, and now he was transitioning into—

God, I had no idea what.

"I thought if Kol could help me with his magic, I could help Marcus just enough to get him to Amiah."

"You used your demonic magic?" Jacob asked.

"Yes." A sob broke free, the sharp breath slicing pain through my chest.

"It must have mixed with Sebastian's teleportation spell and reawakened the lycanthropy in his DNA." Gideon pressed his lips to the back of my head. "You were trying to save him."

Marcus howled, yanking my attention up, and I met Amiah's gaze, her expression hard. Even if my angelic magic hadn't been used up and I had my empathy, I'd have known exactly what she was feeling, and I couldn't argue against it.

Marcus was in agony and it was my fault. Again.

CHAPTER 13

A FEW MINUTES LATER, WE REACHED VOTH'S HOTEL, A massive ten-story 19th century building sitting on top of a gently sloping hill. We avoided the long circular driveway leading to the grand front entrance and headed to the almost as grand side door. Even at this hour, there were lights on in many of the rooms, and warm illumination glowed through the glass double doors at the side entrance. But then Voth catered to supers, including vampires, and likely had entertainment happening all night long.

Except that was going to be a problem. Even if it was weak, red mist wept from me, and given that the Director of the JP Bureau of Supernatural Law Enforcement had instantly known I was an archnephilim, there was a chance someone else would recognize what I was. In our condition, we couldn't handle any more fighting.

"Someone has to go in and get Voth," I said, as Kol parked at the back of the lot but didn't shut off the engine. And while the lot wasn't as full as it had been the other day, there were still plenty of vehicles.

"We have to get you and Marcus inside," Gideon said. "You're not getting warmer even with my body heat."

My eyes drifted shut and I forced them back open. "We can't risk someone seeing me."

And crap, if we lived through stopping Lilith, would I have to spend the rest of my life in hiding?

"Shit," Kol hissed. "And we better hope Voth has a more discreet entrance around back, because yeah, I'm not fighting who-knows-how-many supers when they see you."

"Pretty sure that's not a worry. Voth will kill us the moment we step through those doors," Cassius said.

Marcus screamed and the red mist billowed around him. I clenched my jaw, more tears leaking from my eyes, and the creeping darkness stole my vision for a second.

"Essie's identity is going to get out," Jacob said. "We're going to need to figure out what to do about that."

"First we need to hide and heal." Gideon glanced over the guys and frowned. We were all injured, burned, and covered in blood. We looked like we'd just stepped out of a horror movie. "Cassius, you're up. Tell Voth..." Gideon rubbed his face, smearing blood down one cheek, turning his haggard expression fierce. "Tell him the mated angel is cashing in on his promise."

"This is insane. And we have no idea he's actually in there." But Cassius got out of the minivan and marched across the parking lot.

"We also have to figure out what we're doing about Lilith," Gideon said, his voice soft and far away.

"Gideon, will your angelic nature let you run and hide for much longer?" Kol asked.

Amiah huffed. Guess she didn't think it would.

"If it protects Essie, yes." Gideon's embrace tightened, but thankfully not enough to squeeze my broken ribs. "But I don't think there's anywhere we *can* hide. You heard Lilith. Essie was supposed to be her weapon and she's ready to restart Michael's war. Do you honestly think we can buy a concealment spell strong enough to hide for the rest of our lives?"

The darkness swelled and I bobbed in the not-water... that was the viscous liquid in my nephilim maturation tank. But this time it wasn't warm and comforting. It was freezing, the cold seeping into every pore, every cell, chilling my soul.

"I doubt we could buy one strong enough to last the week," Jacob said from somewhere in the darkness beyond my tank. "I think the best we can hope for is that she's distracted by whatever she's planning long enough for us to come up with our own plan. And even then... Everything I've heard about Lilith said she was a powerhouse before she was imprisoned and now she also has all that extra worship magic."

My father stepped into sight and pressed his hand against the tank. He'd made a deal with Lilith to make me, then hidden me from her. Why had he changed his mind? And if he'd changed his mind, did that mean he wasn't Michael?

"Well, we can't stand up to her," Kol said. "We were literally crushed."

"The JP still has to be warned." Gideon rubbed his hands up and down my arms, trying to warm me up, but the cold was too deep, and his voice was getting farther and farther away. "They need to know Lilith is free and that she's planning something soon, and someone needs to go back for Ephraim."

Except would they even listen to us? The Director had said Gideon was compromised because of our angelic mating brand. Everyone else probably thought that, too.

My father's face re-materialized out of the darkness. Light brown hair with a hint of copper, just like mine, and gold flecks in his angel glow, also like mine. Fear tightened his expression. He glanced over his shoulder and the *pop pop pop* of gunfire sounded in the distance. Screaming drowned it out, tearing at my soul. I had to stop the pain. I had to get out of the tank, had to—

"—have to do something," Jacob said.

"For God's sake, none of you are doing anything," Amiah said, her tone sharp. "You're—"

I lurched back into the not-water. So cold. So damned cold. I was never going to get warm.

"—be ready to gun it, Kol." Gideon tensed beneath me.

Something was happening. We were in danger. I forced my eyes open and dragged my attention out the window to see Cassius running toward us, his expression hard.

"He said he'd help." Cassius hopped into the front passenger seat and glared at me. "Pull around back. He's meeting us at the loading bay."

"You don't believe him?" Gideon asked.

"We'll see what he does when he sees her," Cassius said.

Kol put the minivan in gear and drove across the sloping lot to a blocky modern addition at the back of the hotel. I fought to stay conscious, but the darkness stole my vision again and I was back in the freezing not-water.

One of my guys said something. The minivan stopped moving and the engine died. A door opened and closed and Marcus screamed, wrenching me awake.

We were in an enclosed loading bay, just big enough for one transport truck. Jacob had already gotten out and hefted Marcus—now completely naked—onto his shoulder. Across from me, Cassius leaned through the open minivan side door, the light from his eyes harsh, accentuating his hard glare at me, and hauled out Sebastian. Behind him, his expression just as hard, was Voth.

My pulse stuttered for a second. Even with his power contained—I wouldn't have been able to breathe if it hadn't been—the massive demon was terrifying. Cassius was right. In our condition, we didn't stand a chance against him.

"There's a clinic second door on the left." Voth pointed to an open door a few feet away.

"You have a clinic?" Amiah asked as Gideon lifted me out of the minivan.

"I ran my squad out of here for about ten years after the war. Then just kept it because it's useful for when a fight in my theatre goes a little too far."

Another wave of freezing darkness stole my vision, and another scream from Marcus jerked me back awake.

"—have a transition room, too?" Amiah asked. She sounded surprised.

"Like I said," Voth said, his voice a low, dangerous rumble. "I ran my squad here for a while after the war."

I dragged my eyes open. Voth's clinic was small with barely enough room for two gurneys, but it was packed with as much equipment as Amiah's mini triage in Operations. At the back stood a plexiglass wall, partitioning off the last eight feet of the room, and the only thing inside was a thin plastic-covered mattress on the floor. A shudder swept through me. It looked like a cell.

Voth opened the plexiglass door, and Jacob entered and set Marcus on the mattress, still screaming and writhing, smearing blood from the cuts and burns covering his body over the mattress's white surface.

"You're locking him up?" I said, my chattering teeth making it hard to get the words out.

"Transition isn't just dangerous for the shifter." Gideon

set me on the closest gurney and sagged against it, struggling to breathe, while Cassius set Sebastian on the other one. "When his beast takes over, he could be dangerous."

A tear leaked from my eye and Gideon caught it with his thumb. "A transition only lasts a day or two at most. It'll be okay."

"His first transition lasted over a week," Amiah said, kneeling beside Marcus and placing a hand on his forehead. "Do you have sedatives?" she asked Voth. "Flurazepam or Midazolam will get him through the rest of the morning."

"In that cupboard by your head." Voth jerked his chin at Cassius, who opened the cupboard behind him and scanned the rows of boxes and vials. "There are also needles in the drawer."

"A week?" I could barely get the word out. "He suffered like this for a week?" With his bones breaking and rebreaking and his body ripping itself apart from the inside out.

"Yes." Amiah captured my gaze with hers, but her expression was so strange, or I was just so exhausted I couldn't figure out what it meant. Anger? Hurt? Regret? Sorrow?

No wonder she was so angry with me. She'd sat by his side, listening to him scream for over a week. I'd be furious too if all I could have done was listen and wait, especially when all this pain could have been prevented. I was furious now. Except I could only be angry at myself. Just like the first time, Marcus's agony was my fault.

God, how was he still in love with me? How could he have ever forgiven me? How could he now?

Cassius grabbed a vial and a needle and took them to Amiah, then helped Jacob hold Marcus down. She injected

Marcus and a moment later he went limp, his breathing still ragged, but his body no longer seizing.

"He's strong," Gideon said, entwining his fingers with mine.

More God damned tears leaked from my eyes, and Jacob joined us and placed a warm hand on my shoulder. I shuddered. My insides were so frozen that even Jacob, who needed to feed and should have been cold to the touch, felt warm. "You won't lose him."

"You can't promise that," I said. And they couldn't promise I wouldn't lose him even if he survived.

"Okay." Amiah stood and raked her gaze over us, then strode to Sebastian and placed a hand over his heart.

Blinding light radiated from her palm, but I couldn't shut my eyes, couldn't take my gaze away from Marcus, bleeding, naked, and sprawled on the mattress. Beside me, Gideon's breath rattled wet and heavy, while Jacob's hand on my shoulder trembled. My teeth chattered and my shivering turned the once-spiking agony in my chest to constant gasping pain.

Voth said something and left. I was too dizzy and exhausted to pay attention to his words. I wasn't sure if Cassius went with him or not. One moment Cassius was in the clinic, then I blinked—I guess I'd actually closed my eyes—because when I opened them he was gone.

Amiah stepped into sight and placed a hand on my cold, empty chest above my heart. I had nothing left in me. I didn't even have faint wisps of demonic magic curling from my skin any more.

"Can you warm her?" Gideon asked. I couldn't hear the wet rattle in his breath any longer, so Amiah must have healed him.

"Not if I want to fix her ribs." For a second Amiah looked

exhausted, then my vision wavered and her expression returned to hard and angry. "I haven't got much left. You and Sebastian were in rough shape. I have no idea how you've been running around carrying her."

Agonizing heat screamed through my chest as Amiah shot her healing magic into me, and the room vanished into darkness.

"—sedation won't help with her condition, she still needs to be warmed up," Amiah said, "and I don't know if Voth has heating pads."

"I've got her." Blazing hot hands slid under me and cradled me against a searing chest, his T-shirt sticky with blood. His blood. "But I shouldn't be alone with her."

"Kol." I pressed my hand over his heart. It beat too quickly, and his worry and fear seeped through our barely formed bond. "You're not going to hurt me."

"You don't know that," he murmured. "If Gideon hadn't stopped me in the alley outside City Hall, I would have killed you."

"But you didn't," Jacob said.

"I could have. I even knew it was you, knew deep down you wouldn't hurt me, and I still couldn't stop myself." The muscles in his jaw tightened and little pieces of my soul started to shatter. "It's like there's another me that takes over. The me that would do anything, kill anyone, to never go back to that."

"It'll be okay," I said.

"It won't be. That me is still in here. What happens when I wake from a nightmare and find myself in bed with a —" His breath picked up and his body shook. "With a—"

"A monster?" My throat tightened and I wanted to scream at Kol's heartache, at the tear in his soul, and all the things he'd suffered. And I wanted to scream at the truth.

Michael had made me. I was a creature created from evil magic, who shouldn't exist. I endangered the lives of all my guys, and there wasn't a damned thing I could do about that.

"You're not a monster," Gideon said, his expression stern. He turned to Kol. "And you're not going to hurt her."

"I wish I was so certain."

I raised my gaze to his, his hellfire mesmerizing, stealing my breath and filling me with sudden, aching need. But when I focused past the hellfire, the look in his eyes was so scared it turned my aching need to grief.

Gideon brushed another tear from my cheek—I hadn't even realized it had fallen. "Come on. We're exhausted and not thinking straight. Let's clean up and get some sleep." He turned to Amiah and set a keycard in a numbered cardboard sleeve on the gurney. "When Cassius is done with Voth, tell him to watch Marcus and get some rest."

Kol carried me out of the clinic, my soul begging to stay with Marcus. He needed me. God, I couldn't leave him when he was in such pain. But I could barely keep my eyes open and I couldn't stop shivering. I was useless to Marcus and everyone else. If I didn't get some rest and warm up, I'd continue to be useless. Amiah said the sedative would help him for the rest of the morning. I had a few hours at least to pull my shit together.

We headed down a plain hall, the exposed cinderblock walls painted white, the floor an institutional gray laminate, and the lights above long, glaring fluorescent bulbs. Jacob and Gideon walked ahead of us, Jacob's movements slow as if he were still in pain. At least Gideon looked better. Not perfect, but he no longer held his arm against his side as if his ribs were broken.

About halfway down the hall, Gideon stopped at a plain door with a card reader, unlocked it, and let us into a simple hotel room. The light on the table by the queen-sized bed and the one in the bathroom had already been turned on, revealing a clean and tidy room, decorated in beiges and browns with green accents. A thick curtain covered the window on the back wall, pulled tight to keep out the sunrise which was only a few hours away. The bathroom looked a lot like my bathroom in Operations, just big enough for a sink with some counterspace, a toilet, and—unlike my room in Operations—a walk-in shower instead of a tub. Given how opulent the side door lobby had been, I doubted Voth let guests stay there. If the room was used at all, it was most likely a room for visiting entertainers who were performing in Voth's massive theatre.

"Kol, you and Essie get cleaned up." Gideon looked at the bed as if he wanted to sit, then glanced at his bloody clothes and leaned against the wall instead and held out his wrist. "Jacob, let's see if we can't seal shut the wound in your side that you've been trying to hide."

I opened my mouth to offer my blood, but both Gideon and Jacob glared at me.

"Don't even think about it," Gideon said, and he jerked his chin to the bathroom. "You're barely conscious and you're shivering so hard I'm afraid for your teeth."

Kol's pulse picked up and I was certain it wasn't with desire. "We should wait, or I'll feed Jacob and Gideon, you—"

"She needs you right now," Jacob said, his expression exhausted and sad. "You're the warmest and there isn't enough room for all of us in that shower. Leave the door open. We won't let you hurt her."

"Kol," I said, pulling his attention to me, his face wavering through the encroaching darkness. "I trust you."

"Didn't you hear me in the clinic? You really

shouldn't." But he stepped into the bathroom and sat me on the closed toilet lid. "You shouldn't have claimed me, either."

"Even if I'd had a choice, I would have claimed you." I leaned into him, drawn not just to his warmth but his soul. "You belong. You're mine, just like Marcus and Jacob and Gideon. And I will fix this. I promise." I knew I could help him with my empathic magic—

Except I didn't. Not really. I'd tried to save Marcus and now he was in agony. I didn't want to do that to Kol, too.

Shit. All right. Fine. Even if I couldn't help him with my empathy, I'd find a way to help him. Whatever it took.

He knelt in front of me, his eyes filled with yearning and heartache. "I can't be fixed."

With a sigh, he grabbed the bottom of my blood-encrusted T-shirt and drew it up over my head, but gasped, his gaze on my chest, his eyes wide with—

I had no idea, but it wasn't fear, so I couldn't be injured... especially since Amiah's magic would have healed anything serious.

Which meant my chest had shocked...? Surprised...? Jeez. It had gotten a reaction from an incubus. I didn't know if I should laugh or cry.

"Pretty sure you've seen breasts before," I said through numb lips. Maybe if I made a joke, it would change the mood. "Mine are pretty average." That, and I still wore a bra. I was certain he'd seen me without my top on... hadn't he? Why couldn't I remember? But I could barely concentrate and—

"They're so much more than average," he said, a whisper of his usual wry smile pulling at his lips. "But I was looking at this. It's so beautiful." Kol brushed a tentative finger across my collarbone, drawing a shiver of desire that was quickly consumed by the cold and darkness threatening to overwhelm me. "And so wrong."

I dragged my attention down, my gaze moving in slow motion. Delicate gold threads curled from my shoulder along the top of my right breast. I reached for Kol's T-shirt but he nudged my hands away and took it off, exposing the breathtaking expanse of his sculpted chest and abs. The stab wound in his chest was gone, the only evidence he'd taken the deadly injury the hole in his T-shirt and all the blood crusted on his skin.

Just like me, he had gold threads curling from his shoulder across his collarbone and over the top of his right pec. The mesmerizing design shimmered as if the threads were real gold reflecting sunlight, and I pressed my hand over it, savoring the heat radiating from his body. So warm. I needed to get closer, needed him wrapped around me.

"God, I'm so in love with you," he said as he straightened, my hand sliding down his abs, before he stepped back out of reach. The distance made the cold grow stronger, and even with my jaw clenched, I couldn't stop my teeth from chattering. But he undid his fly and shoved his bloody jeans off his narrow hips, releasing his full thick erection, and for a second the cold and darkness vanished. There was only his breathtaking body and his desire for me.

Holy smokes. My mouth went dry in anticipation, even though I was really too weak to do anything about it. He was so beautiful, so...

The darkness surged, and the bathroom started to tip.

Kol's face lurched into sight, suddenly close—he'd moved and I'd missed it.

"Come on, Essie. Hold on just a little longer. Guys," he called over his shoulder, balancing my weight against his chest. "This isn't going to work. She's barely conscious. I doubt she can stand long enough to get her jeans off, let alone shower. She's been conscious now longer than she ever was when she claimed you two. We need to get her in bed."

Yes. In bed. With all of them. Finally.

Except I didn't have Marcus. He was in Voth's clinic, his body tearing itself apart because I'd fucked up again. I needed to go to him. Now. *Now now now.*

Not while you're useless.

My throat tightened and I wanted to scream at wanting to cry and scream.

God damn it, I could deal with it. All of it. Marcus *would* survive, even if, once I'd regained some strength, I had to go back to the clinic and brand him, knocking myself out for who knew how long. And I *would* stop Lilith. I didn't know how, but I'd figure something out... just as soon as I could stop shaking... and see straight... and—

"Go," Jacob said from out in the bedroom, his voice that sexy rumble I loved so much. "I can hold out."

"Okay." Gideon stepped into the bathroom and stripped. He was bulkier than Kol, his shoulders broader—although not nearly as broad and bulky as Jacob—and just as breathtaking. The light in his eyes blazed, capturing my soul, and I soared in a beautiful summer sky for a second... an eternity...

Kol's heat vanished, and when I dragged my gaze away from Gideon, my incubus was in the shower, quickly scrubbing away the blood on his body, the water and soap sliding over his sculpted muscles.

Oh, wow. My pulse picked up and desire unfurled, hot and needy within me. Gideon unhooked my bra, helped me stand, and turned me into Kol's now clean arms. My back slid against his wet chest and a shiver swept through me, although now I couldn't tell any more if the shiver was from the cold or my desire.

Gideon stripped me of my shoes, jeans, and undies, and Kol helped me stagger into the hot shower spray. He wrapped his arms around me, holding me close, and I leaned my head back, trying to press as much of my flesh against his as possible.

A whisper of his sensual magic slid across my senses, turning my nerves hypersensitive, as Gideon ran a soapy washcloth over my branded arm, sending a tiny tremor of climax shuddering through me.

"Jeez, sorry. I'll pull it back," Kol said, his voice gruff, and the heat of his magic vanished, making me shake with cold even though I was in a steaming shower and leaning into him, his demonic body temperature gloriously warm.

"Please don't. It's warm." And I wanted it. With Kol's magic, I could forget everything, just for a moment. Even if I couldn't do much about the desire it inspired, I could savor the feel of being captured between the hard, slick bodies of two of my guys.

"Okay." Kol's sensual heat swept back in, and a moan escaped my lips.

Gideon stepped closer, his erection brushing my belly, and ran the cloth over my other arm, scrubbing away Kol's and Marcus's blood.

I gave in to the sensation of the pulsing water and the washcloth against my skin, and of Kol's heat and hardness, and Gideon's as well, pressed against me.

Gideon ran the cloth up my belly and circled the soapy fabric over my right nipple and across my new brand. My breath hitched and he dipped in and captured my mouth in a slow, sensual kiss that made me throb. God, I needed him.

I needed both of them.

I needed all of them.

"Gideon," I murmured against his lips, my voice breathy, the darkness flickering over my vision.

"I thought she was going to kill you." He tangled his hand into my hair. "I thought we were going to lose you." The wash cloth landed on my foot with a wet *plop*, and he ran his free hand up my belly to my breast as his kiss turned rough and desperate.

My breath picked up, and Kol shifted his grip to slide his fingers down my abdomen and into my curls. His magic swelled, heating me from the inside out. Gideon kissed me with a desperation that made my soul ache, like if he kissed me hard enough and long enough everything would be all right.

I kissed him back with the same need. I couldn't lose him or any of them. And it had been so close.

Kol brushed his finger over my clit, back and forth, as Gideon stole my breath with his lips. The shower spun, between my exhaustion and need, until Kol's power swelled into a gentle climax that swept through me, bringing with it a soft, warm darkness.

After that, my consciousness flickered between darkness and fuzzy flashes of reality. The guys rubbed me down with a thick towel. Kol carried me to bed, drawing me tight against his hot body and pulling up the heavy comforter. Gideon fed Jacob, showered, then climbed into bed under the covers with us, settling in front of me. Jacob showered as well, and fell asleep on the floor propped up against the side of the bed.

The flashes dimmed and I bobbed in the not-water, a wisp of inky magic curling around me. I needed to push it back, not let Lilith's magic control me. I needed to be at Marcus's side, even if there wasn't anything I could do for him. My soul cried. Our soul bond was different than what I shared with the other guys, but just as strong, and knowing when he woke he'd be in agony shattered me.

My father's face materialized out of the darkness, his eyes filled with fear, and I tried to ask him why. Why had he made a deal with Lilith? Why steal me from her? Why hide me and leave me with a human woman?

But the moment I opened my mouth to ask, a scream tore through the darkness and heart-stopping terror stole my breath.

CHAPTER 14

EVERYTHING WITHIN ME FROZE WITH A FEAR SO ABSOLUTE I couldn't breathe or move or think. There was no light or joy or salvation. The inky magic and the worry about Marcus was gone. There was only fear and emptiness, and screaming, gut-wrenching cries of desperation.

No, please. I promise. I promise. Kol begged. *Please. I won't go back. I can't go back.*

I fought to wake up. This had to stop. He couldn't carry on like this. I had to do something, and my empathy hadn't hurt anyone... yet—

No. I had to try. I couldn't let him suffer any longer. I had no idea how he'd survived like this for so long and how he'd managed to hide it from everyone.

You can't make me. I won't, Kol hissed, and his terror turned to searing anger.

Something heavy crushed my chest.

I won't.

My body burned and I fought to breathe. His rage was overwhelming, threatening to consume me.

I wrenched at my consciousness. If I didn't wake, his emotions were going to shatter me.

My eyes flew open, but the crushing fire didn't vanish. It grew stronger.

I still lay with my back against Kol's chest, but his arms were vises around my ribs. Gideon—lying in front of me—opened his eyes, and a second of panic flashed across his expression before Kol screamed again and Gideon's attention snapped to me.

"I won't go back." Kol's voice broke and his grip tightened. "Please. I can't. I can't."

"Kol, wake up," I gasped, grabbing his wrist and trying to pry at least one of his arms off me.

"I promise. Don't hurt her. Don't—" He tensed and screamed as if he were in agony, and the fire of his rage snapped back to freezing terror.

"Kol, I can't breathe."

Gideon's eyes widened and he shoved the comforter back, exposing all of us, in bed and naked.

"No. You can't— I won't—" A heartbreaking sob escaped his lips. "Don't make me."

"Kol." Gideon grabbed Kol's arm, but Kol wrenched away, yanking me with him, and pressed his back against the headboard, his arms still so tight around me I was afraid he'd break my ribs.

"No," Kol gasped. His eyes were open but unfocused, as if he were seeing something else. "You can't make me. I won't hurt her."

His terror lurched back to rage then snapped cold again, his emotions heaving inside me, freezing and burning, and always with pain, so much emotional pain. I gasped in short, sharp breaths, and specks of darkness danced at the edge of my vision, a sure sign I was about to pass out.

"Jesus." Jacob scrambled onto the bed—also naked because we'd all showered and hadn't had clean clothes to change into.

Kol curled around me, as if he were protecting me from his nightmare, and snarled like an animal, his face a mask of primal desperation and rage. Jacob hesitated, his expression tight, his complexion still a little too pale. He wasn't fully recovered.

"No. I won't let you. Please." Kol's snarls turned to sobs again, his voice so painfully young and broken. God, I had to help him, had to stop this. "Please, don't. Please."

Another lurch of emotions and the heat inside me tightened, whirling into a ball of blazing divine light. Wisps of my demonic magic burst from my skin and the darkness in my vision deepened.

"Kol, please." I clawed at his arm. I wouldn't be able to help him if I passed out. "Let go."

"I'll kill every last one of you," Kol spat. "I swear to God, I'll kill you."

Gideon grabbed Kol's shoulder, and Kol wrenched around and rammed his fist into Gideon's chest, shoving him off the bed.

Jacob lunged in and seized Kol's arm before he could grab me again.

Kol screamed. His fingers dug into my skin and a blazing agony exploded through the new brand on my chest.

"I'll kill you. You can't take me back. I won't go back."

I wrenched out of Kol's grasp and fell off the bed onto my butt as Jacob yanked Kol around and wrapped him in a bear hug, Kol's back against his massive chest.

Kol howled and kicked. His hellfire barely glowed, miniscule pinpricks of red light in his dark eyes, and his breath was too fast. Golden light blazed from his brand, bathing half his face in light and half in shadow from the dimly lit hotel room, and his lurching emotions made the room spin. The burning mix of his rage and my power seared my skin, and the agony in our brand flared, releasing a burst of red demonic mist from my skin.

"Don't touch her. Don't hurt her," Kol begged.

"Kol, wake up." Jacob's intense gaze met mine over the top of Kol's head, his expression clear. This was bad. And I couldn't help wondering if he'd ever seen Kol like this or had realized the depth of his pain.

"Please. Essie. Please," Kol sobbed. Grief slammed into me, stealing my breath, and a thick mist filled the air. My angelic magic surged, swelling to my palms with the gentle heat of strength, not destructive divine light, and I climbed back onto the bed before I realized what I was doing.

"Essie, get back." Gideon jerked to his feet and grabbed my arm, yanking me away from Kol. "Jacob, hold him until I can get Amiah and a sedative."

Kol wrenched in Jacob's grip and slammed his head back, but wasn't high enough to hit Jacob in the face with the back of his head. My demonic mist swelled, whipping around me in a wind I couldn't feel, and Kol's eyes widened. Frozen terror turned the mist to snow that vanished before it hit the comforter.

"No, please. Stop. Stop!" Kol cried.

"Kol, it's okay." I mentally grabbed some of the stillness that always radiated through Jacob's brand and pushed it into Kol's new burning one.

He tensed, his expression stunned.

"Gideon, let me go." Sedating Kol would only prolong his agony and I had the power to help him right now. Except my brand with him was too new, and I couldn't risk it not being strong enough to help him. I needed to touch him.

"No," Gideon said. "He's going to hurt you. We need to sedate him."

"If this doesn't work, then yes."

Gideon glared at me. "He'll never forgive himself if he hurts you."

I pressed my hand over Gideon's, the one that still gripped my arm, and pushed a little of Jacob's stillness into him.

He shuddered and yanked his hand back. "Don't do that. I can't protect you if I'm zoned out."

"Whatever you're going to do, do it, Essie," Jacob said. Kol's breath was picking up again and the wild desperation had returned to his eyes, along with his lurching fear and rage.

I lunged forward before Gideon could stop me and captured Kol's cheeks between my palms. My magic surged. *Please work. Please let me be able to help him.*

My heat flooded him and his body seized. I fought to keep hold of his face while Jacob strained to hold his body.

Kol kneed me in the ribs, and Gideon scrambled in behind me and pinned Kol's legs to the bed.

"Jacob, don't encourage her," Gideon said.

"She's an empath—" The seizure released Kol and he rammed his elbow into Jacob's gut, drawing a grunt of pain. "Maybe she's strong enough to heal him."

"He's already been to all the best empathic healers," Gideon said.

"And he didn't have a soul bond with any of them," Jacob shot back.

Kol snarled and dug his nails into Jacob's arm, drawing blood.

"Essie—" A shadow passed over Gideon's summer-sky

eyes. "He just needs time to regain his balance. It's all we can do for him."

"No, there's a tear in his soul." And I was going to fix it.

God, please, let me be able to fix it.

I closed my eyes and gave in to the angelic light within me. My demonic magic swirled around it but didn't meld with it, as if my empathy was purely angelic. The light poured into every one of my cells until I was nothing but light, a being of pure illumination... with a writhing core of darkness—

I pushed that thought aside and let the light and warmth sweep deeper into Kol, filling him like it filled me. It reached all the way to the core of his being, where the horrible infected darkness lay. A darkness so different than what lay within me. Faced with the horrendous tear in his soul, it was easy to see that my darkness was primal, celestial, neither good nor bad, just like my light. Kol's tear was gangrenous, as if the horrors he'd experienced had warped his core essence, and he'd been holding himself together—probably without even knowing it—by force of will alone.

Please, he cried. *I can't go back. I can't live like this.*

You won't. I promise. My pulse stalled as realization hit me. All this time, I hadn't just been dreaming about Kol. When I'd been shot, he'd poured his essence into me to save me and my magic had held onto it and picked up on his heart's desire. And while I might have just branded him, it was clear my soul had chosen him weeks ago. Perhaps from the moment I'd first seen him, just like I had with Marcus, and, if I was being honest with myself, just like with Gideon and Jacob.

Please, Essie. Please love me.

I do. I always did.

My magic swelled in and around the tear, curling over

the edges and burning into the infection. The darkness shuddered. I was doing it, merding the agony he'd been living with for over twenty years. Finally, my empathy was good for something.

But then Kol jerked. I didn't know if it was just his soul or his body as well. He released a heartrending scream, and the darkness surged. It whipped into me, consuming my light and infecting my essence with a sudden ferocious blast. Horror and agony stole my breath. I was drowning in terror, too small and weak to fight.

No, please. I can't hurt them. I won't hurt them. But I would. I couldn't withstand the pain. I would beg them to stop, tell them I'd be good, let them use me, hurt me, hurt any one they told me to, do anything to make it stop.

I struggled to break free, but Kol mentally clung to me and the infection ripped my essence to shreds, whirling it around and around, giving Lilith's inky magic, magic I'd thought I'd gotten rid of, room to push back inside me. I was no longer a being of light, but of pain, screaming, consuming pain. I couldn't breathe, couldn't think. All I could do was suffer.

No.

I seized a piece of my essence from the infected darkness and clung to it. I was stronger than this. I had to be. For Kol's sake. For all my guys.

Lilith's inky magic whispered the promise of immense power, the power of a goddess, but I concentrated on my brands and kept my soul strong. Becoming a goddess was a lie. I'd only become Lilith's puppet if I let her magic in.

I grabbed another piece of my essence and another, rebuilding myself against the whirling vortex. With each piece, my power grew stronger, brighter, hotter. It squeezed Lilith's inky magic deep inside me until I could barely sense its presence again, and I flooded my light back into Kol, spinning it around the edges of the tear in his soul.

The infection snapped, its darkness slicing at my essence, but I gritted my teeth and pumped in more power. All of my power. I drained myself of my angelic magic, flooding it into Kol, until he was the being of pure light, the infection gone, and I was a being of celestial darkness, not a glimmer of light left.

The tear sealed shut, leaving an ugly scar, but one I knew wouldn't give him night terrors like the infection had, and I collapsed forward, my body too weak to hold me up.

"How did you do that?" Kol gasped as he hugged me tight. He shook as much as I did, his pulse racing. "You didn't just push it back to where I'd tried to lock it away. You took its power. No one's ever been able to do that."

"Half archangel empath," Jacob said, wrapping his arms around both of us.

"For the love of God," Gideon said. "Stop doing things like that."

I turned my head just enough so I could look at him. His eyes were wide and his fear, barely felt with the sliver of angelic magic I had left, cold in my chest... which felt weird. Hollow yet not hollow at the same time. I'd drained myself of my angelic magic again and my weaker demonic magic couldn't fully take its place. I was pretty sure my head would start pounding soon. But it was so worth it.

"Gideon." I held out a trembling hand to him.

He took it and Kol released me enough so I could shift and capture Gideon's lips with mine in a slow sensual kiss that told him how much I cared for him. Strength seeped from him into me and a crackle of electric magic shivered up my arm.

"You know I had to," I said.

"Doesn't mean it didn't scare me." He kissed me again, his passion fueling my desire. I hated that I'd scared him, but I didn't mind the kisses that came with it.

Kol groaned and shifted, his erection digging into my hip. "We need to make some decisions before things go too far."

Right. I was exhausted and naked in a bed with almost all my guys.

And the moment I thought that, the urge to jump up and go to Marcus, sit with him, suffer with him, squeezed in my chest. Except I had no idea when Kol and I would have a chance to seal our bond. There might not be another opportunity any time soon, and I wasn't going to allow a repeat of what had happened with Gideon.

Lilith's inky magic, still clinging to my cells, whispered and cajoled. If I let it in, I'd be able to help Marcus. He wouldn't have to suffer.

No. I concentrated on my brands, rooting my soul deeper inside my body, and held it back, then returned my attention to my guys. After yesterday, I knew both Gideon and Jacob were fine with all being together in bed, and I doubted Kol would argue. But—

I pulled away from Gideon.

"I know we don't have a lot of time, but Kol and I are going to seal our bond." And this was something I wanted to do with only him. "Just us."

Gideon flashed me a warm smile, no hint of jealousy in his expression or radiating through our bond. "We'll give you two some privacy." He lifted his gaze to Kol. "Treat her gently. She almost died yesterday."

The hellfire in Kol's eyes flared. "I'll treat her exactly the way she wants."

"Please don't." Gideon climbed off the bed and grabbed

a towel from the floor. "We all know she has no sense of self-preservation."

"She can draw strength from three of us now. She can have it anyway she likes," Jacob said, pulling me closer to Kol so he could reach past the incubus and kiss my forehead. My vampire still looked pale and exhausted and I was going to need to help top him up—since his hunger was stuck on me and my blood was more potent than any of my mates—but we could deal with that after Kol and I sealed our bond, and after I went to Marcus, and after we figured out a plan to deal with the JP and Lilith, and—

"You two have fun," Jacob said. "We'll leave clothes outside the door."

The guys found robes in the small closet by the bathroom and left, closing the door with a loud *click* that made my pulse jump.

I was alone, naked, and in bed with Kol. My incubus.

"So," Kol said, his voice husky, his gaze capturing mine. "How *do* you like it?"

CHAPTER 15

A SHIVER OF ANTICIPATION SWEPT THROUGH ME, AND THE AIR turned hot and humid. His hellfire filled his eyes with an intense sultry desire, and all thought of being cold and exhausted vanished. He might not be able to do anything about the hollow feeling in my chest, but I already wasn't cold.

"Do you like slow and sensual, like Gideon?"

He skimmed his fingers up my jaw, drawing another shiver, cupped my cheek, and dipped in. His lips brushed against mine, just a whisper of a kiss, making my breath hitch before he pulled away.

His awe and love swelled through our brand, and I leaned into his touch. He pressed his lips back to mine, this time with a full, soft, tender kiss, and the warmth from his brand deepened, turning sensual and unfurling a breath of his magic within me. But his kiss remained tender, reverent, slowly, oh so slowly building my passion, until I was alight and floating with desire.

"Or," he said against my lips, "do you like fierce, like Marcus?"

He cupped my other cheek, capturing me between his palms, and the kiss turned ferocious. His tongue invaded my mouth, and the air around me grew steamy. The desire radiating through our brand surged, making me gasp. He devoured my gasp and stole the rest of my breath as his magic sank lower, drawing a delicious ache. Except his power didn't grow stronger, as if he was waiting to see what I truly desired.

I tangled my fingers into his hair, unable to do anything but hold on and give in to the ferocity of his desire. My insides seared with need, mine and his. The room started to spin and he pulled his lips away and pressed his forehead to mine, his chest heaving, his breath just as fast as mine.

"Or," he gasped, "do you prefer a little pain, like Jacob."

He grabbed my hair, his nails biting into my scalp, and jerked my head back to a painful angle. But a sliver of his magic turned the pain to exquisite need, and my whole body throbbed. He crashed his mouth back onto mine, dominating me with his strength and passion. His free hand scratched down my neck to my breast, and he pinched my nipple, spiking more pain and another bone-melting curl of magical bliss.

Holy fuck.

I moaned into his mouth, every nerve aching for him, my head spinning with sensation. Pain and pleasure, wild dominance, sensual awe. I'd take it all, anyway he wanted it.

His hold on his magic slipped and a whisper of a climax shuddered through me, making me gasp.

He wrenched his lips away and released me, his hellfire licking his cheeks, and I clung to his shoulders to keep steady, lightheaded from his kiss.

"Jesus, Essie." He clenched the comforter on either side of him as if he wanted to touch me but needed to control himself. "It really wasn't sex magic, just the strength of your soul bonds."

"I told you," I said, breathless.

"And your desire is just as strong no matter how I kiss you."

"Probably a good thing, given I'm in love with all four of you."

A hint of a wicked smile pulled at his lips. "Variety is the spice of life."

"So—" Another whisper of a climax shivered through me. "How do *you* like it?"

"Whatever way satisfies you the most," he said, his voice husky.

I bit back a moan. "Whatever way?"

"You want it different every time, I'll do my best." His hands, still clenching the comforter, shifted closer to my legs, his gaze holding me captive.

My pulse picked up with just the anticipation of him touching me again.

"You want to dominate me, you want me to dominate you, you want pain, just ask.' His thumbs brushed the outsides of my knees, and my breath stalled.

Jeez, just a touch. On my knees. God, he could just look at me, he wouldn't even need to use his magic, and I'd come.

"If you want to watch me do one of the other guys—" He flashed a wicked smile that made his eyes light up, and his hands slid to the top of my knees, sweeping a shudder of need through me. "Not sure how they'd take that. It'd probably be better if they did me. But I'm game for that."

I wasn't sure what the others would think of that, but I had a feeling Kol had found a new thing to tease them about.

His fingers brushed up the top of my thighs. "If you want

me to watch while you do the other guys—" He frowned as if he were considering taking that back, and given how he'd been so desperate to get away from me because he couldn't have me, I wouldn't have blamed him.

How ironic that out of all my guys, he'd be the one who wasn't okay with group sex.

"It's okay if you can't watch," I said.

He pressed his palm against my collarbone atop his brand. "You want me, too."

"Yes."

"I'll give you the stars if you ask for them."

"I wouldn't ask for it if it hurts you," I said.

"Watching you with them won't hurt me." He traced a line in his brand with his index finger, his thumb dipping dangerously close to my nipple.

Oh, God. I was going to lose my mind, and I was loving every second of it.

"Because I don't have to just watch any more and *I* can make you come, too."

"Yes, please."

He captured my mouth with his again, his love and passion for me swelling through our brand, and he urged me to lie back on the bed.

His emotions were overwhelming, bright, hot, pure, and amazed. He'd never been in love before, and given what he'd said to me in Lilith's prison, he probably hadn't thought he'd ever be in love.

I tangled my fingers into his hair, deepening the kiss, and let my love for him course through our brand, drawing a startled gasp. Then his sensual magic swelled and all thoughts of love vanished. There was only aching, glorious need.

He kissed me until the room spun again, trailed his lips

across our brand to my breast, and worked my nipple into a tight bud with his tongue. He worshiped one breast then the other, sucking and stroking until I was panting and squirming underneath him, teetering on the edge of climax.

"Definitely not average," he murmured against my breast, then kissed his way down my belly. "Nothing about you is average."

His breath teased my curls and I bit back a moan. Every nerve thrummed for him, my body heavy, liquid bliss. He slid his hands up the insides of my thighs, urging my legs to spread wider and make room for him. With a low masculine hum of pleasure, he slowly—so fucking slowly!—kissed a trail from my knee up my thigh.

"Kol," I gasped. "You're driving me crazy."

"That's the plan." He teased his tongue along the seam where my hip met my torso, making my breath hitch. Another lick and I tangled my fingers in his hair, desperate for his mouth and tongue on me, satisfying me.

"Kol, please." My thumbs brushed the base of his horns, drawing a moan and sending a rush of hot breath over my core.

Oh, God. My climax twisted tighter and another wave of sensual bliss swept over me.

Another teasing lick, so close. I stroked the base of his horns again. Two could play this game, and with a shuddering groan, he swept his tongue over my clit.

Sensation shot straight to my core. I gasped and jerked, unable to hold still. He grabbed my hips and swept his tongue over my clit again. He licked and sucked, building the pressure and speed. I writhed against his grip, every nerve alight, drawing closer and closer to climax. Then he added his fingers, sliding two inside me with a firm stroke and hitting just the right spot.

Stars snapped behind my lids and I hadn't even climaxed yet. He stroked and sucked, his magic whirling into a massive wave that crashed over me with thundering bliss.

He continued to gently stroke me, bringing me down, until the glorious tremors released. Then, with a soft kiss on my clit, he shifted to lie stretched out beside me, his head propped in his hand, staring at me with a slightly dazed smile.

"That's one." His love pulsed through our brand, sending an aftershock trembling through me and stealing my breath. "If it were just me, I'd make you come all day long. But I have a feeling the others might object to that."

And I couldn't stay away from Marcus for much longer. Even riding the bliss of an amazing climax, my insides were twisting with the need to be by his side. He, out of all of my guys, needed me the most right now.

Another aftershock shivered through me, drawing a gasp from me and a heart-stopping smile from Kol.

"I love that sound." He brushed a lock of hair away from my face, and a curl of his magic slipped into me, making me gasp again.

"Just that sound?" I asked, breathless.

"You also make amazing sounds when I touch you." His smile turned wicked and he teased a finger down between my breasts to my abdomen. "And when I kiss you."

His wicked expression grew hungry. Every nerve within me ached, suddenly hyperaware of his touch, his breath, his erection against my thigh.

"You scream their names when you come with them inside you." His hunger deepened and my insides turned to molten desire. "Scream my name."

Oh, yes. I crashed my mouth against his, my need for him making me wild. I didn't think I'd ever get enough of him, of any of my guys. And while a part of me knew that the frenzy of our newly made bonds would fade, my desire for them wouldn't.

Kol grabbed my knee, drew my leg up over his, and teased his fingers through my wet folds. I moaned into his mouth. He was going to drive me insane. Slow and sensual was nice, and I'd take it again, but right now I needed something harder.

With a growl, I pushed him onto his back and straddled him. "You want me to scream? Make me."

"Challenge accepted." He thumbed my clit and sent a shock of magic through me.

My head jerked back and my muscles clenched on the verge of climax again. But he yanked his magic back. It whooshed out of me, taking the climax with it, then surged in again, stealing my breath.

Holy shit.

My hips bucked, grinding against his erection. His eyes rolled back in pleasure, and he sent another pulse of bliss sweeping through me then took it away. With a groan, I wrapped my hand around his length, savoring his girth, knowing he'd fill me completely, and aligned him with my opening.

He gripped my hips, his gaze locked on mine, his desire flooding me. I slid him into me with a strong, sensual stroke, and he curled his magic into the whisper of pain as I stretched around him. Then he urged me into a hard, sensual rhythm, building the climax within me, taunting me, pulling his magic away and teasing it back in, until I was panting and moaning.

The love in his eyes and through our brand was intoxicating. My soul sang at the rightness. This was the way it was supposed to be, who I was supposed to be with.

He was mine.

Marcus, Jacob, Gideon, and now Kol. Mine.

Kol's expression turned fierce and he rolled us over, pinning me under his lithe, sculpted body. He captured my mouth, possessing me with his lips, stealing all breath and thought, and his magic whirled hotter and hotter, making our brands blaze with golden light.

Our breaths ragged gasps, he picked up his pace, his thrusts growing more ferocious, driving me closer and closer to the edge, until my climax slammed into me and I screamed his name.

He thrust again, my name on his lips, and tensed with his own climax, sending a wave of his magic rushing into me, soaring me to new heights. Every muscle seized with a glorious, shattering contraction, and stars exploded behind my lids. All breath and thought vanished. There was only bliss, mind-blowing searing bliss, crashing through me over and over and over again.

When I opened my eyes, I lay in Kol's warm embrace, my head on his chest, my whole body heavy and relaxed and thoroughly satisfied. "Jeez, did I pass out?"

"Yeah." He pressed his lips to my forehead. "Means I did my job right."

Affection and awe seeped from his brand into me, and a wisp of red demonic magic curled from my arm. He trailed his fingers through it, breaking it apart, before it sank back into my skin.

"We're going to need to deal with this," he said, and sadness and fear crept into his affection. The tear in his soul might have been healed, but that didn't mean everything was all right. He'd been living with so much pain for so long.

That wasn't something anyone got over in an hour, let alone days or even years.

I could, however, at least try to alleviate some of his fears before I got dressed and sat with Marcus... who I had to go to. Now now now. Even if he got through his transition and despised me for causing all that agony again. I had to go.

The bedside clock read 11:33 a.m. Amiah had said the sedative would get him through the morning and that was almost over.

I gritted my teeth. Ease Kol's fears, then go to Marcus.

Except we had more problems than just that.

Jeez. One thing at a time.

"You know when you were caught in your nightmare, you didn't try to hurt me."

He traced his fingers from my arm across the heavy bruise forming around my ribs, where he'd crushed me. "I have evidence to the contrary."

"You were trying to protect me. You wouldn't let Gideon or Jacob get near me." I raised my gaze to meet his, determined to will him into believing me. His hellfire was banked, small red pinpricks, but it felt forced, as if he were trying to keep hold of his emotions and had forgotten or didn't know I could feel them through our bond, no empathy needed. "You won't snap like that again."

"I know." The hold on his emotions slipped and his hellfire swelled, along with a wave of desire. "I don't know what you did, but it's gone. The weight and sludge and darkness is gone. I still—" He shuddered and his sadness misted the air around me. "I still remember. I don't think I'll ever forget. But I feel like I can breathe again."

Another red wisp curled from my arm, and he twisted it around his index finger.

"I understand if you need time." I didn't want to give him

time. I wanted him with me just like I wanted my other guys. God, I needed him to help me get through whatever was going to happen with Marcus. But pushing him wouldn't help. "I'm—" My throat tightened and I forced out my words. "I'm a nephilim, and you have every reason to fear and hate what I am."

"Archnephilim," he corrected. "The daughter of Lilith and..." His sadness swelled.

"You can say it. Michael is probably my father." I sat up, pulling my gaze away from him, unable to look into all that love knowing the horrible truth. The gold flecks in my angel glow said I was half archangel—that, and only an archangel's DNA was strong enough to be magically combined with a demon's. Michael had been willing to do anything to win his war. Deciding to sleep with Lilith to create a powerful weapon would have been an easy choice for him.

I didn't want it to be true, but my other paternal options were just as bad and less likely.

Except why did he steal me away from Lilith and hide me with my mom?

"You're not your parents. Even if my soul wasn't bonded to yours, I'd know that." He sat up as well and hooked his finger under my chin, urging me to look at him again. "You'd do anything, fight anyone, to protect the ones you love. Hell, to protect complete strangers. That isn't you *trying* to be good. It's who you are. It's woven into your soul. But until we can figure out how to convince the JP and everyone else of that, you're going to need to pull your demonic magic back."

"Won't my essence still give me away?"

"Unless you look at it closely, it still says you're an angel." The muscles in his jaw flexed and while he didn't say it, I knew he was thinking: for now. "Actually it'd be better if you pulled all of your power back. You're radiating so much power, it's starting to push through the high of your release. And that was so strong I had to feed some of it to the guys again."

"Really? My chest, where I feel my divine light, is almost hollow. I've got almost nothing left after healing your soul."

Kol groaned. "Now you're really going to have to learn to pull it back. If you're almost empty now, I'm going to be in agony when you recover."

"But how is that possible? I wasn't this powerful before." But I already knew how. Lilith had destroyed what was left of my father's spell containing my magic. I'd thought she'd just released my demonic powers, but there must have been more archangel power locked away with it.

And if I let the inky magic in, I'd be even more powerful.

Which wasn't going to happen.

"You also just branded your third mate." Kol traced a line swirling over my shoulder. "I doubt our bond is old enough for me to add to your strength, but you and Gideon have been bonded for over three weeks. You could be starting to feel the effects of that now."

"Please tell me I'm not going to go back to being a bomb." That was the last thing I wanted. It had been bad enough when everyone joked about me taking down a building. A part of me hadn't really taken that seriously. But now, if I was that much stronger... I probably could. And I had no idea what I could do with my demonic powers.

Something I'd have to figure out later.

My first priority was going to Marcus and—

What? Sitting there and worrying. It was the only thing I could do for him.

My insides squirmed. *Get up. Go. Now.*

No. It would be best if I learned to pull my power in so

Kol and anyone else around me who was magically sensitive wouldn't be in pain. And given that I was in a hotel for supers, there could be any number of supers nearby who'd noticed someone powerful was in the building. Which was a complication we didn't need. *Then* I could be with Marcus.

But that didn't address the JP or Lilith.

I drew in a steadying breath, fighting the twisting ache to be at Marcus's side when there were so many other things I also needed to deal with. "How do I pull it back?"

"I imagine I have a box inside me where I keep my magic. Depending on how much I want to use determines how wide I open the box. But others think of it behind a wall, or in a vial. Whatever they need to think about to contain it."

"Okay." The moment Kol had said it, I knew the box idea wasn't right. My magic, when I was at full—or what I'd thought had been full—was a wild blazing sun in the core of my being. I didn't think I'd be able to shove it into a box or be able to imagine a box big enough inside me to contain it. Perhaps a wall?

Whatever I picked, I needed to do it now, get out of bed, and deal with... well, everything else.

No. Marcus. I *needed* to go to Marcus.

I imagined a circle of heavy cinderblocks around me. I had a lot of power, I'd need a strong, solid wall. But my pulse began to race the moment I added the next row of blocks. And it beat faster and faster the higher and thicker the wall became.

My angelic power, what I'd thought had been a faint glimmer, flared and exploded against my mental wall. With a burst of light, my wings released and Kol's eyes flashed wide.

CHAPTER 16

"WELL, THAT DIDN'T WORK," KOL SAID.

"No shit." I shifted back so I wouldn't hit him while I figured out how to get my damned wings back into my body. Which—*ah, crap*—I had yet to do without Gideon's help.

"What were you imagining?"

"A wall." I squeezed my shoulder blades together and imagined my magic flooding into my back.

My wings twitched.

And stayed right where they were.

"Claustrophobic? It's pretty common in angels."

"I hadn't thought I was." I strained to push more magic to the spot Gideon always touched when he helped me. "But I did get an apartment with roof access and a skylight before I'd even known I had wings."

"Which you've only had for a few days." Kol's expression softened. "How are you handling that? I'm sorry, I should have asked earlier. We've had our lives turned upside down, but yours…"

"Was doused in gasoline and set on fire?" I finished for

him. I squeezed my shoulder blades harder, straining to get whatever natural angelic reflex I had to work.

Come on.

Pull them in so you can contain your magic and get to Marcus.

Jeez. Just do it.

The urge to go swelled and my breath picked up. My wings jerked and magic flickered along my spine, then vanished without pulling my wings back in.

"God damn fucking wings." I didn't have the time to deal with this. Marcus needed me, and we had to figure out what we were going to do about Lilith and the JP.

Let me in and you'll have enough power, the inky magic hissed.

No.

I heaved with everything I had and imagined a massive blast of power crashing into my back. Light blazed around me and my wings slammed into me, stealing my breath as if I'd just been punched in the chest.

Kol cocked an eyebrow. "That well, hunh?"

"I'm sure I'll love them more when Gideon teaches me to fly. Until then, they keep getting in the way and messing things up."

"I think they're beautiful," Kol said, and his smile grew wicked again. "And I've heard the base of an angel's wings are really sensitive."

A shiver of desire swept through me at the memory of Gideon stroking my wings the first time he helped me pull them back in.

"Oh, ho!" Kol's eyes lit up. "So they are and you already know. That's going on the list of things we should try. And with Gideon and his wings..."

My body heated at the thought and my breath grew ragged again, this time with desire.

Jeez. I wasn't going to get anything done now that I was bonded with a incubus.

"Later," I forced out. "I promise. First, I need to get my power pulled back." Then Marcus. *Please, God, let him be all right.* I didn't care if he hated me so long as he lived.

"I'm holding you to that," Kol said. "Okay, so the wall didn't work. How about a shield or a vial or a jar?"

But those didn't sound right, either. Even if I tried to imagine just locking up my magic and not all of me like I'd done with the wall, I had a feeling my power would fight it. The only idea that kept popping in my mind was twisting it tight like it had been when my father's spell had contained it. What were the odds that I could twist it back up again?

Given my luck, probably terrible. But it was the only thing that felt right. So I drew in a steadying breath and imagined the sun at the core of my being. It burned, a blazing whirling supernova of half light and half darkness.

I mentally grabbed a thread of each, entwined them into a single strand, and dragged them in the same direction until it whipped into a raging vortex that threatened to tear free from my mental grip, but was at least all moving in the same direction. Clinging to my power with everything I had, I forced the vortex to tighten and curl in on itself, creating a ball.

The ball strained and swelled, and Lilith's inky magic surged and oozed between my cells, sensing a weakness in my concentration.

I mentally clenched down on it and my magic, and with a sharp contraction, my power compacted into a tight supercharged marble, pulsing in my heart, waiting for me to summon it, as if this was how it was supposed to be. I had no doubt it would roar to life the moment I called on it, but I couldn't help the glimmer of pride at successfully containing it. It also didn't hurt that I could feel Kol's pride rushing through our brand as well.

The inky magic's seductive whisper also dimmed, but it wasn't out and I didn't know how to get it out. Which scared the shit out of me.

"What did you pick?" he asked. "You feel like an ordinary angel now."

"I spun it tight into a ball."

His eyebrows rose and surprise flickered through his pride. "No container?"

"It didn't seem right."

"Well, okay then." He blew out a heavy sigh, the whisper of sadness returning. "We should return to real life."

Yes. Go. Go.

Kol got out of bed, strode to the door still naked—God, he was gorgeous—and retrieved a bag of clothes from the hall.

"There's a note," he said, dumping the contents of the bag on the bed. White T-shirts and tan cargo pants. Not really tactical team attire, but wearing all black wouldn't help us blend in with everyone else's summer clothes if that was what we needed to do... not that it wasn't going to look odd with all of us wearing the same thing. "We're to meet the guys in the conference room at the end of this hall, opposite end from the clinic. There'll be breakfast."

"I need to check in on Marcus first." I needed to *stay* with him. Except our troubles weren't going to wait and we needed a plan.

Why couldn't I focus on that? I wouldn't be able to help Marcus if the JP arrested us or Lilith found us.

I grabbed the two T-shirts, tossed the bigger one to Kol,

and set mine aside. Focus on the immediate problem. I couldn't do anything for Marcus—God, I had to do something!—so how did we deal with Lilith? We couldn't let her restart Michael's war and if she was gone, so too would be her inky magic. "We have to figure out what to do about Lilith."

If there was even anything we could do. We hadn't stood a chance the first time we'd fought her. What made me think we'd stand a chance now?

I picked up a pair of cargo pants, looking for more clothes, namely underwear. "We won't be able to stop her without the JP's help. Which is a whole other problem, since all of you just set your careers on fire and became fugitives for me."

Where was the God damned underwear? I needed underwear so I could go to Marcus—

No, come up with a plan for Lilith—

No, figure out how to get my guys' lives back.

"You shouldn't have run," I said. "If you'd let the Director lock me up, we'd have an army to stop Lilith. Hell, we'd have *the* army."

"Essie—"

I picked up the cargo pants I'd already set aside. Undies my size were small. Maybe they'd been caught in a pocket or something.

I needed to get dressed. I needed to go. "We'd have resources and magic and healing. Marcus would be in one of the best transition facilities in Union and—"

I shoved my hand into all the pockets and shook out the clothes. Whoever had purchased the clothes hadn't thought to buy any underwear. And while I doubted Kol minded— in fact, if I recalled correctly he hadn't been wearing any when he'd stripped in the bathroom last night, or rather earlier this morning—I didn't want to be running around without a bra and chafing down there.

"Essie—"

"Where the fuck is the God damned underwear!"

Kol grabbed my hands. "He'll be okay."

"I *know* that," I snapped. But I didn't, and even if he was going to be okay later, he was still suffering now, and I had to fucking think about other more pressing problems.

As if Marcus's pain wasn't pressing.

"You're freaking out over underwear."

I sucked in a sharp breath. What the hell was wrong with me?

But I knew what. Even if Marcus and I didn't share a brand, we were still bonded, and my soul was panicking as if it were Gideon or Jacob in danger. Healing Kol's soul and sealing our bond had distracted me momentarily, but now I had to think about so many things, and yet all I could think about was Marcus.

I could see why Amiah had been distraught over realizing *this* was what it meant to share a soul bond. If all her life she'd thought the soul bond through the angelic mating brand was all beautiful sunshine and fuzzy kittens, seeing this ugly truth would have been a shock.

I sucked in another breath. *I could not freak out. I could not freak out. Please, God, don't let me freak out.*

I squeezed Kol's hands and pulled out of his grip. "I'm okay."

He frowned. Yeah, I didn't believe me, either.

"Fine. I'll *be* okay." I got off the bed and grabbed my dirty underwear and bra from the bathroom.

See. I could think straight.

Thankfully not a lot of blood had soaked through my

jeans and T-shirt, so my undies and bra were mostly blood free, and what blood there was had dried while I'd slept.

I put them on, returned to the bedroom, and finished getting dressed. "I'll check in on Marcus then meet you in the conference room," I said, since I was pretty sure I wouldn't hear a word anyone was saying if we made our plans in the clinic. "We have to figure out our next move."

Kol dipped in and brushed his lips over mine with a whisper of a kiss that shivered desire all the way down to my toes. "I'll let the guys know."

We went down the hall in opposite directions, my stomach churning with worry for Marcus and my heart a confused mix of whispering emotions, joy, grief, anger, desire, and not all of it mine. My powers might have been pulled back, but it looked like that didn't mean my empathy had turned off, and I still had enough angelic juice to *feel* things.

I pushed open the clinic door and a wave of heartache swept over me.

Oh, crap. My legs trembled and I staggered to the first gurney—now empty, Sebastian must have been moved to a room—to catch my balance.

Amiah, sitting on the floor in front of the plexiglass door of the transition room, jerked her head up to look at me. "What do you want?"

Her blue eyes, so much like Gideon's, were red and filled with ice—had she been crying? The heartache would suggest so—and her face was haggard and pale.

"When did you last sleep?" Cassius was supposed to have given her a break, and given that she'd also been in the cafeteria when we'd teleported back to Operations in the early morning, she probably hadn't gone to bed last night. She clearly hadn't changed. She still wore the thin hospital scrubs she'd left Operations in and they still had blood on them. She was running on less sleep than I was. It shouldn't surprise me that her emotions were overwhelming.

"I'm fine."

"Yeah, you look fine," I said, the insensitive words jumping out before I could stop them. Crap. Even if Amiah had been a bitch, I could still take the high road and not be a bitch back. Especially since it was clear the ice and anger right now was hiding emotional pain and exhaustion.

The light in Amiah's eyes flared and she jerked her gaze back to Marcus, who still lay on the thin, bloody mattress with the billowing cloud of demonic mist weeping from and sinking back under his skin. His naked body was a sickening mix of man and beast, his limbs still breaking and changing even though he was unconscious.

"Don't make this harder than it has to be," she said, her tone icy but her heartache swelling.

"You're right. I'm sorry. I'm just having trouble controlling my emotions." And ignoring hers. I clenched my jaw and mentally pushed back the pressure of her feelings and the twisting urge to be closer to Marcus. I shuffled past the gurneys and pressed my hands against the plexiglass wall.

Marcus whimpered and his back arched. His left arm snapped and expanded into a wolf's foreleg, his flesh bleeding and blackened, but fur didn't sweep over it. The red mist whirled faster as if the wind blowing through it had picked up.

God, even unconscious he was in agony. "Is this what transition is always like?"

"Most don't have it quite as bad," Amiah said, a wave of anger cutting into her heartache. "But this is just like Marcus's first time."

"For over a week?" My stomach bottomed out. God, I

couldn't imagine surviving this kind of agony for a few days, let alone a week, without losing my mind.

"The first couple of days were the worst. I suspect it'll be the same here. His body didn't want to accept the change then, and it doesn't want to accept it now," Amiah said. "Then it'll be on and off for the rest of the week."

"And there's nothing I can do?" There had to be something. But a divine light strike and empathy wouldn't help and my demonic magic was the reason he was in this mess. I sagged to the floor beside Amiah. "He's never going to forgive me, is he?"

"If we don't tell him the truth, he might never know."

I jerked my gaze to Amiah, surprised. I'd have thought she, out of everyone, would want Marcus to know that his suffering was my fault, again.

Her angel glow dimmed and her heartache melted into sorrow. "If you hadn't used your demonic magic, he would have died the moment you arrived in the cafeteria," she said matter-of-factly, her tone hiding even a hint of her emotions. "He's alive because of you."

"He's also in agony because of me." Again. And, if Amiah had been telling the truth, he could still die.

Marcus whimpered again and his wolf-like right leg crunched and turned back to a human leg, his flesh torn and bleeding.

"There has to be something." I couldn't just sit there. And really, I had to meet with the rest of the guys and figure out what we were going to do next. It wouldn't help if he recovered to find the situation still just as dire. Except my soul wouldn't let me leave. "What if I branded him? Could I take his pain?"

"Angelic mating brands don't work that way. You have to be destined to be together. Just because you want it doesn't mean it's going to happen." Amiah's sorrow swelled but a shudder of fear swept through it. "Your life already isn't your own. Why trap Marcus, too?"

"You're probably the only angel around who doesn't think the angelic mating brand is a beautiful, sacred thing." But then, when we'd talked in Sebastian's office the other day, she'd been horrified thinking that I'd lost all control of my life. And maybe I had and just couldn't see it.

How did I explain to her how right my bonds were? That I belonged with Gideon, Jacob, Kol, *and* Marcus. Even if we didn't share an angelic mating brand, Marcus was mine and I was his. I knew it in my soul. Every cell in my being knew it.

"If you love him, let him go." Her heartache churned stronger, now cut with a thread of yearning and regret as well as fear. I'd always known there'd been something between them, but this didn't feel like a jealous ex-girl-friend. This was softer, like she desired him, but above all, she wanted him to be happy whether it was with her or not.

"Even if I could let him go, you know he'd never leave me. His wolf has made its choice." I pressed my lips together. Did I say it? Did I push the subject and find out exactly what had been between the two of them? Did I want to face the fact that my reappearance in his life had ended their relationship and I hadn't even given that a second thought until now? "He'd never go back to you."

"He never really was with me," she said, her voice small and tired, the icy mask she'd put up starting to crumble. "I thought if I was patient enough—thought his wolf's mating call couldn't be that strong for you because he wasn't a natu-rally born shifter and eventually he'd see me in that way. I just needed to be patient. And then you branded Gideon and Jacob and not him. I thought—" Her eyes grew glassy, but frustration snapped through me, and her mask hardened her expression again. "You caused him so much pain. He used to scream your name when the lycanthropy was ripping him apart— I know now he's not my destiny, but without a brand, he's not yours, either. If you love him, let him go. Your brands will make you love the others more than him whether you want to or not, and he doesn't deserve that."

Marcus groaned, and his chest rose and fell with rapid, shallow breaths, his expression twisting in agony. The unfelt wind blowing his demonic mist gusted, whipping it around for a second before returning to its uneasy undulations.

"You brand men left and right." She glared at me, but her frustration and heartache belied the anger in her eyes. "Did you really brand Kol?"

"Yeah."

Marcus groaned and the wind gusted again.

"Then that's proof. If you and Marcus were supposed to be mates, you'd have branded him."

Marcus's body jerked taut, and he screamed as both of his legs shattered with a sickening crunch.

"Damn." Amiah jerked to her feet and rushed to the counter, her fear swelling within me, but her body language and expression sternly professional. "He's metabolized the sedative faster than he should have."

My pulse stalled. That didn't sound good. "What does that mean?"

"It means the lycanthropy is more aggressive than a standard transition." She grabbed a needle from the drawer and inserted it into the vial of sedative that had been left on the counter. "He's going to come out of it soon, and it'll be better if he's partially sedated for his transition."

"Partially sedated?" I didn't like the sound of that, either.

Even fully unconscious, he'd been in pain. Partially conscious would be torture.

"He has to be at least semi-lucid to get through it. If we keep him knocked out, he'll never finish transitioning."

"So why did you fully sedate him last night— earlier— whatever."

Marcus screamed again. His chest expanded and ridges formed in his skin, a swirling design of angry red welts cut into his chest.

"If he wasn't out, you'd have never left the clinic, and the rest of the guys wouldn't have left and you all needed to get some sleep." She measured out the dosage she wanted then pocketed the vial along with another capped needle. "Now hold him down for me."

I opened the door as Marcus released another heartrending scream. The welts thickened and turned black. He thrashed onto his chest and the welts rolled over him, crawling over his sides onto his back.

"Roll him over and hold him steady," Amiah said. "I need a vein."

I hurried inside, dropped to my knees beside Marcus, and grabbed his still-human shoulder. His mist whipped around us, and he wailed and heaved against my hold.

"Get him over."

I hauled him onto his back. His arm swept out and the back of his fist slammed into my face. Pain exploded in my cheek and the world spun. Half blind, I threw myself on top of him, pinning him with my body.

Amiah grabbed his arm and captured it under her knees.

His breath heaved and his ribs shattered beneath me. The skin under my hands grew bumpy, the swirling ridges sweeping over his shoulder, and he bucked, my weight not enough to keep him down against his strength.

"Keep him still," Amiah said, fighting to keep his arm steady enough to insert the needle.

But he was too strong. I wasn't going to be able to hold him down, let alone get him still. Not unless I used my magic.

I sucked in a quick breath that did little to steady my nerves and reached for my empathic magic to help push some of Jacob's calm into Marcus. My power flared, rushing out of the tight ball in my heart, sputtered, and vanished.

Shit. I had just enough to feel Amiah's emotions and nothing left to push into Marcus. I'd used everything I had healing Kol.

"Essie, hold him."

"I'm trying."

Marcus bucked again, knocking me off, and howled, the cry half human and half beast. Bones shattered and muscles tore. I jumped back on him and his eyes fluttered open, revealing burning red hellfire.

Everything within me froze. *He's a demon? I made him a demon?* My magic hadn't just reawakened the lycanthropy in his DNA, it had changed it.

Amiah gasped and her fear turned the air frigid for a second before she locked down her emotions. She tightened her grip on his arm, but he wrenched free, his arm half human half... I had no idea what. His whole body was disfigured, his skin covered in swirling ridges and turning black. What the hell was he becoming?

Another scream and he heaved onto his side. His demonic mist whipped around us, sucking all the air into a wild vortex.

"Just hold him. I'll have to do this intramuscular," she said.

I reached for him, but he wrenched to his hands and knees and snarled at me, his jaw misshapen, extending into a snout, the hellfire in his eyes licking across his blackened cheeks.

"Marcus, it'll be okay." I raised my hands. Maybe if I didn't look like an aggressor he'd calm down.

"You can't reason with him in this condition." Amiah grabbed his shoulder, and he jerked toward her, his body breaking and twisting, growing into a massive, furless, muscular mastiff the size of a pony.

Her eyes widened and her fear spiked, no longer under control. She scrambled back.

He swiped an enormous paw at her, his claws tearing into her arm and sending the needle flying across the room.

With a scream, she wrenched her arm tight to her chest, blood oozing between her fingers. She twisted to the side out of the way of another paw swipe and her back hit the plexiglass wall. Nowhere else to go.

He snarled, no sign of humanity in his eyes, and lunged, his massive jaws going for her throat.

CHAPTER 17

AMIAH'S FEAR COATED ME IN FROST AND TURNED THE AIR SO cold my breath misted. She wasn't going to get out of the way fast enough and without her, he might not have a chance of surviving the rest of his transition.

"Marcus, stop." I shoved her out of the way, taking her place in front of Marcus.

His jaws snapped, his canines grazing my throat, and my pulse lurched.

Oh shit oh shit oh shit.

"Marcus, please."

He slammed a heavy paw on my chest, pinning me to the wall, and growled, the sound low and dangerous.

"You can't reason with him. It's not him. It's his beast. He won't be him again until his transition is over." A gut-churning mix of horror and grief joined her frozen fear. She was mourning his loss, as if there was a strong chance we'd never get him back.

His lips curled back giving me a close-up look at those massive teeth that had almost ripped out my throat, and his hot breath blasted my face, each huff fast and flecked with spit. The hellfire blazed in his wide, wild eyes, but there was a glimmer of piercing green in their core, a pinprick of the humanity still deep in his soul.

He was still in there.

He had to still be in there.

Amiah scrambled to the needle and Marcus jerked his head toward her.

"Marcus." I grabbed his head. His body was covered in a short velvet-like fur and not naked flesh like I expected, and his skin was searing hot. I wrenched his attention back to mine with a strength I didn't know I possessed. The red mist sweeping around him curled around my arms and sank into my skin, making my demonic magic burn in my chest. "Marcus, come back to me."

He jerked forward and snapped at me. I flinched, unable to help myself, and his teeth grazed the side of my face but didn't break flesh.

"Marcus, please." My mist whirled into his, swirling around and around.

"He's not in there." Out of the corner of my eye, I saw Amiah slide her hands into her pockets and pull out the vial and extra needle.

But he was in there. I knew it. I could *feel* it. "I'm not giving up on you."

Amiah shifted closer and he wrenched his head out of my grip, his hind legs bunched, ready to leap. The hellfire in his eyes surged, devouring the glimmer of green and any sense that Marcus the man was inside the beast.

My pulse stalled.

I was losing him. If I didn't do something now, the beast would take over and never let him go.

"Marcus." I seized his head again and shoved my forehead against his, his flesh burning hot to the touch in painful contrast to Amiah's frozen fear. "Fight this. You're stronger than your beast."

He wrenched in my grip but I held tight. I would *not* lose him. Not now. Not ever.

"Come back to me."

His claws dug into my flesh, and in the back of my mind, I knew I was bleeding again, but I couldn't feel anything past my desperation and the frigid air.

"Marcus, please." *I can't lose you.* "You're mine."

He howled, the sound deafening and heartbreaking. So much pain and fear and rage.

"You're. Mine." I dug my nails into the thick skin under his jaw and heaved back to meet his gaze, while still trying to hold on. The hellfire raged in his eyes and our demonic magic snapped, stinging my skin.

"Both of you," I growled, my voice, body, hell, my whole essence radiating my determination to keep him and that I loved him. *All* of him. He was my soul mate, and I would *not* lose him. Ever. "Mine."

He stiffened, the fire in his eyes flaring before dimming, exposing the glimmer of piercing human green again.

Essie? he asked, his voice in my mind weak.

Then he collapsed, his weight dragging me to my knees, and melted back into a man, his body temperature returning to normal.

Oh, thank God.

The red demonic storm that had raged around him vanished, now only a few thin wisps seeping from his skin and disappearing in the air. Beneath the blood smeared on his body, his skin was smooth and swarthy, no longer pitch black.

I pulled him into my arms and clung to him. I'd almost lost him. Again.

My throat tightened and tears burned my eyes.

Forgive me. Please forgive me.

Amiah knelt beside us, her eyes wide, and I was hit with a wave of awe and sorrow, the ice of her fear gone. "You really are soul bonded with him. Only his mate could control his beast like that." She pressed a hand against his back, blood rushing down her forearm from four deep gashes, and closed her eyes. Light radiated from her palm for a second, then she sat back on her heels. "Only his mate could have quickened his transition like that."

"What does that mean?" I tightened my grip around him, afraid the answer meant more pain for him.

"It's over. Just like that. You helped him accept his beast, by accepting both of them." Another wave of heartache swelled inside me, but her expression revealed nothing. "Help me move him back to the mattress. He could still be out for a while."

We half carried, half dragged him back to the mattress, and I sagged down beside him. A tear broke free and rolled down my cheek. I had too much emotion churning inside me, not all of it mine, and I couldn't contain it any more.

"He'll be all right," Amiah said.

I brushed a lock of hair from his forehead.

"I know you want to stay with him," Amiah said with a sigh, "but..."

"But I can't? It's too dangerous?" I snapped. To hell with what she thought. Marcus's beast could have killed me and it hadn't. I wasn't the one in danger. And hadn't she just said it was over?

I yanked my gaze to glare at her and tell her I was staying by his side, but my words stalled at the pain tightening her eyes. She held her arm against her chest, her blood soaking into her shirt.

"But I could use a little help. It's hard to bandage your own arm." She forced the words out as if it hurt to say them, and given how in control she always was, asking for my help must have been painful.

"What about your magic?"

"I have enough left so you won't need to stitch me up, but that's about it."

Jeez. Why hadn't I remembered that? I really wasn't thinking straight. We'd been in rough shape when she'd healed us only a few hours ago, and she'd looked haggard when I'd walked into the clinic. She probably didn't have much left. She didn't even have a career any more. In the blink of an eye, she'd decided to come with us and made herself a fugitive as well.

"Why?"

"Because I don't want to bleed on everything." She rolled her eyes and a wave of frustration swept through me.

"No, why did you help us? You didn't have to come with us. You know I'm a—" God, why was it so hard to say? Everyone knew it. It had been clear the moment I'd appeared in the cafeteria and again just now when I'd been with Marcus and my demonic magic had entwined with his.

Except none of her fear had been because of me.

Her expression hardened. "You might be reckless, but it's always to protect people who can't protect themselves. I don't know why you're not like Michael's other nephilim, but you aren't, and I've staked my freedom on that."

"Which still doesn't explain why. The JP will charge you with treason like the rest of us."

"Because I know you and the rest of the team well enough to know you're going to go after whatever beat the hell out of you." A whisper of her fear chilled inside me.

"And if you're going after it, then without a doubt it's evil and *needs* to be stopped."

Yes, but how? I shifted, suddenly uncomfortable with just sitting there. I needed to do something, figure out how to save everyone, and I couldn't do it sitting there with Marcus, since all I could think about when I was with him was him.

"In your previous condition, you wouldn't have stood a chance," she said.

Except I didn't know if we had a chance against Lilith and her witches even if we were at full power. Not without the JP's help. How did I stop Lilith and keep my guys safe? There had to be a way. We all had to get through this alive.

"Helping you was the only sensible option. Now, please." She dipped her gaze back to her injured arm, her emotions a mix of heartache and frustration and resignation. "Even if I had more power left, I'd still need help. My magic is for others. It takes a lot more power to heal myself than someone else."

"Well, that must suck." I forced myself to ease away from Marcus, picked up the original needle—which was only a few feet away from me and farther from her—and followed her out of the transition room.

"I don't usually need to heal myself." Her eyes narrowed, her attention on my chest. "And you're bleeding too."

I followed her gaze to the bloody puncture holes in my new T-shirt. The bleeding wasn't bad and I could hardly feel the pain, so Marcus's claws mustn't have dug in too deep, but I'd ruined another shirt and I hadn't even been wearing it for an hour. Not to mention my cargo pants were also bloody from brushing up against Marcus's body.

My heart squeezed, and I struggled not to think about

him. I wouldn't be able to function if I did, and I had to function, had to figure out a way to stop my mother.

I shuddered.

Yeah, not going to think about that, either.

"There are bandages in that drawer." Amiah pointed to the drawer beside the needle drawer and closed her eyes. Light blazed from the hand keeping pressure on her wound and her body tensed. Then the blaze vanished and she sagged, clutching the counter by the sink with her good hand to keep her balance. Her expression was even more haggard than when I'd first entered the clinic, and with trembling fingers, she turned on the tap and ran her bloody arm under the water.

Behind me, Marcus moaned, making my pulse lurch and my attention jump to him. The urge to take action, to help him, stop Lilith, do something, made my breath pick up even though Amiah had said he was going to be okay.

Except he was only going to be okay from the transition I'd forced onto him. Not from Lilith.

But what could I do? Maybe the other guys had figured something out. Which meant leaving Marcus's side, and what if something happened while I was gone? What if Amiah had lied to me? What if—

Amiah grabbed my chin and forced me to meet her gaze. "He's through the transition," she said, as if she'd been able to read my mind.

A surge of heartache and yearning swept through me. I needed Marcus to be okay above all else… except he was okay. I ached for him, yearned for him—

No, Amiah did. God, it was getting difficult to tell which emotions were mine. She loved him even though she'd known he was in love with me. And now she had absolute proof that I was Marcus's mate. All hope was lost. Even if I never branded Marcus, he was as much mine as Gideon and Jacob and Kol.

"Amiah, I'm—"

A sudden quick blast of her healing magic seared through my body, stealing what I'd been about to say—which was probably best, since I really had no idea what I could say to her.

"I promise. He's going to be okay," she said with another wave of heartache that she kept hidden behind an icy mask of indifference. "Now get something to eat. You won't do him any good if you collapse."

"You should talk." But she was right. I needed to eat and think, and I wouldn't be able to do either if I stayed in the clinic.

I made myself step out into the hall, but instead of going to the conference room, I turned in the other direction, heading to the loading bay and the outside door, away from the weight of Amiah's emotions, and, now that I thought about it, the ocean of feelings coming from the entire hotel.

I just needed a moment. I needed air and sky and a few deep breaths. Then I'd be able to go back in and figure everything out.

Except the truth was that if my guys went up against Lilith again, she'd kill them.

On top of that we were fugitives, wanted by the most powerful law enforcement agency on the planet, and without a doubt they'd use a tracking spell to find us sooner rather than later.

I had to do something.

The emotions from the hotel churned inside me, the pressure building.

Come on, think of something. Save them. Protect them.

How?

I shoved open the security door at the back of the empty loading bay and staggered onto the driveway behind Voth's hotel, momentarily blinded by the hot late-morning summer sun. Before me stretched the vast swath of manicured lawn behind the hotel, and beyond that the forest at the edge of this side of the Quarter. Above, the sky was clear, the same stunning blue as Gideon's eyes, but it did nothing to steady me against the emotional storm inside me.

Come on, Essie, pull your shit together.

But it was all too much. I couldn't ignore it any longer. I couldn't steady my thoughts or emotions, and I sure as hell couldn't get a grip on everyone else's. The pressure grew, raging into a crashing storm, swirling and lurching, hot and cold, burning humidity and freezing mist, all threatening to pull me apart, and Lilith's inky magic chuckled.

Soon I'd give in. Soon I'd be Lilith's. Soon my guys would die.

I screamed, a primal cry of pain and frustration, desperate to get out all my heartache and fear and anger. God, I was so angry. Angry that I wasn't a full angel, angry that my mother was a monster, angry at feeling helpless, and angry that I couldn't figure out how to face Lilith without losing any of my guys.

My demonic magic blasted from my clenched fists and exploded into the ground at my feet, sending chunks of asphalt into the air.

"Feel better?" Gideon asked from behind me.

Gasping, I turned to the door and was captured by his summer-sky eyes. So beautiful. So certain. Our connection instantly righted my internal equilibrium in a way I couldn't. His gaze always mesmerized me. I could look into his eyes forever and never come up for air.

But his angel glow dimmed, a summer's storm settling in

his sky, and I dragged my focus to the rest of him. His arms were crossed, stretching his white T-shirt across his broad shoulders, showing off his muscular biceps. He looked well, but his expression was tight with worry.

"Do you?" he pressed, his gaze taking in my bloody clothes. His worry seeped deeper into my chest and a flicker of lightning crackled through our brand. "You didn't come get breakfast and you weren't in the clinic."

"I just needed—" My gaze dropped to the holes I'd made in Voth's driveway.

"To scream?" Gideon crossed the few steps to me and wrapped me in a strong embrace. "He's strong."

I leaned into him, my ear pressed over his heart listening to his steady sure pulse, embracing his love for me and letting that push out all the other emotions, mine and the ones that weren't mine. All except the one that really stung, the one I'd been avoiding to even think about. "I made him a demon."

"A hellhound," he murmured, his lips against my fore-head. "He'll forgive you. You saved his life. And Amiah says you quickened his transition and he's already through it. So you'll have saved him a second time, too."

"Only for what? To die facing Lilith?" We couldn't let her restart Michael's war, but we weren't strong enough to stop her. "We have to tell the JP about Lilith and get their help."

"I know." Gideon's resignation seeped into me. "Even with Amiah and Cassius on our side, I don't know if the JP will accept you."

"If that's the price I have to pay to ensure Lilith is stopped, I'll pay it," I said. "I'll convince the JP that I manip-ulated all of you."

Gideon grabbed my shoulders and stepped back to look me in the eyes. "You'll do no such thing."

"I'm the only one who has to be incarcerated. You can get your life back."

"You *are* my life." His love for me surged, overwhelming all his other emotions. "Stop with the self-sacrifice. There's a way around this. We just need to figure it out."

His gaze jumped past my shoulder and he stiffened, his emotions lurching to fear. "Oh, God."

I wrenched around, my demonic power rushing to my fists.

A tall, broad-shouldered angel in jeans and a T-shirt strode across the lawn, his angel glow so brilliant I could see it clearly from almost a hundred yards away in the full sunlight. Sunlight that caught in jaw-length light brown hair with a hint of copper. This was the angel I kept seeing in my dreams, the man who'd pressed his hand against the glass of my maturation tank, looking exactly the same as if over twenty years hadn't passed. My father.

Except Michael and Rafael were dead, which only left one other archangel who'd tried to eliminate humanity.

Lucifer.

CHAPTER 18

GIDEON STEPPED IN FRONT OF ME, HIS DIVINE LIGHT SWEEPING over his hand, ready to be blasted. "That's far enough."

"You really think you can stop me, angel?" Lucifer said, his voice a sensual tenor edged with steel.

Oh, shit. Lilith was bad enough, but now we had to deal with Lucifer?

Except I sensed hesitation and worry from him, not rage or ferocity or whatever murderous psychopaths felt. And he had stolen me from Lilith and hidden me.

So what did that mean?

I had absolutely no idea.

"I won't let you take her back to Lilith." Gideon's fear and determination to protect me swelled, overwhelming what I felt from Lucifer.

The archangel narrowed his eyes. "You know what she is. Why are you protecting her?"

"I won't let you take her." Gideon widened his stance and formed his divine light sword. A glimmer of light flared from the brand on his forearm and his electric power crackled up my arm.

"You branded her?" Lucifer's expression flashed from shock to anger and his horror and rage slammed into me, along with a fierce need to protect that was strangely similar to Gideon's.

Had Lucifer really done everything he'd done to protect me?

"You son of a bitch. You branded her." He stormed toward us, his gaze locked on Gideon, murder in his eyes. "And you've done a shitty job protecting her. Look at her. She's covered with blood and has a black eye."

I stepped up beside Gideon and Lucifer's attention jumped back to me with another rush of conflicting emotions and a need to protect.

"You weren't supposed to have anything to do with this world," he said, jerking to a stop a few feet away.

He really *was* trying to protect me.

"What's he talking about?" Gideon asked, his voice low.

Why the hell had Lucifer done what he'd done? He was the original angel who'd fallen and slaughtered thousands. He was evil.

Except the angel standing in front of me didn't look evil and his emotions didn't feel evil.

"Why?" I asked. "Why break your deal with Lilith? Why hide me? Why make me think the world would hate me?" Why God damn everything?

"Because the world will hate you, save for maybe me and your angel." He frowned, his attention on my right arm. "Your brand is bigger than his."

"Essie?" Gideon shifted beside me, his fear growing stronger.

Lucifer's gaze jumped back to mine, and I caught a glimmer of gold flecks in his angel glow. "Is that what she called you? Essie?"

"Esther. You didn't even name me?" I don't know why that hurt so much. He might have donated his DNA to make me, but he wasn't my father. He hadn't raised me, hadn't had anything to do with my life.

"If I did, I wouldn't have been able to let you go." His anger and frustration melted into regret. "If you stayed with me, she'd have found you. But it looks like she will anyway. I'd feared the spell wouldn't be strong enough to contain the power of an archangel and the Hellfire Queen, but it was the only thing I could do."

"That and hiding my memories and manipulating some human woman into thinking she loved you."

His surprise spiked through me. "That wasn't supposed to happen."

"She waited her whole life for you, died thinking you loved her and that you had to stay away because of me." My mom had spent all of my life heartbroken over a lie because she'd been magically manipulated. "She used to cry herself to sleep when she thought I couldn't hear her. She could have been happy. She could have had real love."

"That wasn't my intention," Lucifer said, his voice gruff.

"Well, what was?"

"To give you what neither I nor Lilith could give you. Life. Love. Anything but Michael's fucking war."

"Says the angel who fought for him," Gideon said.

"Not willingly." A shadow passed over Lucifer's angel glow.

"It was *your* war," Gideon said. "You started it. Michael just picked it up years later. I'm sure you jumped at the chance to get out of your cage and finish what you started."

"I jumped at the chance to get out, but it wasn't Michael who freed me." Lucifer's regret swelled and realization hit me.

"It was Lilith. That was the deal you made with her. Your freedom for her weapon."

A whisper of surprise from Gideon sliced through me then disappeared, and he shifted closer to me. He'd just figured out the horrible truth and without a word, reassured me that he stood by me.

"Michael would fuck just about anyone but her. Probably to drive her crazy. Or rather more crazy than she already was." Grief twisted into Lucifer's regret and he rubbed his right forearm, drawing my attention to the pale, delicate scar swirling over his skin. "She'd learned the secret to making nephilim and leveraged Michael by offering her help in the war to use one of his maturation tanks. I'd been locked away from the Realm of Celestial Light for too long. I had no power. Agreeing to Lilith's terms was the only way she wouldn't kill me."

"So why steal me?"

"Because the Angelic Defense was moving in and Michael was destroying all the tanks, killing all of his nephilim." He shifted closer and Gideon tensed. "And you weren't a thing or a weapon. None of Michael's nephilim were, until he finished his process by pulling them from their tanks and shattering their souls. You'd barely had any time in the tank and you were just a little girl. My little girl. And you deserved everything I couldn't give you."

"Because you were a fugitive?"

"Because my soul is broken." He held out his arm, giving me a clear view of the delicate white lines swirling over his forearm.

Gideon drew in a sharp breath. "You survived the death of your mate."

"I went insane and tried to slaughter not just the humans who'd killed her but every last one of them. I deserved to be locked in that cage. Now you're bound by the same curse." His gaze rose to Gideon, his expression fierce, but his fear surged inside me. "I'll bring you back and kill you again in the most painful way possible if you die on her."

Gideon glared back.

Tension filled the air and I opened my mouth before my father—an archangel, so clearly more powerful than Gideon—flattened my mate. But the door behind us banged open and we all jerked to see who it was.

"Hey, Essie—" Kol froze mid-step, his eyes wide, his fear flash-freezing over my skin. "Oh, shit. Lucifer."

"Jeez," I said. "I should have drawn a picture. Everyone seems to know who you are except me."

"Drawn a picture?" Lucifer asked.

"I've been dreaming about you for a week now."

"Ah," Lucifer said. "That's how you knew who I was."

Kol's gaze jumped from Lucifer to me to Gideon. "You should be freaking out. You know who you're standing beside, right?"

"Lucifer," Gideon said, and a wicked smile flashed across his face, along with a burst of mischief. Oh, that was a feeling I never thought I'd feel from Gideon. "Meet your father-in-law."

Kol gasped, his jaw dropped open, and his surprise hit me.

Gideon snorted. "That's payback for how you told me about Jacob."

"Jesus, you've two mates?" Lucifer asked. "And an incubus? Really?"

"Four, actually. And I love him for his personality."

Lucifer rolled his eyes and looked heavenward. "God, help me."

"So, if you're not here to take me back to Lilith, why are you here?" A part of me wanted to believe everything he'd said, that he'd done what he'd done to protect me. But I didn't know him. He could have some other motive in mind, no matter what his emotions were telling me. I was still, after all, a weapon.

"I felt the spell on your angelic magic shatter a day and a half ago, and the spell on your demonic power this morning." Lucifer raked his hands through his hair. "Lilith is going to come after you and you're— I *thought* you were helpless." His gaze dropped to my hands, where demonic mist billowed and a glimmer of divine light heated my palms. "That isn't the control of someone who's had power for less than two days. How long has my spell been failing?"

"At least three weeks," Kol said from the doorway, not drawing any closer. "That's when you bought the enspelled contacts to hide your angel glow, didn't you?" he asked me.

"It was before then," I said. "Blasting myself with the divine light made the biggest crack, but my buzz started about two and a half years ago and my weird empathy manifested before then."

Lucifer frowned. "Buzz?"

"It was like I was constantly holding an electric fence. Nicotine patches worked to calm it for a bit, until we fought the archnephilim— the *other* archnephilim. And then—" I entwined my fingers with Gideon's and looked up at him. "Being near you used to calm it until the zip OD."

"You ODed on zip?" Lucifer's eyes narrowed, his gaze growing fierce again. "You're the worst mate in all the realms. How could you let her take zip?"

Gideon met Lucifer's gaze head-on again. "She didn't take zip, she got dosed, and you've never met your daughter so you have no idea how stupid telling me I should or shouldn't *let* her do anything is."

"Can we please not tell the *archangel* Lucifer he's stupid," Kol said.

Lucifer shifted his attention to me. "The spell was designed to gain strength and further suppress your powers the closer you got to an angel. But if it was already breaking... The zip must have twisted it. Now come on." He held out his hand to me. "Summon your other mates and let's go. I need to get your powers contained before Lilith realizes you're still alive."

A part of me wanted to take his offer. If my powers were contained again and my essence looked like a human's, we could change our names and live a normal life—or as normal a life as a nephilim-in-hiding with an angel, a vampire, a were— hellhound, and a demon could live. We wouldn't face Lilith and my guys would be safe.

But then no one else would be safe. Lilith was planning something that would restart Michael's war and there wasn't a guarantee that the JP would believe us or send enough agents to stop her.

I glanced at Gideon. His emotions had become a strange churning mix of hope and regret, desire and fear, the same as mine. And all from the choice of keeping me safe or saving others. We couldn't have both.

"I have your back," he said.

"So do I. And I'm sure Marcus and Jacob do, too," Kol added.

I turned to meet Kol's dark gaze. His hellfire was banked, but his love radiated through our bond. He was more certain than Gideon about following me down whatever path I chose. Of course, unlike Gideon, he wasn't as psychologically bound to follow the law and protect people.

"We can't let Lilith go unchecked." I turned back to Lucifer. "She already knows I'm alive. She's the one who broke the spell on my demonic magic. She's planning on reigniting Michael's war. Face her with us."

The muscles in Lucifer's jaw tightened and his frustration returned. "I can't."

"Can't or won't?" I asked.

"I was locked away from the Celestial Realm of Light for a long time. I have almost no power. I'd be a liability in a fight, not the asset you want. Come with me. I'll hide your true nature. You're still young, not fully into your power. You won't stand a chance against her as you are."

"If you have no power, how are you going to hide Essie's?" Gideon asked, his emotions turning wary. "And how did you contain it all those years ago?" He frowned. "And are you implying that you can cast spells? That you're a sorcerer?"

"I'm not a sorcerer, I can't channel power directly from the Realm of Celestial Light, but I can weave a spell and use my own essence to power it. I spent a long time in that cage, not unconscious like everyone said I was, and my powers weren't completely locked away. One of my innate magics is to enter and manipulate minds."

"Which is how you locked away my memories and convinced my mother I was her child." Was he manipulating me now? I didn't feel like I was being influenced by him, but I wasn't sure if I'd know if I was.

"Yes. But I couldn't influence anyone in my cage, I could only go along for the ride, and I had a lot of time to kill."

"That still doesn't explain how you cast the spell to hide Essie's true nature," Gideon said, his suspicion growing. "If you don't have any power now, you likely didn't have any power when you pulled her from the tank."

"It doesn't take a lot of power to weave a spell. The big power suck is when you activate it. I wove the spell to hide you and tied it to your magic," Lucifer said, "You were the one maintaining it. That's why the zip OD twisted it. I'll show you, if you don't believe I'm nearly powerless."

He extended his hands, one to me and one to Gideon.

I glanced at Gideon, who gave a tight nod. We took Lucifer's hands, and he gasped, his head jerking back and his angel glow blazing.

"Oh, fuck, I was wrong," he said, his body trembling. "You're more powerful than even she imagined. Once you recover the magic you've spent, you *will* stand a chance against Lilith, even now."

"And you?" Gideon asked, his voice dark. "Stop hiding your power."

"I'm not." Lucifer's frustration grew and he mentally tugged my essence deeper into his, where the whisper of his magic lay. I could sense his essence held the potential for enormous power, a power as crushing and terrifying as Lilith's, but it was like an atrophied muscle, withered from lack of use, and was going to take a long time to recover.

"You're an archangel," Gideon said. "How does that happen?"

Lucifer gently pushed us out and released our hands. "No contact with the Realm of Celestial Light. I don't recommend it."

So he really couldn't help us. Damn. And as much as Lucifer thought I stood a chance against Lilith, I already had proof I couldn't. "So we're back to where we started. Helpless against Lilith and fugitives from the JP."

Lucifer's worry returned. "They know about you, too?"

"We should probably do something about that," Kol said. "I've no doubt they've called in someone who can cast a tracking spell. If our luck holds, they'll have to bring that someone in from Rome."

But if our luck didn't, the spell could be cast at any moment.

"And I think the only reason Lilith isn't coming after Essie is because she's busy preparing for whatever she's planning," Gideon said. "I have no doubt once she's done, she'll hunt us down."

"You're sure you won't come with me?" Lucifer asked.

"Lilith can't be allowed to restart Michael's war."

He held my gaze, the gold flecks dancing in his angel glow mesmerizing. His worry churning in my stomach slowly shifted to resignation.

"There's too much angel in you." He blew out a heavy breath. "Fine. I'll take care of the JP—"

"No killing," Gideon said.

"Wasn't planning on it. I might have a powerful charm that hides me from magical tracking, but the moment I show my face, every agent will be assigned to find me. You'll no longer be their priority. That should buy you some time. And this—" Lucifer drew close and Gideon tensed. "Jeez, I'm more likely to hurt you, lover boy, than her."

"Doesn't make me feel better," Gideon said.

Lucifer huffed and brushed his lips against my forehead. A burst of heated magic snapped in my head and the image of a complicated glyph filled my mind's eye.

"This will give you an edge against Lilith," Lucifer said. "Share that glyph to a witch, any witch, she or he doesn't have to have a lot of power and doesn't need to set it, because you'll only need it once. It just needs to be drawn on your body with enough power to seed it."

"What is it?"

"The spell that made my cage. I had a lot of time to

study it. You're going to need to touch Lilith when you cast it, so cast it fast so she doesn't have time to counter it. But then you don't need to hold on to her, just put every ounce of power you have behind it to imprison her and contain her magic." His eyes narrowed. "Waiting until you've recovered your angelic magic is your best chance at success."

Except I was pretty sure I wasn't going to be recovered by the end of today, which meant going ahead without the necessary strength or sitting back and letting Lilith hurt people.

"And remember to focus. Too much power too quickly will burn you up." His emotions turned sad and he brushed his lips against my forehead again, giving me another complicated glyph.

"What's this one for?"

"It's the spell to contain your powers. I'll always have to hide from everyone, but you don't have to." He shot Kol a hard glare then turned it on Gideon. "If my daughter dies and it doesn't kill you, I will."

"If Essie dies, it means I'm already dead," Gideon said.

Lucifer turned his attention back to me, his emotions returning to sad and misting the air. This was goodbye, and he had no intention of ever seeing me again. "I'm glad I got to meet you. When you figure out what Lilith is doing, call in an anonymous tip saying you saw me there. The JP will send every agent they have."

With a burst of determination, he turned on his heel and strode away, regretting every step he took that put distance between us.

"Well, that was—" Kol's emotions whirled, too mixed up for me to tell what he was really feeling. "I have no idea what that was."

Jacob stepped into the doorway behind him. "Who was that?"

"Daddy," Kol said with a shudder.

"Lucifer." Gideon squared his shoulders. "Did he really give you the spell to imprison Lilith?"

Jacob's eyebrows rose in surprise and his vampiric intensity deepened.

"I don't know," I said. It felt like he had, but I knew nothing about spells and the only person I knew who did was Sebastian. "Is Sebastian awake?"

"He is," Jacob said. "And he managed to get to the conference room for breakfast, but he should probably still be in bed."

Which meant asking him to weave the cage spell was a bad idea. But since I didn't trust any witch Voth might bring in, he was all we had. Here was hoping, given everything we'd been through, that he was still willing to help and that helping wouldn't kill him.

CHAPTER 19

WE HEADED BACK INSIDE THE HOTEL AND DOWN THE HALL, past the clinic—which I made myself go by without stopping because if I did, I wouldn't be able to leave Marcus's side again—and past the room where Kol and I had sealed our bond, to the conference room. It was a plain room with a large conference table and a dozen uncomfortable-looking chairs. A platter of pastries and fruit sat at the edge of the table, along with a carafe and a cluster of coffee mugs.

Sebastian sat in the chair closest to the door, picking at a half-eaten croissant, his skin still dull gray without its usual glow, and his emotions radiating exhausted worry. He wore a white T-shirt and tan cargo pants, like the rest of us, as if whoever had bought the clothes had just purchased a variety of sizes. And I really hoped they'd purchased extra so I wouldn't have to continue running around in bloody clothes.

It was strange seeing him in something other than a button-down and slacks, and he really didn't look like himself.

"How many supers does it take to get an archnephilim to

breakfast? Three, apparently." A ghost of his wicked smile pulled at his lips, but his emotions didn't change. "Or did you stop for a little fun on the way? If I'd known, I would have joined you."

"Sure, you could have met Daddy, too." Kol grabbed the carafe, poured a cup of coffee—his hands shaking—and handed it to me.

Sebastian quirked an eyebrow.

"Lucifer." I pulled out the chair beside Sebastian and sat. "And while he can't help us fight Lilith, he did give us a spell."

Sebastian's worry deepened. "What kind of spell?"

"I'm hoping you can confirm it." I met Sebastian's gaze, staring into his almost colorless eyes, searching for a glimmer of the power I'd seen before. But they were icy and dull. He looked like shit. Still breathtakingly handsome, but handsome that had had the crap beaten out of him. I really couldn't ask him to do anything more than look at the glyph and confirm it was actually a cage spell. "And do you know a witch we can trust to seed it?"

Gideon sat in the chair on my other side, his worry also growing, while Jacob leaned against the wall beside the door, his complexion still too pale. Both of them gave off the sense that they didn't like the idea of bringing anyone else into this, although I wasn't sure if it was to protect whoever we wanted to bring in, since that would make them a fugitive as well, or to protect me and my now-no-longer secret.

"Given your... nature and the fact you're wanted by the JP, I'm not sure I trust anyone," Sebastian said.

"And did you know about my nature?" I asked. But if he had known, why hadn't he said anything?

Sebastian pursed his lips.

So he had known. And he hadn't been afraid of me or turned me in. "Why didn't you say anything?"

Although if he had, I wasn't sure what I would have done. I probably would have figured out how to leave my guys to protect them.

"You weren't ready to know." He glanced over my shoulder at Gideon. "*They* weren't ready to know. I've never felt evil intent from you and I like to judge a person on *who* they are, not *what* they are." His gaze dropped to his half-eaten croissant, and with a sigh, he set it on the plate and held out a shaking hand. "Since you're not holding a piece of paper and Lucifer's power is memory magic, I'm assuming he embedded it in your memory."

"Yes." I took his hand.

A shiver of cold magic caressed my skin and vanished.

Sebastian frowned. "He didn't transmit it through touch?"

"No, he kissed her," Kol said, taking a muffin from the tray and sinking onto a chair.

"Really?" A flicker of mischief flashed through me. "A kiss, hunh? You know they say, once you've kissed a fae—"

Kol cleared his throat. "Dude, you can't compare. Don't even try."

"Right. Soul bonded with an incubus. Because three bonds weren't crazy enough." Sebastian rolled his eyes at me. "All right, lay it on me like Lucifer did."

I leaned in, imagining the first glyph Lucifer had given me, and pressed my lips against Sebastian's forehead. A flash of heated power swept from my lips into Sebastian's head.

He groaned and grabbed the edge of the table, his breath suddenly fast. "Jeez, that's one hell of a spell. Give me a week or so to recover and I can cast it."

"We don't have a week," Jacob said. "Lilith is planning on restarting Michael's war today."

"Well, I don't know of any witch who's powerful enough to cast it." Sebastian picked up his croissant but set it back down again.

"I'm told I just need the witch to draw the glyph and seed it," I said, still not entirely sure what *seeding* meant, only that it required a little magic and not a lot. "Do you have enough power to do that?"

"To seed it for a one-time use, yes. But it would be better if it was fully set. If you're not careful, this spell will burn you up. Setting won't protect you from that, but it's better than not setting it." Frost crept over the back of my hands, the fear coming from all my guys as well as Sebastian.

"You saw what Lilith can do. She has to be stopped." And the fact that she was my biological mother wasn't going to deter me.

Sebastian glanced past my shoulder to Gideon. "You can't possibly be okay with this."

"I'm not." Gideon shifted my chair so he could wrap an arm around my waist and pull me close. "But if not us, then who?"

Sebastian glanced at each of my guys, their expressions grim and determined, before returning his attention to me. "You're all insane. But you're right. If you don't burn yourself to a crisp, you're probably the best ones to go up against Lilith."

"Okay." Kol shoved up from his seat. "So how do we do this?"

"The bigger the glyph, the easier it'll be to control." The mischief returned to Sebastian's expression, and his emotions turned to heated desire. "So it looks like I take Esther back to my room and get her naked."

"You just don't know when to quit," Jacob said, rolling his eyes at him.

"Hey, maybe I'm Esther's fifth soul mate?" He flashed me a seductive smile, but surprise snapped through me, as if he hadn't expected to say that, and his fear dropped the temperature.

Interesting. He desired me, but was afraid of being my mate. And while I was physically attracted to him—who wouldn't be? He was as hot as any of my guys—I didn't have the same pull, the same certainty that I did with the others. I knew in my soul they were mine. And Sebastian wasn't.

I leaned in and trailed a finger along his jaw, bringing my lips close to his. He shuddered again, both his desire and fear deepening. The emotions from my guys swelled into a confusing mix, then one by one settled on acceptance. They didn't know Sebastian like they knew each other, and yet if Sebastian was another mate, they'd accept him.

Sebastian's fear grew, overwhelming his need, but he hummed low in his throat, a sound of sensual masculine desire.

Jeez, he'd do anything to hide his true emotions.

"You know I'm an empath, right?" I breathed against his lips.

"Well, shit," he breathed back. "So, am I doomed or can we just fuck for fun?"

Gideon shifted closer, Jacob's intensity swelled, and the hellfire in Kol's eyes flared.

"Pretty sure I won't need to look beyond my mates for sex. And I'm more than sure that you're not one of mine."

He sagged back with a heavy sigh. "Oh, thank God. Bound to someone for eternity—?" He shuddered. "I don't care how good the sex is, that's a nightmare."

"Okay." Gideon stood, his relief surging into me. "What do you need to seed this spell?"

"A permanent marker and some time." Sebastian glanced at his croissant as if he were going to continue eating then shoved the plate farther away. "How are we dealing with the JP? They've got to have a tracking spell on you by now."

Gideon opened his mouth as Cassius stormed into the conference room. His gaze jumped to me and a wash of mixed emotions swept through me: confusion, fear, relief, and a fierce protective love that I was pretty sure was for Gideon.

"Things just got worse," Cassius said. "Lucifer has been sighted."

Gideon pursed his lips and Kol drained his coffee mug.

"I'll go find that marker," Jacob said, and he strode out of the room.

Cassius frowned. "Why do none of you look surprised?"

"He's running interference with the JP so we can figure out how to deal with Lilith," I said.

Cassius's eyes narrowed. "Why would he do that?"

For a second I contemplated not telling Cassius the truth —and given how I had no problems lying when necessary, I should have known I wasn't all angel. But I was already Lilith's daughter and none of the paternal archangel options were good. Lucifer being my father didn't make things any worse.

"He's my father and doesn't want Lilith or the JP to get their hands on me." I glanced at Sebastian and stood. "Let's get this spell seeded."

Cassius threw his hands up in resignation. "Of course he is. So what's the plan? I can't decide if I want him to lend us his power or not. An archangel would be useful in a fight. A murderous psychopath, not so much."

"The plan is to put Lilith back in her cage." Sebastian stood, using the table to steady himself. His expression tightened with pain, and fear snapped through me then vanished as he locked his emotions down.

Damn, maybe I shouldn't have told him I was an empath. I was sure that was the last I'd feel from him.

"And to do that, we need to figure out where she's going to be," Kol said. "Any ideas?"

Sebastian shuffled to the doorway, sweat beading on his forehead before he'd even made it into the hall.

"You sure you're up for this?" Gideon asked, falling into step beside him.

"I can sit and draw on Esther's back." He huffed. "If you give me a few hours I could probably manage more, but given we don't know our timeline, the sooner I seed this spell, the better."

We stopped at a door halfway down the hall, and Sebastian unlocked it and let us in. The room was identical to the one I'd shared with the guys. The bed had been slept in, the comforter and sheets crumpled, and the bathmat lay on the floor in front of the shower, but other than that it was the same plain, clean room.

Kol propped the door open with a rolled-up towel so Jacob wouldn't have to be let in and leaned against the wall at the foot of the bed as Sebastian sagged onto the mattress.

"So what do we know?" Gideon asked, also leaning on the wall and crossing his arms.

I tugged the comforter and sheets up to make a smoother surface to lie on and pulled off my bloody T-shirt.

Cassius's eyes widened. "I'm not sure I should be here for this."

"He's drawing a glyph," Gideon said. "You're fine."

"You're mated to an archnephilim whose parents are the two most dangerous supers on the planet. I'll let you know when I'm fine."

"Well, if you keep thinking about it that way," Kol said, "you're never going to be fine."

Cassius glared at him.

"So, about the plan." I laid face down on the bed, unhooked my bra, and Sebastian set his hands on my back. Ice trickled into my skin with a whisper of his power, and I turned my head to meet his pale gaze. "Just enough to seed it."

He rolled his eyes at me. "Not a self-sacrificing idiot like your mates."

Jacob returned with the marker and handed it to Sebastian, and the trickle of ice vanished, replaced by the maker's cool tip.

Kol's gaze slid up my body. The heat in his eyes grew and stole my breath, and his seductive power slipped into me and shivered down my spine.

"Jeez," Sebastian huffed. "If you don't want me to mess this up, hold still."

With his lips quirked in his usual wicked smile, Kol mouthed "sorry" to me, although I was pretty sure he wasn't sorry at all. He did, however, slide down the wall and settle on the floor where I couldn't make eye contact with him.

Gideon rolled his eyes at Kol, but a hint of heat darkened his gaze as well when he turned his attention back to me. "Okay, we know Lilith wants to make a statement. She tried to assassinate Ambassador Hollaway so she could attack the funeral and take out as many high-ranking JP members as possible."

"She also said she'd had to move up her plans to today," Jacob added.

"So what does that mean?" Cassius asked, his gaze jumping from Jacob to Gideon to Kol.

"Hey, don't look at me," Kol said. "The only thing I remember from the fight in that lab is freaking out over the maturation tanks. And I'm pretty sure the only reason I didn't have a complete breakdown was because I was in shock over being branded. That whole fight is a blur for me."

Cassius sighed. "Do we know for a fact that she hasn't used the tanks?"

"Nothing is certain," Jacob said. "But the tanks were empty, they didn't look like they'd been used, and all of the equipment was covered up."

"I also couldn't sense any magic in them," Sebastian said, "and those puppies need a lot of magic, magic that would leave a residue for a long time."

"So no nephilim, yet." Cassius pursed his lips and frowned.

Yeah, that was the key word: yet.

"And thank God for that," Kol said. "Her witches feeding off her worship magic are powerful enough. They took out us and an elite team at the same time."

"So is it one or the other for her right now?" I asked. "She can have her army of witches *or* create her nephilim. She doesn't have enough power right now for both?"

"That has to be her plan," Gideon said. "She wasn't going to just kill the JP members at Hollaway's funeral. Most of them are powerful supers with strong essences. She was going to drain them. Probably kidnap them and drain them over and over again until she had enough power for both witches and nephilim."

Sebastian slid the marker over the invisible sensitive spot by my shoulder blade where my right wing formed. Desire shivered through me, and I squirmed, wiggling my toes, fighting to stay still.

Kol groaned. The temperature in the room rose, and Gideon shifted, his breath a little too fast.

"If the funeral isn't happening, where would she go to get an influx of power?" Jacob asked, his voice low and raspy.

"And what would be just as much of a statement as draining JP members?" Cassius added.

Gideon tipped his head back and closed his eyes. "That's also happening today?"

I turned the questions over and over in my mind. If she couldn't drain a handful of powerful supers, would draining a lot of not-powerful supers or even humans give her the power she wanted? What was just as much of a statement as attacking the ambassador's funeral?

Oh, shit. There was only one thing happening today that might fit that bill. "Lots of people and a statement? She's going to attack the unification ceremony. The supers in attendance won't be as powerful as those at Ambassador Hollaway's funeral, but there'll be more of them, and what better statement for restarting Michael's war than attacking a ceremony marking the beginning of its end?"

Gideon glanced at the bedside clock. "That's in just over two hours."

The marker trailed along my ribs, then curled into the small of my back.

"The ceremony takes place in the middle of Unity Park," Jacob said. "There aren't a lot of good places to hide. And even if there were, Lilith would still be able to sense us."

"Well, we can't just walk up to her and take her out," Cassius said.

Except I needed to touch Lilith to cage her and that meant getting close. "I think I *have* to walk up to her. We're not going to be able to catch her unaware with me close enough to touch her, so there's no point in trying to be stealthy."

Gideon ran his hand over his hair, thankfully now not quite as short as Cassius's, and worry but also consideration swelled into me. He was seriously thinking about it.

"Gideon, please," Cassius said. "Don't go through with this. You were all barely alive when you teleported back into Operations. You can't just walk up to Lilith."

"He won't be. I will. I'll hold my power back so hopefully she won't realize how much I have left until it's too late." I wasn't going to mention how I had no idea if I could pull that off. Especially since I also had to concentrate on my bonds with Gideon, Jacob, and Kol to resist the inky magic from taking over my soul, which I was sure would gain strength the closer I got to Lilith. But it was really our only option.

"Are you sure about this?" Jacob knelt by the bed so he could look me in the eyes, his expression tight, his complexion still a little pale. "With a spell this size, you'll need everything you've got, both angelic and demonic magic. If you walk into the middle of the unification ceremony and use both, everyone will know you're a nephilim. You won't be able to get your life back."

"I haven't lost my life. I have you guys." And I wasn't going to think too hard about how I might not have Marcus any more. "I'll tell Lilith I want to join her."

"I'm not sure she'll believe that," Kol said.

"She only needs to believe it long enough for me to

touch her," I reminded him. "You'll need to stay out of sight until I can start the spell, but then you have to take care of her witches. As soon as Lilith realizes what I'm doing, they'll come after me."

"We'll always have your back," Gideon said. "And you're right. If she thinks you're an enemy, she won't let you close, but if she thinks you're her daughter coming to join her cause, you might get close enough to touch her."

"I hate that the plan revolves around a might," Cassius said.

"We all do." Jacob offered me a sad smile. We could all do the math. Even if Lucifer believed I was strong enough to imprison Lilith, that only meant the odds were marginally less terrible. "So we have two hours. We should probably get some rest."

"First I want to check on Marcus," I said. "Then I'm bringing you back to full."

Gideon gave a tight nod and pushed away from the wall. "I'll go talk to Voth and see if he has, and is willing to loan us, anything that might help."

"No, Gideon." I held out my hand to him. I might want Jacob at full health, but I wanted him near me, too. I wanted all my guys. If this didn't go well, if Lilith killed me, or worse, her magic possessed me, this might be my last chance to be with them. "Stay. You, too, Kol."

"And by stay, she means in your own room," Sebastian said.

"I'll talk to Voth." Cassius turned on his heel and left, taking a strange mix of garbled emotions with him. For a moment, I wondered if I'd be able to sort out his feelings if I concentrated, but it was probably rude to be feeling his feelings as it was—something I supposed I'd have to work on if I survived.

Sebastian pressed his palm against the center of my back, sending another whisper of cold magic into me, then sat back.

"Done. Just touch here and think about activating the spell." He brushed a cool finger over a black swirl at the top of my left shoulder. "As long as you have a hand on Lilith when you activate it, it won't matter if she pushes you away. The spell will be locked on her. You just have to pump in enough power to break through her defenses without burning up."

"Gee, it sounds so easy when you say it," I said, not even trying to hide the sarcasm in my voice.

"There's nothing easy about it." Sebastian groaned and bowed his head. "Now get out of here."

I rehooked my bra and reached for my bloody T-shirt with its four claw holes. "Please tell me I can get another one of these. New cargo pants as well would be great."

I really didn't want to put the dirty shirt back on. It was bad enough I'd had to wear my dirty bra and undies. But I couldn't go walking around the halls without a shirt even if it seemed we were the only ones down here, so I pulled it on and stood.

Jacob stood with me, taking my hand in his, and we stepped into the hall. Gideon followed, falling into step on my other side, and Kol drew up close behind me, his body heat radiating against my back.

Their emotions were a mix of worry, desire, and heartache, so I gathered a little of my angelic magic—still not close to being recovered from healing Kol—and pushed my love for them through our bonds.

Kol drew in a sharp breath. His surprise and awe at feeling love made me smile. Gideon turned his gorgeous blue gaze on me, while Jacob's grip on my hand tightened.

"I love you, too," Jacob whispered, his voice that deep rumble that made my soul's vibration align with his.

Forty feet down the hall, the door to our room opened and Marcus stormed out in only a pair of cargo pants hanging low on his hips. Water dripped from his wet hair, trailing a sensual runnel over his chest and making my breath stall. God, he was sexy. All the blood that had caked his skin was gone, and only a red ugly scar the size of my fist lying too close to his heart proved he'd nearly died.

I froze and his piercing green gaze jerked to me, as if he instantly knew where I was. The feralness in his eyes was stronger than before, brutal, as if he could rip me to shreds with just a look.

The temperature jumped to sweltering, sweat instantly slicking my body, but with his hard, ferocious expression, I was certain the heat wasn't desire but rage. We might be mated, but that didn't mean what I'd done to him was forgivable. I'd taken away his humanity and turned him into a demon. He wasn't a despised monster like me, the world didn't hate him, but I didn't know if he'd see it that way.

His stance widened. A whisper of hellfire flared in his eyes and his breath picked up.

"Hey, Marcus," Jacob said, his voice calm and even.

But Marcus growled, his gaze never leaving mine, and he stormed toward me.

Oh, shit.

CHAPTER 20

I squared my shoulders. Marcus's rage seared my skin, every ounce of him radiating deadly ferocity. "I did what I had to do."

"I know," he snarled, picking up his pace.

"Marcus." Gideon stepped in front of me, and Marcus shoved him aside, tossing him into the wall with a resounding crack.

His hands dug into my biceps and he slammed me against the wall, crashing his mouth against mine. I gasped, surprised, and he devoured my breath, kissing me with a wildness that made my senses reel, blazing through me until every nerve was on fire, desperate and needing.

With a snarl, he grabbed my hair, painfully digging his fingers into my scalp, and yanked my head back to deepen the kiss. A whisper of Kol's magic slid into me, turning the pain to delicious pleasure, and I groaned into Marcus's mouth.

He growled back and ripped open the front of my T-shirt with the claws of his free hand. My breath picked up as he shoved his fingers inside my bra and clenched my breast.

His erection ground against me, his need for me over-whelming, and another whisper of Kol's magic twisted the pain into pleasure.

"Marcus." Gideon grabbed Marcus's shoulder.

"Mine," he snarled against my lips, his body trembling as if he were struggling to restrain himself. "You have to know you're still mine and I still want you."

"But I hurt you. Again."

"And you're an idiot to think I won't still love you."

"But all that pain—"

"You saved me. And I knew you wouldn't just take my word for it. We don't share a brand. So I'm cutting to the chase and *showing* you exactly how I feel," he said, his wolf — or rather *beast* darkening his eyes, straining to take over, his rage actually a wild, uncontrolled primal passion. "We both have to show you."

Kol snorted. "Perhaps you could show her in our room. Not out in the hall. You know I'm all for a good display of public indecency, but I'm not sure about Essie and I'm certain this one—" He jerked his thumb at Gideon. "—would hate it."

Jacob unlocked our door and held it open. "We'll give you the room."

"Only if that's what you want," Marcus said to me, not a hint of hesitation or regret in his voice or a change in his searing emotions. "I love *all* of you. Everything you are. Angel and demon and multiple soul bonds. Don't get me wrong, I'll never say no to just the two of us, but I won't say no to anything else."

We only had two hours until the unification ceremony and while I wanted to let Marcus show me that I'd been an idiot to think he'd hate me, I wanted to spend every minute I had left with all my guys.

"I want all of you."

With a growl, Marcus grabbed my hips and urged me up. I wrapped my legs around him and he captured my lips in another breathtaking kiss as he carried me into the hotel room. The rest of the guys followed and I motioned to Jacob.

"Let's get you closer to full."

Marcus turned us and pinned me against Jacob, who brushed my hair away from my neck and pressed his lips against my vein.

My breath hitched, half in anticipation and half in fear. The last time Jacob had bitten me, I'd almost lost my mind.

Jeez. What was wrong with me? I loved the feel of Jacob's magic. Really. But I couldn't seem to push back the memory of what had happened.

"Essie." Kol drew up close and met my gaze, the hellfire in his eyes blazing. "I've got you."

His magic slid into me, melting my fear, and Jacob sank his fangs into my neck. I gasped at the pain and Kol's power grew until Jacob took a gentle pull and flooded me with his seductive magic.

Marcus deepened our kiss and his grip on my butt tightened, his passion fueling mine and adding to the aching need inside me. Another pull on my vein and Jacob's magic twisted tighter.

But my breath picked up, and the fear returned. What if I couldn't release it? What if it built up beyond what I could handle again?

Which was ridiculous. My guys had me. They'd never let it go that far again, and it hadn't been their fault in the first place.

"Hey." Kol gave Marcus a look, and Marcus jerked away with a snarl, his emotions fighting with his beast to give me what I needed even if that meant it wasn't him.

Jacob wrapped an arm around my waist, pulling me tighter against his massive chest and supporting my wobbly legs, and Kol drew close. He kissed me, slowly, sensually, making my head spin, then trailed his lips down my body. He sucked each nipple into a tight peak, drawing all my focus to his mouth on me and away from Jacob's mouth on my neck. With a low hum of pleasure that radiated to my core, he sank lower and slid my pants and underwear down my legs.

Jacob took another bone-melting pull and his magic spun tighter as Kol's lips trailed up my thigh, weaving his magic into Jacob's and sinking both of their powers into me with a seductive, sultry need. I gasped as Kol's tongue brushed me, then I melted into the pleasure of his hot mouth on me. It was glorious the rasp of his tongue, his hands clutching my hips to keep me in place, and his magic combined with Jacob's throbbing inside me.

Kol caressed and licked as Jacob slid a hand to my breast, his magic spinning tighter and tighter, until I was drowning in sensation.

My orgasm crashed into me, sudden and hard, stealing all breath and thought, before I fully realized what had happened. My knees gave way completely, and Jacob tightened his grip, securing me against his muscular chest, his healing magic warming my neck.

Kol's grip on my hips tightened, the only sign my release had affected him, and he slowly brushed his tongue against my clit, drawing out shuddering aftershocks as Marcus stepped close again. He grabbed my chin and turned my head to capture me with a searing, possessive kiss.

The heat of his desire blazed across my already heated skin, and Kol worked me back up to squirming, desperate need with his tongue. I wrapped my arms around Marcus's neck, needing him closer, needing to feel his ferocity driving inside me.

Kissing me breathless, he pulled me from Jacob's arms. Darkness and hellfire and wild desire filled Marcus's eyes. He threw me on the bed, grabbed my ankles, and yanked me to the edge close to him. His gaze locked with mine, the question in his eyes. Did I want this? His beast had more control than he did and there wasn't going to be anything gentle or slow about this.

Just the thought made me throb, aching for all his ferocity focused on me. "Yes." *Oh, yes please.*

With a snarl, he seized my hips and thrust into me, plunging in all the way to the hilt.

A ripple of an orgasm swept through me, my muscles clamping around him already on the verge of release again.

The hellfire in his eyes burned brighter, and his canines extended into fangs. Little wisps of demonic magic curled from his hands and forearms and sank into my skin with glorious, searing sparks.

He pulled out and thrust back in again, hard.

Oh, fuck, yes.

The muscles in his sculpted arms and shoulders flexed as he controlled my body, pounding into me with a wildness that stole my breath. I was awed at how powerful he was and on fire with need. Even without a brand, I could feel the strength of our soul bond blazing in my chest, surging with his love and desire.

Gideon settled on the bed above me, hooked his finger under my chin, and urged my head back. For a second, time stalled and there was only him and his strong, sure love, then Marcus slammed back into me, twisting my desire tighter, and Gideon kissed me. He devoured each gasping cry of pleasure, making love to my mouth slowly, sensually, as Marcus drove me to climax.

The orgasm ripped through me, shooting stars behind my lids and making my head spin. Moments later, Marcus growled and tensed with his own release, his erection pulsing inside me and making me clench tighter around him.

Gideon paused for a second, his lips brushing mine, letting me catch my breath, and the weight on the bed between my legs changed. Large strong hands slid over my hips and along my ribcage to my breasts. Jacob. His erection brushed my wet swollen entrance and I squirmed, my desire picking up again.

Oh, yes, please.

Kol chuckled. He lay on the bed beside me, the hellfire in his eyes so strong it licked his cheeks, his expression blissfully dazed.

"Can't hide anything from you," I said, my voice low and husky.

"You never could before and now I'm free to enjoy it." He nudged Jacob's hand aside and flicked his tongue over my already sensitive nipple.

Oh, yes. I tipped my head back, and Gideon deepened our kiss as Jacob rubbed his tip against my opening. God, I wanted Jacob in me, filling me, but he captured my hips and held me in place, teasing me with his tip as Kol sucked my nipple into his hot mouth.

Gideon palmed my other breast and Jacob slid slowly— so damned slowly—into me, filling me completely. Kol increased the pull on my nipple, twisting pleasure and pain again with his magic, driving me wild, and Gideon commanded my mouth. With a groan, Jacob withdrew just as slowly, drawing out the sensation, then pushed back in.

I writhed against their grips, my senses on overload, their mouths and hands and bodies searing me with their desire. Every nerve, every cell, hell, my whole essence was on fire with need.

Jacob pushed back in again and tightened his grip on my hips, and Gideon and Kol pulled away. With one fluid movement, he rolled us over so I straddled him, and our gazes locked. The depth of his passion swelled through our brand, solid and eternal, and he tangled his fingers in my hair and pulled me down to kiss him.

I melted into his embrace, his hips still rolling in a slow sensual rhythm, sliding his erection out to the tip and driving back in, each thrust drawing out as much pleasure as possible.

Then Kol's hot slicked fingers caressed my back entrance, and my pulse leaped. I had no idea where he'd gotten the lube, but he was an incubus. It shouldn't have surprised me. His fingers teased me, testing my interest, drawing glorious tremors of pleasure and making me gasp.

My breath picked up even faster. The idea of both of them inside me, filling me, almost made me come again right there, but Kol snapped a thread of magic into me and stole my climax, taking me back to the aching edge without letting me crash over.

I groaned, and he slowly pushed his finger into me. Jacob kept his rhythm, and with his thumb rubbed circles over my clit as Kol stretched me, adding another finger, drawing out the anticipation.

God, I ached for him, for more. I almost cried in grief at the loss of the glorious pressure when he pulled out his fingers, but he pressed his thick, slick tip against me, and the cry turned into a moan.

He pushed inside, turning that first moment of pain into

sultry pleasure with his magic. Jacob held steady for me, his thumb skimming my clit, keeping me on the edge until Kol was buried deep, his hips flush with me. It was almost too much to bear, the pleasure mixed with pressure mixed with Kol's bone-melting magic.

"Jesus, Essie," Kol gasped, running his hands up my chest and teasing my nipples. "You feel so good."

Panting, I leaned back into him and gave in, riding their rhythm, my skin growing more and more sensitive with each swell of Kol's power. Every caress of Jacob's thumb or pinch of Kol's fingers or stroke deep inside me spun my desire tighter and tighter. My body was on fire, teetering on the edge of climax. Their rhythm grew faster, turning my breath to gasping moans. Then Jacob tensed with his climax, and my body shuddered, my orgasm swelling in response.

Kol surged a mind-blowing blast of magic into me, and all of my muscles contracted. His grip around me tightened, pulling me close, and he gasped my name, his breath hot in my ear. Bliss crashed over me, shattering me. It was the most amazing feeling, coming with two of my guys inside me, their love and satisfaction coursing through our brands.

I didn't know how long we stayed connected, but too soon, Kol was pulling out and easing me onto Jacob's massive chest. He wrapped his arms around me, and I drew in deep ragged breaths.

"Holy fuck, guys."

Kol flashed me a wicked, satisfied grin and Jacob gave a contented sigh as Gideon stretched out beside me, a whisper of electric power crackling through our brand. He drew me from Jacob's arms into his, and kissed me in his slow, sensual style, drawing out every second, his hard erection digging into the crux between my thigh and torso. Oh so close and oh so far away from where I wanted it.

"You're so beautiful," he murmured against my lips. "I love the way you look when you come."

"Then make me come," I said back, my voice breathy.

"As my mate commands." He settled between my legs, his gaze never leaving mine, and thrust inside me.

The force of his invasion and the intensity in his summer-sky eyes surprised me. His desire for me was just as fierce as my other guys, his love just as sure, but was more reserved than the others. Funny how he was the one I'd been the most afraid of, the one I feared would never accept me, and all I could see in his eyes and feel from his brand was unconditional love.

He trembled, holding himself still, and the anticipation, waiting for him to move, to do anything, twisted my need tighter until I was squirming.

With a breathtaking smile, he dipped down, kissed me, and started to move inside me. His rhythm was slow and powerful, building my desire until I was writhing and gasping underneath him.

The light in the core of my being flared, resonating with the light in his, and all my brands lit up. I could feel all of their love, and the certainty that we belonged together. Fate hadn't led us astray. This was destiny, and even if I'd wanted to fight it, I couldn't.

Gideon's thrusts grew faster, whirling me closer and closer to a climax not just fueled by physical sensation but emotions as well.

Then he tensed, his climax tearing through him, and mine slammed into me a second later, hard and fast, drawing a scream and shattering me again.

My essence and soul spun on light and bliss, and I was

no longer a being of flesh, but one of pure glorious sensation.

After a moment to catch our breaths, Gideon withdrew from me and shifted to draw me onto his chest. Marcus stretched out in front of me and pressed the length of his body against mine, even with Gideon's arm between us, as if he needed as much flesh-to-flesh contact as possible. Kol curled above me, his forehead against the top of my head, his eyes glazed over, and Jacob lay at my feet, his big hand just above my knees between my thighs.

I drifted on boneless pleasure with their bonds—all of their bonds, not just the branded ones—radiating love, satisfaction, and certainty.

I could stay this way forever. I wanted this forever. But if we hid away from the world, Lilith would destroy it, and no matter how much I craved my guys and being satiated like this, none of us could allow Lilith to restart Michael's war.

My love for my men swelled, filling my chest, but so too did my fear.

Please, God. Don't let me lose any of them.

CHAPTER 21

A GENTLE KNOCK ON THE DOOR WOKE ME, AND GIDEON'S GRIP around me tightened as Marcus groaned, his breath feathering warm across the back of my neck.

"I know you're sealing bonds and all that," Cassius said, "but you're out of time. We have to go."

"Fuck," Marcus growled.

Kol mumbled something and a trickle of his magic swept through me, making me gasp.

"Fuck," Marcus said again, his voice raspy, his erection hard against my thigh. "Do you have to make that sound, Essie?"

"Blame Kol," I said as another trickle teased me. "He hasn't got full control of his magic."

"Still?" Jacob asked, his hand sliding higher up my inner thigh, although I suspected he wasn't fully awake, either. "He sent a big surge through the soul bonds before we passed out."

"A couple of surges," Marcus added.

Cassius knocked again. "Anyone? I have clean clothes for Shaw."

Gideon groaned, sat up, and gave Kol a shake, waking him.

"What?" Kol asked, his words slurred.

"You're going to need to bleed that off." Gideon slid off the bed, found his pants in a pile of clothes on the floor, and pulled them on.

"Yeah, sure," Kol said, rolling away from me and drawing in a shuddering breath. "I never thought this would be my problem."

"Who'd have thought we'd find an incubus's limit on sexual energy," Jacob said with a chuckle.

"Only because our soul bonds make everything more powerful." Kol squeezed his eyes shut and more magic swept through me.

A mini orgasm clenched my muscles and I moaned, grinding against Marcus.

"I like this." Marcus pulled me closer and kissed me, his beast's hellfire flickering in his eyes.

I liked it, too, but we didn't have time for more. If we didn't move now, Lilith would kill a lot of innocent people.

With a groan, I eased away from Marcus. Once we'd stopped Lilith, then we could spend all day in bed... because we were all unemployed... and fugitives.

Which was a problem for another day.

Cassius handed off a bag of clothes through a crack in the door just wide enough for the bag without letting him see all of us naked in bed, and Gideon tossed the bag to me. No underwear. Swell. I put my dirty bra and undies back on, and pulled on the clean T-shirt and cargo pants as the rest of the guys dressed as well

Kol still leaked sensual magic that heated my skin and made Marcus stand distractingly close, but it wasn't unmanageable, and his eyes were starting to clear. Thank goodness, because I didn't feel good about letting him go into a fight high.

We strode into the hall where Cassius waited. His angel glow flared when he saw us, and his emotions swirled in a strange mix before settling on fear.

"Voth has Berettas and M4s for anyone who wants them. He also has vests," he said, shoving away from the wall and leading us down the hall toward the clinic and the door to the loading docks.

"We'll take whatever he's got," Gideon said as we hurried into the loading bay. "Anything magical that might be useful?"

Voth, standing at an open locker filled with tactical gear and weapons, looked at us. "The only thing magical I have to offer is this." He held up a glowing marble that looked a lot like the marble imbued with my light magic that we'd used to buy the area containment master ward.

"Is that my power?" I asked. I was still low, so any extra magic would help. Especially if I was going to need everything I had to reimprison Lilith.

He shrugged and handed it to me, as if he wasn't just giving up an extremely expensive power source. "Thought it might be helpful."

The marble warmed my palm, resonating with me even though Sebastian had stripped all of my essence from it before we'd handed it over.

"You're not radiating a lot of power now," Voth said.

I glanced at Kol, who nodded his agreement and took a pair of sheathed knives the length of my forearm out of the locker. So far, I was still managing to contain my power, but I didn't know how easy it would be once I'd recharged.

"Cassius told me your terrible plan. I'd wait until the cage spell is activated and I'd gotten away from Lilith before reabsorbing your power. If you absorb it now, it'll be harder for you to hide it from her."

"And Lilith won't be able to sense the marble?" I asked, pocketing the marble.

"Not unless it's awakened or absorbed." Voth pulled two bulletproof vests out of the locker and handed them to Gideon, who handed one to me.

"I can't." No matter how much I wanted to take a vest and a Beretta. "I can't look like I'm ready to fight. I have to look like I've given in and want to join her."

Marcus growled and Kol tensed.

"This plan just keeps getting worse." Cassius threw his hands up and strode to the front of the loading bay by the security door.

"It's the only way she'll get close," Jacob said.

The muscles in Gideon's jaw tensed and he gave the vest back to Voth.

Yeah, I didn't like it either.

"The SUV is parked outside," Voth said. "I'll give you fifteen minutes then call in the anonymous Lucifer sighting. I also have business I have to take care of, but I'll come as soon as I can." He tossed Cassius a set of keys and strode back into the hotel, passing Amiah who stood in the doorway.

She stared at us, her arms crossed, her expression icy and her fear chilling the air and churning in my stomach. Her gaze darted to Marcus, who was putting on a vest, and a whisper of heartache curled around me before she jerked her attention back to Gideon as he walked over to Cassius.

Jacob belted on a pair of Berettas, drew close, and pressed his large hand against the small of my back. "Are you ready?"

"Nope. But I don't think I'll ever be ready to reimprison my mother the Hellfire Queen."

"I really hope I don't regret this," Cassius growled, and he strode out the door.

We followed him to a silver SUV parked just outside the loading bay door. It wasn't as spacious as a JP vehicle and didn't have a third row of seats, but it was big enough for all six of us if Jacob sat in the back, so it would do the trick.

Fear from my guys chilled me inside and out even in the sweltering SUV, which had clearly been sitting out in the summer sun all morning, but they all kept their expressions tight. If I hadn't been an empath, I wouldn't have known just how worried they were. And I didn't know if that made me feel better or not.

I shifted, unable to keep still as we drove out of the Quarter to Unity Park. Marcus, who sat beside me, squeezed my knee, drawing my attention. His wolf lay just under the surface, a prick of hellfire flickering in his piercing green eyes and sending a mixed shudder of desire and worry down my spine.

"You can call this off any time you want."

"You know I can't." I leaned in and kissed him, savoring the feel of his lips against mine.

Kol, on my other side, shifted closer, and Jacob, sitting in the back, reached over the seats and pressed his big palm against the back of my neck.

Gideon glanced back, the light in his eyes dim with worry, before he sucked in a quick breath and squared his shoulders. "Okay. Essie needs to convince Lilith to trust her long enough to get within grabbing distance. That means we need to stay out of sight. No matter what."

Cassius shot him at hard look. "I really hate this."

"We all do," Jacob said.

"I'll get to her as fast as I can. Hopefully we can get to her before she starts anything."

"There's another word I hate." Cassius stopped at a stop light, his knee nervously bouncing as he waited for it to change. "Might and hopefully. This is a terrible plan."

"You can stay in the SUV," Kol said.

"You know I can't," Cassius snapped back.

The light turned green and Cassius sped through the intersection, faster than the speed limit, but not so fast we'd get pulled over. I was actually impressed that his need to protect lives was stronger than the angelic urge to follow the rules. But then, he was Gideon's brother and more emotionally volatile than Gideon, so maybe it shouldn't have surprised me.

"This is the best plan we've got," Gideon said. "We should park on the far side of the park and make our entrance from there."

"Agreed." Cassius took a corner a little too fast, squealing the wheels, and slowed down a bit. "It'll take a little longer to get to the ceremony's location, but we're less likely to be spotted by any supers."

I didn't like the sound of that. Once again we were leaving our vehicle farther away than I liked and this time we didn't have anyone who could teleport us to safety. But I couldn't argue against it. Better to be farther away than caught before I could even get close to Lilith.

Ten minutes later, Cassius parked at the far end of Unity Park. The tension in the SUV, and the power slipping from my guys with their worry, squeezed my chest, making it hard to breathe.

Kol and I jumped out of the vehicle before it had even come to a full stop, and I sucked in deep gasps of the hot, humid air, sweat instantly slicking my skin.

"Sorry," Marcus mumbled.

Jacob and Gideon gave us apologetic looks, and Cassius gave us a tight nod.

I glanced at the blazing sun. The clock in the SUV had said 3:26 p.m., and the sun still sat high in the sky. With the heat and no clouds, it was a perfect day for an outside ceremony—if possibly a little too hot—and that meant a lot of people would be in attendance.

Gideon and Cassius headed to the path leading into the park, and the rest of us followed. The trees were thicker here than the other side of the park, not so thick you couldn't see through them, but certainly offering better cover. We were a quarter of a way around Unity Lake from the wide, level green space where the ceremony was being held—which was about a hundred yards from where I'd tumbled to a stop after being shot.

I strained to see any sign of Lilith and her witches, but couldn't see or sense anything beyond the slight press of power from my guys and an even slighter pressure from the supers gathered up ahead for the ceremony. No crushing power from Lilith and not a hint of the inky magic inside me.

Were we wrong? Was she going to attack some place else? Was the inky magic gone?

No. I couldn't even pretend that I'd managed to push out her inky worship magic when I'd released my primal scream behind Voth's hotel, and I could only pray I'd be able to hold onto the connection in my brands and keep the inky magic from seizing my body and soul long enough to cast the cage spell.

And Lilith's plan had to be to attack the ceremony. It was the most logical, biggest statement. It had to be.

"Cassius, you, Jacob, and Kol go left," Gideon said. "Marcus, you're with me. Cover Essie and keep your eyes open for JP agents. If Voth timed this right, they should show up in about five minutes."

And me, I was to head straight down the path and draw everyone's attention.

Gideon grabbed my wrist and pulled me close. "If you don't think you can cast the spell, pull out."

"Do you honestly think we'll get another chance?" I asked.

"I don't care." Determination and fear sparked an electric zap through our brand, reminding me that we shared a soul bond and our lives were irrevocably entwined. "You pull out."

I wanted to argue with him, but if anything happened to me, all four of them were lost. Even Marcus. Sure, we didn't share a brand, but I had no doubt his soul would be just as damaged as if he did.

"You have my word." I leaned in, rose on my toes, and kissed him. "Stay safe."

"We need to get moving," Cassius said.

Gideon pulled away, his reluctance to leave me twisting my insides.

The guys hurried off the trail and wove in between the trees, not out of sight, but less obvious, and I carried on down the path. I didn't believe for a second that Lilith would think I'd left them behind, but we were betting it all that me being out in the open and not them would buy us enough time for me to get close enough to touch her.

I picked up my pace, jogging down the path and straining for even the slightest hint that Lilith and her witches were here, my nerves getting tighter and tighter the closer I got to the lake.

Given the time, the ceremony had already started and I

only had four minutes to go before they reached the signing of the unification treaty part of the ceremony. If we were right, Lilith was waiting for the most dramatic moment—the signing of the treaty—to make her entrance.

As I drew closer, I caught bits of the mayor's speech, his voice carrying through the park on the loudspeakers, talking about the grim days when humanity thought all hope was lost. Too many angels and humans had already been slaughtered and Michael had just unveiled his terrible new army of monstrous nephilim.

I shuddered, the grief and horror from the crowd creeping into me even though I was still a fair distance away and my angelic magic was low. And I couldn't blame them. It had only been about twenty years since Gabriel had killed Michael, and the nephilim had been vicious. They hadn't cared for any life, because Michael's whole plan had been to exterminate everyone. Even I was horrified when I watched the videos of what they'd done. But then how did I convince anyone who didn't have a soul bond with me that I wasn't a monster?

My thoughts tripped over that. I still wanted this to work out, to be accepted. I wanted my guys to not have to face a life as fugitives when they'd devoted so much of their lives to upholding the law and protecting people.

And while Cassius, Amiah, and Sebastian trusted me, or seemed to, they'd seen my determination to protect people before they'd known the truth. No one else, when they saw me now, would believe I wasn't a monster. There'd never been a nephilim who hadn't been one, and everyone thought it was the magic that created us that made us evil, not Michael.

I shoved those thoughts aside.

Deal with Lilith, then the rest of the world. And I wasn't

even going to hope anyone would be grateful if me and my guys actually stopped her.

The path curled down a hill and around the squat, red brick public bathrooms. I hurried around the corner just as the crush of enormous pressure pounded into me and the inky magic roared back to life, calling and cajoling and oozing.

I stumbled and caught my balance before I crashed face first to the ground.

Shit.

The mayor started screaming, high-pitched panicked cries that carried over the loudspeaker.

Shit shit shit.

I still had over two hundred yards to go and I couldn't even see the ceremony. The time for a cautious approach was over.

I focused on my brands and my soul's connection to Gideon, Jacob, and Kol, and raced down the path. The pressure from Lilith, her witches, and the gathered supers up ahead swelled, and a blast of smoke shot up from behind the trees where the ceremony's greenspace was. The mayor's screams grew louder, more desperate, and now I could hear others yelling and crying as well, even though they weren't crying into a microphone.

The familiar *thu-thud* of power from a witch casting a spell crushed inside me, threatening my balance again, but I gritted my teeth and kept going.

Another *thu-thud* and another. The magical pressure continued to grow, squeezing until I couldn't draw a full breath and my lungs burned.

I raced past the trees to the edge of the lawn and staggered to a stop, the air freezing around me, covering my arms and cheeks with frost. People screamed and ran, knocking over each other and the white foldout chairs for the important city leaders and the elderly. A toddler screamed for his mommy and a guy picked him up and bolted away. I didn't know if the man was related to the kid, but he was going in the right direction: away from the danger.

Lilith stood at the front on a small stage, red demonic mist whipping around her in a wild vortex, the hellfire in her eyes dripping sparks that hissed when they hit the stage floor. The air around her shimmered as if she stood in the middle of a parking lot on this hot summer's afternoon and not in the park, and the mayor cowered on his knees, his face red and dripping sweat, the mic still clutched in his hand catching every gasping whimper.

A dozen glyph witches with tattoos covering their right arms attacked those fleeing, forcing them back toward the stage with shadow swords and pressure waves and blasts of fire, into the grasps of more witches who snapped shadow whip after whip around the bystanders' necks. They ensnared human and super alike, until each witch had easily captured a dozen people. Half a dozen bat-winged witches lobbed blasts of shadows from the sky, and Lilith cackled, her eyes wild.

The pressure of power grew the closer I got to the fray, and so did the swell of inky magic. If I let it in, I'd be able to stop this. I'd be powerful. I'd be worshiped. I'd—

I skidded to a halt fifty feet from the edge of the chaos.

Lilith threw her head back and raised her hands. Magic pounded in my chest, stealing my breath, and everyone with a whip around their neck screamed. Most collapsed to their knees, a few larger supers staggered a few steps closer to Lilith then collapsed, and another *thu-thud* of power wrenched at my very soul. She was draining their essences, gaining more power. I could feel the pull of the spell even though it hadn't leeched onto me. No one with a whip around their neck stood a chance.

"I see you've come to my party." Lilith's burning gaze jerked to me and her lips curled back in a wicked smile. With a hiss, she flicked her wrist and her whirling demonic mist swept toward me.

CHAPTER 22

I FORCED MYSELF TO TAKE A STEP FORWARD AND LET LILITH'S power curl around me. It burned where it touched my flesh, leaving angry red welts, and sank inside me. It made the inky magic surge and strained my hold on my connection with my guys.

"And here I thought I'd have to go looking for you when I was done with this," she said, her voice dark. "It's always nice when your toys come back without an effort."

I squared my shoulders. "I'm more than just a toy."

And you could be a goddess if you let me in.

No.

One of the witches snapped a shadow whip at me. I jerked my hand up on instinct and a blast of red demonic magic shot from my palm and ripped through the whip. The witch's eyes flashed wide and he shot a bigger whip at me.

I sent another blast of magic through that one as well, then twisted my power before it dissipated and slammed it into the witch's chest, knocking him off his feet.

Lilith watched with narrowed eyes. I couldn't tell what she was thinking from her hard expression, or feel what she was feeling through the frozen fear of everyone else. I could only pray I'd intrigued her enough to get close.

The people around me screamed, their fear thickening the frost on my arms despite the summer's heat, while bursts of pleasure from the glyph witches churned my stomach. I needed to get close. Now. The guys wouldn't do anything until I started the spell and they were probably feeling just as sickened as me.

"I'm your weapon," I said, striding past the witch I'd knocked over. "Your right hand.'

She raised a sculpted black eyebrow and the fire witch turned to face her, as if he'd sensed she wanted his attention. He wore dark shorts and a white T-shirt, blending in perfectly with the people attending the unification ceremony. With the exception of the tattoo on his arm, which gave him an edgier appearance, he looked like an ordinary guy.

He tossed the man he was holding into the arms of another witch and stepped into my path.

"You're not my right hand," Lilith said.

"Isn't that why you made me? You wanted the power of both an archangel and the Hellfire Queen at your side?"

The mayor gasped, his eyes growing even wider with his horror.

The churning in my stomach grew and my throat tightened. I'd never had anyone look at me like that. Sure, there'd been frustration, hate, and fear when I was a beat cop, but never absolute terror. Kol had been the closest when I'd triggered his PTSD, but his reaction had also been filled with rage.

God, I never wanted anyone to look at me like that, like I was a monster.

You're not a monster. You're a goddess, the inky magic

cooed, oozing against my soul, seeping in deeper and dragging my attention from Lilith.

I wrenched my gaze back to her—I didn't know when I'd looked away and I could only pray it hadn't been for long—and forced myself to sneer. The only way I'd get within touching distance of Lilith was if she believed I was just as evil as her.

And to do that, I needed to get the fire witch out of the way as fast as possible before this turned into a real fight. Please let a preemptive strike catch him off guard.

I shot a blast of demonic magic at the fire witch, but in the blink of an eye, he grabbed a tattoo on his arm and hissed the words to activate it. His magic thudded and flames raced through my mist, burning it up just before it reached him.

Shit.

"You're going to have to do better than that if you want to be my right hand," Lilith said.

Shit shit shit. I couldn't afford to get into a magical pissing contest with this guy. I needed everything I had to cast the cage spell.

Unless you let me in.

The fire witch matched my sneer.

A few feet away, a human woman with a shadow whip around her neck collapsed to the ground, her eyes wide and vacant. My pulse stalled. She was dead. They were draining these people to death. Lilith had no intention of taking prisoners to drain and redrain.

"You know my potential." I slowed my pace, now only thirty feet from the fire witch and sixty from the stage. The air was so hot from Lilith's power, it was difficult to breathe, and sweat plastered my T-shirt to my body. How the hell did

I convince her to accept me before anyone else died? "Do you honestly believe I won't surpass him? I've had demonic magic for less than twenty-four hours and I've already started to control it."

The fire witch slid his hand higher up his arm and touched a different tattoo, and time stuttered into slow motion. Two more people nearby collapsed. A woman with the feral eyes of a shifter wrenched free of a shadow whip, transformed into a tiger, and leaped at her assailant. All around me people continued to scream and die and the *thu-thud* of the witches' power pounded again and again inside me.

God damn it. I didn't want to waste power.

But if I didn't make a decisive move against this fire witch, Lilith would never let me get close. The only positive was that the witch couldn't create a massive ball of fire around me without killing the people Lilith wanted to power up from.

And no, I wasn't letting the inky magic inside. Its promises were lies. It would possess me—

Shit. The inky magic was as powerful as it had been in Lilith's lab when it had possessed my body. Lilith might not have my soul, but if she could already control me... unless of course Kol's brand had developed enough that adding it to the other two now helped to protect me.

The fire witch opened his mouth to cast whatever spell had been tattooed in his skin.

This needed to end now.

His magic thu—

I wrenched my hand up, clinging to the connection with my guys to keep the inky magic at bay and focusing on the core of power inside me. Heat and light burst from my palm and a blast of divine light—the last of my divine light until it replenished—slammed into him with all the force I could muster. He flew back, crashing into the side of the stage and taking out all the legs on that end.

Lilith hopped off as the stage collapsed and strode toward me, the hellfire in her eyes flaring.

"Teach me," I said. "I'll be your sword, your vengeance on all who refuse to worship you."

Her wicked smile deepened and the mayor, lying on top of the broken stage, whimpered.

The fire witch crawled to his hands and knees and I hit him with a blast of demonic magic—trying to hold back as much power as possible and yet still send him tumbling.

"I might look like *him*," I said. "But I'm also half yours."

"That you are."

Just one more step. That was all I needed to get within grabbing distance. But God, it felt like I was standing in the middle of an inferno.

I fought to keep my expression hard and concentrated on twisting my demon power tight. I couldn't let her realize just how much power I had—

Which won't be enough.

It will. It had to be because I wasn't going to get another chance to do this.

She held out her hand to me. "Be my highest disciple, daughter."

Behind me, someone yelled, but it didn't sound like a cry of fear or pain. It sounded like a battle cry.

Lightning shot toward us, and Lilith wrenched her hand away and redirected the blast into the ground at our feet.

JP agents from the late-night cafeteria meeting, along with Zuri and Regan, barreled across the lawn toward us, and above flew the Director and the four other angels, their massive white wings brilliant in the summer sun.

"You know the JP won't stop me," she said as the Director threw another bolt of lightning toward us.

"I didn't bring them."

"Oh, no? I saw you wearing their letters when you first entered my temple." The inky magic swelled in my muscles, but my hold on my brands kept it from possessing me. Adding Kol had been enough to help me.

With a snarl, she twisted her demonic magic around my neck and hauled me up until my toes skimmed the ground, even though she stood a few feet away.

Fear sliced through my chest, radiating from my brands, and I fought to break free from Lilith's grip. We couldn't risk my guys being noticed before I'd cast the spell. Except I wasn't sure I'd be able to get within arm's reach now.

I gasped, trying to breathe, and clawed at her mist, but my fingers kept sweeping through it while it still clenched tight. "I didn't bring them. I swear," I said, trying one last time to convince her. "They betrayed me. They learned what I was and turned on me."

"They'll always turn on you, because they fear your power," she hissed, stepping closer.

Just another step. Please. God.

"I'm yours. I swear."

Her gaze drilled into mine as if she could see into my soul and she shifted closer.

Just a little more. If I strained, I might be able to reach her.

"You made me," I gasped. "I was always destined to be yours."

The Director dove toward us and Lilith's attention jerked up. A massive wave of power exploded from her, stealing what little breath I had left, and slamming the Director and the other angels into the ground.

Darkness swarmed my vision. I had to grab her now before I suffocated and passed out.

I heaved against her magic and grabbed her arm, the heat radiating from her flesh burning my hand. With a scream, I slapped my other hand to my shoulder and imagined the cage spell bursting to life. Power exploded within me, blazing through every cell in my body, and crackled around Lilith with blue-white lightning.

She screamed, and a massive blast of power tossed me across the grass. Specks of light and darkness snapped across my vision, and the inky magic surged, determined to take over.

I fought to breathe and keep hold of my connections through my brands and the cage spell.

The witches dropped their shadow whips and barreled toward me, as the JP agents reached the green and entered the fray.

My guys and Cassius bolted out from wherever they'd been hiding, Gideon striking the witch closest to me with his divine light. Kol killed the witch closest to him before I'd fully registered that he'd drawn one of his blades and was on the next witch an instant later. Red demonic mist burst around Marcus's arms and his fingers extended into claws, and Jacob fired four quick shots, taking out two more witches, while Cassius created a fire whip and yanked another witch to the ground.

The Director staggered to his feet and screamed orders to arrest all of us, his gaze filled with rage and locked on me.

But his rage wasn't as terrifying as Lilith's. "You think you can cage me? You think you're strong enough to stop me? You're even more of a fool than your father."

I scrambled back. I didn't need to get to my feet to reimprison her, I just needed to grab the marble in my pocket, but Lilith blasted more power into me, slamming me into a tree trunk. My head snapped back and the specks of darkness in my vision thickened.

CHAPTER 23

THE CAGE SPELL WAVERED, SHUDDERING AROUND HER, threatening to melt away, and I mentally clenched at it, pushing more of my demonic magic into it.

"You're not stronger than me. You'll never be stronger." She jerked her hand and her magic crashed into me, burning into every cell and threatening my concentration.

The inky magic howled with laughter and surged, seizing my muscles. I couldn't breathe, could barely think.

The spell stuttered. I was going to lose it. I needed more magic, except I couldn't move to grab the marble.

I'll give you more power, the inky magic said, oozing against my essence. *Embrace me. Let me in.*

No.

You'd be stronger than her. You could replace her.

"I'm the Hellfire Queen," Lilith said. "The power of every full demon is mine to control." The cage spell's lightning sparked and sputtered, and she pointed at Kol.

He screamed and his body seized. Agonizing lightning exploded through our brand, and red mist erupted from his skin and poured into Lilith.

He crashed to the ground, writhing in pain, and for a moment, my mind jerked to him and only him. There was no fight, no spell, nothing but him, and the strength pouring out of me into him through our brand. He was dying. And fast. She was tearing the life out of him, and I had to save him. He couldn't die. *Please.*

Except the only way to save him was to stop Lilith.

With me, the inky magic cooed.

No. I ground my teeth against the inky magic's lure and the agony tearing through my brand, and strained to refocus on the spell. I pumped more of my demonic magic into it, the ball in the core of my being growing smaller and weaker by the second.

The spell flared around her but her powers swelled, ripping into the cage spell, as if my effort meant nothing.

It is nothing. Nothing compared to her.

"I'm the Hellfire Queen," she roared, and Marcus stumbled.

He screamed as the demonic mist curling around him swept to Lilith and his body jerked, forced into a painful, body-tearing shift. Now that he was past his transition, his shift should have been smooth, painless, but it was like he was still in transition, his bones crunching, his muscles and tendons ripping.

No. Please, no.

Embrace me. You could be the Hellfire Queen.

No. I'd just be the Hellfire Queen's pawn.

I needed to absorb the magic in the marble. It was my only chance.

I heaved against her power and she howled with laughter.

A blast of fire erupted nearby and bystanders, JP agents, and a few witches screamed. The Director shot lightning at the fire witch, knocking him to his knees, but the witches flying above barraged him with blasts of shadows before he could finish off the witch.

Gideon and Cassius sent fire and light up at them, while also trying to protect Kol and Marcus from the other witches, and Jacob had holstered his sidearms—likely out of rounds—and was tearing into more witches with his short, deadly claws.

Lilith clenched her hands and both Marcus and Kol screamed again. "You will bow to me or you will die."

"If I bow to you, I *will* die," I gasped.

"Bow to me,"

"Never." I strained against the inky magic's hold on my muscles to shove my hand into my pocket. The marble was my only hope. The cage spell was sucking up my demonic power. Soon I'd have nothing left and it didn't even look like Lilith was having problems.

Embrace me. Become a queen. Become a goddess.

No.

The spell stuttered.

You can't do it without me. Give in.

God, I wanted to. I could sense the strength of the inky magic, feel it waiting for me to welcome it in. In fact, it was already in. It had hooked into my soul when I'd been in the Cromer Building. All I had to do was embrace it.

"No," I gasped again.

"Then you get to watch them suffer," Lilith snarled, jerking her hand again. Her mist blasted into Jacob, tossing him into the center of the lawn and ripping off the bracelet embedded in his skin that protected him against sunlight.

His skin burst into flames and he screamed. More agony exploded from Jacob's brand, joining Kol's, and my muscles seized tighter, my hand at the opening of my pocket. More strength raced out of me into Jacob.

No. God, no! He couldn't die. I couldn't lose him. I had to save him, do something, God damn fucking do something.

I'm waiting, the inky magic taunted.

Gideon swore and bolted toward him, as Cassius stopped the three witches barreling toward him with a blazing wall of fire.

Jacob staggered toward the closest shade, his skin blackening, the flames fully engulfing him, the strength pouring out of me the only thing keeping him alive.

"He has such strength." Lilith's manic laugher grew. "Or is that yours? How much more can you take?"

Gideon grabbed Jacob despite the flames, and Lilith slammed a blast of demonic magic into Gideon's back with a resounding crack. He screamed and crumpled, taking Jacob down with him.

My whole right side was on fire with pain.

Cassius howled and bolted toward Gideon, but Lilith shot another blast and he went down, too.

"Do you think an angel with a broken back can fly?" she sneered. "Now I've got three of a kind to play with."

A witch shoved his shadow sword into Gideon's gut, not a killing blow, but still painful, and more strength poured from me into him. Jacob dragged himself into a shadow, his bulky body barely recognizable as human.

"I'm going to drain them and drain them and drain them again," Lilith said with a manic laugh. "And you're going to feel all of it until you give in to my will."

My soul wailed, the agony overwhelming.

All around us, people screamed and yelled. Half of the JP agents were battling the witches, the rest gathering around the Director, who stood in a patch of blackened grass, his lightning magic snapping around him.

I could barely think past the pain, barely keep the cage spell in my mind, and even that was starting to slip. The inky magic was going to take over and then all would be lost.

I was out of time. If I couldn't finish this spell, we were all dead.

With a scream, I moved my hand against the pain deeper into my pocket. My fingers brushed the marble, but Lilith snapped a blast of demonic mist at me. Her power ripped open my pocket and tossed me tumbling to the other side of the lawn. The marble landed on the grass at her feet, too far away from me to even try to scramble to it.

"Did you think this would be enough?" She clenched the marble. Light burst from between her fingers then vanished, and she opened her fingers and let the shattered remains of the marble fall into the grass.

Fuck. No.

I couldn't finish this without the marble.

You can finish it if you embrace me.

Wicked pleasure filled her eyes. She'd won and she knew it. There wasn't anything I could do to stop her.

Embrace me. Become a goddess. Be worshiped. Be feared.

A blast of lightning shot through Lilith's chest and sliced into my side. White agony stole my breath. The cage spell sputtered and the inky magic wormed its way deeper inside me.

Shit shit shit.

Lilith wrenched around to face the Director and the JP agents, all powerful supers, the hole in her chest sealing shut as she turned.

The ground was littered with bodies, both victims and witches, and less than half of her witches remained.

"It's over," the Director said.

She laughed at him. "It's just begun."

He wrenched his hand up and shot another blast of lightning at her. She twisted out of the way and the bolt sliced through my shoulder.

I screamed and panic shot through my brands.

Two JP agents with the feral intensity of shifters turned their fingers to claws and leaped at the closest witches, and the Director pressed his attack, shooting more lightning and barreling toward Lilith.

Another JP agent, a woman with glowing angel eyes, whipped a vortex of wind around Lilith, knocking her off balance, and another lightning blast cut through her chest. She stumbled and the cage spell swelled, Lilith's resistance weakening.

A moment of hope flickered through me before her power surged. I didn't have enough magic. Not even if the Director hurt her.

With a howl of rage, her demonic magic tore through the wind and she shot out a crushing blast of power. Everyone fell to their knees, screaming, including her witches. I fought to breathe. Another surge of power and her witches staggered to their feet, half of them attacking the Director and the agents while they were down, the others seizing my guys and Cassius.

She jerked toward me, her power building, the tattoos on all of her witches' arms glowing red.

"You're mine," she spat at me.

"Never."

The agent with the wind magic seized me with a powerful vortex and tossed me farther away from Lilith as the Director shot another blast of lightning at her, cutting into her.

The gash sealed shut and her gaze leaped over the chaos before wrenching back to me.

"You will submit. I'll torture your mates until you come crawling back to me." Her magic exploded with a chest-crushing *thud* into a massive teleportation spell. She vanished with a blinding flash of red light while light rushed from the witches' tattoos. Those holding my guys tightened their grip and her spell ripped into them, taking Cassius and my guys with them.

CHAPTER 24

I COLLAPSED TO THE GROUND, MY BODY TREMBLING, THE GUYS' agony still blazing through my brands, my strength pouring out of me into them. The inky magic threatened and begged, fighting my concentration on my brands—which only made me feel my guys' agony more—and the cage spell sputtered. I clutched at it, twisting it tight into the hollow core of my being, praying I could keep it active with what little magic I had left until I could figure out what the hell I was going to do.

Because I *was* going to do something. I was going to get my guys and end this before Lilith killed more people, and I was going to need the spell to do it.

The Director grabbed the front of my T-shirt, hauled me up, and slammed me against the tree, the force knocking the air from my lungs. The light from his eyes blazed and his lightning crackled with white-blue snaps over his forearms.

"Get her secured and into interrogation." He tossed me into the arms of two other JP agents that I recognized from the fight in the cafeteria. Both men had hellfire simmering in their eyes, but they were complete opposites. The one was so thin he looked like a skeleton with pale skin stretched over his narrow frame, and the other was big and bulky with dark red skin.

I sagged in their grips, my legs too weak to hold me up.

Okay. Think. I needed a plan. I had no idea how long I could keep the spell activated, linked to Lilith, and captured inside my body, and the longer I waited to make my move, the stronger Lilith got, draining my guys over and over again. I also didn't know how much more my guys could take. Sure, Lilith had said she was going to keep them alive and torture them, but she didn't need all of them and she didn't need me sane to be her weapon. In fact, breaking my soul by killing one of my soul mates might become her new plan if I waited too long to go to her.

A third agent, a woman with the feralness of a shifter, pulled out a pair of containment cuffs and my pulse stalled. I wrenched in the men's grips. If my power was cut off, I'd lose hold of the cage spell.

"Please," I gasped. "I'll go willingly. You don't need to cuff me."

Her expression tightened and her gaze slid to my right arm. Blood stained my T-shirt where I'd been hit by one of the Director's lightning blasts. It trailed over my bicep, into the flickering gold light of my brand, and dripped from my elbow.

"She has my mates." My throat tightened and the inky magic pressed against my senses, reminding me I couldn't get distracted for a moment. "I have the spell to stop her, but the cuffs will dispel it."

"What are you waiting for? Cuff her," the Director barked.

The woman grabbed my wrist and I wrenched against the demons' grip, too weak to break free.

"Please. I can't lose the spell."

The demons, Skeleton and Red, shoved me face-first to the ground, and the woman yanked my hands behind my back and secured my wrists. The frozen hollowness in my chest swelled as the containment spell cut me off from my magic.

The cage spell sputtered and shrank, and I strained to pull magic from my brands. Both Gideon and Jacob had given me magic before. But the drain of strength from me to them was too strong. I couldn't pull anything from them, not even magic, without endangering their lives, so the brands wouldn't let me.

Desperate, even though I couldn't feel any power inside me, I imagined shoving everything I had left into the spell to keep it active. My force of will had been strong enough to break through the containment spell on Lilith's prison to claim Kol. It had to be enough now.

Please. Let it be enough. I couldn't lose the spell, not when my guys were in danger. Lilith had to be stopped and the cage spell was the only way.

A spark of demonic magic glimmered in my heart and spun into the spell.

Oh, thank God.

Now I just needed to hold onto it while I figured out a plan.

Except it didn't matter if I had a plan. Not if I didn't have any power.

Skeleton and Red hauled me to my feet, dragged me to a JP SUV, and shoved me inside, one on either side of me. Their power squeezed in my chest, revealing just how magically strong these men were, and their red demonic mist curled from their skin and caressed me.

I followed the wisp of mist as it slid down my body. I

bled from both the gash in my shoulder and in my side, and I was sure my burned hand was bleeding. Which wasn't good. If I had any hope of saving them, I'd need medical attention first. I wasn't rapidly bleeding out, but the longer I sat here unable to apply pressure to my wounds, the more blood I lost. Except I couldn't feel any of my injuries because of the agony screaming through my brands.

I'm coming for you. I promise.

I just had no idea how the hell I was getting out of this mess, and the urge to go to my guys, now—now now now—without thinking things through was overwhelming.

But I couldn't take on Lilith alone. I had less power now than I did before and she still had many of her witches and was regaining power as I sat there. I couldn't just find power and shove it into the cage spell from wherever I was... well, maybe I could. I wasn't sure how the spell worked. But if I didn't have eyes on Lilith, I couldn't guarantee that she wouldn't kill my guys before I finally caged her.

I promise, I'm coming for you.

The pain in my brands flared. My muscles seized and a strangled scream escaped my lips. Skeleton and Red grabbed my arms, their eyes wide as if they were afraid I was going to attack them.

My soul cried. Save them. Do something—

With a whoosh, the pain swept out of me, and the blazing agony was replaced with an overwhelming heartache and a numbing cold that still made it impossible to feel my other injuries. Everything within me stopped: pulse, breath, and thought. The connection with my guys had cut off.

It was gone. Their presence, the pull of strength, and the whisper of desperation, fear, and determination, which I hadn't realized had been seeping through the brands, was gone.

My soul started to shatter and the inky magic swelled.

Gone. They were gone. Another sob threatened to break free and I glanced at my right arm. My brands were still golden. Did that mean they weren't dead?

Please don't be dead. Please.

The inky magic roared with laughter and surged, straining to take over.

I clenched my jaw and desperately reached for my bonds, praying they were still there. They had to still be there. I just had to reach deep enough, concentrate hard enough—

There. Deep inside me. A whisper of our connections.

Oh, thank God. Thank God.

They were far away and cold, but still there, and still rooting my essence and soul within my body, keeping the inky magic out... barely, and that could change at any time.

They had to have shut me out just like when Gideon had blocked me off during the first fight with the glyph witches in the Cromer Building.

Except then I'd still sensed my connection to him. This was absolute. Empty. Crushing. A complete blockage. And they had to have done it to protect me. It was the only reason I could think of for cutting me off like that. Gideon knew the soul-wrenching effect of having his mate mortally wounded. He had to have told the other guys to shut me out, too, but God—!

The female agent and the Director got into the front seats of the SUV and we drove toward Operations. The pressure of magic inside the vehicle swelled, and the demonic mist from the guys on either side thickened.

A whisper of heat sank into my skin and the spark of demonic magic keeping the cage spell alive grew bigger.

Skeleton shifted, and I watched a curl of his magic trail from his hand and sink into my arm. It added to my core of power, just like when I'd been immersed in Ibizual's magic, or when I'd consumed the spell of the demon who'd attacked me behind Hacksaw, or taken it from Mavis while getting the concealment charm.

Lilith had been able to suck the magic out of Kol and Marcus. It hadn't felt as if she'd tried to suck it out of me. She'd said she could only affect full demons and had probably assumed she couldn't pull it out of me. But that didn't mean I hadn't inherited the ability to feed off of demons from her.

Crap. I didn't know how much power I could get from these guys, but if I consumed their magic, I'd look more like the monster they thought I was.

Except if that was the cost for stopping Lilith and saving my guys, so be it.

But even if I drained these demons, would it be enough?

You know it won't, the inky magic whispered. *You need more. You need it all. The only way to be more powerful than her is to embrace me.*

I turned the problem over and over again as we drove to Operations, fighting the heartache of my frozen bonds and the inky magic's lure. How could I get more power, enough power, and soon? Was I willing to drain every demon in Operations? Could I?

More heat sank under my skin, refilling the core of my demonic power, but I resisted the urge to actively draw it in. So far neither demon had noticed, and I didn't want to alert anyone to the fact that I could quickly regain magic and I was strong enough to resist the containment cuffs. Not until I had a plan.

And the best one I could come up with was to somehow convince the Director to help me. It was the only way I could get enough power and enough people to confront Lilith again.

Which I had to do now now now. I had to save my guys, break through the block they'd put up between us and give them everything I had—

Jeez. Focus.

I fought to steady my breathing and control my panic, but it was nearly impossible with my concentration torn in too many directions.

Lilith had gained a lot of power draining the people at the unification ceremony, but she'd also expended a lot teleporting her witches and my guys. If she was ever at her weakest, it was right now.

The woman pulled the SUV up to the side entrance by the secure section of Operations, and the demons hauled me inside and shoved me into the hard metal chair in one of the interrogation rooms.

At least this time I was more conscious, even if I was still bleeding... which I still couldn't feel. And, from the blood trail I'd left staggering into the room, it was too much to hope that I'd also inherited a little of Lilith's super-fast healing.

The Director stormed in and glared at me while Skeleton and Red took up position by the door and the shifter woman left. I didn't know if they were now too far away for me to consume their magic or not, and didn't want to risk notice by trying, not until I'd exhausted every other option.

"So this was your plan all along," the Director said.

"Compromise the city's agents and open the door for Lilith to attack."

"We were trying to stop Lilith."

"It didn't look like that to me," the Director said.

"My guys were fighting Lilith's glyph witches and I was fighting her." I shook with the effort to hold myself together and not break down crying at not being able to feel my guys. "I have a cage spell that can reimprison her, but I can't do it by myself and we have to do it now before she regains her magic."

The Director barked a harsh laugh. "You think I'm going to believe that you actually want to stop Lilith? I know you're her daughter. The agent in charge of the elite team has already made a full report. You're an abomination made from evil magic. You'll say anything."

They're not going to believe you. You're a monster.

I'm not a monster. I might have feared for a bit that being a nephilim meant I was evil and I'd turn into a monster whether I wanted to or not, but I now had Lilith's inky magic trying to worm its way into my soul and I knew what real evil felt like. My soul was nothing like that and never would be.

"Finding out I'm an archnephilim and that Lilith is my mother doesn't make me evil." If he was this certain I was a monster, how the hell was I going to convince him to help me stop Lilith? "It doesn't change the fact that my soul is good, and it doesn't erase all the good I've done as a Union City cop."

The door opened and Yadveer shuffled in.

Oh, thank God.

I clenched my jaw, fighting to not show my relief. If Yadveer read my memories, the Director would have absolute proof of my intentions. But I couldn't look like I wanted it. That would only make the Director think I had a way of deceiving Yadveer's magic.

The elderly lethe demon stared at me with wide eyes containing only a pinprick of hellfire. Even without my empathy, it was clear he was terrified of me.

"You can say whatever you want, but we'll know the truth soon enough." The Director stepped back from the table and crossed his arms. "Read her memories and find out what her plans are."

Which were to stop Lilith. Now. Get my guys. Renew my bonds. Please. I didn't know how much more of the numb chill I could take.

Yadveer glanced at the other chair, but didn't sit. My arms were secured behind my back and he'd have to reach across the table to make contact. Instead, he rounded the table, his breath a little too fast. He didn't want to be this close to me even if I was handcuffed and my magic—supposedly—contained.

They won't care when they learn the truth, the inky magic hissed.

They will. They had to. It was my only hope.

He pressed his palms against my temples, his skin radiating the telltale warmth of a demon, although it was nothing compared to Lilith's burning heat. His body tense, he raised his gaze to the Director.

"I want to know everything," the Director said.

"Fast?" Yadveer asked, his voice hopeful, making it clear that the faster he got my memories, the faster he could get away from me.

"Yes."

Before I could take a breath and steady myself, searing power exploded in my head. I fought to keep hold of my frozen bonds and the cage spell while letting Yadveer see everything. He had to see it all, no matter how ashamed or embarrassed I was. If he didn't see everything, the Director would still suspect me.

His magic burned into my essence and lurched me from memory to memory. Fear. Love. Anger. Joy. My guys. Life before my guys. Bobbing in the not-water. Whirling faster and faster, turning my insides into a raging inferno.

The inky magic swelled, doing nothing to quench the fire, and oozed around my cells, sensing a weakness in my resistance. If I let it in, I'd be powerful.

You've told me that already. No.

I gritted my teeth and clung to the cold connections in my brands. Yadveer and the Director had to believe me. *Please.*

The cage spell sputtered and I forced more demonic magic into it.

Be a goddess.

No.

Be powerful.

No.

Be—

I won't be Lilith's puppet.

My essence heaved and spun. Burning, always burning. And yet the core of my being remained frozen with the absence of my guys. There wasn't a memory or thought or embarrassment or screw up that wasn't seen. My life, with all of my imperfections, was laid bare and Yadveer's power hungrily blazed through it all.

I clung to the cage spell and myself. It was all I could do. I just had to hold on. Just a little longer. The Director needed to know I wasn't a monster, that I was more angel than anything else and that the main thing that drove me was protecting people who couldn't protect themselves.

Someone screamed, and Yadveer's power swept out of me with a whoosh. My body went limp and I tipped out of the chair as Yadveer jerked out of the way, letting me crumple to the floor.

"You—" he gasped.

I dragged my gaze up to him. His shock cut through my chest, his emotion so strong that whatever wisp of angelic magic I'd managed to recover in the short time I'd been in the interrogation room had picked it up through the containment cuffs.

"Show me," the Director said, as if he knew asking Yadveer questions would be useless in his state of shock. He pulled out the chair across from me, nudged Yadveer to sit, and knelt in front of him.

Red hurried to my side and hauled me back into my chair. I dragged in ragged breaths, trying to get the room to stop spinning and my stomach to stop churning.

Please believe me. Please help me. I didn't know how much longer I could hold myself together, not without my full bonds, and I had to save my guys. I had to.

The only way is to let me in.

"How?" Yadveer asked, his gaze locked on me.

The Director grabbed Yadveer's chin and turned his head to face him. "Show me."

Yadveer pressed his palms to the Director's temple, and the Director's head snapped back, his angel glow blazing so bright I had to squint to keep looking at him. His breath picked up and his body trembled.

Please believe me. Please.

With a strangled cry, the Director sagged forward and pressed his forehead against Yadveer's knees.

Red tensed, and more mist curled from him and melted into me.

Yadveer yanked his hands away and the Director groaned, turning his brilliant gaze to me.

"This—" He clutched the edge of the table and used it to help him stand. "This— I need to think about this."

He staggered to the door and my pulse stalled.

He was going to leave and waste time thinking? I didn't have time for him to think about this. My guys didn't have the time.

"Wait." I jerked to my feet and Red shoved me back into the chair, a flicker of his fear chilling my skin. "We have to make our move now. Lilith doesn't just have her own power. She's also using worship magic. She can regain her strength faster than normal."

"Your memories might say you have nothing to do with Lilith or Michael, but I'm not going to make a snap decision. You still had recent contact with Lucifer and used his name to get us to the park."

"Because we couldn't stop Lilith by ourselves."

"I'm aware." The muscles in his jaw flexed. "I can't accept even the slightest risk of letting a monster go free."

"I'm not a monster." God damn it. "I can't do this alone."

You can't do it at all. Not with your amount of power.

The Director's eyes narrowed, his emotions seeping into me. "*You're* not doing anything." He was suspicious and worried. He didn't believe— No, he didn't *want* to believe.

Red tightened his grip on me and more of his magic heated my skin.

"Her witches are down in power and so is she," I pressed. "At full strength, they took out our team plus an elite team. This might be the only chance we get."

God, how did I make him believe me? He'd already seen the truth, that I'd been a child during the war and had nothing to do with it, that I'd dedicated my life to helping others.

"There is no *we*."

He'll never trust you. You'll never get enough power.

And he'd never release me to do it myself.

No power, no help, and I was running out of time. I had no other options. Lilith needed to be stopped and I had the spell to stop her.

There was only one thing I could do.

CHAPTER 25

I HAD TO LET THE INKY MAGIC IN. IT WAS MY ONLY OPTION. IF I could get close to my guys, get them to unblock our connection and concentrate on our bonds, I might be able to hold onto my soul long enough to imprison Lilith. Then...

Then, I had no idea. If imprisoning Lilith didn't end the worship magic spell, and her inky magic didn't disperse, I didn't know if I'd ever be able to get it out of me. I could already feel it clinging inside me, so sticky that I feared it wouldn't matter how hard I scrubbed, it would never go away. I wouldn't be able to live like that, always fighting the inky magic, resisting the evil that everyone believed was inside me. But if my guys could shut me out this completely, maybe with enough power I could make a strong enough block between us that my death wouldn't kill them or drive them insane.

It was a terrible plan.

And the guys would never agree to it. It also depended on a lot of luck, and even then the odds weren't good that any of us would get out of it alive or sane. Not to mention I desperately wanted to be wrong. I wanted to be able to burn the inky magic out of me when I was done and get the life I craved with my guys.

But it was the only plan I had.

Which still didn't address fighting off all of Lilith's witches. If I was concentrating on caging her and holding onto my soul, I'd be open to attack. No matter what I did, I still needed the Director's help.

And the only way I'd been able to convince someone I wasn't a threat was to let them see my soul, like I'd done with Voth.

The Director turned to open the door and I sucked in a thick strand of demonic mist from Red, making him yelp in surprise.

Please let this work. Please let me have enough angelic magic for this to work.

I blasted the demonic magic around my hands, shattering the handcuffs, and rammed my good hand into Red's stomach. His breath burst from his lungs, a blast of hot air in my face, and I shoved him back with a gust of demonic power.

The glimmer of angelic magic I'd felt while handcuffed grew a little stronger, filling my chest with the Director's and the demons' fear and anger. *Please, let it be enough.*

Skeleton jerked forward, his magic rushing around him. On instinct, I twisted my hand, and his power flooded into me, but my concentration on the cage spell started to slip.

Crap.

I heaved the extra power around the spell and twisted it tight, while also trying to release my divine light.

The Director snarled and jerked toward me, lightning dancing over his hands, but I slapped my burned and bloodied hand over his heart and pushed the heat of my empathy into him.

"This is who I am," I said, my good hand wrapped in the front of his shirt, holding him close.

I pushed every ounce of angelic magic I had into him, exposing my soul, my true essence, and the radiant gold threads binding me with my guys.

He gasped, his fear and anger melting into awe, and he held up his hand, stopping Skeleton and Red from hauling me away.

What I had with my guys was pure and primal, and that wasn't something that could happen if my soul was corrupted by evil magic. Yes, I was a being of celestial light and darkness, an impossible creature, but I wasn't a monster. I was a destined being. Evil had conspired to make me, but fate had set me on my path. And that path was to end Michael's war once and for all. Lilith couldn't be allowed to remain free, and I would do everything in my power, sacrifice my life to stop her, even knowing that could irrevocably hurt my guys.

The little angelic magic I had weakened and I strained to hold onto my connection with the Director. I might have changed his emotions about me, but I didn't know if I'd changed his mind. He had to understand I wasn't trying to make him make a rash decision. This was our best, maybe our only chance to stop Lilith from slaughtering millions of people like Michael had. I had to ensure he saw my truth, my need to save my guys, my anger and frustration and fear over how I'd grown up, always afraid, and my overwhelming need to protect people.

"Help me," I begged. "Please."

I had to save them. I couldn't live with this ache inside me. I had a chance to save everyone and I had to try.

Let me in now and you won't have to worry about it.

No. I had to wait until the last possible moment before I

let the inky magic in. Anything sooner, and Lilith would know what I was planning. And if I could get the Director's support, I might not need to let the inky magic in at all.

"I'm holding a spell that will reimprison her, but I can't do it by myself." Not even with all of Lilith's inky worship magic.

The Director's eyes narrowed. "You're not strong enough to cast a spell to contain her. I can feel the pressure of your power weakening, and there aren't any divine light crystals in this operations building to give to you to power up."

Shit. That meant I had to let the inky magic in. And I still needed his help.

"Please. I can't do it alone. My guys shut me out of our brands—"

"They can do that?" His surprise whispered through me.

My angelic magic was almost gone. The cage spell wavered and the cold in my chest billowed. I gritted my teeth. I just needed to hold on a little longer. "If they see me, they can give me magic."

Believe me. Just God damn believe me.

"Vampires don't have magic," the Director said. "And can you pull magic from an incubus through your brand?"

I could pull magic from any demon, but I wasn't going to remind him. "We can discuss the finer points of angelic mating brands later. Do you trust me?" *Just fucking say yes.* If he didn't, I'd have to come up with a plan B and it had been hard enough coming up with a plan A.

He hadn't moved since I'd flooded him with my empathic magic and he hadn't hit me with his lightning. That meant he didn't see me as a threat, but that didn't mean he trusted me with his life or the lives of his agents.

Skeleton and Red stood a few feet away, still ready to strike on the Director's command.

The Director frowned.

God, he still had to think about it?

"Do you trust me?" I pressed. There wasn't anything else I could do to convince him.

"Everything I know says I shouldn't, and yet you've shown me your soul. I *know* you. My soul knows yours. Even if I refuse to help, you'll still go after Lilith."

The interrogation room door banged open and Voth stormed in, with Zuri close behind. They had their powers contained—thank God—but from Voth's dark expression, it wasn't going to stay that way for long.

"You want to let Essie Shaw go," Voth growled, his voice filled with danger.

Lightning crackled over the Director's hands. "You don't have the authority to make demands, and you—" His attention jumped to Zuri, standing in the doorway. "You let a civilian into Operations' secure area?"

"If the Angel of Death has come to defend her, then there's nothing evil about her even if she is an archnephilim." Zuri squared her shoulders. "I already told you when I made my report that Agent Shaw had no idea what she was or who her mother was. I don't believe that knowledge will suddenly turn her into a monster."

A swell of magical pressure shuddered inside me and demonic mist curled around Voth, his hold on his power slipping. "Michael was one of yours, angel. You don't get to judge her on what she is."

"But the only way she's possible is because of black magic," Skeleton said.

"She's proven beyond a doubt that she doesn't have evil intent," the Director replied.

More power rippled off of Voth, straining my hold on the

cage spell. "So you're standing here letting her mates suffer because...?"

"Because we were discussing the plan." The light in the Director's eyes flared.

Skeleton and Red stiffened. I could no longer sense emotions, so I wasn't sure if they were surprised or upset. These men had been in the cafeteria when we'd teleported back to Operations, which meant even though they were acting as regular agents during this interrogation, they were still two of the top leaders of the JP Bureau of Supernatural Law Enforcement.

"Director, are you sure?" Red asked.

"Without a doubt," the Director said. "Agent Shaw, you say we have to make our move right now. What's the plan?"

"That you see Priam," Zuri said to me, her attention jumping to the floor then back to me.

I followed her gaze to the blood splattered at my feet. I was still bleeding from my injuries even though I couldn't feel them past the frozen numbness in my soul.

"How are you not screaming in agony right now? You're bleeding out. Slowly, but still bleeding out."

"The guys shut me out, blocked off our bonds." And if I thought about that, I'd break down. And I would *not* break down. "But I started the cage spell and I'm trying to keep hold of it."

"How long can you hold it?" Voth asked.

"As long as I have to," I said between gritted teeth. "But releasing it sooner rather than later would be better."

But only if you let me in.

"Call Priam and tell him we're meeting him in triage," the Director said to Red, and he grabbed my elbow and tugged me toward the door. "I want a full sit rep, Agent Shaw."

The Director helped me stagger out of the secured section in Operations, with Voth following close on my other side and Zuri and Skeleton behind us.

I repeated how Lilith was using worship magic to become more powerful. "But as I understand, teleportation spells use a lot of magic. If we're lucky, she spent whatever she gained during her attack on the unification ceremony to make her escape."

"But," Voth said, "she now has three angels, a vampire, an incubus, and a hellhound. She's going to be able to replenish her power the moment they're strong enough to drain."

We reached triage, where Priam and Xavier waited for us. Xavier's face paled the moment I walked in the door, even though I was with the Director and Voth and clearly not in custody. Even if I wasn't public enemy number one when this was over, it was going to be a long road, maybe an impossible road, of convincing people I wasn't a monster.

Except the odds of me surviving this were slim. The best I could do was fight to save my guys.

Priam, thankfully without a hint of fear in his eyes, helped me onto a gurney and quickly cut away my bloody T-shirt.

"Is fast okay?" Priam asked, meaning did I mind the burning pain of being healed quickly.

"We don't have a lot of time," I said.

He placed a gloved hand over the wound in my shoulder and lightning roared through me, searing through the hollow chill with blazing agony and threatening my hold on the cage spell.

Darkness swarmed my vision and the inky magic swelled and laughed. Then Priam's magic vanished with a whoosh, leaving me gasping for breath, shivering with cold, and desperately pushing more magic into the cage spell.

"So what's the plan?" Voth asked, placing his enormous hand on my ankle and sending a warm wave of power into me, helping me steady myself.

"Can all demons absorb each other's magic?" I gasped.

"Not many," he said. "But I sensed your ability when we... first met."

And by met he meant when he'd flattened me and my guys in an attempt to understand how an angelic mating brand worked and why he didn't have a soul bond. It was strange to look at the big, bulky, powerful demon and how he looked like he was always on the verge of wanting to rip your head off, knowing his soul ached for a true bond.

But that only made me think of my bonds, drawing my attention back to the frozen numbness of being shut out.

I shoved that thought aside. I had to focus to save them. Just focus.

"I'm guessing Lilith is back in the Cromer Building," I said, as Priam doused some gauze in saline and wiped away the smeared and caked blood around my now healed wounds. "She's expecting me to return to her, so she wouldn't be hiding, but I'll try to use my bonds to confirm their location."

"Can you do that if they've shut you out?" the Director asked.

Priam drew in a sharp breath and met my gaze for a second. Yeah, every angel would probably be shocked to know my guys could block our connection. Well, every angel except Amiah. She'd probably do a happy dance.

"I'm hoping I can. Then I have to walk up to Lilith's door, give myself to her, and finish casting the cage spell."

Zuri frowned. "But if the spell is strong enough to reimprison Lilith, I doubt you'll be able to do anything else. That will leave you wide open to attack."

"I believe that's where we come in," the Director said. "We can't show up with Agent Shaw, and in fact we'll have to keep a few blocks away to avoid detection, but on your signal, we can make our assault and draw most, if not all, of the glyph witches away from you."

"Exactly. I suspect Lilith will think she's strong enough to deal with me on her own." And at the moment she was.

Voth's eyes narrowed. "How do you plan on finishing the spell? You've got almost nothing left."

"I'm going to use Lilith's worship magic against her," I said.

"You can access her worship magic?" Xavier asked, his curiosity, stronger than his fear, pulling him into the conversation. Realization flashed across his expression. "Of course you can. You hold part of her DNA and she always intended for you to be able to access it. She could have attuned the worship magic to include you without ever having met you."

The inky magic howled with laughter. *Soon. Soon.*

"Yes." *Please let my guys have enough strength left to hold me together to cast the spell.* Then, if I couldn't be saved, I could embrace the inky magic fully, shut them out, and burn myself up.

Except I really wanted to be saved.

CHAPTER 26

XAVIER RAN OFF TO GET A CLEAN T-SHIRT, AND THE DIRECTOR, along with Skeleton, left to inform the rest of the JP Bureau's top agents of the plan.

The inky magic kept laughing and laughing, and it took everything I had to keep hold of myself and not let it take over. I was giving it exactly what it wanted and I could only pray I could resist it long enough to not give Lilith what she wanted. But there was no other way. I had no angelic magic left and I wasn't willing to drain demons on the chance that I'd get enough power.

A flicker of agony shot through Kol's brand and my pulse leaped, but the pain vanished as fast as it had appeared, reminding me of how aching and cold I was without them.

My pulse stalled with the realization that whatever was happening, it was horrible enough to weaken his will.

But this was a chance to confirm where they were.

I scrambled to regain hold of our connection. I just needed a moment, just enough to confirm where they were.

The frozen numbness swelled, and I shoved at it, determined to break through.

Just give me a glimpse.

The numbness trembled.

Please.

Then the agony roared back into me, stealing my breath and making my muscles seize. But instead of breaking the block between me and Kol, I was connected with Gideon... and he'd let me in on purpose.

His pain, rage, and determination pounded through me. But so too did the knowledge that he knew I wouldn't be able to leave them to Lilith, no matter what he or the other guys wanted. He knew I'd come after them no matter what and he was showing me where they were and what I was walking into.

The foggy image of a vast room filled my vision, blocking out everyone in triage. Its stone floor, walls, and ceiling were covered in glyphs. About a hundred people in robes lay prostrate on the floor in front of Lilith, who sat on a large stone throne raised up on a wide dais. Power whirled around her in a wild vortex, tugged at her hair and the hem of her gown, and sent the sparks from her hellfire whirling up to the ceiling to rain down around her, snapping and hissing when they hit the stone floor.

Her fiery gaze slid to me— or rather Gideon's gaze, and captured my soul, her essence burning into me as if she were looking at me through Gideon's eyes.

With a wicked smile that made the inky magic purr with pleasure, she flicked her finger.

Oh, shit.

More searing agony exploded through me, consuming the frozen numbness, and Gideon screamed. She tore into his essence, ripping away chunks, adding it to the vortex, and I fought to breathe.

I'm coming for you. I promise.

The connection snapped closed, engulfing me in darkness and then frozen numbness. I sobbed, my soul shattering at his pain and the distance between us, and blinked my vision clear.

Voth and Priam stood on either side of the gurney, their expressions tight with fear.

"What the hell was that?" Priam asked, pressing his hand against my forehead and sending a warm thread of magic into me, looking for physical injuries.

"Gideon let me confirm where they were." And everything within me cried that I had to go. Now. I couldn't wait for the Director to gather the other agents. Every second meant Lilith gained more power and my guys grew weaker.

"And?" Zuri asked, her expression just as tight.

Xavier returned with a T-shirt and handed it to her, who handed it to me.

"They're under the Cromer Building." I dragged on the new T-shirt, even though Priam hadn't finished helping me clean off the blood, and I slid off the gurney.

The room tilted and Voth grabbed my arm, steadying me. He sent another wave of magic whirling around my heart and easing my trembling muscles.

"Thanks."

"You shouldn't face Lilith alone," he growled.

I took an unsteady step toward the door. "Take care of her glyph witches fast and I won't have to."

Voth's expression darkened.

Yeah, we both knew I couldn't count on that.

"Whatever happens, Lilith and her witches must be

stopped." I drew in a ragged breath and tightened my hold on the cage spell. "Whatever the cost."

I took another unsteady step, and another, straining to look steadier and more confidant than I felt. My insides squirmed with the need to go to my guys, to finish this, to —*please, God*—survive this.

Zuri fell into step beside me and pulled out a set of keys from her pocket. "It's the blue sedan. I didn't have time to return the keys after the disaster at the park."

"Thanks." I took the offered keys and strode into the garage, each step taking me closer to my guys and giving me more strength.

I *would* save them. I *would* reimprison Lilith. I *would* do what I had to do to ensure the safety of the city, the world, and my guys.

The Director and half of the high-ranking agents he'd brought with him from Rome were gathered around the SUVs. Some wore tactical gear. Many didn't. Their conversations stopped the moment I stepped through the door, and all eyes turned to me.

Even without my empathy, I could tell the emotions were mixed. Which actually surprised me. Some of the agents—most of them angels—looked at me with disgust. Given that I was an abomination to beings of celestial light, that didn't surprise me. I broke their rules. Most angels had trouble with that. But the three demons, Red among them, and the one vampire present watched me with cautious appraisal, as if waiting to see what I'd do.

They're still never going to trust you, the inky magic hissed.

So be it.

"Tell us when you're ready to strike." The Director handed me a com, and one of the angels stiffened while the vampire's posture relaxed even more. "We'll go in on your word."

"The glimpse I got looked like she had about a hundred witches." I inserted the com in my ear. "Check."

"You're good," he said, as bits of the other agents' conversations filled my ear.

My hold on the cage spell flickered, and I gritted my teeth. "Can you put me on a separate channel?"

"Are you sure?" the Director asked.

Yeah, being put on a separate channel meant I wouldn't have the reassuring chatter of my backup, but— "I'm kind of concentrating on a lot of things right now. Blocking everyone out on top of that is just going to make everything more challenging."

He gave a tight nod. "I understand. Switch agent Shaw to a separate channel," he called out, then turned and barked orders at the agents.

The chatter in my ear cut out, and I got into the blue sedan and drove out of Operations' secured garage, my soul sobbing while I strained to hold myself together. The late afternoon summer heat turned the car sweltering and sweat slicked my body, but my insides were so cold and numb I could barely feel the heat and didn't bother to put the windows down, let alone turn on the air conditioning.

So much had happened in so little time. It hadn't even been a month since I'd walked into Abe and Pam's pharmacy and got caught up in my worst nightmare—permanently soul bound to an angel and immersed in the supernatural world.

Now I didn't want to imagine my life without Gideon, without any of them. I craved Marcus's ferocious passion, Jacob's intense desire, Kol's sensual playfulness, and Gideon's unwavering devotion.

God, I loved them so deeply. There was a chance I might be able to live without them, but I didn't want to. They were a part of my soul, and blocking me out cut to my core, even if it was just to protect me.

Just like I knew blocking myself from them and burning myself up was the only way to protect them if the inky magic didn't dispel once I'd imprisoned Lilith and if I couldn't push the magic out of me.

I tried not to think about that as I drove out of the Supers' Quarter to the heart of downtown, the churning in my stomach growing the closer I got to the Cromer Building.

By the time I parked on the side of the road across the street from my destination, I had a death grip on the steering wheel to keep my hands from shaking.

I had to help them.

I had to stop Lilith.

I wasn't going to be strong enough.

My mind kept whirling—*save them, save them, whatever it takes*—and my insides ached, my body strangely frozen and numb, and yet covered in sweat from the heat in the car. I got out of the vehicle, hoping the breeze would at least make my hands feel less clammy.

But there wasn't even a whisper of wind, as if the world held its breath, waiting to see if everyone in this city and in this realm could carry on, healing the wounds of a war that had only ended about twenty years ago, or if they were going to go back to fighting for their lives.

I dragged my gaze over the street. Even though it was dinnertime, the area should have been busy. Unity Park was only a few blocks away and the restaurants and shops in the areas were still open—

The sign in the store window beside me said CLOSED and

only the night security lights were on. In fact, all of the stores and businesses around me looked closed. There were also no pedestrians and very few cars on the road.

A cruiser rounded the corner and pulled up beside my sedan. For a second, panic made my pulse trip. I didn't want to have to deal with anyone who knew me when I'd thought I was human. That was time I couldn't afford to waste.

I tried to roll my shoulders without looking like I was rolling my shoulders to ease some of the tension in my neck. The odds the officer knew me were slim. This part of the city wasn't in my old precinct. And—thank God—when the officer put down her window, I didn't recognize her.

"There's an evacuation order for downtown. It's not safe to be out here—" The woman's gaze locked on my face and her eyes widened. Guess she'd finally noticed my glowing eyes. "I'm sorry, agent," she said, assuming because I was an angel in the human part of town that I was a JP agent.

"That's okay, officer." I fought to not show my fear and desperation. "You'll want to keep a secured perimeter around this area. The rest of the JP team will be here shortly."

"We haven't gotten word of an operation."

Crap. Of course they hadn't. Jeez. I'd spoken on auto pilot. I should have just kept my mouth shut. Because it was best if she and the rest of the UCPD kept their distance. There wasn't any way a normal human would stand a chance against Lilith's glyph witches. Of course, I wasn't sure if the top leaders of the JP Bureau of Supernatural Law Enforcement stood a chance, either. Not without me imprisoning Lilith and terminating her worship magic spell... if imprisoning her ended the spell.

Except if I failed, there wasn't any way I could keep Union City's humans out of the fight. We'd needed everyone, supers and humans, to defeat Michael. Lilith's war would be the same.

Be a goddess. Be strong.

Save them.

The cage spell flickered.

"It's nothing that requires UCPD backup." I gave her a tight nod and strode across the street to the Cromer Building. It wasn't great that she knew where I was going, but I couldn't stand there any longer and wait for her to leave.

I pulled open one of the many glass doors and marched into the building's empty, spacious, multi-story glass and metal lobby. Unlike the level below, the main floor's construction had been finished to sleek and modern perfection, glass and steel and marble, in white, grays, and black.

The weight of enormous power crushed inside me and the inky magic swelled, pressing against my essence and straining my will the moment I crossed the threshold into the building. All this power could be mine if I let it in. I wouldn't have trouble holding onto the cage spell if I just let it in.

Ahead of me, in the center of the lobby, stood the fire witch with his arms crossed and his lips curled in a sneer.

He wore the same dark shorts and white T-shirt he'd worn at the park—the T-shirt now with a large grass stain. His dark eyes narrowed and he released his hold on his power, adding to the crush inside me

"I thought you said you were something," he said, his voice a raspy hiss. "You didn't even last an hour before you came crawling back to her."

I fought to breathe and look like I wasn't affected. "And I thought you were her right hand. Looks like you're just her errand boy."

Come on, just take me to Lilith. I didn't have the willpower to stand there having a pissing contest with him.

"I'm whatever my goddess needs me to be. Just like you." He turned, strode deeper into the lobby to a bank of elevators, and pressed the call button. "You can't fight it. But I'm glad you did."

I followed, pushing through the power as if it had physical mass. The elevator door opened as I got there and I staggered inside with him.

"I'm going to enjoy watching her break you." He opened the panel with the floor buttons, revealing a single button, and pressed it.

"Well, that's handy," I said. "A button behind the buttons."

I didn't know if the Director and the other agents would be able to deal with Lilith's witches before I had finished the cage spell... or was dead... but on the off chance, he needed to know how to get to me and my guys.

The fire witch shot me a dark look, and the elevator went down, deep under the building, the pressure of Lilith's power, along with the fire witch's caught within the confines of the elevator, growing by the second. The strain of concentrating on my freezing, aching bonds, and holding the spell, made me tremble, and my breath turned into shallow gasps that I couldn't hide from him, making his sneer deepen.

When the door finally opened, I staggered out into a long, wide hall without waiting for the fire witch. The floor was large polished granite flagstones, and the walls were stone with swirling glyphs carved into them. Torches in wrought iron holders placed on both sides of the wall about thirty feet apart illuminated the way with a mix of light and writhing shadows, making me feel like I'd entered some ancient temple.

But then this *was* a temple. I'd already seen Lilith sitting on her throne in her throne room, the walls covered in glyphs and the witches bowing to her. They referred to her as their goddess, and with all the worship magic at her disposal, she *was* a goddess.

And *I* needed to be stronger than her.

The inky magic chuckled. *Embrace me, and you will be.*

I'd also be Lilith's puppet if I couldn't keep hold of myself.

The fire witch led me all the way to the end of the hall to a pair of enormous metal doors.

My pulse pounded. I needed to get eyes on my guys, then find a way to call in the Director without giving myself away. If I pushed power into the cage spell first, Lilith's witches could just blast me into submission before I'd even started.

The fire witch flicked his finger and released his magic with a crushing *thu-thud,* and the doors slowly opened inward, revealing the enormous chamber, the floor, walls, and ceiling covered in glyphs, exactly as I'd seen it through Gideon's eyes.

Wrought iron chandeliers with dozens of candles lit the room with the same flickering illumination as the hall, their smoke making the air hazy, and the acrid reek of sweat, blood, and desperation filled my nose. The hundred witches still lay prostrate on the floor in perfect lines, leaving a wide center aisle and drawing my gaze up to Lilith, sitting on her large stone throne, radiating enormous power, heat, and darkness.

CHAPTER 27

THE THRONE SAT ON A RAISED DAIS WITH FIVE WIDE STONE steps, and the glyphs behind her pulsed with a mix of red demonic magic and smoky black worship magic. Marcus, in his massive hellhound form, lay on the floor at the foot of the dais, a thick chain around his neck securing him to a metal ring attached to the floor.

He stiffened, and for a second I worried that Lilith had a containment spell on the chamber that only allowed her and her witches to cast spells.

Shit. That was something I should have thought of. I wouldn't stand a chance against her if I was also trying to push the cage spell through a containment spell. I'd barely been able to hold onto it with the cuffs on and I doubted the spell on the JP's cuffs was as powerful as the spell on Lilith's prison.

Except I still didn't have any other option but to confront Lilith and I couldn't back out now.

I tried to draw in a steadying breath, but could only manage a shallow gasp that made the fire witch chuckle with dark pleasure as I stepped across the threshold into the room.

No chill or hollowness. At least not any more than what I already had with my guys blocking their bonds.

Thank God. My chance went from none back to slim again.

The hellfire in Marcus's eyes grew as I took another step, but he didn't get up or move. I couldn't tell if he was injured or not, but if Lilith had control of his ability to shift, then Marcus needed to be smart about when he made his move... if he *could* make a move.

Up at the front of the room on the right-hand wall hung the rest of my guys, along with Cassius and Ephraim.

The churning cold and fear in my gut hardened, a whisper of emotions: agony, rage, and terror made my throat tighten. I gritted my teeth. I couldn't attack Lilith. Not until the glyph witches were out of the room.

Yes, my guys were alive, but they were in rough shape, bleeding and bruised and barely breathing. They'd been chained with their hands above their heads, high enough that only their toes skimmed the floor, making it difficult to breathe, and the glyphs behind them pulsed with demonic and worship magic in time with the glyphs behind Lilith.

Jacob looked the worst, his skin blackened and oozing blood. What I could make out of his charred T-shirt was half burned, half pasted to his bulky body, and so, too, were his cargo pants. Beside him, Kol raised his head.

I gasped, unable to stop myself.

His face was one big ugly bruise, with one eye swollen shut. They'd beaten him after they'd captured him and drained him so deeply he couldn't heal. Which meant Lilith was already well on her way to regaining the power she'd spent to teleport out of the park.

Gideon hung beside Kol, his face almost as battered, his clothes also bloody from dozens of gashes. He trembled, the muscles in his arms flexed, the tendons and veins raised as he fought to hold himself up so he could breathe. With his back broken, he wasn't able to support himself with his toes like Jacob and Kol.

Cassius, beside him, was in the same situation, arms bulging, his face red with exertion, while Ephraim, at the end of the line, had collapsed. His head lolled forward, and I couldn't tell if he was alive and was in no position to check.

Lilith leaned back, her magic sweeping through her hair, the pressure increasing in my chest and straining my hold on the cage spell. "You're not crawling."

I strode to the middle of the room. "Let them go and I'm yours."

She flicked her finger, the glyphs behind her exploded with red light, and the glyph behind Gideon burst to life. He screamed and his body jerked, his muscles seizing. His gaze locked on me and the connection through our brand grew colder. He wouldn't let me take his pain, wouldn't let me give him strength to survive this.

God. I wanted to yell at him, at all of them, and at Lilith. But shutting me off was the only way Gideon thought we could win.

Except Lilith was expecting me to be writhing in agony at Gideon's pain. She had to be. She knew the effects of the angelic mating brand and if I didn't react, she'd know every-thing wasn't as she expected.

With a strangled cry, I dropped to my knees and bowed my head.

"Your bonds make you weak," she said.

Another *thu-thud* of her power, and Jacob screamed. The chill in our bond deepened as well and my throat tightened, my thoughts whirling. They were in pain. They were dying. I had to save them. I had to—

"Move in now," I whispered, praying Lilith wouldn't be able to hear me over Jacob's and Gideon's screaming.

The inky magic laughed with gleeful anticipation. I was going to let it in. It would have my soul and I'd be Lilith's puppet.

No. Not yet. Not until Lilith sent all her witches to confront the Director. My guys and I just needed to hold on a little longer.

Kol started screaming and everything within me joined him. I could stop this. I had the power inside me to stop this. I just needed to let the inky magic in.

God damn it, just wait. Just a little longer.

"I'm yours," I gasped to Lilith. *Please, stop.*

"What was that?" Lilith asked. "I didn't hear you."

Another scream from Gideon and I pressed my forehead against the carved granite floor. The plan wouldn't work if I didn't look like I was in agony and weak, and it took everything inside me not to pump every ounce of power I had left into the cage spell right now.

"You need to speak up over the screaming, daughter," Lilith said.

The fire witch grabbed my hair, digging his fingers into my skull, and yanked my head up.

"What are you?" Lilith snarled.

"I'm yours. I'm your weapon."

"You're mine to do with as I please. Just like your mates," Lilith said.

"Thank your goddess for using you." With a thud of magic that stole my breath, the fire witch sent flames burning down my neck, searing my skin. I fought my scream, but it tore free, a strangled sound that made Jacob heave against his shackles.

I gritted my teeth. Where the hell was the Director? Putting me on a separate channel from the rest of the op might have been good for my focus, but I had no idea what was going on unless the Director made an effort to communicate with me.

Except it hadn't been that long since I'd given him the signal and he'd had to stay a few blocks away to avoid notice.

"Thank your goddess," the fire witch pressed.

"Thank you," I gasped.

Lilith jerked to her feet, her hellfire flaring, sending sparks showering around her. "Not good enough."

The prostate glyph witch beside me tensed, and the fire witch's sneer deepened.

"You need to learn your place." Lilith gave a nod so slight I almost missed it.

The fire witch wrapped his arm around my burned neck and hauled me to my feet, choking me. I rammed my elbow into his gut and heaved forward, tossing him over my shoulder onto the stone floor.

Lilith barked a harsh laugh. "Oh, you're going to have to do better than that, Bates."

The fire witch, Bates, snarled something and grabbed a small tattoo on his right arm as the other glyph witches bolted out of the way, gathering by the pillars at the sides of the room. His power thudded in my chest, stealing my breath.

What little demonic magic I had left swelled, ready to blast at him, but the cage spell sputtered.

Shit.

I scrambled to bolster the cage spell as Bates's spell slammed me into a pillar.

Agony sliced through my chest and my head cracked against the stone, sending flashes of light and darkness dancing over my vision. The cage spell sputtered again and so too did my hold on my frozen bonds.

The inky magic dug in deeper, grinding against my will, begging, cajoling, promising I'd be strong if I'd just let it in.

Let me in. Fight back.

Not yet. I had to wait. I'd fail if I didn't wait.

But I was going to have to let it in soon. Holding the cage spell active inside me had drained almost all of my remaining demonic magic. If the JP didn't arrive soon, I was going to have to go ahead with the plan whether the other witches were there or not, or I'd lose the spell.

Bates pressed a red tattoo on his shoulder and hissed a quick word. Fire roared around his hands like Cassius's fire magic, and he snapped a whip of fire at me.

I wrenched out of the way, shooting agony through my chest—another God damned broken rib—and the whip sliced into the pillar. Sparks flew through the air from the impact, stinging my skin. I scrambled to get to cover around the pillar, but Bates jerked his hand. The whip sliced into my shoulder. Blood rushed down my arm and the acrid scent of burned flesh filled my nose. The cage spell sputtered.

Shit shit shit.

Bates snapped the whip again. I heaved to the side and the whip hit the floor with another shower of sparks. I couldn't keep this up. My lungs burned, desperate for more air, but I couldn't draw a full breath against the pressure of magic power inside me and out.

Jacob and Kol screamed and heaved against their shackles, while Gideon gasped, still fighting to keep himself up so he could breathe.

Come on, Director. Any time now.

I shifted to put the pillar between me and Bates, but his whip seized my ankle, searing my flesh, the pain stealing the rest of my breath and straining my hold on the cage spell.

With a snarl, he yanked me out into the open.

"Your place is bowing before your goddess," he said, flicking his wrist and wrapping his whip around my neck. I tried to scream, but I had no breath left. I barely had enough thought to hold onto the cage spell. The inky magic swelled and its power seeped into me, the fiery pain burning away my resistance.

A ghost of demonic mist rushed around my hands, ready to strike Bates, but I shoved it back.

Not yet. Not yet. Just a little longer.

He wrenched me across the floor, too fast for me to get to my feet, grabbed my hair again, and shoved my face against the flagstones. "Thank your goddess for letting you live. Thank—"

"My goddess," a reedy masculine voice said from somewhere behind me, his words coming out fast and sharp. "The JP have entered the building."

"About time," Lilith snapped.

The inky magic roared with laughter.

Shit, I should have thought of that. Why didn't I think of that? But I'd been focusing on too many other things at the time. Of course Lilith expected me to lead the JP there. She had to have assumed they'd arrested me in the park, so I'd either escaped and they'd followed me, or I'd made a deal and shown them her location.

Bates yanked my head up, his fire whip digging deeper

into my neck, the flames searing agony over my jaw and cheeks and down my chest.

Lilith gave me a sickeningly sweet smile, her eyes filled with malice. "The Joined Parliament's bureau will be in chaos when I kill their top leadership, and then I'll release you on the world."

"Never," I gasped.

"You don't have a say in the matter." She flicked her finger and light burst from the glyphs behind my guys. Their muscles jerked taut and they screamed.

I heaved in Bates's grip. I had to get free, had to stop her—

I had to wait for her God damned witches to get out of the room.

Come on. Tell them to go. Please.

The inky magic churned as whispers of rage and fear ghosted through my chest, my guys' pain so strong I was picking up their emotions through our blocked bonds. The cage spell flickered, snapped back to life, then flickered again.

I was out of time.

Lilith swept her gaze over the witches gathered by the walls. "Kill the JP agents."

The witches threw off their robes and raced to the door, and Lilith turned her gaze back to me. "Bates, break her. She's a weapon. She doesn't need a whole soul or mind."

"As my goddess commands." The fire in his whip surged and so did the agony. Darkness danced across my vision and the cage spell burst into smoky nothingness inside me.

No. Please no.

I screamed, and let the inky magic in.

CHAPTER 28

THE INKY MAGIC EXPLODED INSIDE ME, A FEROCIOUS POWER that stained my soul. Every cell was blackened with its malicious intent and filled with Lilith's essence. I was finally hers to command, and she'd been waiting for this moment all along.

"That won't save you," Lilith taunted, and my body jerked up to my hands and knees. "That's my worship magic. I control that power."

"I know." I heaved at the power and spun it into the cage spell. I needed to save it above all else.

"You're not strong enough to take it away from me."

"I am with my bonds." The cage spell flared, a blazing ball inside my chest, but the inky magic whirled into a vortex of overwhelming power, too strong for me to grasp hold of and push fully into the cage spell. It tore at my soul and essence, consuming pieces and adding them to Lilith's inky reservoir.

"Your bonds make you weak."

My body crawled toward her, blood from my burned neck splattering on the floor. I fought to keep myself in place, control the inky magic, anything to keep hold of myself. Please, God, I couldn't let her possess me.

Bates released his whip from around my neck, and snapped it down onto my back. I screamed. Every nerve was on fire and I couldn't catch my breath. Too much pain and pressure and inky magic. And I had to hold onto the spell. Just. Hold. On.

Marcus jerked to his feet and snarled, wrenching and clawing at the chain around his neck, but couldn't break free.

"Stay," Lilith hissed, and red demonic mist twisted around him and yanked him down to the floor, drawing a yelp of pain. "You're all weak."

The glyphs glowed blindingly bright, making my guys scream, and a flicker of electric magic cut through my arm as agony tore through me.

Save them. Save them. They're dying. I have to save them.

The inky magic's hold on me weakened and I jerked to a stop before Gideon clamped down on our bond again, the sudden aching cold stealing my breath.

I wrenched my head against the inky magic's control and looked at him. "Release it."

"No," he gasped. "It'll kill you."

"It'll save me. I can't resist her without you and the connection within our brands."

"You can't resist me at all," Lilith said. I heaved forward, back onto my hands, and Bates kicked me in the ribs, knocking me over.

White lightning shot through my chest, and the inky magic's vortex tore more pieces from my soul. I was losing myself, who I was, what I remembered, who I loved.

"Please, Gideon, Jacob, Kol. Focus on our brands."

"I love you," Gideon said, and lightning exploded inside

me. My muscles seized and for a second there was only him and his pain.

Then Jacob and Kol released their hold on our bonds and I was burning in the center of the sun, my soul ignited, their brands pulling strength from me. But in that center with me were my guys—Gideon, Jacob, Kol, and a whisper of Marcus because we didn't share a brand—and the raw primal power binding us together.

The surety of our bonds filled my burning soul, holding it together against the inky magic's vortex. I clung to my guys, their love, their determination, and used that strength of spirit to weave my essence into the inky magic and spin its vortex into a tight supernova in the core of my being, just like the rest of my power. A supernova more powerful than anything I'd ever contained before that threatened to burn me up.

Lilith howled, and the inky magic strained to control my body, but my guys held me steady.

I heaved to my feet and shoved power into the cage spell. It burst around Lilith in a crackling nimbus of blue-white lightning, but her demonic magic roared with a chest-crushing *thud* that weakened the spell.

I gritted my teeth, fought to stay standing, and pushed more power into the spell to keep it going.

Bates jerked forward and snapped his whip at me, but I sent a blast of demonic mist, powered by Lilith's inky magic, into him. It threw him to the back of the room, slammed him into one of the enormous metal doors, and took it off its hinges.

"You think you can cage me?" Lilith's demonic magic tore into me.

I staggered. Behind me, I felt the *thu-thud* of magic, but couldn't move to get out of the way.

A fireball exploded around me. The heat started to sear my skin but my power roared stronger, rushing out of me in a great wave and sweeping Bates's fire away from me.

My hold on the cage spell weakened and Lilith's demonic magic surged. I wasn't going to be able to fight Bates and cage Lilith at the same time. I needed all my concentration on the cage spell. I needed my guys to be fighting.

"Brace yourself," I yelled at them, and shoved power into the bonds. Gold light gleamed from their brands. Jacob's vampiric intensity swelled, his monster fully released, and the light in Gideon's eyes turned into a blinding halo and his wings burst from his back. With a gasp, Kol's head jerked up and his hellfire flared from his good eye.

I shot a blast of demonic magic into the chain securing Kol as Gideon sliced through his restraints with a blade of divine light.

Oh, thank God. They'd either kept some power back in reserve, or my surge into them hadn't just given them strength but replenished some magic as well.

"We've got Bates," Gideon said, sagging to the floor and sending a blast of divine light into Jacob's chains. "You cage Lilith."

"You can't cage me," Lilith snarled. "I'm the Hellfire Queen. I'm more powerful than you. You think stealing my worship magic will make you more powerful?" She fisted her hands and the inky magic seized my body and dropped me to my knees. "It just makes you mine."

"No," Jacob said, and the power in our bond grew stronger. "She'll never be yours."

"Never." Kol glanced at me, his one eye still swollen shut, and the power in our bond grew stronger as well.

Another *thu-thud* of power from Bates behind me, and

Gideon blasted divine light, as Jacob and Kol charged toward him, somehow moving with speed and power even though I knew they were still seriously injured. Marcus snarled and lunged toward Lilith, but her demonic magic wrenched him back, making him whimper.

I clung to my bonds, anchoring myself in the raging power burning inside me, and pushed more magic into the cage spell.

The blue-white lightning around Lilith flared and thickened, the spell gaining strength, but she squared her shoulders and whipped more demonic magic around her, burning through the lightning as fast as it formed.

Out of the corner of my eye, I saw Jacob slash at a fire whip with his short sharp claws, breaking it apart, as Kol leapt in, ramming his fist into Bates's face. Gideon blasted more divine light, hitting Bates in the chest and knocking him back.

Bates grabbed a tattoo and a massive invisible weight slammed into me. Jacob and Kol staggered and dropped to their knees, and the next blast of light from Gideon fell short, exploding on the floor at Bates's feet.

I wrenched my attention back to Lilith. This would end if I caged her, and I fought to strengthen the spell.

"That power belongs to me." Lilith heaved at the inky magic and my grasp on it weakened. The cage spell sputtered.

Shit. I scrambled to regain my grip on the inky magic. My muscles trembled and my insides burned. I couldn't afford for her to take back her worship magic.

Screaming, I shoved my soul fully into the inky magic. It twisted around my essence and I wrenched the power out of her grasp and shoved it into the cage spell.

Lilith hissed and fisted her hands, yanking demonic

magic from Marcus and sucking out his essence. With a howl, he collapsed on his side, writhing on the floor, his massive black chest, covered in all those swirling glyphs, heaving with shallow, ragged breaths.

"Release the cage spell and I'll let him live." Lilith reached out her hand and Kol screamed, his demonic magic rushing out of him into her. "I'll let them both live."

But the moment I released the spell, we were all dead. I had to cage her before she killed Marcus and Kol. It was the only way to stop this.

Please, God, let me stop this.

I pushed more power into the spell. All the power I had as fast as I could. The inferno inside me burned into my essence and soul, and poured out through my body. My skin blistered and burst, the agony excruciating, but I had to overpower Lilith and finish the cage spell.

Lilith roared, a primal cry of rage, and wrenched her power out of Bates. He gasped a strangled cry and collapsed, and her strength started to overpower mine.

I fought to hold on. Darkness swam across my vision and the inky magic tore away more pieces of my soul, but Lilith's skin also blistered and burst. Blood trailed down her face, and her expression grew wild, and yet still she pushed more power into her defense.

"You will not cage me," she yelled as she released a massive blast of power, burning it into the inky magic.

But I shoved my magic against hers, pushing it back into her, and her eyes flashed wide with surprise.

Fire exploded from her body. With a scream, she spun her power into a whirlwind, sucking at the flames, but the fire kept burning, brighter and hotter. Wailing, she thrashed against the inferno, but it consumed her, burning her into a smoldering pile of ash.

She'd chosen death over imprisonment.

I sagged forward, my insides still burning, and the inky magic grew.

Mine. All mine.

It tore the rest of my soul to shreds, sweeping it around in its vortex. I fought to cling to my bonds but they kept slipping out of my mental grasp. I wanted to kill, to rule, to be worshiped—

No. Please. That was the inky magic. That wasn't me.

Of course it's you. You're a monster.

I'm not. My soul is good.

Not any more, the inky magic laughed.

I fought to pull my soul back together, but my bonds were no longer strong enough to keep me whole. I was drowning in sticky, malicious magic and was too exhausted to resist. The only thing I could do was shut my guys out and finish burning myself up.

I heaved my head up and locked gazes with Marcus. I couldn't do this alone. I wouldn't be strong enough. I loved him so much. All of them. I had to do this to protect them. If I let the inky magic take over, I'd become a monster just like Lilith, and I'd take them with me.

Tears streamed down my cheeks. There had to be another way, but I could already feel the magic taking over, and soon I wouldn't have enough strength to finish this.

A small, distant part of my mind found it funny that once again I was going to sacrifice myself to save my guys, as if my final battle with the archnephilim had been practice for this very moment. I'd proven I'd had the nerve once before. I just had to do it again. Except now I had so much more to lose.

"I love you. All of you."

I clamped down on my bonds. An icy hollowness

snapped through my chest and the guys started yelling. Kol grabbed my arm, but I tossed him back with a blast of magic.

"Essie, stop," Jacob begged.

"I can't fight it. I won't become like her." I gathered the power inside me. One quick blast and, please God, let that be enough to end it. "Our connection isn't strong enough. It's taking over."

"No, please." Kol's heartache cut through my block and my throat tightened.

"Block me out. You'll survive if we both block the bonds."

I shoved another wave of power out around me and pushed my guys farther back, then released the rest of the magic inside me.

Marcus howled and lunged toward me, shifting at the same time as Gideon snapped the chain securing him to the floor with a blast of divine light.

"Don't you fucking dare," Marcus growled, cupping my cheeks.

"No." I tried to shove him back, get him out of the way of my inevitable fiery explosion, but all of the inky magic was already released and burning through me.

No, please. He's not supposed to die with me.

Flames licked over my skin, making both of us scream, and I fought to pull the magic back, change its direction, anything to save him. The block I'd put in my bonds shattered and the strength of my guys' souls flooded into me.

They yanked the inky magic into our brands, and the primal magic binding our souls together consumed it. Gideon's brand lit up, then Jacob's, then Kol's. The magic poured into my chest, and roared around my heart.

Marcus groaned and his grip on my cheeks tightened.

Golden magic burst from his bare chest over his heart, and twisted into a beautiful complicated sigil, binding our souls together with an angelic mating brand.

With the combined strength of all my guys and the primal magic binding us together, I burned out every last speck of inky magic, and collapsed into Marcus's arms.

CHAPTER 29

TWO WEEKS LATER, I SAT ON A BLANKET IN THE SHADOW OF A large maple with my back against Jacob's broad chest and his arms around me. It was a glorious summer's day, hot and humid, and I'd decided to wear shorts and a barely-there body-hugging halter top that showed off almost all of my brands.

The sky above was a perfect clear blue, just like Gideon's eyes, and less than an hour ago, I'd been soaring with him— after a lot of stumbles and help—for my first flying lesson. He, along with Kol, was now at the Tasty Tacos food truck ordering lunch while we waited for Marcus to finish letting his beast loose in the wolves' forest.

The last few days had been a strange mix of writing reports, being interrogated— or rather *interviewed*, and doing nothing because we'd all been put on medical leave until the JP decided otherwise.

I didn't remember much after Lilith had burned herself up by channeling too much magic and I'd branded Marcus. It had all been a frozen, agonizing blur. My burns had been so bad, and there'd been so many other serious injuries between my guys and the other agents, that the angels with healing magic had kept me sedated while they drained, regained, and drained their magic again and again to heal me and everyone else.

So when I'd woken, it had been almost a week later, and much to my surprise, I hadn't been handcuffed to the hospital bed. All of my guys had been in the room with me, waiting for me to wake, none of them in handcuffs, either.

My head had been pounding and was still a little sore. My magical channels had been burned so badly that both Amiah and Priam had said it would take months, maybe years... maybe never to regain all of my magical strength. Which didn't leave me helpless, just not as likely to accidentally take out a building, and I could live with that.

I'd learned the team, along with Cassius and Amiah, had been reprimanded but not arrested or fired, and that I was still an agent.

That shocked the hell out of me. I hadn't thought it was possible for the JP to completely accept me. Sure, the Director had been willing to support me to stop Lilith, but that didn't mean he trusted me.

Except I'd shown him my soul and he'd become one of my strongest supporters. With the help of an angel with an empathic power, he'd shared the experience of my memories and empathic soul-baring, and the rest of the surviving members of the JP Bureau of Supernatural Law Enforcement's leadership were on my side as well... and I wasn't going to think about all the people who now knew a lot of really embarrassing things about me.

It also didn't hurt that Voth, the Angel of Death—a moniker he'd picked up during the war for all the nephilim he'd killed—was another strong supporter and he'd threatened the lives of any JP leader who thought to arrest me.

He'd also told them they were idiots if they didn't keep me on as an active agent. I'd already proven I'd go up against terrible odds and face anyone—even my mother—to save lives. If that didn't prove my soul was good, he said, he had no idea what did.

Unfortunately, video from the fight in Unity Park had gone viral. The only saving grace was that one of the many videos released included the whole fight: both the horrible part where I'd told Lilith I was hers and wanted to join her, as well as when I'd denounced her and swore I'd stop her.

I wasn't surprised at the fear and hate the video received. The inky magic hadn't been wrong. People were afraid of me. They might always be afraid. I reminded them of the worst time in their lives and was the same kind of super that had slaughtered thousands.

But the inky magic hadn't been right, either. There were a lot more people who'd commented positively on the video, and many—mostly shifters but surprisingly a few angels, too—were furious on my behalf that Lilith had vowed to torture my mates. Soul bonds were sacred and rare, and many of them were amazed I hadn't completely lost it under those conditions.

It also didn't hurt that the JP had, at the Director's insistence, agreed to have their most powerful empathic angel judge my soul. A process which thankfully wasn't as intrusive or embarrassing as what I'd done to prove my innocence to the Director.

It did, however, confirm with irrefutable evidence that I didn't have evil intent, and the Joined Parliament had made an official statement about me, providing the evidence the empath had gathered. And while the JP technically didn't lie, they did leave out certain details which I had no doubt made the public assume they'd had a bigger part in my life than they really did.

They'd said I'd been a nephilim taken out of her maturation tank as a child, and had had nothing to do with the war. True.

Except there was no mention of *who* pulled me from the tank.

They'd said I'd been raised to help and protect people. Sort of true.

But they certainly hadn't mentioned who raised me, likely hoping the public would assume they'd had a hand in my upbringing.

They'd said—after the Director shared my conversation with Lucifer with them—that they'd learned nephilim became monsters because Michael shattered their souls, and because Michael had never gotten his hands on me, my soul was still whole. True.

And then they provided the evidence from the empathic angel.

I was, without a doubt, not a danger and would never be a danger to the law-abiding citizens in the earthly realm. The empathic soul examination and the video of me vowing to stop Lilith were proof.

I was certain not everyone believed them, but Voth, a notorious war hero known for killing nephilim, had made numerous television appearances spreading the JP's official statement.

It wasn't a guarantee that everything would go smoothly from now on—nothing in life was guaranteed—but it certainly helped having the JP's official and very public support. And for the most part, shocking me even more, the world accepted the JP's statement.

I was not a threat, or a monster, or a war criminal.

Yeah, I also got that in writing. Best to have as many bases as possible covered.

The Director, along with Zuri and her team, including Ephraim who'd barely survived, had returned to Rome shortly after the empathic angel had proven my innocence, and I'd tried to come to terms with everything that had happened.

I wasn't a naturally born nephilim. I didn't even have any human DNA in me. The world of the supernatural was still terrifying, but, given that I was the daughter of the Hellfire Queen and the archangel Lucifer, I was one of the scariest things out there now.

That didn't make me feel better. But it did make me feel more confident in my ability to protect those who couldn't protect themselves.

I ran my finger over the new thick silver bracelet around Jacob's wrist with the prongs digging into his skin every eighth of an inch. His charm protecting him against sunlight had been replaced, he'd recently fed, and the calm certainty of his love for me radiated around my heart.

"It's almost a shame they reinstated us," he said, his soft low voice rumbling through me. "I could spend every day sitting in the sun with you."

"Pretty sure you'd eventually get bored."

"Of you?" His arm around my waist tightened. "Never. And I'm sure we wouldn't just be *sitting* every day."

He brushed his lips across the back of my neck, drawing a shiver of desire.

Yeah, there wouldn't be much sitting at all, and if he kept that up, there wouldn't be any sitting right now. But then Kol would want to join and he'd convince Marcus to join, too, and Gideon would get angry and everyone in the park would see a whole lot more of me than I really wanted.

"Well, Kol would be happy." I leaned back and kissed him, letting my love and desire for him swell through our bond.

"I have a feeling Kol wouldn't be the only one," he groaned, his breath fast.

"Yeah," I sighed as I leaned my head against his shoulder, savoring the feel of his large body against mine, his arms embracing and protecting me.

The giggles of a young child carried over the rumble of cars on the busy street nearby and the conversation of the half dozen other people standing in line at the taco truck. Marcus, in his massive hellhound form, burst out of the underbrush on the other side of the lawn with a naked child, probably about five or six, clinging to his back. Two more kids about the same age, also naked, chased after him, and three wolf pups nipped at his heels.

He tipped the child off his back onto the grass and gently headbutted another kid as six adult wolves, half the size of Marcus, broke through the trees. They shifted back into their human forms, a mix of men and women, laughing and chatting and pulling on the clothes they'd left with their picnic baskets.

"Okay, that's enough," one of the women called to the kids. "I'm sure Marcus didn't come here to play with you." Her gaze jumped to me and I tensed.

Everyone in the Union City wolf pack knew Marcus was mated to me, the archnephilim. My face had been plastered on every newscast for the last two weeks—which meant I was never going to be doing undercover work again. But that was a small price to pay for not being public enemy number one.

Except I still couldn't stop the instinctual reaction of anticipating hate and fear. I'd spent my entire life hiding what I was without even knowing *what* I really was, and had been told over and over again that the world wouldn't understand me. Now I kept expecting to wake up and find that my amazing new life had all been a dream.

The woman waved and gave me a warm smile, shocking me, then turned back to the kids. She knew what I was and didn't care.

"I feel your surprise through our bond every time someone welcomes you," Jacob said. "Is it that shocking that someone would see you for who you really are? You stopped Lilith. You prevented another war. Most of the supers in Union City think you're a hero."

"Yeah." Although I suspected my positive welcome had a lot to do with Voth. I had a feeling he was the one who'd spread all the extra details about my fight with Lilith. The tale had grown to near epic proportions and it had only been floating around for a few weeks. Even those who lived and worked in Operations whispered it with awe. The one detail, however, that always remained true, because in retrospect it was pretty epic—or pretty foolish, depending on how you looked at it—was that I'd been willing to do anything, even burn myself up, in order to stop Lilith... my mother.

Something I didn't think I'd ever fully come to terms with. I was the daughter of the Hellfire Queen and the most notorious fallen angel in human and angelic history. And yet I didn't feel any guilt over Lilith's death. She'd been determined to kill everyone, and every cell in my being knew she'd needed to be stopped. That she'd chosen to burn up instead of being caged wasn't something I'd had any control over, and while I might have half of her DNA, she hadn't been my mother. My mother had been a kind, protective human woman who'd given me everything she could. Just like Lucifer had hoped for when he'd left me with her.

Marcus nudged an eager child out of the way. He'd been worried that the Union City wolf pack wouldn't accept him because he was no longer a werewolf, but the pack had welcomed him with open arms... although some of the single ladies had been disappointed that he was off the market.

He strode toward us, his powerful muscles bunching and releasing, the sun catching in his short velvety fur, accentuating the swirling glyphs in his skin. As far as anyone knew, he was the only hellhound in the mortal realm, and now one of a few remaining hounds in all the realms.

Tests had proven his DNA had completely changed from human with the lycanthropy infection, to fully demonic, and no one could explain it. And I didn't care. He was alive, healthy, now with the extended demonic lifespan, and still mine.

He shifted, the movement fast and smooth, as if his body turned to liquid from one step to another and then back to flesh again. His piercing green gaze captured mine, making my pulse stutter, and I dragged my attention away from his eyes to appreciate his lean-muscled body and the delicate golden glyph above his heart before he put on his clothes.

He cocked an eyebrow, his beast's feral intensity rising, and pulled on a pair of shorts, covering his growing erection.

With a low growl, he knelt before me and captured my lips in a fierce, breathtaking kiss. "God, I love you."

"Ooo, are we showing Essie our love for her again?" Kol asked as he sat beside me, handed Marcus the tray with our food, and kissed me, building up my barely-contained desire for him and the rest of my guys. A whisper of his heated magic unfurled low within me and a moan escaped before I could stop it.

He sat back on his heels. The hellfire in his eyes licking his cheeks revealed his desire, while his lopsided grin revealed his awe and joy. It had only been a few weeks since our brand had formed, but I had a feeling he'd always be a little surprised that he, an incubus, had fallen in love.

He'd been in the worst shape when I'd woken in Operations. Amiah and Priam—and a few other angels who worked at Mercy Memorial and had been reassigned to Operations by the Director to deal with all the wounded—had taken care of Gideon and Marcus, and they, in turn, had helped Jacob. But Kol had been unwilling to go to someone else to get the sexual energy he needed to properly heal.

I'd yelled at him over that. I understood his nature, and while I didn't exactly like the idea of him turning to someone else, the idea of him spending almost a week sitting at my bedside in agony bothered me more.

He had shrugged and changed the subject with a kiss that turned into more and went a long way to healing him.

And here I'd thought Marcus would be the most stubborn of my mates.

Gideon, also carrying food and drinks, sat by my feet and set the tray on the blanket between us. A crackle of electric power teased over my forearm and his desire seeped through our bond.

He was the most reserved of my guys, at least when it came to large displays of public affection, but that didn't mean he didn't crave me. His love radiated through our bond as strongly as the other guys, and the moment we were out of the public eye he freely kissed me in his sensual, languid style that always awakened the divine light within me and made me squirm for more.

He'd said he and Cassius had talked during the week I was unconscious, and while Cassius no longer looked at me like I was going to murder his brother, his demeanor toward me remained cool, verging on icy, and his emotions seethed with anger and frustration.

But he was icy and angry with everyone, not just me, and really, the anger was probably at himself. Gideon had forced him to make a choice and he'd gone against what he believed in to protect his brother. That kind of choice could make a person question everything he thought was true about himself, and that wasn't something easily dealt with.

Amiah also remained brusquely professional, her emotions harder and icier than Cassius's. But her world had been rocked as well. She'd been determined to protect a man who could never have loved her back, and now, with my angelic mating brand on Marcus's chest, any last shred of hope was gone. My empathic healing magic kept flaring up when she was near, desperately wanting to help her, but I was the last person she'd want help from so I kept my power restrained.

"So we have a decision to make," Gideon said, handing me a paper-wrapped burrito. "Head office approved our request to renovate the fifth floor."

"You're kidding." Kol grabbed a cardboard tray with his brisket tacos. "What did we have to give up?"

"Nothing." Gideon opened his bottle of water and took a long sip.

"Nothing?" Jacob asked. 'The reno is going to be expensive. I was sure they'd negotiate."

We'd proposed a plan to strip the suites on the fifth floor in the southwest corner of Operations to create an apart-

ment for us. We wanted a main bedroom as well as indi-
vidual rooms so each of us had our own space. We'd also
thrown in some fancy bathroom plans for multiple bathrooms, private access to the roof, along with a private
rooftop patio—because hey, if we were going to ask, why not
start by asking for everything—and a skylight over the open
concept living room/dining room/kitchen area.

None of us had expected head office to say yes. In fact, I
had been expecting them to outright refuse us. I'd already
caused them an enormous amount of trouble with my very
existence, and I was pretty sure they considered the debt for
stopping another war paid by ensuring the townsfolk didn't
come after me with pitchforks.

"We're a mated quintet." Gideon's love for me swelled in
my chest. "That's never happened before, and despite me
being the only full angel in the group, we're still sacred."

"I wonder what else we can get out of that?" Kol's eyes lit
with a wicked gleam, and I could just imagine all the crazy
requests he'd make just to see if they'd say yes.

Gideon rolled his eyes at Kol, probably thinking what I
was. "We're not going to abuse this," he said. "The only
other thing we should use this for is leverage to leave the JP
if that's what we want."

Which was the other option on the table. Yes, we were
still a JP team, but was that what we really wanted? The job
was dangerous and the JP wasn't without politics. With the
second spell Lucifer had given me, I could hide my true
nature and we could move someplace where no one knew
us. There'd still be a chance someone would recognize me,
but without my glowing eyes and a new haircut, people
would be more likely to think I *looked* like the nephilim and
wasn't actually *the* nephilim.

I hadn't asked Sebastian if he would cast the spell, but as

a full fae sorcerer, I was sure he had more than enough power to do it.

He'd popped by two days after I'd woken up, looking like his usual sexy self. The soft glow radiating from his skin was back to normal, or rather normal for the faekin he was pretending to be, and his ears were a little less pointy than a real fae's. He hadn't gotten close enough for me to look into his eyes and see the vast universe of power, and he'd kept his power and emotions locked down tight, but I had no doubt he was back to normal. After a brief hello and a wicked smile, he'd given Gideon a bill that Gideon had said head office would never pay, then he'd left.

"So?" Marcus said.

"Do we stay or go?" Jacob asked.

But I didn't want to run and hide any more. I couldn't. That life was over. I wasn't the same Officer Essie Shaw whose only goal had been to help people while flying under the radar. Hell, I wasn't even the same species, or at least the species I'd thought I was. I no longer had to keep everyone at arm's length for fear they'd learn my secret, nor hide from all things supernatural. For the first time in my life, I was free to choose whatever path I wanted.

And I was in a position where I could help so many people.

I knew my guys would give up everything and follow me to the ends of the earth, just like I would for them. But I'd never ask them to. They'd joined the JP to serve and protect, just like I'd joined the UCPD.

"I made a promise to myself to help those who couldn't help themselves," I said. "I want to keep that promise."

I met Marcus's piercing gaze, his feral passion making my pulse pick up, and Kol released a shuddering breath, drawing my attention to him. The hellfire in his eyes flickered and danced, and his sensual magic whispered low within me.

Leaning back, I looked into Jacob's eyes, black still pools focused entirely on me. His yearning merged with the heat building within me, and then Gideon's magic crackled through our brand, stealing my breath. I slid my attention to him and soared in a perfect summer sky, wrapped in desire and love and trust.

I wasn't despised, I wasn't weak, and I was no longer alone. I belonged with these men and they loved me for who I was, the good and the bad. Destiny had conspired to give me everything I'd thought I'd never be able to have. I'd just needed to accept myself, both my darkness and my light, to attain it.

OTHER BOOKS BY TESSA COLE

THE NEPHILIM'S DESTINY SERIES